Karen

A DANGEROUS MAN

The sheriff tugged Kane around by the wrists, so that the captive's face was in the light. He was much closer now to Rilla, and she caught a clear, three-quarters view of him.

His features were calm, quiet, serene, in spite of everything. If he had not been so blatantly masculine, so disheveled and bruised, she might have said he was beautiful. His thick, nearly black hair had been brushed back carelessly except where it waved in rebellion just behind his ear, and the sharp angles and planes of the bone structure beneath his skin were clear and distinct. He was the most breathtaking dark angel Rilla had ever seen.

She couldn't think of why he'd frightened her, why she'd thought him wild.

Sensing her stare, he glanced up and caught her looking at him. Then Rilla knew, and she recoiled in confused shock.

He had the eyes of a sinner.

———

Also by Lisa G. Brown

Billy Bob Walker Got Married

Available from HarperPaperbacks

CRAZY FOR LOVIN' YOU

Lisa G. Brown

HarperPaperbacks
A Division of HarperCollinsPublishers

This is a work of fiction. The characters, incidents, and dialogues are products of the author's imagination and are not to be construed as real. Any resemblance to actual events or persons, living or dead, is entirely coincidental.

HarperPaperbacks   *A Division of* HarperCollins*Publishers*
10 East 53rd Street, New York, N.Y. 10022

Cover illustration by Jean Monti

First printing: April 1994

Printed in the United States of America

HarperPaperbacks, HarperMonogram, and colophon are trademarks of HarperCollins*Publishers*

❖ 10 9 8 7 6 5 4 3 2 1

For my family on the Ridge, especially Pa Bill and Mema Dot, and for Kathy Watts, who believed in Jubal's story the first time.

1

Martha Denton, the matron of Rose Hall, taught her young ladies three cardinal rules: Say "yes" to Jesus and "no" to anything else masculine; Always put paper over the seat in any suspicious-looking bathroom; and Never, ever raise your voice in temper.

Terrill Carroll was breaking the last one with all the strength she could muster, right to Mrs. Denton's face.

"What do you mean, nobody is coming to get me?" The anger in the voice of the tall girl was echoed in her clenched hands, her tense stance, the blazing blue of her eyes as she faced the heavy body and stern posture of the matron.

"I didn't say 'nobody' was coming, Terrill." Mrs. Denton's own voice was soothing, her face kind. "Let's just calm down. I know you've had some shocking news this week—"

"You just said Tandy had called. That she couldn't be here." Terrill made an impatient, frantic gesture with her hands as she stood in the middle of her pile of suitcases. "I should have had my own car a long time ago. Henry made sure I didn't have one so that I couldn't come home. But I'm not staying another night. I'll ride the bus, or take a rental car. He can pay for it. I *have* to go home. Aunt Tandy said I could." Her voice cracked and wobbled a little; there was a trace of panic in it, mingled with dark determination.

The matron responded reassuringly, "And you will go. A neighbor of yours—a Mr. Lionel Johnson—is here, waiting to take you. Your aunt spoke to me on the phone earlier, and she confirmed that he—"

"Mama's dead, isn't she? I knew Henry wouldn't let me come home again unless the worst possible had hap—"

"Terrill, no! *No.* Your mother is still very much alive. Your aunt said that there had been a break-in, a robbery, at Henry's—at your father's mill last night." Mrs. Denton juggled words and phrases carefully; talking to Terrill when she was this upset was like walking in a minefield.

"Henry's my *step*father. Or my uncle. Whatever you want to call him. But never my father. And it's not his mill." The girl's back stiffened even more, but her voice was fraying into tears around the edges.

"All right. Fine. I know how you feel about the situation. After all these years, I've pried enough bits and pieces out of you to understand. But the fact is that your *step*father had to remain at the mill today instead of staying with your mother. Your aunt is with her. She asked this Mr. Johnson to come and get you in her place. The poor man is waiting for you, Terrill."

"I just want to go home," she repeated, and wondered if she'd really said it a million times or if it just felt that way.

A middle-aged man stood in a dark suit and tie like an ink blot in the delicate, icy pinkness of the front hall. He looked up in relief as they approached.

"Here she is, Mr. Johnson. Terrill."

He appeared slightly taken back, whether at the sight of her or at the hand she extended, she didn't know.

"Mr. Johnson?" Terrill's voice was a little uncertain, unlike her strong movements, her sure posture.

He took her hand belatedly. "That's right. I'm Lionel Johnson. We live a mile or so down the road. My daughter Tess—"

"I remember."

He relaxed a little, then laughed. "Well, you've got one on me. I remembered you as a skinny little kid, maybe fourteen or so, with the biggest blue eyes I ever saw. Why, you're as tall as your aunt Tandy. You even remind me of her. . . ." He let his voice trail off, and his face was suddenly doubtful.

He doesn't know whether he has insulted me or not, Terrill thought with a flash of black humor. And the emotion helped soothe the turmoil of the other, more intense feelings that boiled inside her. "I don't know if Aunt Tandy will thank you for finding a resemblance."

Her dry words startled him; he finally laughed. "It's just something about the way you stand. Sort of strong, that's all."

Headstrong, that was probably the word he really wanted to use. Or maybe defiant. Terrill had been called all of that too many times before. But at least it was an improvement over what people called Tandy. They said she was prissy and high-minded, rigid and righteous.

At least that was what they used to say. Maybe now things were different. Terrill was about to find out, and the thought made her throat close up again.

"Why don't you go to your own room for a few minutes, Terrill?" Mrs. Denton asked kindly. "Wash your face. Let yourself calm down. You might want to freshen your makeup. While you're doing that, Mr. Johnson can put your suitcases in the car."

Never cry enough to smear mascara, Terrill thought as she climbed the stairs. A lady never shows her emotions in public, Mrs. Denton would say.

Well, she must have somehow missed most of those ladylike qualities when God was handing them out. He'd given all the gentleness in her family to her mother.

Katherine.

No. She splashed cold water furiously on her face.

Fifteen minutes later, as she came down the stairs, she caught the tail end of a conversation going on between Mrs. Denton and Lionel Johnson.

". . . and she was a regular little hellion four years ago. That was when she finally ran away from home. Trying to worry the life out of Katherine, Henry said." Johnson's voice held foreboding.

Mrs. Denton practiced what she preached; she did not gossip. Her mouth was pursed into a near prune. "Terrill has worked very hard, Mr. Johnson. She had some difficulties at first here, but she has become one of my brightest hopes. She's only twenty and already a senior at Belmont College. Very intelligent. Very determined."

"She's living here and going to college?"

"It's an option that several of the girls have chosen over the years. We're very glad Terrill has stayed. This is her home. She rarely gets to visit with her family. She's been good to tutor some of the younger ones, too. The girls who come here need many kinds of help."

"I guess so . . . and I guess I'm one of the lucky ones. I've got a daughter, too, but she's never given me one lick of trouble. Don't know what I'd do if I had one like Terrill."

His satisfied voice made the girl on the stairs so angry that she was thankful: anger, she'd discovered, sometimes burned away hurt.

"In fact," Johnson continued, "Tess is here in Nashville, too. At Vanderbilt. Expensive as hell, but if it's what my little china doll wants . . ." He laughed, then pushed his coat back to shove his hands into his pants pockets. "The people down at the bank say I'm going to have to quit calling her that now that she's grown, but I told them, 'It's my bank—'"

"I'm ready." Terrill's words from the top of the stairs broke off Lionel's. Relief washed over Martha Denton's face as she moved to meet the girl.

"Have a good trip, Terrill. Our prayers will be with you and with your mother."

"Thank you."

The Terrill who stood in front of Mrs. Denton now was calm, adult, controlled. The matron smiled and nodded approvingly. But just before the girl stepped out the door of Rose Hall, Mrs. Denton let one word burst without volition from her throat.

"Terrill!"

The older woman hurried across the pale tiles of the foyer, her heels doing a staccato click, her silk dress rustling. She reached for the girl who was a whole head taller and hugged her tightly.

"You're frightened, I know. But you'll do fine. I can remember you at sixteen—the way you cried in the night when you thought I didn't know. But you made it, my dear. All grown up. You'll make it through this, too."

Terrill's slender fingers clutched the matron's

back as she finally returned the unexpected embrace. "I hope so," she whispered painfully. "I hope so."

Awkwardly, Johnson cleared his throat. "Well, let's get going. We've got a two-hour drive, and I reckon you want to get home and see your mama."

Carroll Mill was one of the few industries in Cade County; it had been the pride and joy of Terrill's father, Luke, and her grandfather, Melvin Carroll.

It hadn't changed much over the last four years, even if Terrill had barely had time to glance at it in her short trips home. The office loomed to the right, with its vinyl siding and brick front. It was at the corner of the yellow, dusty yard, not far from the one lone tree in the middle of the grounds, a huge sprawling oak ten times her age that had been spared the mill saw because her father had loved it.

Far to the left were stacks of fresh-cut oak and birch, yellow and fragrant. Beyond them were older, graying bundles of lumber, some of them warped and useless. To the back of the yard lay the big barnlike structures of the buildings that made up the mill itself; just now they were empty, closed for the weekend.

On the right—that was the view Terrill liked. Several piles of logs stood waiting to be sawed, but beyond them was a stand of maples and poplars, just beginning to turn to vivid reds, with little splashes of orange mingling with green against the blue sky. The land dipped into a hollow, and just beyond that rolled the farm.

The place had belonged to Grandpa Carroll; Luke had bought it from him two years before Grandpa died. These days Henry ran Luke's mill, Aunt Tandy ran Katherine's house, but nobody did much of anything for Grandpa's farm. The fields were rented out or cut for hay only occasionally, to keep them from going wild, and the hay was sold. No cattle were kept here now.

It wasn't all that rich a farm. It was too hilly and too dramatic. If it had been better, Grandpa Carroll and Luke might not have turned this section of it, where it touched Highway 37, into the sawmill and a lumberyard some twenty years ago. But the farm was a pretty place, maybe the prettiest in the county.

Down the highway from the mill just a little way—two hundred yards or so—was the long, shady, gravel road that led back to the Carroll farmhouse, with its glistening white paint, black shutters, dormer windows, and long porch.

Home.

Her home, and Daddy's mill. It was reassuring to see the place, the big, bold, black lettering across the front that proclaimed to the world that this was "Carroll Lumber." And beneath that, as if he'd never died, was Daddy's name; the sign had always read in smaller letters, "Owner, Luke—"

"Stop!" Terrill said abruptly, sitting up with a snap on the wine-colored seat of Mr. Johnson's Buick Electra.

"What?" he asked, startled by the way she broke the silence that had wrapped them most of the way from Nashville.

"The mill. I want to stop at the mill," she demanded impatiently, staring at the place as if she'd never seen it.

"But your aunt's expecting you home."

"I want to see the mill," she repeated. *"Daddy's mill."*

Johnson said with a sting of anger, "No need to be so high-handed about it. But I figure that I can cut you a little slack, considering the situation with your mother. We'll stop." He pulled in the yard, right under the big oak.

Terrill sat there looking up at the sign until Johnson looked up at it, too, his face puzzled. It was clean and freshly painted, and it read clearly, "Carroll Lumber. Owner, Henry Carroll."

Johnson cleared his throat. "Looks nice. Real nice. Henry's running things just like Luke did. He takes being his brother's keeper to heart. You and your mama have been real lucky to have Henry. I told him myself at the last Jaycees meeting, 'You're a good man and a good Christian, Henry, taking on Luke's wife and child like you have.'"

Terrill stared at Johnson as if he'd grown two heads, and he edged away a little in confusion.

Then she jerked open the door of the car and flung herself out of it without a word. Behind her, she heard his muttered comment. "I don't care if that girl is grown, she needs a good, old-fashioned spanking," he was saying to himself as he followed her up to the office.

There was pure rage in Terrill's throat, choking her. Henry had taken Daddy's name off his own mill. But it was more than that—he was trying to cut Terrill off, too. Again.

No. I swear, not this time, Henry. She could think no more than that through the red emotions that swirled inside her. Did Mama know? Probably not. It would make no difference to her anyway. But Tandy—how could she let this happen? Luke had been Tandy's brother, too, just as Henry was. She owed his memory something.

Terrill yanked open the door to the office. The first room was a sort of reception area. It had a couch, a water cooler, a secretary's desk, and a smaller desk off to the side.

No one was in the room, but it echoed with the sound of the voices coming from the office, which lay just past the half-opened door in front of her. She crossed to it, shoved open the door, stepped in, and spoke simultaneously, all in a rush, before she got afraid to say it. "I don't understand why your name is the one on the sign, Henry. I won't let you—"

Terrill broke off, her voice just stopping as the full impact of the scene in front of her hit home, as four faces turned toward her.

One was Henry's. She knew the expression he wore as he faced her: it was barely contained dislike.

Two of the others were equally startled. They were the faces of men in police uniforms. One had been down on his haunches in front of an open safe—a robbery, Mrs. Denton had said—and he was just rising now from that position. The other looked like Terrill's idea of a marine sergeant; his craggy, square face and flattop haircut were familiar. He was the sheriff from Bethel, Standford or something by name.

But it was the fourth man who stopped her cold, the one with his back to her as he stood rigidly, looking out the window before him. The one wearing the silver handcuffs that pulled his arms back and clipped his wrists together tightly.

"Terrill!" Henry said in reprimand. "What are you doing here? Go on to the house." His voice betrayed a little nervousness. He didn't want her here. The thought made her dig in her heels stubbornly. Then Johnson peered around the corner of the door, and Henry snapped at him as well. "You're supposed to take her home, not bring her to the mill in the middle of all this. I've got enough trouble for one day already."

Johnson shrugged. "She was bound and determined to stop. I didn't think it'd be a problem, but I forgot about the break-in. How much did they get, Henry?" He looked around appraisingly.

With reluctance, Henry said, "Several thousand dollars."

Johnson whistled and raised his eyebrows. "If you'd bring it down to the bank every day like I've told you—" He broke off at Henry's darkening face and looked over instead at the one caught in the handcuffs. "So, it was Kane," he said to the sheriff, then added with a wealth of satisfaction, "Again."

Ned—that was his name, Terrill remembered now—Ned Standford said in resignation, "Well, if it was, we can't prove it."

Johnson's mouth tightened. "What do you mean?"

"No fingerprints of his are anywhere to be found. Nobody saw Kane near the mill."

Johnson snorted. "Kane's an old hand at this. He was probably long gone before you all ever pulled up. That money's stashed away somewhere."

"Well, it's not at his mama's house, if that's what you mean. We searched the property, and him, too, when he finally came rolling in at dawn. Besides, he's got an alibi." For the first time, the sheriff looked at his prisoner as if he were in the room instead of invisible. "Idn't that right, boy?" He prodded the "boy" once in the side with the short, fat billy club he held in his hand.

The one they'd called Kane looked at Standford slowly, then Johnson. Then he turned silently back to the window. Johnson's face darkened at the rudeness.

There was something frightening about this Kane. Maybe it was the tension in the long, lean body, or it might just have been the unkempt look about him, the way his shirt had been dragged off one brown shoulder, the way his thick dark hair waved untidily down over his nape.

It could even have been his hands, with their agile fingers that kept flexing, as if he longed to have them around somebody's throat.

"What alibi?" Johnson demanded.

"He was with Bobo Hackett at the time of the robbery—"

"Good God, Ned, surely you don't believe Bobo, do you? Why, he's as thick as thieves with Kane here."

"Yeah, maybe," the sheriff said. "But this alibi holds water, 'cause Kane rode to the Lonesome Pine with him. People saw him there. Then Kane says he went off with one of the girls for most of the rest of the night, and she dropped him off at Ida's store on the Ridge. He walked from there home, right into my deputies. And I reckon," the sheriff added knowingly, "that he's got proof of the girl."

He lifted the billy club and laid the end of it against Kane's cheek, pushing his face around toward Johnson and lifting up his chin. "Idn't that a beauty?" Standford asked dryly. "You oughta see the rest of him. He got in a little tussle with one of my deputies this morning—that's why he's wearin' cuffs—and they about tore his shirt off. His back looks like he's been scratched by a wildcat."

"You mean an alley cat, don't you?" Johnson said contemptuously.

Terrill couldn't see whatever it was on Kane's throat that had warranted such attention, and she wasn't really listening, anyway, because she'd been stunned by a brief glimpse of the man's profile. She thought she'd caught a fleeting impression of shocking good looks. Surely not on this half-wild animal.

Maybe the sheriff read her thoughts, because he let out his breath and said in resignation, "Most of my trouble is the way he's packaged. With a face like his, you can't trust women."

"He's nothing special," Johnson said derisively. "But he's got all the signs of being with some woman. So what makes you think she's lying?"

"I don't—and I don't even know who the 'she' is. He's took it into his head to play the gentleman," the sheriff returned. "Won't give us her name."

"Like it'd matter," Johnson said. "All those girls he runs around with are from the Ridge, and they're all tramps."

"Not all of 'em," Standford replied shortly.

His tone must have brought a half-forgotten memory back to Johnson, because he said lamely, "Sorry, Ned. I forgot—your mama was from out there, wasn't she? That's not a problem, just as long as it doesn't make you go easy on Kane."

Standford didn't bother to answer.

"Besides, your mother was a Pickett. But his mama—" Johnson looked over at the darkening face of the prisoner. "She married Morgan Kane. Come to think of it, though, Jubal here doesn't look like anybody I ever saw. He's sure not like his daddy. Maybe his mama—"

"Shut up!"

Terrill jumped; she knew Kane had to speak sometime, but these first two words of his were too furious for her to control the reaction. His voice was choked, husky, rough. A blood vessel throbbed in his temple.

Both Johnson and the sheriff fell back for an instant, silent, then the sheriff said sharply, "Lionel's not too particular about how he talks to you, but don't you pull this act with me, Jubal. I don't want to hear any garbage about defending your mother's honor. You want to be good to Maggie? Then you clean up your act. She'd rather you do that than waste time gettin' mad at what somebody says." The sheriff turned back to Johnson. "And you stay out of this, Lionel. You've got no call to—"

"I've got a right to dislike Kane," Johnson said hotly, his face flushing at the sheriff's reprimand. "The decent folks in this town want him gone. It ought to tell you what kind of trash he is when not even a two-bit whore from the Lonesome Pine wants to be his alibi."

Kane sucked in his breath in a sharp hiss; the side of his face that Terrill could see was blood red. He got out harshly, "Maybe it wasn't a two-bit whore I was with." There was a taunting edge in his voice.

Johnson looked at him blankly.

Kane added suggestively, outrageously, "Maybe it was—a little china doll."

Johnson's face went white, then mottled purple. All hell suddenly broke loose. Henry exclaimed, "For God's sake, Kane!" The sheriff swore; so did the deputy at the safe, who'd been silent up to that point.

But all of that was swallowed up in Lionel Johnson's roar of rage. Like a mad bull, he lunged for Kane's throat, and Kane, unable to balance or protect himself, hit the floor with a crash as Johnson tackled him, then followed him down. His face red, his eyes bulging, his hands like claws around Kane's neck, Johnson straddled the younger man's stomach, meaning to choke him to death.

The sheriff threw himself forward, yanking at Johnson's shoulders, just as the deputy tried to get between the struggling pair.

"He just said it to get at you—can't you tell that?" shouted the sheriff. "Lionel, don't do something crazy!"

The deputy gave a short, sharp jab at Johnson's throat, and when the blow connected, the man gasped for air, turning loose of Kane's neck to grab at his own. Then Henry moved at last, taking advantage of Johnson's loosened grip to haul him off Kane and hold him away forcibly.

Terrill backed up against the far wall, feeling for the door that had to be somewhere behind her, stunned by the violence that had exploded so rapidly in the room.

Kane was quietly gagging on the floor in front of the desk. The sheriff reached down and hauled up the long body by one shoulder. Kane lurched sideways, and the sheriff righted him.

"Well, you got what you were asking for, didn't you, boy?" Then he took pity on the one before him, who was still breathing raggedly. "The next time you decide to play a little game like this one you just played with Johnson, get smart. Make sure your hands are untied." Standford reached irritably for his own pocket. "Here. Turn around. I'll take the cuffs off. I can't find a reason to keep 'em on you any longer."

He tugged Kane around by his wrists, so that the captive's face was in the light. He was much closer now to Terrill, and she caught a clear, three-quarters view of his features.

That view riveted her attention and dropped a sentence into her head, the one she felt as if she'd been fumbling for ever since he'd turned toward her earlier: this Kane had the face of a saint.

The unbidden, exotic thought embarrassed Terrill, but it was still true. His features were calm, quiet, serene, in spite of everything. If he had not been so blatantly masculine, so disheveled and bruised, she might have said he was beautiful. His thick, nearly black hair had been brushed back carelessly except where it waved in rebellion just behind his ear, and the sharp angles and planes of his bone structure beneath the brown skin were clean and distinct. He was the most breathtaking dark angel Terrill had ever seen.

She couldn't think why he'd frightened her, why she'd thought him wild.

Sensing her stare, he glanced up and caught her looking at him. Then Terrill knew, and she recoiled in confused shock.

He had the eyes of a sinner.

They were hotly, brilliantly green, long and slanting, and they completely dispelled any idiotic notion that their owner was a soft, angelic sort. Set in vibrant contrast with their dark lashes and with the stillness of his face, the life and fire of those green eyes knocked the breath out of her.

He belonged in handcuffs, she thought in panic—don't turn him loose.

But he was already hunching his shoulders forward, rubbing his reddened wrists. Then he asked sullenly, "Can I go now?"

"You can't let him just walk out," Johnson protested, pushing Henry away and trying to stand. "Not after what he said about my daughter."

"You've done enough, Lionel," answered the sheriff in exasperation. "You said nearly the same thing about his mama."

"You're telling *me* that you're defending Jubal Kane?" Johnson demanded in shock.

"I'm not defendin' him. Don't get so het up over it, anyway. If I don't get Kane for this today, I'll get him for something else tomorrow. It's just a natural fact, ain't it, boy?" the sheriff addressed Kane. "You'll wind up one of these days just like your daddy did—dead in some worthless fight. Go on—you're free. For right now, anyway. Malone"—Standford turned to the deputy—"drive him home. And no more rough stuff, either."

Terrill pressed back against the wall by the door, but as Kane strode past her, she sucked in her breath sharply. She saw what the sheriff had pointed to earlier under his chin. Right beside the hollow in his throat, where Johnson had nearly finished the job of tearing the shirt off of him, was a dark, blood-red mark, and Terrill knew exactly how it had got there.

The sound of her quick-drawn breath brought those blazing green eyes up to her face. When he realized what she'd seen, he raised his hand, and his long fingers audaciously brushed the place. She stood mesmerized, then Henry said sharply, "Terrill!"

Kane pushed on out the door, and she turned slowly to her stepfather.

"That one," Henry said, motioning after Kane, "that one you leave alone. Do you hear me?"

2

As if embarrassed by his outburst, Johnson insisted on being the gentleman and taking Terrill on to the farmhouse while Henry finished up with Standford.

"I'm sorry you saw that . . . that scene," he offered frostily as they pulled back out on the highway, only to stop a few yards down to make the turn into the Carrolls' long drive. "But it's just as well you find out early who and what this Kane is, since Henry has crossed the line from Christian charity into plain stupidity and given him a job. Kane can be violent."

So can you, Terrill longed to retort, but she prudently said nothing. All she wanted was to see the house and the farm and wallow in the thought that she was back from exile—she was home.

It was here, all the memories made into reality—all hers again.

The trees and the ridges in the distance; the dry, brown cornfields that led north, toward the Red

Fork River; the far, dark hollows—these were old friends.

Now she could see through the gates, all the way down to the end of the road, where it loomed like a gentle dream—the white farmhouse.

The rockers still sat on the long porch, just now moving a little, as if to welcome her. And in the side yard, there were sheets on the clothesline, swelling in the cool September breeze like multicolored sails.

I won't cry, she thought fiercely.

"It might not be a good idea," Johnson was mumbling uneasily, "to tell your aunt Tandy—or Katherine—about the run-in with Kane. It'd just upset them. And Tandy—"

Terrill might have laughed at the sheer terror in his voice at the thought of Tandy's ire, but all she could do was nod wordlessly, struggling to tamp down her emotions.

The car had no sooner slid to a stop in front of the house than the screen door opened, and Tandy herself stood there, motionless, a tall, thin woman in a brown skirt and neat shirt. Her short brown hair was molded in place—no wind dared to ruffle it, or could have.

Staring at her through the window, Terrill already knew that Tandy would be wearing Bluegrass cologne. She always had, and it and the scent of her Merle Norman makeup clung to every memory Terrill had of her stern, constant aunt.

She was smiling.

Terrill fumbled for the car handle, shoved it up, and climbed out.

The smell of leaves, and grass, and purple petunias blooming at the edge of the yard hit her in the face, and she could have sworn that a wisp of Bluegrass reached out for her.

"Welcome home, Terrill," her aunt said, her voice a little unsteady as it floated across the yard.

"Thank you," she answered simply, and this time nothing could stop the tears that streamed down her face.

"Well, now," Johnson cut in jovially, trying to ignore the weeping girl beside him, "where do you want me to put Terrill's luggage?"

"Oh, upstairs. In her old room," Tandy answered. "We appreciate your going to get her." She stood watching her niece as Terrill touched the white gate lovingly, looked around at the flowers, stared at the house.

"Well, come on in," Tandy said at last, quietly. "No sense in dawdling around." But as Terrill stepped up on the porch, she leaned forward to brush a kiss on her cheek. "It's good to have you home."

Inside the screen door, the oak floor gleamed with polish and the grandfather clock stood ponderously beside the stairs.

Terrill sucked in a deep breath. "I just—need to get used to things," she managed.

Tandy's face held a flash of understanding. "Don't be afraid to see Katherine, Terrill. She's waiting to see you, there, in the bedroom."

Terrill swallowed. "Now?"

"It won't get any easier if you put it off." That was typical of Tandy—the truth unsalted and unvarnished, no matter how bad it hurt.

Terrill couldn't move for a second or two to get to the bedroom door; memories and emotions swamped her. In her mind she could see her mother, delicate, blond, and angelic, and remember how she'd once yearned to be like her. The town adored her, children in her toddler Sunday school class loved her, her husbands—both of them—worshiped her. Instead, Terrill had been born hot-tempered and smart-mouthed.

But then she'd learned her mother was too gentle, too weak.

Too afraid of life alone, so she'd married Henry.

Too afraid of confrontations, so she'd sent Terrill away.

Sacrificed a daughter for a husband.

But Terrill wouldn't think of that now.

Mama was dying.

Down the hall a few steps, to the left. Terrill's feet dragged as she neared the open door. But as she hesitated, hovering, Katherine's voice called out eagerly, "Tandy? I heard a car. Was it Rilla? Do you see her coming yet?"

The childhood nickname made Terrill's throat close up an instant, but she swallowed twice and answered lightly, "No, she doesn't, because I'm already here, Mama." She stepped into the bedroom.

Katherine's face blazed with relief from the bed, where she sat nearly upright against the piled pillows. "Rilla," she said thankfully. "Welcome home." She stretched both arms wide, and after a second's hesitation, Terrill walked into them.

And all the while, her mind reeled in a terrible shock. Oh, God, she thought to herself frantically, what are you doing to Mama? Katherine was so thin, so fragile.

It was truth, then, what they had told Terrill. Death was in this room. She could feel it as she pulled Katherine tight: the thin, brittle splinters of bone in her mother's shoulders, her matchstick arms as Terrill's fingers closed around them.

This was all that was left of Katherine's life.

Terrill felt the agony tearing through her own stomach, cutting through her heart. She pulled her fingers away quickly, breathing harshly.

Katherine was smiling. "It's so good to see you, honey," she whispered. "I hope you didn't mind having to leave Rose Hall and Belmont. I know Mrs. Denton . . . had hopes . . . you'd get your degree this year." Her voice kept catching in her throat, the sounds coming out in little spurts.

Terrill shook her head. "I'll finish the degree sooner or later, Mama. I'm too close even to think of quitting. But now all I want is to hear you tell me that I'm really home, this time for more than two weeks."

"Really home," Katherine promised solemnly.

There was a long, awkward pause, which Terrill finally broke by standing and looking around. What to say—to do?

"This room has—changed a lot," she offered at last. "It used to be painted."

Katherine looked around, too, surveying the buttery-colored wallpaper with its green vines and tiny roses. "We had this done—more than a year ago," she said, her voice fluttery and weak. "Last summer. Surely you saw it when you came home—for Christmas."

"No," Terrill answered flatly. "Henry doesn't like me to come in this room—to get between the two of you—remember?"

After another silence, Katherine spoke a little nervously. "We need to talk, Rilla. Things will change—"

But Terrill interrupted her. "Why didn't somebody tell me you were sick, Mama?"

Katherine let her first words die on her lips, then she sighed. "I didn't know myself . . . what was wrong . . . until twelve weeks ago. They told me . . . maybe cancer. Then later they discovered a second cancer, this one of the stomach." Her eyes closed a minute. She said flatly, "There's . . . no hope."

Fury cracked through Terrill. "Everybody else knew, even Mrs. Denton. But not me, and I'm your daughter. I had the right to be there the day you found out."

Katherine rested her head on a pillow behind her and replied wearily, "Believe me, Rilla, you didn't miss much by not being at the hospital. I never want to go there again."

Terrill's heart twisted, and she sank onto the bed again. "I'm sorry, Mama." She wanted to explain, to say she was sorry for everything—for her temper, for never being the kind of daughter Katherine wanted, for the rotten hand life had just dealt Katherine.

"It doesn't matter," her mother answered, and her nearly transparent fingers reached out to caress her daughter's cheek. "You're home now, where you're going to stay. This time, things will be different. Everybody will . . . give a little."

Even beneath the despair and the heartbreak, Terrill felt the old burn of resentment. She had been the one to give the last time—she had been the one forced out of her home into a boarding school.

But that was in the past, she told herself firmly. Mama had called her home. She'd stood up to Henry. Maybe she loved her daughter a little after all.

A little might be enough.

Upstairs in her old room, Terrill did what she always did when she came home. She touched things, caressing them like old friends with the palms of her hands.

There was the old iron bedstead that had once belonged to Grandmother Carroll, now painted a soft, glowing pink. The curved dressing table with its long mirrors on each side was pushed against one wall. Soft, ruffled cushions were piled on the window seat where she'd sat dreaming as a child, looking out over the hollow that lay between the house and the mill.

How many nights had she lain here in this room, listening to the wind as it grieved up out of the hollow, watching the white ball of the moon as it blazed above her? She remembered lying awake once when she was six, the night of her birthday. That was the day her uncle showed up at the house she and Luke and Katherine shared with Grandpa. He had stumbled unawares into Terrill's birthday party.

She was already half-afraid of the quiet uncle, the one member of the family who totally ignored her. But that day she'd run laughing out into the hall, holding a glass of strawberry punch, and slammed right into his knees, splashing his glistening shoes. Henry had yanked her up, glaring at her.

"You little brat!" he'd muttered, and the adult dislike in his eyes had scared her to death. She knew even then that his emotions ran far deeper than one spilled cup of strawberry punch warranted.

Terrill had struggled away, running from him, and that night, here in this room, she'd tried to tell her mother.

"Oh, honey, I don't want to hear such silliness," Katherine had answered, laughing. "Your uncle Henry's so wrapped up in his career as a big-time accountant over in Knoxville that he doesn't have time for children, that's all."

But Terrill had watched Henry uneasily on his infrequent trips home, and by the age of eight she'd realized that he never showed the dark side of his personality to her mother. By ten she'd even learned why: he loved Katherine.

Then everything came apart.

Grandpa died of a heart attack, and then her father, Luke, died in a logging accident.

And suddenly Katherine was accessible to Henry. Terrill could find no escape from him as he closed in.

She'd fought her mother's marriage tooth and nail.

"Please, Rilla, try to understand," her mother begged night after night. "Luke is dead. Grandpa Carroll is dead. We've got to hold the mill together. Henry can. He's doing it for you, honey. Someday it will be yours. You're Luke's only heir."

"He's doing it for *you*, Mama!" Terrill finally screamed. "To get his hands on *you*. To go to bed with *you*."

Katherine gasped, paled, then blushed a fiery red. "What are you saying, Terrill? You're only fourteen. I won't have you talking like this."

"It's the truth," Terrill said defiantly. "He wants you, and he hates me. Just like he hated Daddy. I won't have him for my father."

"Please, Rilla," Katherine began again.

Terrill jerked away from her mother's hands. She was already taller than Katherine, a leggy, coltish girl with a wild mane of blond-brown hair.

"And you don't want him because of the mill, either. You'll *like* getting in bed with him. But I hate both of you."

By the time she was sixteen, she had conceded the battle: Henry had won.

He was always smooth and right, and she had not

known how to fight back except through rudeness
and flippancy and belligerence. It was either that or
cry and beg them to want her, and she had too much
pride ever to do that, even if she'd thought it might
have changed things.

They'd sent her to Rose Hall.

And now they'd called her back home.

That night Katherine came to the supper table,
with Henry supporting her. She ate very little, but
she sat on a chair with a pillow behind her. Terrill
didn't want to be here, just a few feet from her
stepfather as he presided over the fried chicken
and the pecan pie, but, reluctantly, she slid onto
her chair and suffered through Henry's mumbled
prayer. It didn't take long for Katherine to tire, and
Henry helped her back to her bed midway through
the meal. He returned frowning, barely eating
himself, but just as he pushed away his half-full
plate, Tandy's voice stopped his leaving the table.
She asked abruptly, "What happened at the
sawmill today?"

"Nothing much. Standford looked over the place.
Asked a few questions."

Tandy sipped her tea, then squeezed a lemon slice
into it carefully, all before she said in a meaningful
voice, "And did they question—"

"Yes," Henry cut in impatiently before she could
finish. "They questioned Jubal Kane. That is what
you're about to ask, isn't it?"

Tandy picked up her glass with a clinking of the
ice cubes. "It just makes good sense to be careful any
time one of those Kanes is involved in something,
Henry."

"He had an alibi."

"Hmph," Tandy said scornfully. "The fact is that no good—"

"Ever came off of Sullivan's Ridge," Henry said in a sarcastic singsong repetition. "I've heard it all before, Tandy."

"I was *about* to say that no good ever came out of Lineville."

There was a long pause, while Terrill looked from Tandy's stubborn face to Henry's aggravated one.

"Who's Jubal Kane?" Terrill asked at last, and Tandy gave a loud exclamation. "What's he done?"

"See?" she said to her brother accusingly. "She's not home a day, and she's already asking about the likes of him."

"Oh, I doubt Terrill's so pure that just hearing Kane's name is going to contaminate her," Henry said.

She hated his superior tone; it was the one he used when he did the most damage. She struck back with the one piece of information she was pretty sure he didn't want Tandy to know: that she'd already come face to face with Kane.

"If being two feet from him at the mill today didn't do me any harm, then no, I don't guess hearing his name over the supper table will, either."

It got the response she wanted; Henry's face darkened ominously, and Tandy stopped all motion, sitting stiff as a board in her chair to ask quietly, "What did you say?"

Terrill fell silent. She had said enough.

"I asked what you meant by that remark," Tandy repeated.

"She meant to make trouble," Henry said heavily. "Lionel stopped by the mill before he brought Terrill home. Kane was there with the sheriff. That's all."

"He took her to the mill when all the riffraff of Bethel was there, too?" Tandy said in a slow-rising anger.

"I don't consider myself 'riffraff,' Tandy," Henry said testily.

Tandy took a deep breath. "You should have sent Terrill directly home the minute she got there. You have a responsibility to her, Henry, and to her mother—"

"Don't talk to me in those high-and-mighty terms, Tandy," Henry said coldly. "You've got no right. Nothing happened to your precious niece. Nothing to upset your brother Luke's daughter. As for responsibilities, I'm running the mill. I'm paying the bills—"

Terrill cut in sharply, "And you're paying to keep me a long way away."

Henry's face was stiff with temper, but Tandy plowed on. "We're not talking about your ability to make money, Henry. We're talking about your hiring Kane—and your firing him."

Henry struggled visibly with his resentment at Tandy's persistence before he spoke. "I'm not about to fire Kane. He's good at his job. Nobody in this county has been able to keep that old loader running except him. He's saved me a fortune in mechanic's bills. And he works cheap."

"And that's so important to you that you asked—*asked*—for his release and gave him a job? After what he did to you?" Tandy snapped. "I'll never understand, Henry. And he probably stole you blind last night."

"No. He's smarter than that. He has to work for me if he's to stay out of prison, if he's going to make it through his probation time without trouble. He knows if I complain, he'll go back, and there'll be nobody to help his mother. Just like before. Is that the way you want it, Tandy? Maggie Kane—who's worked all these years cleaning your church—now practically starving to death, too proud to take charity?"

Tandy opened her mouth once again, then shut it slowly. Henry had hit her on a weak spot; Terrill could tell it, and he knew it as well.

"Anyway," Henry added ironically, "Kane's better with his hands than to set off that burglar alarm, even if he hadn't been up at the Pine when it happened."

The expression of distaste that momentarily marked Tandy's face was gone so fast that Terrill barely caught it. "So that's his alibi. Well, the crowd up there doesn't hold much water with me. But I hate to think of his mother trying to clean again, as crippled with arthritis as her hands have become. Maggie was always a good sort. If only the mill weren't so close to the house, especially now that Terrill's here—"

"I'm twenty years old, Aunt," Terrill cut in. "I'm not the little girl that you sent away. Jubal Kane—whoever he is—doesn't scare me."

"Well . . ." Tandy's words trailed off indecisively. "How much money was stolen, Henry?"

"Enough," he said shortly.

"And that was?" his sister demanded pointedly.

"For God's sake, Tandy," Henry answered in irritation, throwing his napkin onto the table. "Do we have to discuss this over supper, too, along with everything else?"

She said nothing, merely waiting.

"Thousands of dollars," Henry said at last, capitulating ungracefully.

Terrill slowly set down her own glass.

"Thousands?" Tandy echoed. "But how? Wasn't most of it in checks—"

"No. Most of it was cash."

"Cash! But why?"

"I had held out the money to pay those men you took upon yourself to talk to last week when I wasn't here. The ones that *you* bought timber from. I didn't know if they'd take a check or not when they got here with the logs."

"Of course they would have," Tandy said, frowning. "Carroll Mill has a good name. You never discussed paying them in cash with me. I could have told you that—"

Henry stood up, his face angry and dark. "In the name of heaven, Tandy, I'm not a snot-nosed kid who has to run to his big sister to make decisions. What do you know about business, anyway? You've spent your life as a bookkeeper. So why don't you just stay out of the mill?" he said brutally.

"I'm not policing you, Henry—"

"Good."

"—but I think I have a right to be told about anything involving such big sums of money," Tandy continued firmly.

"So the next time a 'big sum' comes my way, I'll tell you. Don't grieve over the money so, Tandy. The insurance has already agreed to cover it as early as next week, before the logs even get here. I talked to Tom Haskel from the firm today. Any other questions?" He looked from one to the other of them, then turned and went out.

"He didn't eat much," Tandy said wistfully in the silence, looking over at his half-full plate. "But I have the right to ask questions."

And so do I, thought Terrill. "Where's Lineville?" she asked curiously.

The question drew Tandy's attention back to her. "I beg your pardon?"

"You said, 'No good ever came out of Lineville,'" Terrill reminded her patiently.

"And that's a natural fact," Tandy snapped. "It's a prison on the Tennessee and Kentucky state line. Henry's up and hired a man who spent two years there."

"Oh." So the green-eyed captive today really was as bad as he had looked.

As an afterthought, she asked Tandy, "What did he do? To go to prison, I mean?"

"He robbed the mill," Tandy said flatly. "Nearly three years ago. And cut up a deputy in the process."

"*Daddy's* mill?" Terrill asked in shock.

"That's right."

But Terrill remembered something else. "Aunt Tandy, today when we were at the mill, it had—the sign had Henry's name on it." She watched her aunt's face, waiting for the simple explanation. Waiting for her to say that it was all Henry's idea.

Instead Tandy's face flushed a little and she bit her lip nervously.

Still Terrill waited.

"I suppose I knew I'd have to be the one to tell you," Tandy said at last, reluctantly. "Katherine has given Henry full control over the business, Terrill."

"Full control!" Terrill echoed, her voice incredulous, then hurt. And that made her angry at herself: surely she'd learned enough to know that something like this was bound to happen, that there was no point in wasting emotions on it. "So Henry runs the business completely now for Mama."

"More than that," Tandy said firmly, looking her niece in the eye. "No more shilly-shallying. The truth is that Katherine has willed the mill over to Henry. It—it will be his. It *is* his."

Terrill went even whiter. "And Daddy? He's just forgotten forever? She never even thought once about him? That it was his, even if Henry always wanted it?"

"Luke has been dead these seven years, Terrill. What is there to think? Henry's done better than—"

"Don't say it!"

"Better than Katherine did with the mill, even with me trying to help. I don't like to admit it, but it's the truth. And she's made provisions for you, too."

"I don't want them. Not a single thing from her," Terrill said fiercely, trying to choke back the hurt and the anger. "This is not about money. This is about Henry taking Daddy's place, and mine. It wouldn't be so terrible except—he meant to do it. So where do I go, Aunt Tandy? Where do I belong?"

"Don't be so dramatic, Terrill. You belong here, with Katherine."

"No, I don't. I haven't in years. Not since the day that you and Mama and I went to Nashville—to shop, I thought. Instead"—Terrill stood, moving so roughly that she jarred the silverware on the table, and her hands gripped the back of the chair—"you took me to Rose Hall and left me."

"Please, Terrill," Tandy said pleadingly, looking up at her niece. "You wouldn't let us talk to you or try to explain that day."

"There was nothing to explain. Mama was crying, so you had to tell me what was happening, that all of you were pushing me out. I might as well have been dead, like Daddy."

"You know that's not true. Katherine and I came to see you week after week, and you refused even to talk to us. It wasn't until you came down sick with pneumonia and couldn't run from the infirmary bed that you even let Katherine touch you. You knew why we sent you to Rose Hall, anyway. You and Henry had been at each other's throats, tearing this family apart."

Terrill pushed the chair in under the table carefully. "And I had tried to run away," she said without emotion.

"You *did* run away," Tandy corrected. "That was when we decided you had to go to Rose Hall, the day you ran away because Katherine tried to send you to visit with me at my house in Bethel."

"He was sending me to live with you for good, Aunt Tandy. He wanted me out because Mama was going to have a baby. *His* baby."

"If they were sending you away for more than the summer, I never knew it."

"Henry told me," Terrill said passionately. "Standing right here in this kitchen."

"So you left. A sixteen-year-old girl, gone three days. Gone so wrong, Terrill. We thought you were dead. They—they dragged the river for your body. Do you know how terrified Katherine was, how sick *I* was, until we found you half-starved and hiding in that old picnic shelter down close to the Red Fork River? What could we do but send you to Rose Hall?"

"You could have loved me. Said, 'Rilla, this is your home.' That was what I wanted. But instead I got sent away. And Mama lost the baby three weeks later. One more thing that Henry could blame me for. One more reason to hate me."

Tandy hesitated, speaking carefully. "He doesn't love you like he should. But, honey, you were never very lovable around him, either. Poor Henry—even his own father—your grandpa Carroll—turned against him in that last year before he died. I never understood it. But, please, Terrill, for Katherine's sake, try to make things work. Take the love she's trying to give you, even if you think it's late. Love is hard to come by in this world."

3

When Ned Standford pulled up in front of the little gray house shrouded by darkness, Maggie Kane was waiting for him at the door.

"Ned's here," she told her son Jubal, who lay on the couch in the tiny living room with one bruised arm resting in exhaustion across his forehead and eyes. "I knew he'd come."

She opened the door before Ned could knock and stared at him solemnly a minute. Then she said, her voice quiet and resigned, "Ever' time you come to my door, you bring trouble."

"Sometimes it's not of my makin', Maggie," the sheriff said quickly.

"And last night? Who's to blame for that?"

"I didn't tell Foster to rough up your boy. I swear it. I jumped him about it, too."

"Him and that Malone man—that other deputy—they never give him a chance. They caught him when he came in the door, took him by surprise. When he tried to get free, before he even knew who they were, they beat him half-senseless. I was tellin' 'em and tellin' 'em to stop, but they—"

"Ma!"

Jubal's voice cut across her furious, painful words as he stood slowly, his shirt open, his hair ruffled.

In relief, Standford spoke directly to him. "I want to talk to you, Jubal. That's all—just talk."

"I got nothin' to say to you, except I didn't steal Carroll's money," Jubal answered flatly, his face like stone. But his hands tightened into fists at his side.

"I believe you," said Standford.

Kane stared at him scornfully.

"I do," the sheriff insisted.

"Why?" Kane asked in patent disbelief.

"Not because you're such a good, law-abidin' citizen," Standford replied ironically. "But because I know how much you hated Lineville. That place is pure hell."

There was a moment's silence, and then Kane swallowed heavily. Standford motioned outside. "Can we talk out here?" he asked. "Just for a few minutes. I'm not your enemy, Jubal. But you know that. So just stop fightin' me for once."

At last, with a hard, jerking movement, Kane acquiesced. Maggie stepped aside to let him out the door, and when he stood on the porch beside the sheriff, reluctance written all over him, she closed the door and turned out the light.

Out in the darkness, Jubal heard the long call of a faraway whippoorwill across the top of the ridge and his own too rapid, harsh breathing. To the back of Maggie's house, he could see where the land lifted even higher, all the way up to Copper's Bluff, now just a black, looming, impossible promontory against the shadowy night sky, its edges ragged with trees so big they looked like towering temples.

"Well, what you want?" Jubal asked impatiently.

"I want to know why Henry Carroll hired you," Standford said bluntly. "I've been wonderin' all these months."

Kane moved away sharply. "You'd have to ask him."

"I have, but I don't get any real answers. Everything about this setup bothers me. Three years ago you rob the man, he's hotter'n hell about it—wants them to throw the book at you. They send you to a rough little hellhole of a prison. But then Carroll goes to Lineville just two years later and tells them he'll guarantee you a job if they'll give you early probation, on account of Maggie and all. Because he's had a change of heart. It don't make a damn bit of sense."

The sheriff glanced over in the shadows; Kane didn't move. "You know what the town's saying, Jubal? They say you're Henry's charity case. They say he's helpin' *you* in the hopes that God's gonna help him and make his wife well again. How's it feel to be somebody's Christian duty, boy?"

Kane shrugged. That was all. But he didn't like Standford's words, and the sheriff knew it, so he plowed on. "You been workin' at that mill several months now. You got any idea who mighta robbed Carroll last night?"

"I don't know," Kane replied tonelessly.

Standford moved at last, his voice frustrated. "Not givin' anythin' away, are you? Lineville smartened you up considerably, didn't it?" There was an unwilling touch of pity in the words, but he still gained no answer from the poker-stiff figure at the other end of the porch.

"I got one or two more things to say to you, Jubal," the sheriff said determinedly. "Stay out of trouble.

Just keep thinking about that probation. This county's real leery of you, and if you turn up involved in just one more mess, they're gonna put you away for a big chunk of your life before you even get it started. Do you know how to stay out of trouble? Sometimes I don't think you do. So I'm gonna do you a big favor—I'm gonna tell you. You keep away from some of those so-called friends of yours, for one thing, and you keep away from the Pine, and most of all, you keep away from little bitches like Tess Johnson."

Kane sucked in his breath sharply, but Standford ignored him.

"It was a fool thing to do, to tell Johnson about her. You're damn lucky he hadn't figured out yet what she does on all these weekends that she comes home from Vanderbilt." The sheriff glanced over at Kane. "An' don't get ideas about that Carroll girl, either. I don't care if she does look like honey and lightning all poured together. She's trouble. That's why they sent her to that school. Fancy or not, it's for kids who're givin' problems. Watch your back, Jubal, and watch your step."

Standford started down the rickety little wooden stairs that led off the porch, then he turned for a parting shot, one hand resting on the big blue-black butt of the gun that protruded from his holster. "Because if you don't," he said on a note of warning, "I'll come and get you myself. And I hit a damn sight harder than those sorry deputies of mine."

Jubal leaned back against a porch post, watching Standford leave, aching all over. It wasn't just the bruises he'd picked up at dawn from Foster and the other deputy, although they'd nearly killed him.

No—he'd taken punches before.

Most of this hurt came from wondering how many more times he was going to wind up at the mercy of this county.

Three years ago, when Jubal had been twenty, it had refused any kind of plea for leniency.

"I want Kane to pay," Henry Carroll had told the jury, his face full of the righteous indignation of the wronged. "If we don't stop his kind the first time, everybody gets hurt."

His kind.

Cade County understood Henry's words exactly, and with that understanding came remembrance.

They remembered that one of Jubal's grandfathers had been a bootlegger and a whiskey runner, and that his daddy, Morgan, had died in a gunfight as an accessory to armed robbery.

"An apple doesn't fall far from the tree," Jubal had actually heard one of the jurors tell another.

But nobody—not even Jubal's reluctant, court-appointed attorney—had defended Jubal or his family by telling what had actually happened, that Morgan had been sitting in Sammie Belden's old truck, half-drunk and with his deer rifle across his knees, the night Sammie went into the Fina station for a carton of Lucky Strike cigarettes and decided to ask for a little more than his change.

Morgan got caught in the crossfire between his buddy and the owner of the station, who took Sammie's request in an unfavorable light.

Sammie survived to do time at Brushy Mountain State Penitentiary, and nobody much even questioned the station owner, who was one of the Allardts and therefore automatically in the right.

Jubal had been only three years old when Morgan died, but to Cade County he clearly had no choice about his destiny: genetics alone determined that he was bent straight for hell, they said.

And life out on that hilly, rocky, poor arm of the county that stretched up toward Kentucky had just finished the job, just put Jubal so close to the devil that you could feel the heat when he moved. They said that, too.

He was a Kane. No matter that he'd never been in any serious trouble before; bad blood was bound to come out.

A wild ridge runner from Sullivan's Ridge—and all of them knew that no good ever came off of Sullivan's Ridge.

And, finally, they said "Guilty."

Then they sent him to Lineville.

The sole individual from Bethel who ever thought twice about Jubal while he was there was Standford. Jubal could remember the one time that the sheriff had actually intervened for him. . . .

"What happened to your face, boy?"

Standford's words rang harshly in Jubal's ears as they sat opposite each other in the quiet little room. Just the two of them and a poker-faced guard over at the door.

"Ain't nothin' happened to it," Jubal answered at last, keeping his voice emotionless.

"Don't lie to me. You took a fist, hard."

Jubal straightened, his body too slender in the dark T-shirt. "So what? It's got nothin' to do with you. Just get the hell off my back, okay?"

Standford shrugged. He'd come dressed as a civilian in a plaid shirt and khaki pants, for which Jubal was devoutly thankful. All he needed was for word to get around that he'd been talking to a cop. A lawyer, the inmates at Lineville would understand—but not a sheriff.

"It's nothin' to me if they're beatin' up on you around here, kid."

"That's right. It ain't. So what'd you come for?"

"I want to know why you didn't tell the jury that somebody else was in on that little deal at Carroll Mill," the sheriff said abruptly.

Jubal jumped a little—or maybe it was just his skin flinching, the movement was so small. "I don't know what you're talkin' about," he finally answered.

"Oh, don't you?" Standford's words were dry and sardonic. Then he dropped the game; he got direct. "We finally found all those little things that Carroll reported missin' from his office, including that solid gold antique watch that used to belong to his old man."

His blunt features under the flattop haircut were suddenly sharp; his decisive voice prodded Jubal to speak. But Jubal stayed stubborn and silent.

"A fisherman hooked the sack out of the mud at the bottom of the Red Fork last week. Who threw it there, Jubal? We know now that you didn't hide it somewhere on the mill property. And you sure as hell never got a chance to get to the river. We caught you dead to rights in the office."

Jubal swallowed, but he never moved or spoke.

"Why didn't you tell that jury there was somebody else that night?" Standford asked quietly. "Instead, here you are, taking all the rap. And the other person is somewhere out there scot-free."

"It woulda done no good to tell 'em. The jury meant to put me away. It was in their faces. And there wasn't a damn thing I could do about it."

Standford took the truth as stoically as Jubal's words.

"All right. It's done. So now we'll deal with the present. You were takin' some classes—workin' in the shop, too, the warden said, up until last week. But today he tells me you've been in solitary for seven days for fightin'."

"It's no big deal."

"Didn't you hear what I said? I know why." Standford stood abruptly, then said in angry exasperation, "Goddammit, Jubal, somebody—one of *them* out there—made a—a pass at you, didn't he?"

The sheriff was blustery and rough in his embarrassment; the red tide that came up in his face was echoed by the one in Jubal's as he looked up, then away.

"I—I don't know what'n the hell you're talkin' about," Jubal stumbled, but shame was eating him alive.

"Yeah, you do. I shoulda known it, soon as I found out they didn't put you in the section with the first-timers. The warden said since there wasn't a man in Lineville over twenty-five anyway—since it was for young offenders—it'd make no difference. But young men are just as mean as old ones." Standford laid his big hand on Jubal's shoulder, shaking him a little. "How'd you keep him off, Jubal? You might as well tell me—I'll find out somehow anyway."

Jubal choked, finally forcing out the words. "A knife. I made it," he said roughly, looking away. "I knew . . . he was gettin' ready to try something."

Standford's hand tightened. "You're tough, that's for sure. Ridge runners gotta be. But don't worry. I'm gonna raise hell around here. You're gonna get moved to the facility for first-time offenders. And I don't give a damn what Henry Carroll, or anybody else, says about it, either."

Standford kept his word; they sent Jubal down the road to Dormitory C, where he was one of the oldest inmates. He entered the place with a reputation for being quick with a homemade knife and more than willing to use it.

The others mostly just left him alone. But in the smothering confines of that prison-within-a-prison, Jubal did learn one thing of the greatest importance. He learned that he had to get out of this place. And stay out.

Lineville couldn't hold him forever; he'd do whatever he had to do to walk free again.

And, finally, he had. He'd agreed to work for Carroll himself. He'd virtually made himself a slave to a master, but after two years in prison he would have worked for Lucifer if he'd asked him to.

Thinking about the downward spiral his life had taken, standing in the dark on Maggie's porch, Jubal wished—God, he wished—he could just climb up to Copper's Bluff with the clouds and vanish.

Forget what he owed Maggie. Forget mistakes. Forget people like Henry Carroll and Lionel Johnson . . . and their daughters.

But, instead, Jubal kept remembering. More than anything, he kept seeing the revulsion and fright and distaste that had been written with blinding clarity in the face of the girl as she'd stood in the door of the mill office that morning. For one split second, under the blaze of her wide, dark blue eyes, he'd felt scorched with shame, and he'd wanted to hide the bite on his throat and the manacles on his wrists.

Heat and anger had torn through him, coming to his rescue. She had no right to look at him as if he were half human, an untamed creature that both fascinated and repelled.

She looked at him the way Tess treated him.

He dropped his face into the crook of his raised

elbow a minute, then winced as he brushed his bruised cheek on the hard bone of his forearm.

"You all right?" Ma's voice right behind him made him jump a little. She had opened the door silently.

"Yeah—yeah, I'm okay."

But when he stepped back inside the house, in the brightness of the lamps, she looked at his face and said involuntarily, "You're gonna make it, boy."

He said in quiet pain, "You been tellin' me that all my life."

"I tell you the truth," she said, lifting her hand to brush her twisted, arthritic fingers across his high cheekbones, somewhere just under his tired eyes. "You're a good boy. The one Jesus gave me—"

"Ma, please." But he stood there in resignation, making no more than the token protest. He knew the story, knew what she would say. She told it to him at every crisis of his life, even when they'd come to take him to Lineville. It was her litany of comfort, so he let her continue.

"When I found out I was carryin' you, I told Him none of my troubles would ever matter to me again, if He'd just give me a special son. One who was gonna do better and be more in his life. And I asked Him to put a sign in my baby's face."

She laughed a little, looking up at him. "Green eyes, Jubal. Just as bright as new leaves even on the mornin' you was born. Like none I've ever seen. They're my sign. You ain't meant for no jail. They ain't one little part of you like your daddy, or your brother Frankie. You're marked for better things."

"Ma." His voice was flat. "I'm nothin' special. I never will be."

"You will someday. I'll know when. Something's gonna give you a chance. It'll happen."

He looked down at her a long, long moment. Not even a lifetime of hardship had robbed her completely of an old-fashioned prettiness. She had a neat, slightly rounded body and a cap of silvery hair, chopped off under her ears and softened by a natural curl. She was the sum total of all the love he'd ever known in his life, but she looked at the world with a faded hazel stare that was too inward to catch view of the fact that she was hopelessly out of date.

Sometimes Jubal wanted to shake her, to tell her to wake up and join real life, to ask her if she'd ever heard of things like fast cars and faster women.

But she'd always been there for him, so he just said quietly, "I'll be all right."

She nodded, folding her hands up under her apron as if to hide their uselessness, and she said calmly, "Yes. You will."

Then her gaze fell on the mark on his throat that he couldn't get his collar up high enough to hide. "But I don't reckon there's any need in you comin' home lookin' like this anymore," she said, nodding in distaste toward the place.

Even after everything, he couldn't stop the flush that rose hotly to his face. "No, ma'am," he mumbled meekly enough, and he felt twelve, not twenty-three.

4

"*Kane, you come* with me and Hackett."

Carroll's voice issued the command carelessly. When Jubal looked up from the oily, greasy engine parts that he worked with every day, the parts that were scattered across the worktable in front of him, the man was already vanishing from the door of the little shop that sat at the back and to the side of Carroll Mill's office.

Carroll never even looked around to see if Jubal was following his orders. But then he didn't have to; he knew he would.

Reluctantly Jubal reached for the shop rag, wiping the oily slickness from his hands. This engine was due to be put together by Saturday; why didn't Carroll just leave him alone back here in the shop, isolated from the rest of the mill, and let him do his job?

Instead Carroll was waiting, and beside him, Bobo Hackett had both feet planted firmly under his rotund, St. Nick figure. He had a jovial face, too, partially hidden by a bushy red-blond beard that bristled out over the flannel shirt he wore.

Once Jubal had thought Bobo was a pretty good old boy, maybe a buddy.

He'd gotten a lot smarter since.

It said a lot about Carroll that he hired men like Bobo—but, hell, who was Jubal to complain? Carroll had hired him, too.

Ridge runners, the other men called the two of them, always pairing them together. It was only halfway meant as a joke.

Jubal mostly just ignored it, just as he'd ignored the pugnacious overtures of a few of the workers who were itching to show the sawmill world that they were better men than this twenty-three-year-old kid with his tough-guy, bad-boy reputation.

Just stay out of trouble, he kept telling himself. *Probation's up at Christmas—then you'll walk.*

He always reminded himself of that when Carroll ordered him around the way he was doing now.

"I want you boys to go up to the house," Carroll said calmly, running an ink pen into his shirt pocket with his right hand.

Bobo stared. "*Your* house, Mr. Carroll?"

"Where do you think I mean? There's a hospital supply company up there with some things for my wife. A hospital bed so that she can be raised at night. To—help her breathe." Carroll's face darkened. "They'll need help. Take the truck"—he nodded toward one of the mill's company vehicles—"and go on up there. Move what they tell you."

Jubal didn't budge. What was Carroll thinking of, to send him to the house?

"You got a problem, Kane?"

"Yeah. I can't go in there. I never been any closer'n

a hundred feet to your sister, but I can already tell you—she's gonna raise hell over me comin' into her house."

"Do you think I care?" Carroll said irritably. "It comes down to this—you're all I've got available right now. So get the hell up to the house."

Jubal's face felt tight with anger, but he started walking.

"Wait. You—Bobo. You'd better do the talking," Carroll called brusquely. "You just do the job and stay out of the way, Kane. I'll call Tandy and tell her somebody's co—"

Carroll was already halfway to the office when the last word was obscured by the sound of a giant saw that was turned on in the nearby shop. The black shadow of the oak tree, its limbs nearly bare of leaves, fell across Carroll like a dark bar as he passed under it.

"Son of a bitch," Bobo muttered under his breath. "C'mon, Jubal, let's get it over with. Man, I dread facin' that puckered-up sister of his."

But Jubal had forgotten Tandy Carroll in the sudden rush of another memory. Was the girl with blue eyes—the one he'd seen here nine days ago— was she at the house?

God, he hoped not. All he needed was another run-in with her scorn and contempt.

They went first to the side door, which stood open to reveal the neat kitchen beyond, but the screen door was latched. The front door, though, had been propped open wide; the van in front of it had its doors open as well, and several heavy pieces sat inside it.

"Miz Carroll?" Bobo called through the aperture. Jubal stood back, waiting. "We're here to help move a bed."

The woman's voice called back in answer, "It's the second door past the stairs. Go right on through the hall."

And that was exactly what Bobo did. Jubal followed him, a dark shadow on his heels.

He'd never been inside the Carroll house, and it made him uneasy being here now. He hoped he didn't break anything. A gleaming oak floor ran left into a formal dining room, where a cherry table gleamed under its load of two crystal candlesticks and a vase of cut flowers. On the right was a living room, where a delicate floral sofa and pale blue armchairs stood grouped around a wooden-and-glass table. A copy of a magazine named *Southern Living* lay on the table; another paperback folder, this one full of music sheets, stood on the big piano that was pushed against a far wall.

Jubal wondered if he had gotten all the grease off his hands and shoes before he followed Bobo down the pristine hall in front of him. He could hear Tandy Carroll talking in a distant room, apparently on a telephone. There was no sign of the girl.

But his relief was short-lived. He found her in the bedroom instead, where she was caught between the two beds, one a tall, four-poster affair that she'd stripped clean of bedclothes. She stood with her back to them, clutching the sheets to her as two men in white adjusted the stern silver lines of the standard hospital bed they'd already set up.

Katherine Carroll lay in it; she reached for her daughter's free hand as one of the men rolled up the head.

"How's that?" the other one asked cheerfully, his voice too loud as he addressed Katherine. "All right for you?"

"It's fine. Fine." Her own voice was weak and husky.

Jubal had never seen the woman before except in a picture that sat on Carroll's desk. The huge blue eyes and the golden cloud of hair were the only features he recognized in the paper-thin face.

"We're here to move some things for you," Bobo repeated again to anybody who'd listen, but mostly he spoke in the general direction of the tall girl.

She twisted a little, surprise written on her face. Jubal, hanging behind Bobo's broad girth in the door, caught only a flash of blue—darker than her mother's—as she did. He'd thought more than he wanted to admit about her. He didn't like her much, that was for sure.

"Oh, it's the men from the mill. Aunt Tandy wants the bed moved to the attic at the top of the stairs. And I think—we need to move this chest of drawers, too." She looked inquiringly at one of the men in white, who nodded.

"That's right. We've got a standing set of shelves for that corner for several pieces of equipment the doctor wants left here."

"Then move the bed first. I'll empty the drawers—"

"No need to do that," Bobo interrupted. "We'll just take 'em out, move the frame, then put the drawers back in one at a time. C'mon, Jubal, grab that end of this mattress."

The girl's head came up sharply from her inspection of the chest, and she searched for an instant, until Bobo moved and her gaze fell on Jubal's face. Her eyes were startled, surprised, tentative, as they met his.

Well, he didn't have to wonder anymore if she knew who he was, or what her reaction would be. She took two steps back as he moved up to the foot of the bed—and her gaze slid farther, to his throat, seeking the mark there as if to prove he was the same man she thought.

But he dropped his head so that even if it had still been there, she couldn't have seen it.

A flash of anger shot through him, identical with the one he'd felt that Saturday. Damn Tess for marking him like some animal, and damn this girl for noticing.

"Better show us where this goes," Bobo said as they heaved up the top mattress.

"Oh—here. Follow me," the girl said hurriedly. She had to brush past Jubal; her scent was clean and light as she did, but she kept her head turned away.

They made several trips up the stairs to a door at the far end. Another short flight of steps up was the attic, with its walls sloping to the ceiling and its big expanse of space.

By the time they'd broken down the bed and moved its rails and headboards separately, the men from the supply company were through. They went out to speak to Tandy, still in that distant room.

The girl—she had on close-fitting jeans and a T-shirt—was pulling drawers out of the chest. As Jubal moved up to help her, she twisted too fast— maybe to get away from him—and dropped one corner of the heavy drawer.

He grabbed at it as it fell out of her hands, but too late—one end hit the floor, and a thin fabric bag spilled out, breaking open and scattering its contents across the creamy carpet.

She muttered something under her breath, and he dropped to his knees to try to gather up what had spilled. It was strange stuff—the sack had contained old leaves and dried purple flowers and sticks and twigs.

"Just let it—go," Katherine told him from the bed. "We'll vacuum it. It was . . . an old potpourri bag . . . anyway. Been there since . . . last summer."

"A what?" He let the crumply, papery substance fall from his hands as he looked up at the woman watching him. Katherine Carroll had luminous, gentle eyes.

"A potpourri bag," she repeated.

He'd be damned if he let on that he didn't know what in the hell she was talking about.

The girl on his other side hefted up the drawer with her shoulders and one knee. "You put it in drawers to make clothes smell good. It has dried herbs and flowers in it."

Her voice was clear and cool, so uninterested and so very superior.

"Is that so?" he asked flippantly, trying to hide his embarrassment at his lack of knowledge, and twisted up to grab the heavy drawer that was slipping from her grasp again. At least here was something he could do better than she did.

He was so close to her when he looked up that he could see a tiny pulse pounding in her throat, just at the edge of the heavy mass of honey-brown hair.

Maybe she wasn't so superior and uninterested after all.

"What are you doing here?"

Tandy's sharp, startled voice cut the tension between them. Both Jubal and the girl jumped, and he nearly let the drawer slip again.

But he looked back at the woman with silent defiance. It was a look he'd perfected out of sheer necessity at Lineville.

Nobody answered until Katherine finally spoke in mild surprise. "He's one of the men . . . from the mill, Tandy. Henry sent him."

Tandy swallowed the words on her lips and forced pleasantness into her tone. "I see. Henry sent him, did he?"

"Me'n Bobo Hackett." There—he'd gotten out the words, hadn't let this stern old woman intimidate him.

"The other man's still in the attic," Terrill offered in a rush, her fingers tightening on her end of the drawer.

"Why don't you put that heavy drawer down, Terrill?" Tandy said quietly. "Let Mr. Kane and Mr. Hackett do their job, so they can get through."

And leave your house, Jubal finished in his own head. The woman on the bed looked like an angel; this one was a witch. He had a good idea which one the girl was like.

She released the drawer abruptly, and he shifted to take the weight. Without a word or a glance, she left the room, left him facing the still, disapproving face of Tandy Carroll, who stepped aside and motioned him through the door.

Upstairs, he met Bobo coming out of the attic.

"You better watch your step," he told the older man. "There's a drill sergeant down there now."

"Ah, shit, not her," Bobo muttered in protest. "I thought we'd get outta here without seein' the woman."

Jubal was going down empty-handed and Bobo was coming back up the stairs with another load when they met again. "Well, you're outta here, kid," he told Jubal.

"What?"

"Carroll just came in. She's givin' him hell over havin' you in the house."

"What does she think I'm gonna do?" Jubal asked, half in anger, half in despair. "Rob her? Rape her?"

"I hope you ain't that desperate for a woman," Bobo retorted.

Without another word, Jubal turned down the stairs. He couldn't get out the front door—Tandy and Henry were there.

". . . and if you're determined to keep him on as a hand, I can't stop you. But it makes no sense to send him right into your home when somebody else will do. I found him not a foot from Terrill—"

Jubal cut across her words. "I'm leavin'," he said roughly. Instead of pushing his way past the two of them, he took the more dignified exit, heading toward that side door they'd come to earlier in the kitchen he could see from here at the stairs.

He would have made it scot-free, except for the girl. She was standing near the sink as he strode through the room.

His sudden entrance, his hurried movements—they startled her. "What's wrong?" she demanded, her eyes turning in her mother's direction.

"Nothin'. I just want out before I get sick."

She moved quickly out of his way as he lunged for the latch on the screen, but as he pulled it open, he felt it—her gaze on his throat again. This time he caught her staring before she could look away, and the temper inside him broke.

"Here," he said furiously, yanking down the shirt to bare his throat and part of his shoulder. "It's gone. Now will you quit starin'? Are you satisfied?"

"I don't know—what you're talking about," she whispered huskily, but her cheeks were flushed and her eyes wide and dark.

"Oh, yeah—you do. What d'you want, anyway? Me to tell you how it got there?"

"No!" She pressed back against the end of the kitchen counter that blocked farther retreat.

"No?" He let his gaze drop down her face—to her lips, her throat, her breasts—then back to her lips. They were trembling. Maybe she was afraid of him, like her aunt. Something dark and mean took hold of him, and he said suggestively, "Or I could show you, maybe."

She sucked in a harsh wave of breath, and this

time it was fury that flushed her cheeks. "You deserve to have your face slapped. But I'm not going to waste my time getting mad over a man who's so ignorant he doesn't know any better than to say something that . . . that rude to a stranger."

Her words—her fight, her spirit—were a shock. He'd expected something clever, something hiding a sting, something full of sexual innuendo. He'd been expecting an answer like one Tess would have made, he realized suddenly.

Not this direct, clean, swift retaliation.

"I ain't—I'm not ignorant," he shot back, his own face staining darkly.

"No? You didn't even know what a potpourri bag was," she answered. Her words were quiet, but they rang with triumph.

He swallowed. Couldn't speak. Couldn't stem the rush of embarrassment that swept over him. So he reached again for the latch and flung himself out the door.

He wasn't going back to work today; he was going where he belonged, back to Sullivan's Ridge. Away from people who distrusted him and despised him just because of his name. Away from this *Better Homes and Gardens* house.

And away from girls with eyes as darkly blue as the twilight sky and tongues that held the sting of a scorpion.

On Sunday, Terrill climbed the steps to the First Baptist Church with Tandy and actually took time to look around, to enjoy the big building where she'd once sat beside Katherine and Luke and listened to Grandfather Terrill—the one she'd been named for—preach.

The bright sunshine of the morning, the tiny chill in the air, the voices ringing in song—those lulled Terrill into a sense of peace.

It lasted until late that afternoon, when she and Tandy sat with Katherine.

"Did you . . . did you see anybody you knew at church?" she whispered a little drowsily. She'd had pain in her back so much today that Tandy had reluctantly given her half a dose of the pain medicine that was supposed to be used only at night.

"No."

"Tess Johnson was home. She came to show off her new boyfriend, I suppose," Tandy said dryly. "You know her, don't you, Terrill?"

"Not in years." She remembered the girl with the shiny cap of black hair, the perfect makeup, the expensive, fashion-plate look. Beside her had been another equally gorgeous human being, his brown hair the same exact shade as his suntanned skin, a creamy suit and tie showing his build to advantage.

Terrill understood now how ludicrous Kane's words that first day were. The idea of Tess Johnson and Jubal Kane was preposterous.

"Luke came . . . to church and just walked in and sat right down . . . beside me the first time," Katherine said suddenly.

Silence.

Terrill's throat closed up.

And almost as if she'd been disloyal, Katherine asked anxiously, "Where's . . . Henry?"

"Still down at the mill. I don't hold with working on Sundays, but something unexpected came up, he said," Tandy answered soothingly.

Terrill's carefully blank face made Katherine say, looking at her daughter, "Henry's working—hard . . . to keep things going for you . . . honey."

Terrill still said nothing.

Then Tandy urged, "That's good of him, isn't it, Terrill?"

"It's his way . . . of showing that he does care," Katherine added. "About you, Rilla. Why . . . else would he work . . . so hard?"

Terrill wanted to be good, to say something reassuring, but before she could stop it, her tongue was saying something else. "Is that why you've given him the mill? Why Daddy's name has been painted over? Why you took away what was his?"

There was a long moment of strained silence. Then Tandy said from her position on the rocking chair at the door, "I had to tell her, Katherine."

Katherine whispered, "Henry says . . . it has to do with buyer confidence."

"Buyer confidence!" Terrill echoed scornfully. "In Cade County? Because Daddy's dead and Henry's alive?"

Katherine spoke at last, her voice a long shiver of sound. "I loved . . . Luke. I did, Rilla, no matter what . . . you think. . . ."

It was unsettling, the way Katherine suddenly went to the heart of things these days—she, who had always been so anxious to avoid an argument or a confrontation. And it made Terrill angry. Why hadn't her mother always done it? Why now, when it was too late?

"Now, Katherine," Tandy said soothingly. "We know that. Terrill knows that."

"No—she doesn't," Katherine choked out. "I ne-never realized un-til—" Then she began to cough and choke in an agitated fervor.

"Her medicine . . . Get the rest of the medicine," Tandy said sharply to Terrill, who had half risen from her own chair, guilt-stricken.

They got it down Katherine at last, and as she lay quietly, drowsily, on the pillow, her face wet with tears, she said faintly, "I *did* love . . . him, Ri . . . Rilla."

The remorse that gripped Terrill made it hard for her to speak, but she said at last, "All right, Mama. All right."

Maybe Katherine didn't even hear the muttered words; she was slipping in and out of euphoric sleep. But Tandy heard them, and she nodded a little in approval, motioning Terrill into silence as they sat at the bed.

They were still sitting there when Henry came home. Terrill gave him his ground without a word, just getting up as he came in the room and walking out, but she unwillingly heard the sound of his kiss on Katherine's face. She heard Katherine stir on the bed. And she heard Henry say, "Hello, darling."

"Luke."

Katherine spoke the name clearly. It stopped Terrill in her tracks.

Henry straightened slowly, backing away. Somewhere behind her, Terrill heard Tandy say pleadingly, "Henry."

He turned then, facing Terrill and Tandy in the hall, his face white. His single look at his stepdaughter told her his thoughts: *You. It's your fault, Terrill.* And maybe it was, she thought to herself. Maybe she was what was wrong in this house.

"It's the medicine," Tandy told him anxiously. "I had to give her more than usual. She's—getting worse. She won't even remember this tomorrow."

"But I will," he said through clenched teeth, then he pushed past his sister and went outside. Terrill heard his car pulling out of the drive a minute later.

"Go on to bed," Tandy said wearily. "Get a good

night's sleep. We may have to get up tonight with Katherine."

Instead, Terrill stared at the ceiling for hours. For one minute she had looked at her uncle and her mother, and they were just Henry and Katherine. Two people whose lives were tangled tragedies. Almost—almost—she'd felt sorrier for Henry.

She lay awake so long, in fact, that she didn't sleep until nearly dawn, and she awoke to her alarm knowing that she had to see Katherine, no matter what time it was. Hesitantly she looked in her mother's room. She didn't know what to say except "I'm sorry, Mama."

But she didn't get to say anything. Katherine's eyes were closed, her face a white, waxy mask. And Henry was there.

She backed out hastily, but today, instead of ignoring her, he called after her, came after her, catching at her arm as she got just to the door. She flinched in surprise and fell back against the door frame. He released her instantly; he too had no taste for the physical contact.

"I've got something to say to you," he said shortly.

"What law did I break this time?" Terrill answered, flippant and rude.

"Stay out of Katherine's room after supper," he said abrasively. "That's my time with my wife. *Our* time. I won't have you intruding anymore. Tandy said you upset her last night. That's just part of the reason she had the attack. Stay in your room."

"Who do you think you are to tell me this?" Terrill breathed, low and enraged, shocked by his words. "She's my mother. I know everybody wishes I didn't exist, but I do. I'll go in any time I please. Do you hear me?"

"And she's my wife. This is *my* house."

"Like it's *your* mill?" she asked sarcastically, trying not to cry. "You're pathetic, Henry. You're living Daddy's life. You've got his mill and his wife—and you pretend they're yours. But you've not got me. Not me."

Henry answered without a flicker of emotion, "Haven't you figured it out yet, Terrill? I don't want you. Nobody does."

Terrill drew a deep, ragged breath. No need to hurt; no need to feel as if she'd been slapped to her knees. She didn't need anybody.

She had herself.

It was enough.

She would make it be enough.

Just as she tried to get beyond the door, she saw Katherine over Henry's shoulder. Not asleep. Her eyes were wide and blue and full of some inner pain—but Terrill had no time now to think of Katherine's pain.

Now she had to deal with her own.

5

Two days later Henry put Terrill to work at the mill office on Mondays, Wednesdays, and Fridays. He was getting her out of the house part of the time, and he made it clear that he would go even farther.

"You give me one reason to send you back to Rose Hall—just one I can use with Tandy—and you'll be gone," he told her quietly as they stood alone together in the kitchen on the morning she was to begin the job. "You may be an adult by law, but I still hold some degree of control over this house."

Tandy, who walked in a minute later, mistook their confrontation for a silent companionship.

"Well, this is wonderful. You're both up early. Maybe you can even ride over with Henry, Terrill," she said cheerfully.

"I have several errands to run this morning before I go to the mill," Henry answered, his voice brusque.

He was pulling on the light jacket he held in his hands.

"I want to walk," Terrill told Tandy. "It's not half a mile if I cut across the field and go along the edge of the hollow."

"Walk!"

"Daddy used to walk over every morning," Terrill reminded Tandy, and her words challenged Henry, daring him to take offense. But he did nothing except leave the room, heading outside.

"And I suppose this idea you've got about walking is the reason you're dressed like a—a . . ." Tandy didn't finish the sentence, instead letting her gaze slide disapprovingly down the plaid cotton shirt with its rolled-up sleeves, the blue jeans, and the leather high-tops.

"This is comfortable."

"I've never held with a secretary looking like an escaped teenager. You need a suit—or one of your Sunday dresses. Hose and heels."

"But I'm not the secretary. Rosalie is. We both know the reason I'm at the office is that Henry wants me away from Mama. It's just to get me out of the way."

Tandy stood silent, looking into Terrill's blue eyes. Then she put the coffee cup she held on the table. "Maybe that's true, Terrill. But fighting his every move like this is foolish. You were angry that he'd cut you out of the mill, but here is your chance back in. And I think you'll enjoy getting out of the house. Won't you?"

Terrill took a deep breath. Why was she arguing? All that Tandy said was true. "Yes," she mumbled reluctantly, running her hand through the top of her hair to rake its heavy, rippling waves off her face. "I just feel guilty about it. I came home to be with Mama, but sometimes I think I'll go crazy if I don't get outside. There are days when I have to get away from what's—what's happening in that room."

"That's normal. Just know that you'll be better for her when you are here if you have gotten away for a while. Dying is just one of the parts of living; go on to the mill and remember the others. I won't worry about you there, either, because you'll be working right in the same building with Henry. He has promised me that he'll keep an eye on you."

There's a comforting thought, Terrill wanted to tell Tandy wryly, but she'd said enough, so she took off across the fields, letting her long legs cover ground in free, loping strides.

Out here, she could almost forget.

It felt good—so good—to walk like this. The September wind brushed against her face, tugged at the sleeves of the warm shirt, lifted strands of her hair. It was urging her to turn loose. To think of nothing but this place.

The woods were wet with an early morning moisture, and the dampness carried up the rich, fecund smell of decaying leaves from the chilly dark hollow as she skirted it, high along its edge. Terrill stopped for an instant to suck in the scent, to turn her face up to the cool rays of the autumn sun and shut her eyes to feel it. All sensation, remembering . . . this place.

A blue jay screeched in the distance, but when Terrill looked to find him, there was a hawk instead high against the blue sky, circling and soaring, letting his wide wings stretch and reach.

He could have gone anywhere, that huge bird, but instead he kept narrowing the concentric rings, looking, seeking, until he homed in on one tiny point somewhere below him and dropped in a glorious fall to his destination.

Sometimes being free didn't mean escape; sometimes it meant coming back to one place. The place that you belonged, that you loved.

The place that set you free.

The place that had its roots in you so deep that it kept pulling you, tugging you back insistently.

At Rose Hall, she'd been marking time.

At Belmont, she'd been waiting.

Circling, sweeping the sky, getting ready to free-fall to where she wanted to be.

Now here she was, high on this edge, with the sweet wind welcoming her.

Those realizations hit Terrill as hard as if the hawk had swirled and swooped to snatch her, and the sense of freedom was suddenly so exuberant, so bright, that she laughed.

I'm where I want to be, she thought.

And she held out her arms as far as they would go and twirled around and around in the field, a ballerina in blue jeans.

Weightless for a minute.

No rules from Rose Hall. No schedules at Belmont. No instructions from Tandy. No grief over Katherine. No oppressive hate from Henry.

Maybe she stood there for five minutes. Maybe for ten.

When she began to walk again, her feet were lighter.

Even being in the same vicinity as Henry would be bearable if she could hold on to this sense of rightness. Of being complete.

She had not counted on where her walk would bring her out—right at the back of the office, in the graveled lot where the men who worked for the mill parked their vehicles.

Three of those men had not yet gone out on the

job; they stood talking at one of the trucks. For one startled moment the four of them stared at each other. Then the oldest, a gray-haired, bewhiskered, skinny one with a knobby nose and equally knobby hands, nodded at her.

"Mornin'," he said civilly enough.

She returned his nod a little uncomfortably. "Good morning," she said, and wondered suddenly if she should have done this Tandy's way after all, in a suit and a car. The old man didn't bother her; what bothered her was one of the others, a blond-haired, ruddy-faced individual whose stare had gone from surprise to appreciative assessment.

"And who might you be, honey?" he asked quizzically.

"Terrill Carroll," she answered, looking back at him steadily.

He raised his eyebrows; she tossed back her hair and walked on.

Whoever the blond man was, she didn't like him. Before she went to Belmont, she'd been around very few men. But in her short two years there, she'd met this type too many times.

Once up the steps and into the office, she forgot him. He was out there, she was in here. And Rosalie Anderson, who'd been a young girl when she first went to work for Grandpa and Luke, was waiting for her inside.

"It's been a long time, Rilla," she said emotionally, reaching out to hold the girl by the shoulders. "Look at you. All grown up. Seeing you in this mill—just the way you used to stand here—makes everything seem right."

"I hope you don't mind my getting dumped on you," Terrill offered hesitantly. "They keep trying to figure out where to . . . to put me."

"Mind? No—I'll like the company. The only other female I see much of around here is Tandy. And now, since Katherine . . ."

She let the words drop off, and Terrill waded through them. "I doubt that I'm as good with books and figures as Aunt Tandy. But I can type, and do billing, and I know the cuts and the timber—"

"There'll be plenty for you to do," Rosalie interrupted confidently. "Like answering that"—she nodded toward the ringing phone—"so that I can get started. I always make coffee the very first thing." She twisted to grin at Terrill as she took off toward the big supply closet. "Don't you tell the feminists, now."

Terrill did as she was instructed and answered the phone.

It was a good beginning, and the day got better: Henry left at eleven on business, locking the door to his own office behind him.

Terrill breathed more easily.

When two o'clock came, Rosalie left the office, too, to make an afternoon run to Citizens Bank.

For a while Terrill just looked around herself, remembering.

But it was different now: this place belonged to Henry. She was just an employee here, doing a job. There was a businesslike briskness to things and an efficiency that Luke's office hadn't had. Maybe Henry really had come into Luke's life—every part of it—and done better.

The door opening behind her made Terrill jump, and it dragged her away from her dark thoughts.

"That was a quick trip—"

She stumbled over the sentence, staring in shock. Rosalie hadn't reentered the office.

A man had. Tall, slender. Dark hair. Blue jeans and

T-shirt. He was looking down, fitting paperwork into a folder—and the sound of her voice pulled his head up.

Green eyes. He had green eyes.

What was he doing here? She meant to ask him, but nothing came out of her mouth.

Confused himself, he glanced around. "Where's— the woman there—" His head indicated Rosalie's desk.

"She'll be back," Terrill managed. She would *not* let her eyes drop from his, not to his throat or anywhere else. No more chances for him to make remarks.

They stood there a minute.

"So, where do I sit?" he asked at last.

"What?"

"Sit," he repeated patiently. "You're at the desk I usually use."

"The desk you—Why are you here?" she demanded.

"I work here."

"You work in the mechanic shop."

He frowned. "Once in a while they let me out," he returned ironically. "I come here some afternoons to fill out these"—he held out the folder of papers— "and pick up those." His head movement indicated another package, firmly sealed, that she remembered Henry placing on the filing cabinet as he left.

Her gaze was disbelieving and reluctant.

"I ain't bit anybody yet," he snapped at last. "What are *you* doin' here?"

She swallowed once. "I'm supposed to be here. I'm . . . I'm working here."

"Well, that makes two of us, then. And you better let me get *my* work done, or Henry Carroll's gonna have my hide."

They eyed each other, he challenging, she belligerent, and a silent moment ticked by.

Then Rosalie pushed open the door. "Thank goodness that the cashier—" She stopped short at the sight of Kane. "Oh, it's you. Aren't you here early?"

Kane gave a shrug; that was all.

Rosalie frowned, and her voice was reserved and wary. "I forgot to tell you, Terrill, that Kane here comes in for about an hour every day or so."

"He says he uses this desk." Terrill spoke to the other woman as if he weren't even in the room.

"That's right. Mr. Carroll doesn't let anybody else do the paperwork for Kane's job," Rosalie said, making it plain that she didn't like the situation at all. "We can get another small desk put in here for tomorrow—but today—" She looked at Terrill ruefully. "He can't use mine," she said, nodding at the computer terminal on it.

Without a word Terrill pushed from her desk, standing to walk away. She brushed past him, trying to stay as far away as the space would permit, and after a moment's hesitation he scooped up Henry's package, walked to the chair she'd vacated, and sat down, spreading out the contents of the folder.

Terrill yanked open the smaller filing cabinet at the side of the desk. She could do this work now instead of later, she reasoned. Inside her head, though, she wondered furiously what was wrong with Henry Carroll that he just let ex-convicts wander into his office and make themselves at home.

She shot a quick glance over at this particular ex-con as he spread out the papers, his dark head bent.

Just how old was he, anyway? There was a youthful line to his jaw and his profile that belied the aura of danger that clung to him.

But Terrill turned quickly back to her work when

he shifted. She didn't want to look at him; she didn't want to be around him.

She would just do her job.

Kane would do his.

The only problem was, she couldn't figure out what his job was.

"What does that man do around here?" Terrill tried to make the question casual after Kane left.

Rosalie sighed. "He's a mechanic. But he does a lot more than just work on our equipment. We don't need a full-time mechanic. Or at least we didn't, until Mr. Carroll got some kind of contract with a big company; I don't even know where. It's to rebuild engines and ship them to another state. Lots of money in it—if you can do it. Kane can. Then he fills out warranties on each and does the paperwork to see that they're shipped. It really doesn't have anything to do with the sawmill at all, except that Kane works on both."

"It's just a way for Henry to make money hand over fist, with Kane," Terrill said in slow realization.

"I think so. That boy's quiet enough, but that's the kind you've got to watch. My grandson went to school with one of Kane's brothers. Nothing but problems, that's what my Joel said about Frankie Kane. I'd be just as happy if Mr. Carroll found somebody else to do the work," Rosalie finished, smoothing back her carefully permed hair as she got ready to leave for the day. "Kane had better be grateful to have employment. There's not much of it in this little county, especially for a Kane."

"Except . . . Henry's such a good man that he gave him a job."

Rosalie picked up her purse and looked at Terrill

slyly. "Good man or not, Mr. Carroll knows how to make money. Jubal Kane is here because it's profitable for him to be. Not that I've got anything against profit," she added hastily, remembering that this was Henry's niece.

So much for Christian charity, thought Terrill as she watched Rosalie leave.

Jubal was late with the paperwork, and once he'd rushed it to the office, he wished he'd never turned it in at all, because if he hadn't, somebody might have had time to tell him that there was a new face in the office. He might have had time to prepare himself for the shock that ran down his whole body when he looked up and saw the incredulous eyes of Terrill Carroll.

She didn't want him to be there. That much was clear from the way she turned a little from him as he passed her, from her slight edging away.

I don't want you here, either, he thought furiously, thank you, anyway.

He tried to ignore her, and the temper she set off in him, the rest of the time he had to spend in the office. But that afternoon, in the parking lot, he heard more than enough.

Dusty Bainbridge said to the departing workers in general from his own car window, "Carroll's step-daughter's workin' here now. Terrill, that's her name. I heard she was some kind of wild child growing up. She's a doll these days, ain't she? Just the way I like 'em."

Somebody—Red Sinclair—spoke up. "You like 'em any way, Dusty."

"Maybe so. But the pretty boy over there got to see her up real close. What'd you think, ridge runner?" Dusty's voice taunted Jubal, pushing, waiting.

The rest of the men waited, too.

Jubal just slid in his truck and out of Dusty's reach, the way he'd been doing for months now, conceding victory to the other man.

6

After two weeks, Terrill had her days at the mill under control.

She continued to walk through the increasing chill of the mornings, and now she was comfortable crossing the parking lot under the gaze of the men. Only two of them still made her uneasy. The dark, green-eyed one never seemed to watch her, though, even if he happened to be in the lot when she crossed it. The other, the blond named Dusty, mostly annoyed her. He whistled once, but she refused to let him make her rush, so she forced her steps to be comfortable and unhurried, and she ignored him.

Terrill had been listening to Henry's warning: she meant to make no waves anywhere, especially not with one of these men.

Ironically, the one who bothered her the most was the first one, the one who cooperated fully with her ignore-and-be-ignored campaign.

Kane did his work, coming in to sit at a little table

Rosalie had pulled up near Terrill's desk, right under the eagle eye of the older woman, who watched him as though he were a wayward child. He kept his mouth shut; he never made a move toward Terrill. Finally Rosalie relaxed her vigilance.

And Terrill learned that if she let her hair fall to the side as she worked, it wound up a silent curtain between them. But even with her head turned away most of the time, she caught little things about the man beside her.

He surprised her by possessing a sort of careless, lazy intelligence that showed up even in the short time he was near. The work he did was quick, his handwriting neat. He had a habit of cupping the back of his neck in one long-fingered hand and frowning a little when he worked. He was left-handed, decidedly so.

But he didn't look right. Not here in this civilized little office, doing paperwork.

He was too tall. Too masculine. Too—untamed. Sometimes she'd slide a glance over at him, almost able to picture him in a hot blood lust, ready to kill.

But there was more to the knowledge she gained about him, more hints about his life that showed up physically.

She knew the old brown jacket he wore on cold mornings—ugly and too big for his slender frame.

And the shoes. There were two pairs of them, one a pair of high-topped sneakers—once white, now nearly gray—that said clearly in their worn-over state that Kane had a habit of putting his weight on the outside of his foot when he walked. The boots were in a little better shape, but the heels were worn down.

Combine his clothes and his shoes with his too long, shaggy hair and the smell of woodsmoke that sometimes clung to him on cold mornings, and it all added up to one thing: poverty.

But Terrill never wasted much time looking at Kane, because if he ever caught any of her sliding glances, he stared back at her insolently and silently. If he was aware of his sorry state, he gave no hint of it.

He rarely gave a hint that he even knew she was around.

Like Rosalie, Terrill began to relax a little more when he came in; he wasn't paying enough attention to warrant her nervousness.

Rosalie Anderson was taking longer than usual on her daily afternoon bank errand, so it was just the two of them alone in the quiet room.

The girl across from him was restless today, her mind on things that had nothing to do with a sawmill office.

Jubal sensed all of that as soon as he sat down near her. It was an unwilling knowledge; he didn't want to know her at all. But some sort of peculiar osmosis was occurring day by day at those two desks; things seeped through to him.

He knew the clean, sweet smell that always surrounded Terrill; maybe it was the thick, rich fall of hair that held that scent. He knew the way she pulled the gold chain up from her throat and hooked it around her chin, tugging its diamond back and forth across the taut yellow links when she read something.

He knew that she hardly ever smiled, that she did her work efficiently, that her fingers were long and delicate, that she doodled in big circles when she talked on the telephone.

Knowing those things didn't bother him; what

irked him was the way he sometimes felt tuned in to her emotions by their proximity, which always happened when it was just the two of them, working in silence nearly side by side.

They never spoke to each other.

He'd heard her and Henry in a quiet but heated argument one day, and she'd been belligerent and fidgety the whole hour afterward when he sat beside her. Now he figured that they argued a lot or maybe were engaged in some contest of wills: she was belligerent a lot, too. Defiant. Defensive. She never said anything, but on those days her eyes shot blue fire at him if he moved.

He didn't like it when Terrill Carroll was quiet, either. She was too quiet, as still as a mummy, wrapped in sorrow. He suspected on those days she was thinking about her mother. When Terrill sat deathly still, staring at nothing, Jubal almost wished for her defiance instead.

She made no move toward him. He had to admit grudgingly at last that in that respect, she and Tess were different.

In fact, after three weeks Jubal was a little aggravated by the way he was apparently invisible around her. He found some consolation, though, in the fact that she did it to everybody, that tuning out. He'd seen more than one of the men angle for her attention as she walked across the mill grounds on some errand or another; Terrill never noticed any of them. She was democratic in her rudeness.

In fact, she could be a downright smart aleck if pushed; she proved it the noon that she had a run-in with Dusty, when he deliberately stepped in front of her as she walked across the mill yard.

The day was warm, and several of the men—Jubal included—had opened their lunches under the nearly bare oak tree. Terrill stepped out of the office, examining whatever she had in her hands. It looked like the payroll sheets for the week.

Dusty watched her like a wolf about to pounce. Exactly why that aggravated Jubal, he didn't know. He had no right to fault Dusty: he watched her, too.

But it was nearly impossible to ignore the girl, he told himself defensively; the blue jeans clung to her long legs, the fold behind her knee nearly white with wear, the fabric smooth over her well-shaped hips and thighs and calves. The sides of her hair were pulled up to the top of her head and held by a shiny, flat clip that let the waves tumble down her back, nearly to her tiny waist.

She was blue eyes and blue jeans, tawny hair and golden skin; tall and slender and somehow wild when she moved.

A sleek tiger—that was what she reminded Jubal of. He had no doubt at all that she was giving Henry and Tandy Carroll fits. She would probably give a man fits, too. Jubal didn't intend to find out.

But Dusty did. Irritated by the way she'd turned a deaf ear to him for weeks, he came slowly to his feet as she advanced. Just as she got even with him, Dusty took two huge sideways steps.

She slammed into his body, dropping some of the papers, startled into looking up into Dusty's grinning face.

"Well, well, well. Miss Carroll."

Jubal saw her brown throat move as she swallowed once. Then she bent, picked up the papers, and rose coolly to her full height again.

"Did you want something?" she asked, so quietly he had to strain to hear it, just as the other two men were doing. She turned a little away from them, trying to stop their hearing.

"Well, now, that's a good question," Dusty drawled suggestively, his own voice clear. "What do I want."

"And what's the answer? Let's hear it—before I get knocked down. You keep running into me, making sure that I know you're around," she said hurriedly.

"Look, little girl, you banged into *me.*"

Her face flushed. "*Little girl?* Well, I'll have to be more careful, won't I? I wouldn't want to hurt a decrepit old man like you."

One of the listening men gave a huff of laughter, quickly smothered.

Dusty's face turned as red as hers. "You got a smart mouth, did you know that?"

"Thanks," she said calmly. "It's trying to keep up with my IQ." Then she brushed past him, her easy walk carrying her rapidly away.

"Bitch," Dusty muttered.

Jubal felt an odd sense of satisfaction in the girl; Terrill had not even been flustered by Dusty's come-on.

"You better give up on that one," Red Sinclair advised, his mouth full of a bologna sandwich. "She's high society. And even if she wasn't, she's the kind that bites and scratches."

"She's the kind that needs a man, I don't care how high she is," Dusty retorted. "If she filled out those jeans any better, I'd be dead. I'd give a week's pay to get those legs around me. And I will yet."

Jubal kept eating, saying nothing. As always. Staying out of trouble.

He didn't like Terrill Carroll. She didn't like him.

But there was something about her that made it wrong to talk about her the way Dusty did. Maybe it was her reserve or the pain he saw in her face sometimes.

Maybe it was the way she stayed so apart from the world.

Or it could be that the anger Jubal felt toward Dusty came from a far baser reaction: for one flashing minute, he'd imagined what it would feel like to have her long, slender body tangled with his.

The thought bothered him a lot. It lingered in his head, even that afternoon as he drove away from the mill. If he wanted a woman, he didn't need to think about the Carroll girl.

He could have Tess. Lord knew she was surely enough for any man.

Except . . . she left him nearly as empty as he felt before he was with her.

He'd been a fool to rise to her bait. To let her catch him. He should have known she didn't really want him, the person he actually was.

But she'd been handy, and willing, and he'd been weak.

It had begun last summer, three weeks after he'd come home from Lineville, when he'd finally given in to the urgings of Bobo. He'd gone back to his old hangout one Saturday night.

Saturday nights were meant for the Lonesome Pine, anyway. Exactly when they had come to mean that, Jubal didn't know. It was just a tradition, sort of. His brother Frankie had always hung out there, then his brother Jarvis.

Jubal had been in and out of the Pine since he was a kid; neither of his older brothers had ever had any compunction about dragging him in with them if one of them stopped for a beer and he was along.

The Pine had energy—a hot, vivid, Saturday-night style of life—and there the others like him, a lot of them from the Ridge, hung out and did whatever sort of socializing they did. Girls were always there, too, and some of them had a decided yen for him. There, at the Pine, he was a person, somebody others liked and wanted to be with—not a hood to be afraid of or a loser to treat with contempt.

But upon his return, the place had surprised him by being so changed, so full of people—and so many of them from a different side of the county.

"What in the hell are *they* doin' here?" he had asked Bobo, motioning toward two or three tables of young college types.

Bobo had shrugged. "Livin' wild, they think. Reckon it's hip now for them to party with us rednecks. Autry don't care. They got money to burn. Mostly they leave us alone."

But *she* hadn't.

He'd gone out to his truck that hot June night and found an unsigned note slid down between his windshield and the wiper. It had been suggestive and inflammatory: "Everybody says you're bad. I'll bet you'd be very, very good, Jubal Kane."

He examined it as if it were a bomb. Who? *Who?*

Maybe it was a big joke.

So he tore it up.

But a week later she made another move. He came out of the Pine early, and there she was, leaning up against his truck, cool as ice cream in the heat in her low-cut cotton top. As expensive as a sleek, imported race car.

Her face was childishly sweet and pouting under the stylish cut of her coal black hair—and she stopped him cold in his tracks, stunned out of his skull.

The banker's daughter. He couldn't remember her name, but he knew who she was. Everybody in town did.

Lionel Johnson's little china doll.

And while Jubal stared, she took the paper she held in her hand—another note—and slid it under the wiper. Then she turned, sauntered over to her big Buick, and got in. Waiting.

The note told him exactly what she wanted in clear, explicit terms. Then she asked where she could get it.

So he told her, and she followed him when he left, right up to the deserted old park high on Mason's Point.

Jubal had never had too much trouble finding girls. He'd been with a few since he'd turned sixteen. But by twenty he'd been in Lineville. At twenty-three he had a lot of time to make up for and a lot of knowledge to gain.

He didn't realize that, though, until his encounter with Tess Johnson on the backseat of that Buick. He came away from the experience a little dazed and a lot wiser.

When it was over, when she finally let him go, she got in the driver's seat of the car, her clothes in place, her silky black hair only a little rumpled, and laughed up at him as he leaned against the hood of his truck, the one parked in the shadows at Mason's Point alongside the car. He reached for a cigarette in his shirt pocket and tried to light it nonchalantly.

"Are you glad I followed you, Jubal?" she asked him provocatively, archly.

"Yeah," he said at last, pulling on the cigarette. What was he supposed to say? You scare me to death? I wish I'd never started this?

"So am I," she said on a breathy note. Then she gave that excited, triumphant laugh again and riffled her hair back. "My God," she murmured. "I can't believe it. I did it."

Slowly he lowered the cigarette. "Did what?" he asked warily.

"I just made Jubal Kane."

She was still laughing as she started the car engine and pulled off into the night, while he stared after her with his forgotten cigarette burning in his fingers and a very, very sick taste in his mouth.

She was blasé and sophisticated about it; he tried to be.

She ignored him for two or three weeks. Once she came to the mill with her father and walked right by him, pretending not to see him.

The he found her watching him again a few nights later from a corner of the Pine, and at what was in her face, he flushed hotly. He turned an even more brilliant shade of red as he realized how juvenile and revealing his reaction was, and he let her have him again, just to prove that he didn't care. That he was tough. That sex was just sex. Except it wasn't; it was terrible and getting worse with every encounter. She was beautiful, and delicate, and expensive. But she was also brittle and self-centered. And worse—she was using him. Literally using him and his body, just because he had a very bad reputation and a very good face.

The last night he'd been with her, she'd been wilder than ever, biting him, raking his back, twisting under his hands until he wondered if he'd bruised her the same way she'd marked him.

He tried to pull away; he didn't want a trumped-up rape charge.

"Where are you, Jubal?" she demanded imperiously, catching at his arms, her body a pale, slender shape in the dark car. "Off in your head somewhere? Do you think you can ignore me?"

"Dammit, Tess, turn loose," he muttered.

"Turn loose?" she echoed. "I'll let you go when I'm through."

Leaping upward at him, she wrapped her arms around his neck tightly, fastening her mouth to his throat. For a minute he thought she was kissing him. Then he realized her intention, and swearing, he reached up to pull her mouth away. Instead she wrapped herself around him—even her bare ankles wrapped his—and she sucked at his throat like some thirsty vampire determined to be satisfied.

The damage was done.

He forced himself not to react, to hold himself above her in a curious detachment, staring at the dark night sky. Then Tess pulled her lips away slowly and peered up at him, defiance mingling with an excited fear.

"That's just to remind you of me, Jubal, while I'm gone this week." Her fingers stroked the blood red mark. "To give you something to really brood about when you're like this."

"What are you doin' out here with me, Tess?" he asked quietly. "And why should I remember you? I'm nothin' to you. Am I?"

He asked the last insistently, and she laughed.

"You see, Jubal? I can make you care. You can't stay away from me, back in your head somewhere, no matter how hard you try." She laid a hand against the thudding of his heart.

"You didn't answer my question," he said stubbornly.

"What was it? Are you anything to me? You know you are. Sometimes, when you really mean it, you're the best I've ever had. And I'm the best you'll ever have, Jubal."

That had been the night she'd dropped him at Ida's store, and he'd walked home to find Foster waiting for him, the night he'd taken a beating and been dragged to the mill on a burglary charge.

Weeks ago.

Tess might be at the Pine again tonight; it was Friday. If he went and she was, she'd be madder than hell that he'd stayed away. But sooner or later they'd wind up out at the Point.

She'd make his blood rush like a heat wave through his veins and his heart beat enough that he'd think he was doing more than just passing time.

More than surviving.

But when it was over, when the white-hot burn faded, he'd be colder than before.

With a hard jerk of the wheel, Jubal pulled the truck off the road and drove it down the two dusty ruts that led to the river. The late afternoon sun glowed weakly across the water, glinting off a rowboat at its edge. Far in a distant field, a cow made a loud, low sound of protest, and an old red barn advertised JEFFERSON ISLAND on its side.

Jubal crawled up on a big rock in the shelter of the sprawling trees, watching, thinking, smoking.

When he remembered Tess, he didn't know what to do. She was destroying him, and he was cooperating fully.

"'Lo, Jubal."

The quiet voice startled him, making him twist to see who'd found his hiding place. The old black face under the white hair belonged to Rainey Lewis; it was his little boat that was tied at anchor in the water below.

"I didn't hear you comin'."

"Look like to me you ain't hearin' much a' nothin'," Rainey returned.

"Maybe not. You goin' fishin'?"

"Not tonight. Tonight, I'm checkin' the water to see how deep and warm it is. I got a baptizin' come Sunday."

"You still preachin'?" Jubal asked the old man lazily, blowing smoke as Rainey bent heavily over the water and dipped a big black hand in it.

"Little cool," Rainey observed as he wiped the water off his palm onto the knee of his khaki work pants. "But it'll do. Yeah, I'm still a'preachin'. Church is mighty small, but this county ain't got many black folks. Reckon I've got about all I'm gonna get."

"Maybe some of the white ones'll listen to you," Jubal offered humorously, grinding out the cigarette on the rock.

"You ain't never," Rainey pointed out mildly. "And I been talkin' to you since you was a kid."

"You and Ma," Jubal agreed in resignation. "Reckon I just ain't into this baptizin' stuff. I can't believe God's gonna wanta know if I've been dunked under water before He decides where I'm goin'."

Rainey hitched up a suspender strap. "Maybe baptizin' ain't for God, Jubal. Maybe it's for us, so we can say, 'From this minute, I try a different kinda living.'"

"There's just one kind of life, Rainey," Jubal said moodily. "And I'm not doin' too good at it."

"The world's a pretty hard place," Rainey agreed, coming to lean on the rock beside the man who sat on it, his knees pulled up, his elbows across them. "My son Jonah—he could tell you. You remember? You used to fish with him. Hardest-workin' boy I got, and he can't get no jobs around here. You did that much, at least."

Jubal made a quick, negative movement. "I got it because Carroll wanted a desperate man—that's why."

"I seen the time Jonah's been pretty desperate, too. But it don't do no good. He can't change his color. So he'll be leavin' soon, too, just like his brothers and your brothers did. Came to me yesterday. Said, 'Daddy, you baptize me good, 'cause I'm getting ready to get on outta here. I'm gonna be a different man somewhere else.'"

"Maybe he will."

"Maybe. But most of the time we got to prove ourselves right where we stand."

"What if we stand—and stand—and finally just fall?"

"Prop yourself up on something, Jubal. You just got to be careful you don't sit down and quit. Don't settle for things that ain't no good for you. Reach for the best you can get."

"Don't start on me, Rainey," Jubal warned passionately, sliding off the rough rock, letting his boots dig into the soft moss around it. "Don't give me all those lines that Ma does. You know what's the worst about it? Sometimes I half believe her. I think I'll get a different life. I think, I want a—a different kind of woman than I ever met to love me. But they don't love anymore, so what's the use? It's all a lie. What's Ma doin' to me, Rainey?"

"She's making you believe."

"She's making me *crazy*. And you know what? Just as soon as I can, I'm gonna copy Jonah. I'm gonna get the hell out of here."

Without another word, Jubal pushed away from the rock and strode to his truck. Rainey was just a rosy shadow against a setting red sun as Jubal drove away.

"You was meant for better things," he heard Ma say.

"Reach," he heard Rainey say.

He didn't believe either of them—but he wasn't going to the Pine. Not tonight.

7

It had been a hellish week.

Katherine stopped eating on Tuesday.

"At least try, Mama," Terrill pleaded with her.

"For what?" Katherine asked wearily. "I'm tired . . . of trying. It makes me sick."

Tandy coaxed to no avail.

Finally, on Thursday night, Henry shut himself in the bedroom with his wife. He spent half the night getting her to eat one cup of oatmeal.

Katherine managed to keep it down; the next morning she ate a little more.

Nearly as tired and exhausted as Henry, Terrill looked at his worn face at breakfast the next day and for once felt gratitude toward him. That was before he spoke to her.

"Katherine stays upset all the time about you, Terrill. I don't want her upset again. She's too weak. Make certain you remember that."

"I'm not the reason she quit eating."

"You're the reason for more than you know," he said tersely.

The day dragged. It was a bright, sunny one, still and cool. Through the tiny window behind Terrill's desk, she could see the walnut tree near the road, already bare of leaves. Beside it, a sweet-gum tree was fading into late fall colors and a few leaves were settling onto the dry grass under it.

Autumn already in Tennessee.

The sun was so warm on Terrill's back as she worked that it made her drowsy. That afternoon Rosalie left early and Henry was so quiet back in his office that Terrill's head nodded. All the nights with Katherine were taking their toll.

When Jubal entered the quiet office a few minutes later, he thought for a minute that the place was empty. Then he saw the girl slumped over the desk.

Sound asleep.

He slid quietly into the desk beside hers with the folder, picking up the other sealed folder Henry always left for him. For a while the only sounds in the hot room were of his pen scratching on the paper and of her gentle breathing.

With her guard down, Terrill Carroll seemed smaller. Vulnerable. And while she slept, Jubal could relax and finally do what curiosity demanded: take a long, hard look at her.

She looked . . . good. Not pretty, not glamorous, none of the standard words. But she took the eye. There was an attraction to her all the more potent because she was so careless about it, because she chose to ignore her own looks. Something rich and vibrant clung to her.

Her hair was a heavy, rippling mass as it lay over her arm on the desk. Molasses—it was the color of pure molasses. Her eyebrows were the same color, strong and arched. And her lips were full, barely open now as she slept.

He'd done enough of this damn looking. On the thought, Jubal grabbed the finished papers and the folder and straightened too rapidly. His hip hit the corner of the desk, jarring it, and she came wide awake.

Unguarded, her eyes were huge dark pools of soft blue as she looked up at him. Mesmerized, he stared back.

Then she realized who he was. "Oh! You!" she gasped, and tried to stand in one rush. Instead her feet tangled and she stumbled a little, knocking over a cup of Rosalie's coffee that stood on the edge of the desk.

It splattered across his shirt and puddled right in the middle of the papers he held, generously sprinkling another stack right beside him on the desk.

With a curse, he shook his own off.

"What are you doing, watching me?" she whispered, shoving her hair back on both sides of her face with her hands.

"I wasn't watchin' you," he protested hotly, letting the wet papers drip out to his side. "You were asleep. I had to come in here to—"

"Kane!"

Carroll's voice came from the adjoining office, where he stood waiting in the door that had just opened as Jubal turned toward him.

"Yeah?" he answered warily.

"I need to see you . . . now." Then Carroll's black eyes took in the whole scene—Jubal's anger, Terrill's guilty face, the wet papers, the spilled brown liquid.

"Is that today's paperwork? What have you done, Terrill?"

His heavy, accusing voice made the girl flush and bite her lip defensively. Where was her smart mouth now? There was a moment of silence, and then Jubal did something he didn't even understand his own motives for doing.

"I . . . I hit the desk," he told Carroll. "Knocked that drink over by accident. I'll—I'll redo these papers if I need to."

Carroll looked at him a moment, then at the startled girl. "We'll see," he said finally. "But for now I want to talk to you . . . in here. Terrill, clean up that mess."

Why had he done that?

At first the thought was fuzzy and half-formed in Terrill's head as she struggled to come awake.

When had he come in? How long had he been standing there?

She sucked in her breath, remembering how shocking it had been to open her eyes and look straight up into his.

An ocean of green fire.

She'd nearly fallen into it, right down into him as he stood there so close. Just the two of them, breathing, watching, circling.

Why had he lied for her?

She kept glancing over at the closed door between the two rooms.

And then she heard their raised voices, not distinct but clearly argumentative. Whatever was going on, Kane was in trouble.

"What in the hell d'you mean, you won't do it?" Carroll sat up slowly, dangerously, on his chair, facing the one who stood opposite him.

"It ain't my job to haul engines," Kane answered stubbornly. "That's what Bobo's here for."

"Bobo does what I tell him to do. Just like you. The paperwork's ready. Bobo's already loaded the truck. And he tells me you can drive anything. The Peterbilt should be a cinch for you."

"It's not the drivin' that worries me," Kane cut in. "What worries me is that something's not right here. Why me?"

"There's only you and Bobo. And I've got plans for him somewhere else. You don't even have to worry about a commercial driver's license. I've got things all taken care of."

Kane didn't answer for a minute; he didn't do anything, just standing there in silence.

"You know what, Kane?" Henry said at last, examining the gold writing on a pencil he held as if he'd never seen it before. "That damn quietness in you gets next to me sometimes."

"I can't help that. I don't like this," Kane returned. "Just like I didn't like it a few weeks ago, when somebody broke in here and I got accused."

"That's your problem," Carroll said smoothly, but a muscle twitched in his cheek, pulling his mouth into an ugly grimace as he spoke. "Mine is making sure you do the job I've laid out for you. You get yourself down here tonight, get in that truck, deliver those engines to Kentucky, and bring me back the paperwork from the buyer. It'll be sealed in plastic, inside a manila envelope."

Then Henry leaned back sharply on his chair, rolling the pencil between his hands, the change in his pocket jingling at the quick move.

"And if I don't do it?"

"Then I don't need you," Carroll answered. "Maybe Lineville does."

Kane's whole body jerked. "This is not right."

Carroll stood up and dropped the pencil on his

desk. "I'd hate to see you go back to that prison for such a little thing," he said casually. "What's your mama going to do? Clean the bathrooms at the church, like she did when your old man got killed? Take in more sewing? Or she could do what she refused to do while you were serving time—she could take charity from Tandy's ladies' aid group."

Kane's face flushed red hot, and he sucked in his breath in a sharp hiss. "Shut up. By God, Carroll—"

"Save the indignation for somebody else," Henry cut in, cold anger in his voice. "For right now, all I want is for you to do a simple job. Get here tonight around eight."

Kane struggled with himself a minute. "I don't like you one damn bit, Carroll," he said resentfully at last.

Carroll shrugged. "You're young. You'll find out before long that you just do what you're told in this world when somebody else holds all the aces. I hold them where you're concerned, and I don't care whether you like it or not."

Kane slammed out of Carroll's office, color high in his cheeks, his eyes blazing. Anger was written all over him.

Terrill watched him for an instant from beside the door, where she stood with her jacket, ready to leave, and after a pause he took a deep breath and straightened.

That was when he saw her. They stood there: the girl by the door, waiting; the man across the room, blind with anger.

Then she demanded at last, "Why'd you do that?"

"Do what?" he asked roughly, raking his hand over his face, trying to push down his emotions.

Her tone was nearly truculent. "You lied to Henry.

You don't need to protect me. I can take care of myself. So why'd you do it?"

Jubal thought to himself that her attitude was exactly what he should have expected from one of these high-and-mighty Carrolls.

"'Cause I wanted to," he answered shortly, moving forward in a sudden lunge. At the door, he looked over at her and added, "You're welcome."

Terrill watched him go, his long body moving in a slouchy, sulky sort of grace.

On Friday nights it had become Terrill's job to cook supper. Henry was late coming from the mill, and finally Tandy gave up waiting on him and sent Terrill in to Katherine with her meal on a tray. Late as it was, her mother was still not hungry, pushing the food around aimlessly.

"This week has shown me . . . I don't have long to settle things . . . between you and Henry," she said abruptly. "Are you happy here . . . Rilla?"

A little surprised and uneasy, Terrill answered, "Sure, Mama. I'm happy."

"But you and Henry—you're not getting along any better this time, are you?" Katherine asked at last, hopelessly.

Terrill's face stiffened. "I don't want to talk about it, Mama. We're—doing okay."

"No, you're not," Katherine objected. "Are you trying, Rilla—really trying?"

Terrill busied herself picking up dishes, looking down so her mother wouldn't see the quick flame of anger in her face. "You say he's good to you. Maybe he is. But not to me. And I don't see what difference it makes now. You knew the way I felt about Henry when you married him."

"I thought . . . you would get over it."

"And what about him? Was he supposed to get over it, too? You're doing it even now, Mama, defending Henry. To you, it's always been my fault."

"No—no. Now, too late, I know that—he was in the wrong, too. And . . . so was I," Katherine said, and unshed tears shone in her eyes. "I should never . . . have let him send you to Tandy's that summer. I should have made you understand that you were still my daughter . . . no matter how many husbands or babies came after you."

Terrill stared at her mother. "Mama—"

"No—don't stop me. I want to talk. I thought a child would help Henry, that if he had his own, he'd accept you more . . . easily. At first, he didn't . . . want a baby. Not right now, he'd say . . . I want you to myself a while . . . longer." Katherine paused. "But when I . . . got pregnant, he was . . . thrilled."

"I don't want to hear this," Terrill interrupted, putting her hands up over her ears.

"But you . . . need to. You need to understand . . . how it is with Henry. He loves me . . . more than Luke ever did—"

"No!"

"I'm his . . . whole world. If . . . if I had died first and left Luke, he would have . . . suffered. But he would have . . . survived. But sometimes I think . . . I wonder what will happen to Henry when I'm dead. He needs . . . somebody—"

"All he ever needed was you," Terrill cried, her chin jutting out defensively, her hands dropping. "And it never mattered that you belonged to Daddy first. I was there, Mama, the day Henry and Grandpa had the fight. I heard it all."

"What are you . . . talking about?" Katherine

gasped, her thin fingers pushing against the sheets of the bed beside her.

"I was ten. You thought I had already gone with Grandpa and Daddy to the mill that Saturday morning, but I hadn't. I was still in the backyard, in the grape arbor, when Henry pulled up in the drive. You were cutting back the rosebushes, and he . . . he walked over to you. I guess he thought the two of you were all alone. You turned—slipped on the walk and—he caught you. And all of a sudden, he— Henry kissed you. And *kissed* you." Terrill nearly choked on the words.

Katherine's face was white. "I didn't ask for Henry . . . to do that, Rilla," she whispered.

"No. You pulled away. Told him he would hate himself the next day. And I can still hear what he said. 'How can I hate myself for touching what is mine, Katherine?'"

Terrill remembered that scene with such clarity that even now she could feel the shock. Henry's voice had been calm and controlled, but the air had had a heavy, waiting, explosive quality to it. . . .

"I don't know what you're talking about, Henry," Katherine had said shakily.

"Don't lie to me, Katherine. I've loved you since you were fifteen, but you were too young. You knew I was waiting, holding on for *you*. And for all my waiting, I got nothing. Luke stumbled across you. My God, Katherine—why Luke? He never even finished college. His biggest ambition was to start that sawmill with Daddy. I just came home one weekend—and got the news that Luke had run off with Katherine Terrill. You'd—" Henry's voice was beginning to break, to shatter into little shards of sound. "You were eighteen years old—he just reached out and took you. You knew I loved you; it was in your face."

"Just because I knew didn't mean I loved you back, Henry. Maybe I tried to, but I love Luke more. Loving him is so easy. I don't have to try. I just *love* him."

"No, you don't. You can't. But I've had to watch him touch you, and you get pregnant with that daughter of his. God, Katherine, have pity. *Touch me.*" Henry's hands caught at Katherine, pulled her up against him as she struggled.

No, no more, Terrill thought frantically, and twisted to find an escape. Instead, through the leaves and the lattice she saw Grandpa walking into the yard from the mill, probably looking for her, wondering what had kept his granddaughter from tagging after him as she always did on Saturdays. Terrill saw his face when he looked up and glimpsed Katherine in Henry's unrelenting embrace, too.

"Let me kiss you—once in fifteen years. Let me say 'I love you.' Let me—"

"Henry!" Grandpa's voice was a roar of sound, his face under his cap was white, and his lips were drawn back in a thin line as he strode across the yard.

Henry's own face streaked red from the sudden check on his heavy emotions; then he pried his hands from Katherine and drew himself up in tall pride.

Grandpa stared at him, temper and incredulity mingling.

"Go in the house, Katherine," he managed at last.

"Please, don't hurt him," she whispered, her eyes full of tears as she looked at her father-in-law pleadingly.

"Just go on in, like I said. And don't talk about this to Luke. Not any of it. Do you hear me?"

When the back door closed behind Katherine, it was just Grandpa and Henry, and the silent, scared, angry ten-year-old girl hidden in the arbor.

"Luke will kill you for what I just saw."

"Let him try. She'll cry for me if he does. It might be worth it."

"Holy Jesus, what's got into you?"

"Maybe I'm tired of sitting back and watching Luke take things away from me. You're just alike, the two of you. Two good old boys, happy here in your narrow little world, where you've kept your favorite son. Went into business with him. Not that I mind— the two of you deserve each other. But I minded about Katherine. Luke just took her."

"You'll be damned in hell for this, Henry. I never thought once that you coveted your own brother's wife."

"Thinking has never been your strong suit," Henry returned hoarsely. "You're a blind, stupid old man."

Without a word, Grandpa opened his hand and slapped Henry. The sound of his big rough palm connecting with his son's cheek rang across the yard, startling in its clarity.

Henry's head bounced sideways, and he kept his face averted for a long, tense, silent moment before he slowly looked back at Grandpa. Before he slid his hands carefully down into the pockets of his light spring overcoat. "What I would have expected from you, *Daddy*," he said ironically.

"Get out," Grandpa ordered roughly. "You come back here again to try this, and I'll throw you out myself."

Henry smiled. "Even if you could, it wouldn't make any difference. Someday I'll have what's mine. Katherine—and anything else I want. . . ."

"And that's exactly what he got, wasn't it, Mama?" Terrill asked passionately as the painful memories slid away into the corners of the room, as Katherine let hot tears slid down her face unchecked. "Poor, innocent Daddy. He was completely bewildered by the way Grandpa and Henry suddenly hated each other. And Grandpa's will. When he died six months later, there was all sorts of money left to Tandy, and his half of the mill left to Daddy. But for Henry, just one sentence: 'Stay the hell out of Cade County.' Daddy and Tandy didn't understand. They even tried to give Henry part of their inheritance. He wouldn't have it . . . but now he's got all he wanted."

"What, Rilla? A dying wife? A wife who loved Luke first . . . and best . . . even when she knew Henry had loved her forever? Henry's just a man."

"A possessive, jealous one," Terrill returned. "He had to push a sixteen-year-old girl out, even though he already had you. There were days when I hated—" She broke off, jumping to her feet.

"It's all right, Rilla," Katherine murmured soothingly from the bed. "I want to know the truth—"

Terrill turned back from the window in a jerky rush. "No, it's not all right. D'you think I want to tell you this now? Now, when it doesn't matter and it can't be changed? Maybe it makes you feel better. Well, not me, Mama. All it will do for me is make me feel guilty because I've told you the way I feel and worried you when you're dy—" She choked on the word.

In the long silence, Katherine twisted in the bedclothes and whispered painfully, "How did we come to this?"

No answer from Terrill. Her throat hurt too much. And in her heart, the desire to crawl up in Katherine's arms, to wipe out everything with forgiveness and love, warred with the bitter resentment and loneliness of the last four years.

"I need you, Rilla," Katherine said at last, awkwardly.

If she had said "love" instead of "need," if she had

reached again for the girl who stood frozen by the windows, everything would have been different. But she didn't.

"I needed you, too, Mama, for years," Terrill answered at last, her voice strained and unnatural.

Katherine shut her eyes a second.

"I don't expect you to understand," Terrill told her. "You've always had somebody to love you and protect you. How could you know what it's like to eat and sleep when you're only doing things just because you have to fill the time? I play the piano now—did you know that? It was because it was better to take piano lessons on Sunday afternoons than to watch television. I was in two recitals. Not for anybody except me, just because I wanted to."

"You never told me—"

"You never asked me," Terrill cried, moving closer to the bed. "You were the one who talked. Whatever you wanted to say, I just listened and answered."

"I wish—I could . . . see Luke tonight," Katherine gasped, struggling upright in the bed, shoving at the covers.

"Why?" The words rushed out of her, like water pouring from a shattered dam. "You've given everything that was his—or mine—to Henry. Even the mill."

"That's . . . not true. . . . Luke might . . . show me what . . . you want from me. . . ." She put her bare heel flat on the floor, as though testing its sturdiness.

"I don't want anything," Terrill returned passionately. "You let me come home. That was enough. I never meant to blame you again, just because you were weak, too weak to fight Henry."

Katherine stood slowly, the yellow of her gown the only color about her. She clutched at the bedpost unsteadily with one hand.

"Mama," Terrill said in belated alarm. "Lie down."
What had she said?

"No—I won't," Katherine answered huskily. "I've
got to reach . . . you. Somehow." Her breath came
and went in hard, shallow expulsions that shook her
whole body and punctuated each word. "I loved
Luke. I love you. I—*do* love you. *Now.*"

"Don't—"

"Believe me." Her voice was insistent, and she
turned loose of the bed to take a step toward Terrill.
"I can . . . prove it. I . . . know a way to . . . show
you. . . . I . . ." Her words spiraled higher and more
frantically, and she stumbled, flinging out a hand to
clutch at the little table by the desk. As she caught at
it, it tilted, and the lamp sitting on it wobbled like a
spinning jack, just before everything crashed to the
floor. Katherine fell, too, like a burst balloon, before
Terrill could reach her. "Mama!"

The next instant all hell broke loose. Henry must
have come in from the mill; he was at the bedroom
door, his face strained and, as he saw Katherine,
incredulous.

"Katherine!" His voice shook, and he spared one
glance at Terrill that said she was at fault.

Remorse and guilt washed over her; looking at the
pitiful jumble of sharp bones and silk that her mother
made on the hardwood floor, Terrill was terrified of
what she had said.

Tears were seeping from under Katherine's
closed eyelids, and her back was heaving.

"What have you done?" Henry accused, taking
long, anxious strides to bend over Katherine. Tandy,
too, had come to the door, and her face and her
reactions were nearly exact replicas of Henry's.

He gently rolled his wife over by her thin shoulders,
murmuring softly, "There, there. Don't cry, Kathy."

Then he hoisted her up and stood heavily, with her cradled against his chest like a beloved broken toy.

Terrill stood watching, eyes wide and frightened. Then Henry lifted his face from Katherine's hair and looked at his stepdaughter.

"I'm—I'm sorry," she made her numb lips say.

"Get out," he said quietly. But menace was in every inch of his body.

Then the woman in his arms moved. "No," she protested. "It was . . . my fault. Rilla," she added beseechingly, her eyes strained as she looked at her daughter anxiously, "I just want you to believe me. I love you. And I loved Luke. I never stopped."

Henry stiffened, unconsciously pulling her more closely to his heart, and Tandy in the corner began a soothing murmur of "Now, now, Katherine, now, now."

"Get out," Henry repeated, and the fury Terrill could feel bubbling up inside him sent her backing to the door.

"No, Henry, I've got to talk to her," Katherine said pleadingly, like a child who couldn't understand, a lost soul in a world that was moving too fast. "About why I sent her away. About how I'm going to make things right. . . ."

"Let's get you back in bed," he said tightly, and Terrill fled.

Twenty-seven minutes later, Katherine was asleep, victim of some sort of medicine Tandy had nearly forced down her throat. She had grabbed at Tandy's hands, begging her to bring back Terrill.

And whispering Luke's name, over and over.

At last Tandy stood from the bed and sighed in relief. "She's asleep," she whispered thankfully.

"Out until tomorrow morning." Outside in the hall, where Terrill shivered in despair, she caught the words and began to breathe again.

Henry said nothing. Instead he rose purposefully from the chair and turned with deliberate intent. Terrill, hearing his movements, flew up the stairs, scrambling for her room.

"Henry—where are—what are you doing?" she heard Tandy ask in alarm. "No—don't do something rash, Henry. Let's find out first what happened—when you've rested a little. Maybe it's not totally her fault. Katherine was determined to talk to her. Henry, please."

Up the stairs he advanced. Terrill waited, her heart jarring her with its sick pounding as she listened to his footsteps.

He stepped across the threshold, an invader in his stepdaughter's room. "Witch." He said it without any emotion. "You're the one. You took my baby. Now you had to bring *him* back."

"I didn't mean to say all those things," Terrill said in a quavering voice.

Again Tandy's voice—her hands—pulled at him from behind. He pushed her away, focused totally on Terrill.

"No—not a witch. A *bitch.* A little bitch. I should have got rid of you long ago. Katherine might still be well if it weren't for you—and him. Don't you think I know what's pulling her into the grave? It's *him.* A damned ghost. And you . . . his shadow."

"What are . . . what are you talking about?" she faltered. Henry looked like something mad, ready to leap at her.

"I told you downstairs," he said, and his voice was as smooth as silk. "Get out."

There was a dead silence—then a shocked gasp from

Tandy. "No, Henry," she cried, clutching at her niece's arm.

But Terrill shook off her aunt's hold and stood stiffly before Henry, searching his face. "I did something wrong tonight, but throwing me out won't help. You're not even doing it because I hurt Mama. You're trying to push me away from her," she said in bitterness. "You can't hold her tight enough to make her forget me, can you? Or Daddy. She said she loved us—she still loves—"

He hit her. For all her newfound insight, he knocked her to her knees in the floor.

It was over before they hardly knew it, and Tandy gave a cry of protest. Henry visibly forced his hand to hold back. Terrill didn't cry. Instead she stared at him with wide, strained eyes full of hate and fear, one cheek blood red.

"Do as I told you," he intoned. "Get out. Or do I have to throw you out?" And he raised his hand again, palm open.

Then, at last, she struggled up and pushed past him, shoving Tandy away and ignoring her cries of "Terrill! Stop!" as she rushed for the door.

"Run, Terrill," Henry shouted, suddenly exuberant and furious, following to call down the stairs after her. "You always wanted to run away. Do it. There'll be no sheriff come after you this time—by God, I swear it!"

She slammed the kitchen door shut on his words, running into the chilly night.

8

Jubal had been swearing steadily to himself, every vicious, raunchy word he knew, since he'd left home tonight.

He didn't like unexpected night work, even when things went as smoothly as they were now. The Peterbilt was giving him no trouble; there was little traffic on the winding, circuitous, torturous route that Henry had chosen for him to follow.

It was an easy trip, with nothing for him to do but smoke an occasional cigarette and lumber through the night with a radio station that called itself "the Beaver." But there was too much time to think. It was either burn with fury at Carroll or let his thoughts stray to the girl.

She had voluntarily spoken to him today. Hadn't wanted to, had been downright ungracious about things. Her voice had held pure puzzlement when she'd asked him "Why?" He'd surprised himself and her, too, with his answer: He'd wanted to. He had wanted to protect her as she lay there sleeping like a baby from the darkness he felt in Carroll.

And it was not only dangerous to feel this way, it was stupid. Nobody who looked and acted the way she did needed—or wanted—protection.

It wasn't too safe to sit here behind the wheel of the big truck and concentrate on her, either.

He found the place that was his destination. It looked exactly the way he expected, and he didn't like anything about it. It was just a tiny, one-room, shacky-looking office in the middle of a cleared, dusty yard, a long way down a gravel road.

Before he was through unhooking the trailer, a black pickup truck was pulling in. Jubal moved back into the shadows warily, waiting. The driver of the truck got out in the night, called out loudly, "Hey! Where are you, Bobo?"

Jubal answered reluctantly. "Here," he called back. "Bobo couldn't come. Carroll sent me."

"Yeah?" the man asked dubiously. "Carroll said he might have to send somebody new tonight. Where's the paperwork?"

Jubal got it, handed it over to the stranger in silence. The man went back to his truck, looked it over with the aid of a tiny flashlight, then returned with a brown envelope in one hand and, in the other, a clipboard, which he thrust at Jubal. "Here. Sign on the bottom line."

Jubal stared at him. "You're crazy," he said derisively. "I ain't signin' anything."

Making an angry gesture, the man retorted, "Carroll needs to get some men with brains—real brains—to work for him. Look, you, I wouldn't hand *this*"—he nodded at the packet in his hand—"to the president without his signature. You could just run off with it, and I'd have no proof I ever gave it to you. So you either sign you received it—like Bobo does—or you get back in that truck and haul this load right back to Carroll."

Jubal didn't move.

The stranger snorted and shook his head in frustration. "Tell Carroll this deal is off. And I wouldn't want to be in your shoes when he hears about it." He was halfway to his truck when Jubal gave in.

"Wait."

"Yeah?"

"I want to see one of those papers with Bobo's signature."

Without a word the man held out the clipboard. Jubal glanced first at him, then down at it. He had to twist to hold the papers in the headlights of the truck. There were three receipt bills; the first two did indeed have Bobo's name at the bottom.

Jubal acquiesed unwillingly. "Okay," he muttered, and scrawled his own name, making it nearly illegible. He didn't like this at all, too leery of the sudden trip, this dark yard, the bland, anonymous buyer.

Silently he exchanged the clipboard for the envelope.

"There's the payment," the man said shortly. "Carroll's expectin' it just like it is, sealed like this."

"He'll get it that way," Jubal retorted.

"And tell Carroll I don't like paranoid drivers. Send Bobo the next time." Then he turned away, leaving Jubal to climb back in the Peterbilt.

"Yes sir," he muttered to himself. "I'll sure tell him, sir. Me, I'm just the dumb mechanic. Somebody better tell Carroll that, too."

His anger kept him awake through Glasgow, and Gamaliel, and across the state line; then it began to rain, a steady downpour his windshield wipers had to push away again and again. The rain and the drugging, monotonous clacking of the wipers slowed him down, so that it was two-thirty or so when he pulled into the yard at the Carroll Mill.

He was supposed to slide this folder under the door to Carroll's inner office; he had a key to the front room so he could get inside that far. The key was one Bobo usually carried. Jubal had inherited that along with Bobo's job tonight.

He made a quick run through the rain to the little porch. Under its stoop, he shook the water out of his face, his heart pounding. If somebody saw him here now after that still unsolved robbery those weeks ago, he'd never get through explaining. I don't like this, he thought again. Then his shoulder brushed the glass pane in the top—and the door opened.

The door was open. Already unlocked—and open.

He balanced there, on the balls of his feet, staring in dread at the narrow fan of light that marked where the door had gapped a good four inches.

Something was wrong.

Not again. He wasn't getting involved in somebody else's schemes and going to jail for it, not ever again.

So what was he to do? Afraid to move forward, afraid to run, waiting for the loud screeching of the burglar alarm. His palms were sweaty as he waited, and there was no sound except the rain.

Then, out of the corner of his eye, he saw it, down close to the floor.

A foot. A white sneaker.

Someone was standing, heels pressed against the wall, right there in the shadows, not a yard from him.

He made a sudden fast dive that shoved the door open and grabbed for the ankle above the foot. There was a muffled cry as he yanked the watcher off his feet and slammed him to the ground. He heard his grunt and the hard expulsion of his breath.

Then the other person began to fight and twist frantically in the darkness, kicking Jubal backward, off balance, out onto the little porch. But he didn't loosen his hold on the leg; he pulled his captive with him.

The two of them, locked together, rolled onto the porch, then off the steps into the rain and into the scraggly wet grass. For a minute it was all struggling, panting, heaving confusion. The he pinned the body under him, subduing the flailing legs under his own, yanking the scratching hands up above his assailant's head.

At last he sucked in several gulps of air and lifted and twisted to let the purple glare from the security light fall over his shoulder, to stare down into the face of the stranger who'd been waiting for him inside the office.

Amazement hit him like a knife between his ribs; he was looking down into the terrified face of a girl.

Terrill. Terrill Carroll.

For a long, shocked moment he just stared incredulously at her, at the wide frightened blue eyes, watching him; at the hair spilling out on the wet ground, its strands darkened now to a deep brown by shadows and rain; at the panting, up-and-down movement of her chest beneath the round, scooped neck of her white blouse.

At three in the morning, out in the pouring rain, he was straddling Terrill Carroll.

"You scared the hell outta me," he said at last after he got his voice back. "What're you doin' down here?"

"Let go of me," she demanded instead of answering, her voice tremulous. She fought for a minute against his hard grip on her wrists.

"I asked you a question. What are you doin' here?" he asked again, shaking her a little.

"I've got a right to be here. It's my . . . mill. Get off! Let me *up*. You're hurting me."

He stared down at her a minute longer, then slowly relaxed his hold on her arms and sat up a little, but still straddling her stomach. The rain beat a tattoo down his back and ran down his coat collar, just as it fell on his face and neck.

Beneath this weight, Terrill could barely breathe, and her terrified heart was trying to knock up and out of her throat. The dark face of Kane was scary enough, but having his hands on her, his body right against hers, was enough to make her teeth chatter. At last, frantic, she bucked up, trying to rise, but his weight wouldn't let her.

"Let—me—up!"

"I asked you a question," he said shortly. "I want to know what you're doin' here."

"None of your business," she retorted faintly. "What are *you* doing here?"

"I had to deliver a load," he answered. "For Carroll. I just got back from Kentucky."

"Sure." Even breathless, her voice was sarcastic.

"You don't believe me? There's the truck." He jerked his head in the general direction of the big truck yard. "Engine's still hot."

"Okay. Fine. Whatever you say. I want *up*."

He moved at last, and Terrill pulled in a deep, grateful breath as he rose to his feet. She didn't like lying sprawled out in front of him, so she scrambled up quickly and made a frantic lunge for freedom, trying to escape him.

But he was expecting it, and his hand shot out and grabbed her right above the elbow. "Uh-huh," he said shortly. "You're not going anywhere."

Her quick shiver made him give her a hard pull back toward the office. "C'mon. Let's go."

"Who d'you think you are, hauling me around this way?" she blazed, but he yanked her up the steps, even when her reluctant feet stumbled, and thrust her into the dark office. Then he entered, too, shoving the door shut behind him.

Her only avenue of escape was blocked off, she realized, shivering and clasping her arms around herself. Backing away, she got as far from him as she could, stopping only when her calves in the wet jeans bumped the couch.

There was a long silence as the rain beat down on the roof; then she spoke, belligerently.

"Get out. I don't have to tell you anything."

"You meetin' somebody down here?" he asked suddenly.

"What?"

"Look at you." He gestured in the shadows at her disheveled state. "You look like you climbed out a window and came to meet somebody."

His meaning hit her, and she felt her cheeks getting hot in the darkness from anger and embarrassment. "I'm not meeting a guy, if that's what you mean. And I didn't climb out a window. I went out the kitchen door."

In the silence this time, he took a step closer to her, and she could hear him breathing. Maybe she'd said the wrong thing. She spoke again, hastily.

"I want you to go away. I won't tell anybody else what you were doing down here, okay? We'll just forget that we—ran into each other like this."

"Maybe you'll forget, but I won't," he retorted. "What d'you mean, 'what I'm doin' down here'? I *told* you why. Ask Carroll if you don't believe me. What d'you think I'm doin' here, anyway?"

She didn't answer, and he was getting mad. The way she edged around him, the way she jumped every time he moved, he had a pretty good idea of exactly what she was thinking.

"You think . . . you think I came to rob the place. Maybe to get what I didn't get the last time. You remember that day, don't you? I remember *you*— the way you stared at me. You looked scared. What you scared of, Terrill?" he taunted mockingly.

She meant to deny that she was afraid, but instead she burst out, "Aunt Tandy says that you—"

"What?" Jubal demanded in rising anger. "What does Aunt Tandy say?" Stubborn silence. "You're not gonna tell me? That's okay. I bet I can guess. She says I've been to Lineville. Am I right?"

Terrill made no answer, so he laughed a little. "Yeah, I'm right. You've heard of that place, now, ain't you?" After another silent moment he asked more forcefully, "Ain't you?"

"What am I supposed to say?" she returned. "Everybody has." She shivered again. He was tall, far taller than she'd ever realized, and there was an iron strength in him despite his slenderness.

"Aunt Tandy said I went to jail for a robbery. Didn't she?"

Terrill hadn't really wanted to remember what crimes lay in his past or, for that matter, for him to remember them, either, and his sudden jerky movement made her jump a little.

But all he did was move his feet apart and lift his arms out to his sides. "You think I'm here to steal? Who knows what I might be gettin' away with me? Go ahead, then. Search me."

"W-what?" she faltered.

"You don't believe me when I tell you the truth. So go ahead. Search me. Find out for yourself."

"Stop it," she whispered.

"You're awful quick to accuse me. Don't you want to know the truth?" He stepped right into her, then reached out and grasped her chin. "You're so damned sure I'm gonna hurt you. I—"

She winced involuntarily as his fingers grasped her jaw, then she twisted her face away a little. The light from a big digital wall clock that read 3:15 A.M. hit the side of her cheek.

He remembered then how she'd had heavy shadows on her left cheek outside—at least that was what he'd thought then. But in here, the shadows were still there, except they looked like bruises.

"What's wrong with your face?" he asked abruptly.

"Nothing. What's wrong with yours?" she said bitingly, and pushed his hand down.

Jubal let her go and moved away, but just as she began to breathe in relief, he flipped on the tiny lamp that always sat on the secretary's desk. Even its small glow hurt their eyes, making them both blink.

Terrill jerked and tried to cover her cheek with her hand, but Jubal had time to see all he needed to: there was a deep, purple bruise from her jaw to the corner of her eye, the length of a man's hand.

"Who hit you?"

"Turn off the light."

After a hesitation he did as she asked, and they were swallowed again by dusky shadows.

"Who hit you?" he repeated insistently.

She laughed a little. "Nobody. I—I was trying to find my shoes to put them on here in the dark, and I stumbled, and I—I fell against the desk—"

"You're lying," he said flatly. "He did, didn't he?"

"I don't know what you're talking about."

"Henry Carroll."

No answer, but he heard her swallow. Then she shivered violently.

"I want my coat."

"Your coat," he repeated blankly.

"It's there. Beside you on the desk."

He found it, started to hold it out to her as she reached for it from her safe position, then remembered his original grievance. He folded it over his arms instead.

"You can come and get it," Jubal said flatly.

She took one little step. Suddenly angry, not just at her but at himself for baiting her and for feeling more than he should at the sight of her cheek, Jubal flung the coat at her abruptly. "Here. Take it. You could come all the way over here and pull it right out of my hand and I still wouldn't hurt you. Don't you get it yet? I don't want to hurt you. I'm sure as hell not gonna hit you, like he did."

She stooped to pick up the coat. "What makes you so sure Henry hit me?"

"Because I know him."

"But the whole town knows him. He's a . . . good man," she said slowly, testing him.

He laughed a little under his breath. "Well, maybe the whole town ain't workin' for him. He don't care what I think, so I get to see him a little clearer than most. He don't worry about me. Who's gonna listen to anythin' I say? I'm a no-name. A nobody."

Terrill didn't know why her fear was slowly evaporating. Maybe a little part of it was still there, but somehow she was beginning to believe he really wasn't going to hurt her. And he knew about Henry. Somehow he knew, this Kane.

"Kane," she said slowly.

He looked at her warily; she wasn't calling him, that much was clear.

"You're not a no-name. See? I know more about you than Lineville," Terrill offered tentatively.

He'd never thought about it before, but the way she said it, he didn't like it.

"My name is *Jubal*," he said fiercely.

Terrill stared at him. "All right."

"No, it ain't all right. I'm not your—your dog. I don't want you callin' me 'Kane' like I am, either." There was a long, impatient pause. "Well, can't you say it?"

"Yes," Terrill answered quietly. "Jubal."

He looked away from her, swallowing heavily. "I really did make a run for Carroll tonight, you know. I was supposed to bring *this* to the office"—he found the long brown envelope, still in his pocket—"and slide it under his inner office door. It's payment for the load."

She stared at the envelope a moment but made no answer, staying stubbornly quiet. Then she turned away.

Quick as a cat, he tossed the envelope onto the desk and caught at her arm. "No, you don't. Tell me."

Rebelliousness rose in Terrill, but she wanted desperately to tell *somebody*, and the conflicting emotions warred inside her.

"I—" The words wouldn't come.

The his hand reached up, and carefully, slowly, his fingers brushed her cheek, and before she even had time to realize what was happening, the words and—worse—heavy, choking sobs tore out of her.

"He . . . hit me be-c-cause he hates me. It wasn't . . . because of what I said. She loved . . . Daddy, and she used to love me. He hit me . . . to—to push me away again. He won't. I won't let him—"

Jubal's hand froze on her cheek. He'd never expected such a gushing of emotion. It frightened him, her crying, tearing out of her as it was. Nothing pretty or delicate in it. It was for real. My God, this was the Carroll girl, who'd run away from home and who had him and half the men around scared of her tongue.

She was crying so hard that she was shaking, choking on the heavy sobs. Dammit—what was he supposed to do? Maggie never cried—the more things hurt her, the more stoic she became. And now here he was with a girl who'd come to pieces at an hour they should both have been home in their beds, and she was probably freezing in the cold, damp clothes she had on, to boot.

No girl ought to cry the way she was crying.

He did the only thing he could think of, and it was nothing more than a quick, instinctive reaction: he reached out and pulled her up against him.

For a second or two she strained away, then she collapsed against his shirtfront, and he wrapped his arms tightly around her in the darkness. They stood there for a long, long time, until her sobs began to die away and fade a little, and Jubal had time to think about a lot of things.

Like about how warm she really was lying there against him. How tall she was; her head tucked right under his chin, and he was tall himself. Her hair was soft, too, as soft as he'd thought it would be as he'd watched it day after day as it hung between them.

But most of all, he began to think about what he'd like to do to Henry Carroll, and how hard he must have struck her to leave such a huge mark. He tightened his hold on Terrill a little, trying to comfort her with rambling comments that sounded as if he were talking to a baby: "Cry. Just go ahead and cry. It'll be okay. You're okay."

"No, I'm not," she said chokily at last. "I'm so mad—I wish I could tear his eyes out."

He almost laughed in relief. She sounded more like the girl he knew, a little hiccupy, maybe, but normal. But he didn't turn loose of her just yet.

His arms were comforting enough that it took several minutes for Terrill to want to move away, for her to realize exactly what she was doing. She was cuddled up against Jubal Kane as if she belonged there. He was warm beneath the dampness of his shirt, and his heart was thudding under her ear. He smelled different. Not like anybody she'd ever been around. Like the outdoors and the earth and the rain, and he smelled of sharper things, too, of cigarettes and smoke and diesel.

And his arms and hands were soothing as they wrapped her to him, as they caressed her hair and her back. It had been a long time since anybody had caressed Terrill—a long time since she had let them. The way he touched was different as well, like none she'd ever felt before. His hands were calming, tender. Not like the open-palmed pain of—

She drew in air sharply, as if a knife had stabbed her.

"What's wrong?" he asked above her.

And it was easy to tell him, standing there with her face buried against him, her hands pushed under the warmth of his arms. She told him about Katherine, about the way she loved her and how she hated her. Funny, though—it was difficult to feel that hate now that she had time to remember. She had burned for years to tell Katherine the way she felt; she had choked back the hot words a thousand times, staying far away from any conversation that even came close to her real emotions for fear they would spill out.

But tonight she had spewed out her anger like hot coals, and now she knew: she hadn't wanted to hurt Katherine after all.

She told all of that to Jubal Kane, and he listened and held her. So she told him more. She told him about Henry, and of what had happened, of how she'd run from the bedroom and out into the night.

Terrill hadn't been afraid of the night; it and the wind were freedom from Henry Carroll, and the road she had walked was familiar.

In the pocket of her jacket were keys to the office. Tandy kept a set of them hanging in the pantry on a hook beside the coat rack, and maybe more to spite Henry than anything else, Terrill had grabbed them on her way out.

She was panting, sticky with a cold sweat and wet with rain, when she got to the sawmill office, where she'd come in and sunk wearily on the couch. She'd fallen asleep there, too tired to do anything else, and hadn't awakened until the sound of a heavy truck in the distance had aroused her.

Now, suddenly, she remembered her fear, and a few other realities hit as well: this was Kane. She was letting *Kane* touch her. The one who'd worn handcuffs with such easy familiarity here just a few weeks past.

With a quick movement, she pushed away from his body a little, and he let her go, his hands still holding her arms lightly. She looked up at him, studying his face. It was dark in this room, just before dawn, and difficult to see anything except the green glow of his eyes. The security light shone through the window, and the rain reflecting on the pane made snaky black patterns on the side of his face.

"I don't even know why I told you all this," she said at last in the heavy silence. "I guess because of where we are. Maybe because everything's mixed up tonight. This morning. Whatever."

"Don't feel bad about tellin' me. Not now. I knew most of it, except how things were with you and your mother."

She pulled away completely and reached for her coat a second time. As she put it on, Jubal spoke again.

"I don't know what you're plannin', but you can't run away again. You gotta go back. You know that, don't you?"

"I'm not running," Terrill told him decisively. "Not this time. If I do, he wins."

"That ain't a good enough reason," Jubal said quietly. "The thing is, if you run, you lose." Somebody had said this to him not long ago. Who?

She considered his words a minute. "What do you know about running?"

"I've wanted to a few times," he answered honestly.

"Did you really do what they said you did? Is it true?" Terrill asked diffidently. She wanted to believe he was innocent. It would be easy to believe it here.

"Yeah, it's true." At her quick jerk, he said defensively, "What'd you expect me to say?"

She shivered a little and tried to laugh. "That was the wrong answer."

"Maybe it was the wrong question," he replied shortly.

"So now you're back to trying to scare me again. Well, listen, Kane, I'm never going to be as scared as

I was when I realized I'd left the door unlocked and somebody was standing at it. When I saw it was you—"

He broke into her angry words. "I think I like you better when you're cryin'."

Terrill flushed; she hated the thought of how weak-kneed she'd been minutes earlier, of how she'd clung to him.

"Don't expect me to cry again," she said flippantly. "Not in a hundred years."

He might not have heard her; he was watching her face. Thinking what? she wondered uneasily.

So here she was back, Jubal was telling himself. The Terrill he knew, cool and brash.

But tonight he'd seen a real girl under all that bravado, one so full of passion for the ones she loved—or hated—that she'd nearly burned up in his arms telling him about it. Past the pretense, she cared and felt and cried.

She made his heart hurt, and she was probably going to hate him when she had time to remember all she'd told him here in this mill office. Jubal didn't want that to happen. Not now. He wanted her up against him again, trusting him, clinging to him.

What he really wanted, most of all, was to kiss her.

The sudden realization surprised him.

That was absolutely the one thing he must *not* do. He was leaving Cade County soon, he'd been burned by one girl like her already this fall, and this spitfire wasn't about to let him touch her: those were the reasons he shouldn't kiss her.

But her lips were soft and trembling. The one reason he wanted to—and it kept tilting the scales in its favor.

"I'll take you home," he said. That was all.

She started. "Home?" Her voice held uncertainty.

"You said you'd go back. And you have to tell your mother all the . . . the stuff you told me."

She bit her lip a little, then she laughed. A little nervous, a little embarrassed. "All right."

"Will you do it?"

"Go home? Yes."

"No. Tell her."

"I'll try."

She said it seriously, looking right at him as though she were taking some kind of vow, and the scales tipped a little farther. He moved abruptly. "Look, I need some sleep so I can be Carroll's best little mechanic. I gotta come in at ten to do a repair job on a loader. Hurry up."

"I'll walk."

"It's rainin'," he pointed out patiently.

"I like rain. I like walking in the dark," she persisted. She couldn't tell him the truth—that there'd be hell to pay again if anybody saw him bring her home.

He shook his head in exasperation. "I believe you," he answered humorously. "But the temperature's droppin' and the wind's up. Besides, my truck's right here. It's been parked at the corner of the mill ever since I left here for Kentucky."

There was no help for it; she had to tell him now.

"They might be waiting. Tandy would still be up and see us."

A slight pause while he considered her rushed words. "See who you're with?"

That hateful, drawling tone made her want to smack him. "She'd be mad if I was with the angel Gabriel at this hour," Terrill retorted. "And you're not exactly him, so she'd probably shoot *you*. Then me. And I'm saving myself for Henry—he's been waiting so long to do me in, I'd hate to deprive him now."

Jubal didn't know when he started to laugh; his crack of amusement burst from him much as her tears had earlier. He didn't know how, but she'd said the right thing. It felt like—like he was just a regular person, and she was treating him that way.

"We'll go past the end of your drive, on the highway," he said at last, his voice still rumbly and smiling. "If we don't see anybody, I'll turn off my lights and take you to the gate. Just that far."

He wanted to take care of her, just for tonight. It was the same emotion that had been born as she'd slept at the desk. The thought was nearly funny: him going soft over a girl almost as tall as he was, one who bit and scratched at anybody who tried to get too close. But it would just have to be funny; it was still the truth.

"C'mon," he said, opening the door for her.

"You're the most stubborn person I ever met," she muttered at last, a little angrily.

"You oughta know about stubborn," he said significantly.

She gave a quick, reluctant laugh, then broke into movement. She raced out the door while he shut it, then across the yard through the rain. He motioned her toward the old red truck parked at the back. After yanking open the passenger door, he held it for her, then slammed it shut behind her. He opened his own door and slid in, under the wheel.

Terrill didn't think she liked being in this truck, in spite of the shelter it offered. Something intimate was involved in sitting in another person's vehicle, even in daylight. Now, caught here together in the darkness, she and Kane were just too close, and it wasn't fear of his admitted criminal offenses that made her stomach knot up. His scent was in the truck, accentuated by the dampness and the heat rising from his clothes.

He made no more moves toward her, only started the engine, and finally they pulled out onto the road. She shot a glance over at his hands, at the long, agile brown fingers wrapping the steering wheel. He had a scrape across his knuckles on his right hand that looked painful, but the hand had been gentle against her when he held her.

She hadn't expected that gentleness from one like him.

They drove to the turnoff to her house; all was quiet, and nobody was waiting. So he turned into the gravel road, keeping his word: he turned off the lights on the truck and stopped a good distance from the house, at the first gate.

The porch lights were on, and that fact told Terrill that Tandy was waiting. She was ready to admit it: she was glad somebody was there.

Her conscience told her suddenly that Kane had been there for her, too, whether she'd wanted him or not. In fact, he'd been working double time on her behalf, she thought as she remembered how he'd helped her earlier today, or yesterday, whichever it was now.

If she was ever going to say it, now was the time, but she was out of practice. "I was wondering how I could thank you. Not just for tonight, but for today, too. When you told Henry that you spilled the coffee."

I know a way for you to thank me, his mind replied instantly, and he couldn't stop his eyes as they dropped to her lips in the shadowy truck.

She moved uneasily. "I wish—"

"What?" he asked her at last, still watching her lips.

I wish you weren't Jubal Kane with a reputation as long as the Mississippi River, and that you'd said "no" when I asked you if you'd really done all those things, Terrill thought, and I wish you weren't quite so close. . . .

A little chill ran up her arms. Then he looked up, right into her eyes, and her heart did a funny flip-flop.

Or maybe I wish you were closer.

The idea sprang up unexpectedly, just as had the quick tension, all a part of the moody, rainy night. She turned quickly toward the door, but not quickly enough. He caught her arm.

"Wait," he said, and her blood began to strum thickly in her ears. "This is it, I reckon. The only time we're ever gonna be together, alone like this."

Her heart beat thunderously right at the base of her neck instead of where it belonged, down in her rib cage. She didn't answer, just stared at him like a frightened, blue-eyed kitten.

What would Dusty and the rest of them say, he wondered fleetingly, if he told them sass-and-brass Terrill was all show? That she was scared to neck with him?

"Just one time," he whispered. "Just so I'll know what it's like."

She knew what he intended, but she couldn't seem to move away. She watched his dark, still, beautiful face lower toward hers, saw the brilliant flame of his green eyes intent on her lips.

Jubal Kane was about to kiss her.

Then his mouth touched hers, and she couldn't see any more. She could only feel: his breath warm on her cheek, his hands on her shoulders, his body so close that her fingers brushed his shirt, and her own heart slowing down painfully, because it couldn't beat its way through the clogging, thick richness that flooded around it.

Jubal wasn't sure how long his mouth held hers. There was only one word flashing on and off in his surprised brain as he caught her breath with his mouth: innocence. He'd never tasted it before, hadn't even known it had a flavor all its own, wasn't sure he even believed in its existence. But he recognized it on her lips. He must be mistaken. Nobody like Terrill could be this cleanly, purely sweet. Even if he were willing to admit he'd been wrong about a few things concerning her, she still looked too good and ran too wild—it was four o'clock in the morning, and she was out in the rain, kissing him, for God's sake. That was proof enough.

He had to get away. He gave a hard jerk out of her arms, then discovered she wasn't holding him. They gazed at each other a long, shocked minute.

"You didn't have any right to do that," she spoke first, clearly.

"No." He admitted it now that it was too late. But he couldn't get the words "I'm sorry" unstuck from the roof of his mouth, despite the feeling that he was really going to be. "Don't worry, I don't expect you to remember any of this on Monday. Or ever," he said brusquely. "And I ain't gonna do it again."

She was still too close to him.

"Jubal," she whispered, as though she hadn't heard his words and couldn't stop her own, "you have the greenest eyes I've ever seen."

Whatever he'd been expecting her to say, that wasn't it. Only Ma ever talked about his green eyes, and it felt weirder than hell to hear the words on the lips of the girl he'd just kissed, and wanted to again.

Then she opened her door, and in one smooth movement she slid out into the early dawn and the rain. The last he saw of her as she vanished into the misty darkness was the flash of her white shirt, where it hung outside her jeans and below her jacket.

His hands were shaking when he tried to start the truck. "Weirder than hell," he repeated to himself.

9

Terrill shut the door behind her. In the dim glow of the light above the kitchen sink, she saw the figure at the table, its shoulders square and determined.

"You . . . you have rain in your hair." Tandy's voice was a little slurred as she spoke to her niece, maybe from exhaustion. Surely she would never get emotional enough to sound this ragged.

Terrill shrugged, and tiny rivulets of water trickled down the front of the short leather jacket she wore. "You didn't stay up to tell me that." She meant to be flippant; instead her voice was ragged, too.

"I've been sitting here, Rilla, telling myself that I would wait for you until morning. If you came back, I'd ask no questions. If you didn't, I'd go to the authorities and tell every unpleasant detail. Yes, even about what Henry did." Tandy raised her voice a little to answer Terrill's question before she spoke it. "And I remind myself that you're twenty years old. An adult. And that I might behave the same way you did tonight if I got pushed enough."

"You, Aunt Tandy?" Terrill said in doubt.

"Oh, yes. Me. You see, there was a time when I got shoved aside, too. And it hurt. Luke agreed to let me own a third of the mill, but your grandpa Carroll wouldn't hear of it. A woman's place wasn't in a sawmill, he said. I'd been working as an accountant at the bank since I got out of high school, but he thought I couldn't handle it. He never gave me a chance, or any training at all so that I might have."

"I don't understand what—"

"It's just time to tell you some things," Tandy interrupted flatly. "Come and sit down here."

Reluctantly Terrill made her feet walk forward. She sat down tentatively on the edge of the chair farthest away from her aunt.

"When Luke was killed, and Katherine didn't know the first thing about running the mill, I told her I could. I was certain I could make the mill work."

Tandy leaned back a little, straightening her shoulders against the tall back of the kitchen chair. "I was wrong."

Two spots of hectic red splotched over her cheeks, each one riding high on the cheekbone. "I didn't know the first thing about cutting or buying or anything else. But I could have learned all of that. Unfortunately, I antagonized the workers right away. I discovered one with liquor in his work truck. I believe I delivered a rather stinging lecture on the evils of alcohol, as well as on the unnecessary use of profanity on the job. They were all . . . excessively vulgar in their conversation."

Silence reigned in the kitchen for a long, long moment before Tandy licked her lips nervously and spoke again. "I looked like quite a fool. I was the town joke for a while. Prissy old-maid Tandy Carroll, running a sawmill full of men. Reading them Sunday school lectures."

"I'm sorry," Terrill whispered at last, seeing the pained embarrassment on Tandy's face clearly, feeling it for her. What else could she do?

Tandy stood abruptly, walked over to the sink, and looked out the low window. "Don't be. The last laugh was on them, because then the town began to joke that it took a mighty strange man to work for a bossy, self-righteous woman. The talk got to some of them, and finally one named Mike Manchester blew up at me when I reprimanded him because he made an error in a bill. He salvaged his pride by telling me in front of the other men exactly how much I needed a good strong masculine hand, and exactly what . . . what *other* part of the male anatomy I needed a dose of. He got quite graphic."

In between the flashes of searing pity and mortification, Terrill felt for her aunt, she wanted to give a hysterical burst of laughter at her oh-so-prim word choice. She hastily put her fist to her mouth, biting it a little.

"I fired him immediately. Unfortunately, his replacement had very little actual experience. When he and his crew got in a bind while they were out cutting, he made a poor judgment call and there was an accident. One of the workers lost his right hand and nearly his life, he sued Carroll Mills, and our insurance paid him off. But the damage was done. Men quit like flies.

"Oh, I tried to save things. Katherine and I both went to the bank and asked for a loan until we could pull things back together. I've never quite forgiven Lionel Johnson for his refusal. 'You were meant to work with figures, Tandy, not men,' he said. 'Come back to the bank job. Give up the mill.' Before I was through, I'd pulled every cent I had out of his bank, intending to use my own inheritance for the mill.

"Then, Katherine intervened. She talked to Henry, and I was left out of the decision. Katherine wouldn't let me put my money into the mill. She said she was afraid I would lose it, too.

"Henry said he could straighten things out. He gave up his job to come back and run the place. I'll never forget how . . . how jubilant he was about it that first week. He asked me, 'Do you think Daddy knows that I run his mill now, Tandy? I'm a better man.' And I answered, 'A better man, Henry?' He looked at me, sort of startled, as if he'd just realized what we were saying to each other, and said, 'A better man than he ever knew I was.'"

There was a long silence. At last Terrill said slowly, "So Henry was the salvation of the mill. I still don't see why he had to marry Mama."

Normally Tandy would have ignored the bitterness in the words, but not this time. "She knew he loved her; I didn't realize he did until Luke was dead, but I think she's always known. Maybe she felt guilty using him for the mill. But you know what I really think, Rilla?"

"You think," Terrill choked out, nearly gagging on the words, "that Mama loves him."

Tandy turned to her niece, where she'd risen again from the table, and took a step or two toward her. Her voice held pity and compassion when she spoke. "Don't take it so hard, Rilla. She still loves Luke. Some women can love twice in a lifetime, and each love is different. One takes nothing from the other."

"Not me," Terrill said on a hard sob, holding her coat tightly around herself. "Not me. One time, that's all I'll ever love."

Tandy looked at the set face of the girl, at the brightness of tears in her eyes. "Maybe you're right," she answered quietly. "For you, maybe once will be all."

Then she continued, "But the point is, you and Henry both love Katherine. You're the only part of her he'll have left soon. He has to start dealing with you, without anger, as an adult. You two need each other. You can't afford to destroy one another."

"I hate him."

"Just like you hate Katherine?"

Terrill's breath rushed out in a ragged sob of protest, and she held out her hands as if to push Tandy's words away. "I don't hate Mama," she whispered painfully.

"You haven't got long to make her believe that," Tandy answered somberly. "And I don't want any more repetitions of tonight. Do you?"

Terrill shook her head wordlessly.

Outside, a rooster crowed in the distance. His raucous squawk broke the tension in the room.

"Well," Tandy said on a tiny half laugh, "I've never said this to anybody at this hour of the morning before, but you need a good night's sleep, Rilla. Rest awhile. Don't worry about Henry. I'm going to talk to him, too."

Terrill started to turn away, then remembered. "Aunt Tandy," she said hesitantly, "I'm sorry about the mill. About what the men said to you."

"I guess it was an education of sorts," Tandy said, then added kindly. "Go to bed before you drop, child."

Her mother was watching from the pillows as Terrill stepped into the room that morning at half-past ten. Katherine's eyes were so bright and intense, they appeared to be the only spark of life in her entire body.

"M-Mama," Terrill faltered, then drew a step closer. "I love you, Rilla."

The unexpected, abrupt declaration made her steps stumble a little.

"And I'm . . . sorry we got . . . separated along the . . . way." Katherine finished up her confession huskily.

"I—" She couldn't say it; even now Terrill couldn't get out "I love you." She would, but not today. Today she hurt too much. She said instead, haltingly, "I'm sorry, too, Mama."

"So—now—could we . . . could we just talk?" Katherine asked hesitantly. "About everything."

Terrill sank onto the edge of the bed. "I'll tell you about piano lessons," she offered tremulously, trying to smile.

"Your face," Katherine said slowly, reaching up a hand to turn Terrill's reluctant head toward her.

"I—went outside last night. After our argument. It started raining, and I slipped and . . . fell," Terrill told her. It sounded good; she'd planned it carefully.

Katherine looked at her for a minute; disbelief and a quick flare of something else—understanding?— lit her eyes. "All right," she said, as though the two of them had made an agreement. "Don't do it again."

Terrill pulled her head away. "I won't," she promised steadily.

"I . . . I want to tell you . . . about Luke . . . and Henry . . . and all the things I never talked about . . . before." Katherine said finally, and searched her daughter's face with her eyes. "I need to tell you, Rilla, but only if you need to hear."

Terrill nodded. She felt a thousand years old and tired with the long fight that had gained her just one blinding truth: Katherine had only the past to share with her daughter—there would be no future.

A few eddying days for Terrill to remember with pleasure—or regret. A kaleidoscoped circle of time with her and Katherine at its center, their past, their present, their future, all compressed into it, filling it. A memory to take out someday and let its dried fragrance blow around her.

"I want to hear, Mama, and I want to talk, too," Terrill answered steadily, and words—Jubal Kane's words—came back to her unexpectedly. "If we don't, nobody wins. I lose. And I'm losing enough."

The fragile sunrise promised a red-and-gold autumn Saturday, but by the time Jubal dragged himself into work, rain had moved in again, and the skies were full of clouds that were a dark, metallic gray in hue.

It made no difference to Jubal; he still had to repair the loader. As he worked patiently with the tiny bolts in the shop at the back of the lumberyard, the rain beat down on the tin roof. Its patter finally turned into a roar, sometimes nearly drowning out the only companion he had, the radio that set high on a shelf above his head. That, too, made no difference; he was only barely aware that some man was singing about "the back side of thirty, the short side of time" in the middle of the downpour, anyway.

Jubal was thinking.

Not about his work.

He was thinking of the way Terrill Carroll had felt when he'd pulled her up against him. Of the way her eyes had watched him. And—why not admit it?—of the way that thunderous thing that had started out as a kiss had felt. And tasted.

Six hours later he was still running his tongue over his lips, trying to recall that delicate, sweet taste again.

The fourth time he caught himself doing that, he dropped the started he was rebuilding onto the worktable and swore to himself.

"Having problems, Kane?"

The sarcastic voice of Henry Carroll made him jump and turn. The man had just come in and stood in the door watching him, his bright yellow rain slicker the only spot of color in the dark, grease-stained shop.

"No," Jubal answered shortly.

"Good," Carroll drawled. "And last night? Any problems there?"

For a minute Jubal couldn't even remember what the man was talking about. He stared at Carroll blankly.

"With the run to Kentucky," Carroll supplied dryly, and there was a hint of knowledge in his voice that set off warning bells in Jubal's ears.

"Oh, that. No. No problems."

"Um. I just wondered. Here's your check for the week. There's overtime for last night. Guess you were real busy—you earned it."

Jubal reached out slowly to take the proffered check, and his jaw tightened as he glanced down at Carroll's hands. They were big, heavy, powerful. And her face was fine-boned. Delicate.

Don't hit her again, Carroll. Not unless you want to get hit back, he thought.

Maybe Jubal had thought about Terrill so much that morning that he mentally forced her to see him in town that afternoon. He'd never found her there before, but then he rarely ever went himself.

But the heavy rain brought the loggers and the rest of the crew in even earlier than usual that Saturday, and everybody got to go home a little after eleven.

Only Jubal kept working, until at last Bobo Hackett stuck his head in the shop door.

"Hey, kid," he greeted Jubal. "Noon. Time to quit, even for you."

Jubal finished tightening a screw with his black, oil-slicked fingers.

"Put that damned stuff down," Bobo said irritably. "It makes me nervous just watchin' you with that tedious work. You got the patience of a saint, y'know that?"

Jubal glanced up at Bobo, one eyebrow raised derisively. "Yeah, that's me. A saint. I'm so damned saintly that last night I took your place in a run to Kentucky. And I didn't like it."

Bobo backed up against the doorjamb in the tiny shop, knocking over one of the diesel canisters that lined the wall. "Carroll's the one that decided you'd go. Not me. Says he wants you to know the whole routine. Seems like he's took a real likin' to you," he added ironically.

Jubal put down the parts. "You tell him you want that run back. Hell, that man at the yard had me signin' papers like this was *my* business."

Bobo fumbled for a cigarette. "Standard stuff. I've had to do it, too. Quit worryin' so much, Jubal. I was needin' a favor, but I wouldn'ta come by if I'da known you were so hell-fired grouchy."

"What favor?"

"Nothin' much. My truck's in the shop. I was wonderin' if you could take me to meet Lily."

Lily Clayburn worked as the cashier at the City Cafe, on one side of the town square, just down the street from McDowell's Drugstore. Tandy Carroll's white Ford Taurus was pulling into an angled parking space right in front of that drugstore when Jubal came out of the City Cafe fifteen minutes later.

But it wasn't the car that froze him in place, or even the driver. It was the girl on the passenger seat. Her hair had been pulled back in some kind of complicated, heavy braid, but the dampness in the air had loosened it, made it cling and curl loosely around the face like a soft halo.

Honey and lightning, somebody had told Jubal. Somebody had been right; he could almost taste the sweetness, feel the kick in his stomach.

She didn't see him as she got out, as he stood under the white-and-green-striped awning that ran the length of the block over the various businesses, so he relaxed slowly back against the hard brick of the City Cafe's outside wall and surveyed her.

There was pleasure in watching her lithe walk and her graceful movement, so he decided he'd wait a while, just to get another chance to see her when she came out again.

He lit a cigarette while he waited, bent his right knee to prop the sole of his boot on the wall at his back, and watched the cigarette smoke drift away into the drizzling rain. Two old farmers passed him, arguing over the political race for county road commissioner. A mother and two children hurried by, one crying over a Tootsie Roll pop he'd dropped in the road. James Lawson roared up to the stop sign at the corner in his '66 Ford Mustang, complete with ear-splitting, straight-out exhausts.

And still Jubal waited, barely conscious of them. When the drugstore door opened, he was ready. And she was every bit as beautiful as she had been minutes before—hours before—days before. Except that now, turned a different way and listening to her aunt, she was walking into the gray, rainy light, and the dark bruise on her face showed up clearly.

He let the cigarette burn while he examined her

cheek, totally unaware of the world around him, until Bobo opened the door of the cafe and shouted, "Hey, Jubal, come 'ere a minute."

She heard the shout, too, and she looked up quickly, eyes searching for him. Maybe there was a hundred feet between them. It didn't matter. Even through the rain dripping off the cracks in the metal awning, he saw her flush and swallow, and look away and look back again. Nothing cool, or hard, or sarcastic about her now.

You remember. You remember how that kiss was, too, he told her silently.

Then Tandy Carroll saw him standing there and frowned, and Terrill turned away from him, back to her aunt, for all the world like hers had been an idle, curious glance.

But she knew better, because he knew better.

The restlessness that ran in his blood the remainder of the day wouldn't leave, no matter what he did. At dusk he drove out the Ridge to Ida Fuller's store, where Ida was locking up for the night, hunched down in her tweed coat as she fooled with her keys.

Bobo and two or three of his cronies were out on the porch, getting ready to make their weekly trek to the Pine.

"Come on with us, Ida," Bobo said teasingly. "I bet you could dance up a storm if you wanted to."

Ida pocketed the keys and looked down her bony nose at him. "I reckon I'll do my dancin' in heaven. And if you keep hangin' around at that place, you'll be jumpin' around tryin' to cool your feet. Goin' straight to hell, all of you, if you don't watch it."

"I've been there, Ida," Jubal retorted. "Guess I'll take the Pine."

He'd made up his mind: no more of this damn silly mooning around over Terrill Carroll. She'd made him edgy all day, but she could never be anything to him, no matter how enticing her lips were.

He was going to the Pine; maybe that was where he belonged. Tess would probably be there. He had to face her sometime, and he was in the mood to take whatever she was offering and to hell with it. Anything to scratch the itch that wouldn't let him calm down.

Tonight the crowd was a little louder and a little rowdier than usual, mostly because Autry, the proprietor, had a live band there, several hairy sorts with cowboy hats pounding out "Dumas Walker" in the smoke and the noise at the far end of the room.

She came in the way she always did, with an expensive set of friends, and as if they'd been waiting for her, the band took off into "Pretty Woman."

Her hair gleamed with blue lights under the entrance illumination. Four others were with her tonight. She usually came with a crowd, always with a man in tow.

One of the men, the suntanned one in the neatly creased shirt and corduroy slacks, didn't seem to like the Pine much, but he liked Tess, and he liked whiskey. He kept one proprietary hand on her somewhere, the other on his glass. She let him, drinking from a hot-looking mug herself, smiling at him as she ran one finger around the rim.

Old stuff. Obvious stuff.

Then, after a while, she began to search the room with her eyes. Jubal knew who she was looking for, and he stayed stubbornly still on his chair, half-hidden by the haze and the dark shadows along the walls where he sat. The man with Tess touched her knee, then her side.

She found Jubal at last, and she smiled a little, like a smug cat. So satisfied.

Suddenly it was too hot in there, too loud, too smoky.

Abruptly Jubal shoved away from the wall and stood. Bobby Delaney, startled out of his concentration at the pool table nearby, looked over at him, squinting like a red-eyed owl. "Who lit a fire under you?" he asked lazily, a little surprised.

Jubal shrugged. "I'm just going outside so I can smoke my own instead of everybody else's," he answered easily.

He pushed his way to the door, and when he opened it the cold air outside hit him like a revivifying snort of ammonia, almost painful in its clarity.

He found his old truck where he'd parked it, out near the highway, and stood for a few minutes, bracing his hands on the cold metal. At his back was the pounding of the band's drums, and the muffled sound of loud music, and the flashing neon sign. And for the first time in his life, he hated the Pine.

The highway stretched before him, deserted and black; far in the distance past the trees, he could see where the land began to lift into Sullivan's Ridge and, beyond that, up to Copper's Bluff.

Two men went past him, talking, laughing. If Jubal had looked at their faces, he might have known them; but he never moved, never turned away from the view of the highway and the Ridge and the cold October night.

There had to be something more. Maggie was right. There had to be places where the air was sweet, and the music was enticing, and a blue-eyed girl with innocent lips would reach out to touch him—

"So you finally made it back to the Pine." The female voice came from behind, accompanied by the weight of her hand as it rested familiarly, unexpectedly, on his arm.

He knew who it was before he even turned, and his disappointment was so strong, he nearly choked on it.

"What are you doin' out here?" he asked her. In the garish, flashing lights of the bar, Tess's hair looked nearly red, not blue.

"I came out for the same reason you did," she said invitingly, and her hand slid from his arm to his jacket front. "But we can't be caught out here together. I'll be at the Point in an hour or so. I've been waiting for you. Weeks. You'll have to pay for making me wait, won't you?"

Jubal didn't make a move toward her, just stood there passively under her palm, under the sound of her husky, suggestive voice. "You've got company with you. He might be gettin' lonely for you, don't you think?"

She laughed a little. "He has a bottle for his company. And I'll get rid of him, anyway. He's got nothing to do with us."

Her hand had climbed nearly to his throat by now, and the other one had settled under his coat, at his waist. Jubal could smell her perfume, mingled with the whiskey on her breath, and his stomach churned a little. She didn't have the right to touch him like this. He was a person. A man.

He couldn't stop his own convulsive movement; he caught both of her wrists in his, pushing her hands off him.

She looked up at him imperiously for a moment, then she laughed. "I think you're jealous, Jubal."

"Of that man in there? No." He spoke without any

emotion. Nothing but truth. "I'm just sorry for him."

She searched his face for a moment, then lifted herself to touch his cool lips with her own warm ones. He didn't move, didn't open his mouth even when her tongue insisted.

Slowly she pulled away. Strands of her black hair brushed his face, and he reached up one hand to push them away, too. Deliberately.

Temper flamed across her face. "Who do you think you are? You're just Jubal Kane. I can do whatever I want with you. Because—what are you going to do about it? Nothing. So don't get on any high horse with *me.*"

He wished she were a man; he would have hit her. Instead he forced himself to reach for his cigarettes. "I am who I am, Tess. But I don't have to come when you call. You don't own me."

She tried to calm down, tried to smile at him. "Oh, for God's sake, Jubal, let's don't get heavy here. I want you. That's enough. I'll meet you at the Point in—"

"I don't give a damn how much you want me," he cut in brutally. He was sick—sick—*sick* of this. "I don't want *you.* Don't you get it? So don't come for me anymore. Don't call the Pine anymore. I do my own calling."

He turned away and took three steps to the truck door, trying not to see her stunned, furious face.

"You—you—" She could barely speak, but she came after him, hitting him viciously in the back with her fists, pounding at his shoulders.

He let her, taking the hard blows stoically, lighting a cigarette with his hands cupped around it, all before he twisted away and spoke. "Just remember what I said, Tess. No more." Then he opened the door, got in, and turned on the ignition.

She pounded on his window, screaming at him, "You'll pay for this, Jubal! I don't need you. I never did. You were just an easy lay, because I wanted to see what it'd be like to do it with a dumb redneck. Go to *hell!*"

Instead he drove away.

A mile down the road, he rolled down the window and sucked in all of the cold air his lungs could hold. That need to breathe was always with him when he had to prove to himself that he was free. That he was able to make his own decisions. That he wasn't a puppet on somebody else's short strings.

He thought he was about to feel very, very good.

Maggie had fallen asleep on her chair, one of his shirts that she had been mending in her lap. Once she had been a seamstress, and her handmade quilts had been the finest in the county. Ida had taken one and entered it in the county fair one year, and it had won hands down. Blue-ribbon "Wedding Ring." All of that was before Maggie's fingers had stiffened from arthritis.

It was just another unfair bit of life: she was a person who worked with her hands, who touched and soothed and created with them. Now it was all a struggle, but she kept on with dogged determination, even if mending, and not creation, was all she was capable of anymore. More mending in the world, anyway, she said.

The fire in the Ashley wood stove that had been inserted into the old fireplace was burning low. Jubal had left wood beside it for her to put on the fire before she went to bed. It was oak, and pine, and hot-burning hickory that he himself had cut for her and stacked at the side of the house.

After pulling on the big gloves that always lay on the hearth in the winter, he opened the door quietly and loaded more wood into the stove. But the red coals of what had once been a log broke and shattered into a thousand flaming pieces. When he turned back to Maggie, latching the stove door as he did, she was awake, sitting upright, looking at him.

"Sorry, Ma," he said, dropping the gloves into their place.

"What time is it?" she asked dazedly.

He glanced at the clock on the mantel. "Nearly ten."

"Nearly ten," she repeated. "You're home on a Saturday night and it's just—" Too late she broke off her hasty, surprised words.

He flushed without knowing why. "I thought I'd go up toward the Bluff," he offered at last.

"The Bluff. Copper's Bluff?"

"Yeah. Just to . . . to be goin'." She hadn't asked, but still he told her.

"It's too late to climb all the way to the top of it," she said slowly, "but you could make it to the first ledge. You remember how it is, don't you? You ain't been in a long time. Not since you got back from Lineville."

Not a word that questioned. No comment that it was late. None of the normal curious inquiries as to why he'd come home.

"I remember," he told her.

On her face was a spreading warmth, and as she stood, pushing the sewing off her lap, she was smiling a little, nodding in agreement.

"Reckon you better put on some warmer clothes, then," was all she said. "I'll fix you some coffee, and there's that old bedroll that used to belong to Jarvis, if you're plannin' on stayin' up there the rest of the night."

He laughed. It felt good, that laugh. Full of relief and satisfaction.

"I won't get there 'till nearly dawn, Ma," he protested.

"Dawn's as good a time to sleep as any. It'll come easy when you lay down up there."

She looked at him as he stood before her, the son who towered over her. "You all right, Jubal?"

He didn't lie. "I don't know what's wrong with me."

"I do. I told you—there's some places you don't belong. The sooner you figure out which ones they are, and walk out of 'em, the faster you'll get in the right frame of mind."

"For what?" he asked wearily, but he grinned at her. "What you got planned for me, Ma?"

"I don't rightly know—yet," she answered solemnly, then the hazel eyes behind her glasses twinkled just a tiny bit. "But I'll let you know when the revelation hits me."

"That's what I'm afraid of," he told her wryly.

The cold wind in his face took the place of the heat at the Pine. The smell of autumn and the rich muskiness of fallen leaves swept away the sick sweetness of Tess's perfume that had clung to his own clothes after he'd left her. The black night blotted out neon; the wh-wh-whoo of a woods owl scorned pounding drums.

The faster he walked, the harder he breathed, the wetter his back became under the coat—the more clearly his brain worked.

He was alive.

He hadn't been this sure of the fact in more than three years.

He could live his own life. Maybe he didn't have to get pushed around.

Terrifying to feel the pound of blood and the sweep of breath this strong.

But what was even more frightening was to have all the pieces fall into place with one sharp, jolting click, to have knowledge burst upon him like an electric bulb cutting through darkness.

He knew now what was wrong with him. As he climbed and fought his way up to the lower ledge of Copper's Bluff, he knew why he was so wired, and—most remarkable of all—happy.

It was because, nearly twenty-four hours ago, he had kissed Terrill Carroll and found her lips sweet. Pure. Clean as the morning.

Don't put any hope on that kiss, he told himself. *Don't put any faith in that girl.*

But there was an abstract joy he could let himself feel: what was in her kiss and on her lips made him realize that maybe, maybe, there really was something bright and decent out there somewhere.

On Sunday morning an attack of sanity hit Terrill as she sat in one of the long rows of padded pews at Bethel First Baptist.

While the minister preached, she looked around herself. The people here were the kind she'd grown up with, the kind she would become: prosperous, clean-cut, normal. The women were perfumed and well dressed, the men neat and ambitious. Up-and-coming middle-class successes.

What had ever possessed her to feel such an overpowering attraction to Jubal Kane? That kiss had left her restless, some part of her that had never been alive before struggling to come awake. Such a pull had been between them.

And she didn't want it, didn't want to be attracted

to a person like him. Terrill wanted to be good, to love somebody like . . . like the handsome man who sat beside Tess Johnson two pews ahead. Or maybe she'd love one of the three who'd come calling on her since she'd been at Belmont. They had plans; they were mainstream and right.

But not one of them had made her twist and turn in the darkness of her room, remembering. Not one had branded her with a single kiss until she had dreamed of it. Over and over again, she'd seen his face bend toward hers, felt his lips brush hers.

But it had been a nighttime aberration, because when she'd seen him in town leaning against that wall, smoking, he'd looked half-wild and rednecky. He'd frightened her with his watchful gaze, and she'd remembered then that the dark, shadowed, mesmerizing stranger with the tender hands was only Jubal Kane. That he'd had a bite on his neck, scratches on his back, and handcuffs on his wrists just weeks ago.

He was no good. Worthless.

She had to remember that and stay away from him. And if that long, silent stare he'd leveled on her meant that he had other plans because of one simple kiss, she'd disabuse him of the idea quickly.

The minister was finishing up his prayer; Terrill echoed his amen with one of her own.

Jubal was primping in front of the mirror in the tiny bathroom Monday morning. He didn't mean to. But he had three clean shirts hanging in his closet. Nothing great, just like usual—three flannel shirts. Today, though, it took him fifteen minutes to decide that the red plaid looked better than the blue. And he rolled up the sleeves to the elbow carefully, instead of letting them flap about his wrists.

The boots were old. He'd never realized before how old or how worn over, and he frowned at them. Even polished, they were ancient. But his other choice, the old high-topped tennis shoes, were even worse.

He settled for the boots.

And he combed his hair furiously, brushing it straight back over and over, cursing under his breath at its heavy brown-black waviness that wanted to cling to his temples and curl around his ears. In the mirror, above his high, jutting cheekbones, his eyes blazed with anxiety.

"Your breakfast is ready," Ma called at last, and he flung open the door of the bathroom in exasperation. "Well." She said it blinking, looking at the scrubbed-clean face before her, at the carefully shaved jawline, at the neat, shining dark hair. "You goin' to church on a Monday?" she asked humorously.

"Ain't goin' nowhere," he muttered, flushing. Why did she have to comment today, when she'd kept quiet Saturday night? "It's my hair. I don't like it, Ma."

She blinked again. "You're worried about your hair? You?" Her voice rose in astonishment.

He took a deep breath. "You think I look all right?"

Maggie Kane surveyed her twenty-three-year-old son.

"A girl," she said in sudden knowledge, and her voice caught on the word.

He flushed and tried to protest.

"Don't. I've raised three other sons. I know the signs." She looked him over one last time and tried to say calmly, "You'll do. You'll do fine."

*   *   *

Things were not going well in the office today. Rosalie was gathering up things, getting ready to leave. Terrill wanted to beg her to stay. The man at the desk beside her was working quietly enough, but she could almost sense an intensity about him—which was ridiculous. He was behaving just as he always did, wasn't he? So it had to be a weakness in her. She wasn't fighting that weird attraction hard enough.

Terrill struggled with her need to look at his face for nearly twenty minutes; it was as great a battle as she had ever put up. At last the chains that drew her to him became too tight, and, reluctantly, she turned to see Jubal Kane.

He was writing, but as soon as her gaze hit the side of his face, he stopped, alerted, and looked back.

Still. Serene.

But she knew—he was questioning her, searching her, pulling at her for something.

She turned away, and the minutes wore on.

Maybe she had somehow signaled him with that one look, because when Rosalie vanished into Henry's office for last-minute instructions about something, he spoke, his voice low.

"Terrill."

She stopped all movement, her hands freezing in their task, and slowly she confronted him.

"How's your face?" he asked her, motioning toward her cheek. "Does it hurt?"

Her hand flew to cover the dark bruise. "It's okay. No, it doesn't hurt."

"Oh." He was at a loss a minute, then he said slowly, "I thought about it a lot. About . . . about you. And about . . . everything."

His eyes fell to her lips for an instant. Maybe he had meant to tease her; there was a tiny smile hovering around the corners of his mouth. But Terrill, already in a panic, cut him off completely.

"Listen, Jubal Kane," she said fiercely, "you said you'd forget it. That you didn't expect me to remember. So I don't." She swallowed once. "I'm sorry, but that's the way I want it."

Then she picked up her papers and turned to flee to the corner where the filing cabinet was, leaving him at the desk, unmoving and still.

Jubal got out of the office. Somehow. All he remembered was that he tripped over Dusty as he shoved his way out the door, and Dusty showed his typical signs of belligerence. Jubal ignored him.

Once in his truck, he sat gripping the steering wheel. Embarrassed. Furious. And, mostly, hurting.

You stupid fool. You actually thought that girl was different. That a kiss had made a difference.

He was a fool. A fool. *A fool.*

The next day at work, Carroll announced that he needed him to make another run to Kentucky Friday night. Then Carroll waited, almost as if he were daring Jubal to protest, baiting him.

"All right," Jubal said without emotion.

What did he care what he did?

10

At seven o'clock in the morning in the middle of the kitchen, Tandy had on a three-piece navy suit and matching shoes. Her purse sat on the counter by the door. Terrill stopped and stared as she entered.

"Are you going somewhere?" she asked in surprise.

"Katherine had a terrible night," Tandy answered instead, running her fingers across her cheekbones as if she could rub away the weariness in her face. "I don't know how a woman that small can suffer so much."

Terrill's hand went to her shirtfront, to clutch the buttons convulsively. "She's—"

"She's better."

"You didn't call me."

"I'm too tired to be anything but blunt, Rilla. Henry doesn't want you anywhere in that room at night. Sometimes I think grief has turned his brain. But I see no point in stirring up more misery by calling you in."

"But she could have died!" Terrill gave the nearest chair a hard shove, her movement frustrated.

"No. I've seen that before, in my own mother. I'll make sure you know when the time comes." Tandy reached for her purse.

"Where are you going?"

"To Nashville. To the hospital. We called the doctor, and he wants to see Katherine today. He says he can help so that she won't get so worn down with the hurting."

"And Henry?"

"Henry has the Lexus ready. Katherine's in it, and they're waiting." Tandy looked directly at Terrill, and she waited, too.

Terrill knew already what was about to be said. "And you want me to stay here," she managed, her voice nearly calm.

"There's no room in the car," Tandy tried to explain. "Katherine's lying on the backseat. And this way, if there's a problem at the mill, Rosalie can call here and leave a message with you."

"Call here! It's Friday, Aunt Tandy. I go to the mill on Friday," Terrill told her, but she knew what Tandy was working her way toward. She understood so well.

"You certainly don't need to go today," Tandy returned decisively. "Henry won't be there to keep an eye on you, and besides—" She broke off abruptly.

"And besides, I'm only there on sufferance anyway," Terrill finished flatly. "It's not like I do anything important."

"I didn't say that, Rilla. Just . . . well, never mind. But Katherine wants to see you."

Tandy opened the door for her niece, then motioned her outside. After a moment's hesitation, Terrill stepped past her into the cool, cloudy morning.

In the drive the car sat waiting, a silent Henry at the wheel. Terrill opened the back door, and Katherine smiled at her from the pillows they'd propped against the other, locked door.

"Rilla," she whispered in relief. "You'll be . . . all right here at home? By yourself? I didn't want you to sit in a waiting room all day."

"I'm grown, Mama," Terrill said in mock exasperation. "Not afraid of the boogie man anymore." Her hands clutched her mother's a minute.

Katherine nodded, and Terrill pulled herself backward out of the car, pushing the door shut behind herself.

Tandy hesitated before she shut her own door. "We'll be at St. Thomas, Rilla, if you need us. I'll call you later today to let you know about things."

Watching the car pull out onto the highway, Terrill made herself stand tall and straight. She'd get over this, too, as she had a hundred other little hurts.

Now it was just her at the house. Maybe it had never been her alone, here at home, in her entire life.

It was too quiet standing in the drive as leaves fell around her, the place silent and waiting behind her. It was solitary.

Terrill turned, looked at the white farmhouse, at the wide yard, at the hollows and hills beyond it, and then another sensation hit her: it was good sometimes to be alone. Nobody else's expectations. She could do what she pleased. Be what she wanted.

She opened every door, walked in every room except Tandy's and Henry and Katherine's. She climbed to the attic. She even went outside to the apartment above the garage that Grandpa had built for himself after Grandma died.

In it, she found memories. A box of pictures, all

of Luke. Luke and Katherine, so young, on their wedding day. Luke holding his new baby daughter, grinning from ear to ear. Luke and Grandpa. Tandy with a big hat one Easter Sunday, standing beside Luke and his two-year-old child as she peeped over a new stuffed rabbit.

One man's lifetime, shoved into a box, into a closet, into a closed, tiny apartment. This was what was left of Luke. Maybe it was all that was left of anybody when all was said and done.

She took the pictures back to her own room. In the bottom of the box were older pictures, mostly of her grandparents. Other lives. Under them there was a yellowed calendar advertising a place she'd never heard of. "Jenkins and Long Hardware," read the calendar. And below the name, in black numerals, "1943."

1943.

Terrill's fingers traced the numbers. Who had breathed then? Another woman like her, struggling to find what she wanted, who she was, where she belonged? Somebody else wondering what existence was all about?

She was only twenty: she wanted to live. She didn't want to be faced with mortality.

In the silence of the house, sounds from the sawmill echoed across the hollow. The loud crash of logs being dropped from a truck, the whine of the huge saws, the occasional sound of a man's shout.

The hard conversation of real life, that was what was going on at the mill. Not the silence of this house, filled with only the sound of the clock ticking away another calendar year.

Life just kept moving on; it slid by whether you did what you wanted or let circumstances and other people decide things for you.

Jubal Kane was over there, at the mill. Serious, silent, shut up inside himself. Just as he'd been every day since she'd made it plain that she expected him to leave her alone. But for a few minutes last Saturday morning, when his lips had touched hers, she'd felt like a race car that had finally been allowed to hit top speed. She'd been living. The seconds that had ticked by then had been the beating of her own blood. Real life, internalized.

She wondered for a split second what he was doing right now. Terrill hadn't realized before, but he was half the reason she liked being there: at the desk, she could gaze at him. Nothing more than that, but it had become a daily habit. The kick start that set her heart beating.

He had no right to look the way he did, like some fallen angel. He was just a poor ridge runner, working in a sawmill, driving an old pickup truck, running wild on the weekends. She didn't want him, but she'd like to look at him, even if he wouldn't look back at her anymore. She had stopped his doing that with her words Monday.

The phone rang at eleven.

"Rilla?" Tandy questioned. "They want to do a minor surgery on Katherine today, to put in a nerve block to stop the pain."

"Surgery! But what if she doesn't make it?"

A slight pause before Tandy spoke reluctantly. "She's already in surgery now, Rilla. Henry gave them permission to go ahead."

Just like that. *Just like that.*

"I see."

"But this means that we won't be back until tomorrow morning. Maybe you could call the Johnsons. Lionel could come and get you to spend the night with them. Tess will probably be home."

"I'll be fine here," Terrill answered, shuddering a little at the thought of calling Lionel and his perfect daughter.

"But I—"

"If I need something, I'll call them, all right? I know you want to get back to Mama."

"Things are going well. The surgery's almost over. I won't call again unless . . . unless there's a problem. Bye, Rilla."

Terrill hung up the telephone, easing it into its cradle gently, because inside her there was no gentleness at all.

Just anger, that age-old resentment, and rebellion.

Why did she keep trying to do things their way? They never stopped to consider her. There were things she wanted. She didn't need anybody else's approval.

She wanted to live.

She was going to, in spite of Henry and Tandy. Because of Katherine, because she proved that people died, whether they'd lived some first or not.

1943.

It made no difference if even the very memories of the people who'd lived then had been wiped out, if they'd lived the lives they'd wanted.

As soon as Terrill shut the door of the house behind herself, she broke into a run, out of the prison. Just as the sun had broken through the clouds, leaving puzzle pieces of an autumn blue sky showing.

She would look at him, just once.

It had happened a dozen times before, all of them aggravating: they hadn't shipped all of the parts to the big Cummins engine that Jubal was supposed to assemble. This time two of the fuel injectors were missing.

That meant he had to spend half his day making a trip to Edmonds to pick up replacements, but that was all right. At least he'd be too busy to get the paperwork together; he wouldn't have to go near the office today.

Carroll was gone anyway, he'd heard. Nobody to check up on Jubal.

So he pulled on his old jacket and headed for the parking lot. Halfway across it, he saw her.

Terrill.

She was running through the adjacent field, her hair whipping behind her.

He knew the exact minute she saw him, too. She stopped abruptly, looking right at him. *Why don't you look away?* he wanted to demand. And he stared back at her, across the hundred yards that separated them.

But she didn't back down. Instead she suddenly began to walk again, right toward him.

Confused, he hesitated, waiting. *Why wait?* he asked himself. *So you can let her cut you dead like she did Monday?*

He moved then, ignoring her approach, opening the truck door. He'd be damned if he'd even show he knew she was around.

"Jubal."

His name on her lips stopped him completely. He stood stiffly, caught between the open door and the truck for a minute, then he got in. Deliberately dumb.

But he didn't shut the door.

She *had* called his name; it wasn't his imagination. "Jubal."

He nearly jumped. So close.

Twisting his head, he saw her. She was standing right beside the truck. He could have reached out and touched her, could have laid his fingers over the pulse beating in her throat, could have felt her breath as she dragged it noisily into her lungs.

She'd run. To catch him?

They looked at one another.

His eyes were so cool, his face like haughty stone, Terrill thought nervously.

"Are you speakin' to me?" he drawled at last.

"You know I am."

"What d'you want?" He was as rude as he could make himself be. Why were her eyes so wide, so blue, so pleading?

"I just wanted . . . to talk to you," she stumbled.

"Where are you going?"

"To Edmonds, to get a part for the engine," he returned at last, slowly. "What d'you mean, you wanted to talk to me? You know damn well you don't."

"About Monday . . . and . . . and Saturday morning, Jubal, I—"

He cut off her hurried, embarrassed words. "I don't think I *remember* anything about Saturday," he said harshly. "I don't know what you're talkin' about."

His eyes challenged her to deny his words. Terrill took a deep breath, then let it out. "Yes, you do. And I do, too. But you scared me."

"*I* scared you? I didn't do a damn thing," he answered passionately, pulling himself out of the truck. She took a step back so that she wouldn't be right against him.

"You . . . you—" Her gaze dropped to his lips, and her face flushed pink.

She remembered that kiss. He thought it again,

the same way he had all week. She was running from that kiss.

But she'd hurt him too much for him to consider what her reaction meant.

"You mean because I kissed you?" he said flippantly, and he laughed. "Where you been all your life, Terrill? It was just a kiss. Not even a big deal of one."

The lie was hard to get out, but it did the trick: her face flushed an even darker hue, and she backed up again.

She couldn't even think of a sharp return, so they just stood there facing one another, Jubal challenging, she embarrassed.

Then she walked away.

He'd just gone a round with Terrill Carroll and scored a decision. Or had he lost?

He wanted to know why she'd come running to him.

"Wait," he got out, striding after her. "Terrill, wait."

He caught her arm; she went still before she faced him, and her expression made him drop his hold on her.

"What are you doin' out here?" he demanded.

"Just walking."

"Walking! I thought you were in the office."

"No. They took Mama to the hospital. Aunt Tandy thought I should stay home today because Henry wasn't here to protect me from all the bad influences." This time she was the flippant one.

"Well, this one's leavin', so you can stay."

"Leaving! It's not even noon."

"I've got to go to Edmonds, like I said. So you'll be safe. No need to be scared—not of me, or a kiss," he said deliberately.

Her chin came up. "You made your point, Kane."

Okay, he'd let that one slide, the way she said his name. A blow for her that time.

"So go on," she invited, flinging her hair back, tucking her hands into the pockets of her jacket. Then she looked up at the sun as it struggled past the clouds. "It's a good day to be on your own."

Try as she might, she couldn't keep the wistful note out of her voice.

Jubal heard it. What? What did she want? What was wrong?

The noon whistle shrilled across the air, marking lunchtime.

"Terrill, if nobody's at home, if you're not supposed to be at the mill," he began, trying to feel his way through the emotions, trying to understand what it was she wanted from him, "you—"

She watched him, puzzled.

"Come with me," he burst out at last.

Her eyes widened. Maybe she hadn't even know that was what she was asking him for.

"I can't."

"Why not?"

She didn't know, and she stared at him in wide-eyed indecision.

"The men will be here in a minute for lunch. You have to do it *now*," he said urgently. "Nobody will know. Don't you want to?"

She laughed suddenly. I'm going to do what I want, she thought in quick-born exhilaration, and I want to go with Jubal.

"I'll come," she whispered, and an answering excitement spread across his own face.

He held open the door of the truck for her, and she stepped in.

11

They pulled off the sawmill grounds the back way, circling behind the offices so that no one could see them. There were no screaming police sirens or protesting relatives or flashing blue lights. Nothing to indicate that this was risky. Wrong.

As they hit the highway, Terrill glanced over at the tall man folded behind the steering wheel and felt a tingle of nerves. "I didn't know it would be so easy to ride off with you," she offered. "So quiet."

He looked at her, then flashed a grin. "The noise starts when we get back—if they catch us." Then his smiled faded. "Maybe I wasn't thinkin' too smart when I asked you to come, because if anybody finds out you're with me, you might get in a lot of trouble. If"—he took a deep breath—"if you want, I can take you back now."

Terrill looked out her window. "Do you want to do that?"

"Take you back? Hell, no, but—"

She turned to give him a dazzling smile. "Good. Because I don't want you to."

In relief, he let out the breath he had taken earlier. Through the little town, the two of them were silent. Waiting at the stop sign on the corner, Terrill looked at the town square: the courthouse with its dull red brick, the monument in front commemorating the men from Cade County who'd died in Vietnam; the post office; the Dollar General Store; the drugstore; and the City Cafe.

"I saw you standing there"—she motioned—"last Saturday in the rain." She wanted to explain how last Saturday had shaped this whole disastrous week, but she didn't dare.

"Yeah. I saw you, too. But I'd seen you when you went in the drugstore with your aunt. I was waitin' for you to come out." He barely dared to make the admission, and he didn't look at her when he said it, too afraid he'd told too much.

People were going in the cafe, and a man in a three-piece suit and a plaid golf cap had twisted about on the steps of the bank to call back an answer to Lionel Johnson, who stood in the door.

Terrill laughed suddenly. Jubal looked over at her questioningly as he shifted the truck into gear and it rolled forward.

"It's Friday," she said. "Friday afternoon, and all these people are doing all the things they're supposed to. Following the rules and the timetables and going to work. But me, I'm free." She laughed again, a quick sound of breathless excitement.

Jubal shook his head dubiously. "I hope you feel this way tomorrow." Everything had consequences; he knew, whether she did or not.

"I won't be sorry. Not tomorrow, or the next day," Terrill retorted certainly. Then she shifted, turning directly toward him, and she waited until he looked over at her inquiringly, blue eyes meeting green. "Unless I can't trust you," she said frankly, and pink color stained the high line of her cheeks. "Unless you do something to make me regret coming with you. Will you?"

"You mean am I gonna make a pass at you," he answered bluntly, and he couldn't keep a tiny touch of anger out of his voice. "No, I'm not gonna try anythin'."

"Oh." She wanted to kick herself; the "Oh" had sounded just a little disappointed instead of relieved—and she *was* relieved. "I didn't think so."

"Would you ask another man that question, if you'd gone with him?"

He was angry, Terrill realized, and something like hot quicksilver rushed through her. "No," she replied honestly. "But I've never done anything like this before, nor spent half the night talking to another man at the mill, either, or let him ki—"

He knew what the word was despite her best efforts to swallow it hastily; and she knew how much her answer pleased him—when he glanced at her, his smile had changed his entire dark face. She tore her gaze away, shivering a little, and said, "I'm cold."

Jubal reached down and flipped on the heater, and it blew into noisy life. She felt its warmth even through her jeans and held her fingers down to warm them, too.

"Where did you say we're headed?" she asked whimsically.

"Edmonds," he answered.

Edmonds was much larger than Bethel—a small city, in fact—and it held a lot more places to go. "Okay. And what will we do when we get there?"

He said simply, "Whatever you want."

So they drove. And they kept glancing over at each other in the middle of meaningless bits of conversation.

They might have been halfway to Edmonds when it really began to hit Jubal exactly what he had done. No, they. *They* had done. The two of them had just walked off. He had opened the door, she had climbed in. Terrill Carroll and Jubal Kane. Together. Nobody knew except them, but still the thought shook him. She had come with him.

Maybe she wouldn't have except for the way things were at her house. But he didn't care what her motives were. Maybe he was only an escape for a while for a restless, overwrought girl. He'd been worse. But today he had a chance. He was going to show her that Jubal Kane could be just as straight, just as decent, just as trustworthy, as any of them. He meant to make sure she didn't get any rude awakenings from him or that there'd be any regrets for this day.

He had five hours with her. The prince couldn't have had any more time than that with Cinderella.

Five stolen, illicit hours.

It was Jubal's turn to laugh to himself.

"I have to go here," Jubal said as he pulled the truck into the big parking lot in front of the parts dealership. "I might be a while. Sometimes they're busy and I have to wait. Do you want to stay in the truck?"

Terrill looked at the big supply store, at the paved lot, at the rows of cars. "Can I come with you?"

"Sure. I'd rather you did. But it's borin'," he answered apologetically.

"That's okay."

He met her as she circled the truck, and he wanted

to reach out and take her hand, to pull her with him, but he stopped the gesture before he'd barely made it. She was along for the ride, and that was all, he reminded himself. No need for him to grab at her.

After he told the man at the long parts desk inside what he wanted and that man had gone off to locate it somewhere back in the warehouse, Jubal turned his attention back to the girl beside him.

"Rosalie said you put together engines for Henry. Where'd you learn to do that?" Terrill asked curiously.

He laughed. "Sometimes it feels like I was born knowin' it. My brothers were always foolin' with cars and tractors. Jarvis drove a cattle truck for one of the Henigars one summer. It kept breakin' down and he kept fixin' it, and I was always there with him. I got better at it than him. Then I had a class in it in high school and another when I was at Line—" He broke off the work awkwardly. What in the hell had possessed him to bring up the prison? She was antsy enough as it was around him.

But at least she didn't edge away this time as if he half terrified her. Instead her face went still and her eyes got wider and bluer as she watched him. He ducked his head away.

"You went to Cade County High?"

"Yeah."

"How old are you, anyway?"

"Twenty-three."

"I'll be twenty-one in April," she offered, then smiled. "I might have gone to school with you if they hadn't sent me to Rose Hall. You'd have been a big senior, and I would have been a lowly little sophomore. Maybe we would have been friends."

He thought of the six hundred and sixty-two students who'd attended Cade County High along with him. He could barely, barely remember Tess

Johnson. *She'd* been a sophomore when he'd been a senior.

"No," he said abruptly, straightening off the counter where he'd been leaning. "We wouldn't have."

"Oh." She pushed her hands down into her pockets and considered his set jaw and his dark face as he looked away from her stubbornly. "Why not?"

He laughed, but it wasn't a laugh she liked much. "Now why do you think?"

"Because I would have been from town and you would have been from Sullivan's Ridge?" she guessed.

"That's part of it. But the biggest part is—I'm me and you're you. I didn't talk the same, or look the same, or do anything else right." He spoke without emotion, then looked around. "Where'd that salesman go? All I needed was a set of injectors, not the whole engine."

But she persisted. "So you don't talk exactly the way most people do. What do you—"

"Nothin' wrong with the way I talk," he interrupted belligerently, frowning at her.

"You said it. I didn't," she pointed out reasonably. "Just like you said you didn't look right. You look . . . you look good to me," she stumbled, her cheeks flushing. She had little or no experience at all with men, especially not with one as touchy and defensive as Jubal.

His frown faded, to be replaced by surprised pleasure. But he shook his head. "No. I was all wrong. Like that." He pointed to the name brand emblazoned across the heavy cotton sweatshirt she wore. "I bet that means something."

Terrill glanced down at herself in surprise. "It's just a word. 'Espirit.' It doesn't mean anything."

"Sure," he said wryly. "But when I was sixteen, everybody else thought it did."

"When *I* was sixteen," Terrill answered him slowly, "I had a navy uniform every day. If I'd once had a chance to dress like you are now"—she nodded at his plaid shirt, at the dark T-shirt under it, at his blue jeans—"I'd have loved it."

"Yeah." His derisive voice said he didn't believe one word of it. "Well, you'll have to talk to Ma about it. She gets most of my clothes. I don't know where."

Terrill looked at him a minute, from his head to his toes. Uncomfortable, he moved his feet. Today he had on the old boots.

"Not my shoes. I think I got them at a place out on the county line," he mumbled. He wanted to tell her that he was saving his money, that he needed a nest egg to tide Ma over after he left the mill, until he found another job.

But it was his business, not hers. He didn't even know her, and he'd get over this sense of shame that was washing through him as she looked at him so carefully.

"Here's the parts you needed, buddy," the man behind the counter said unexpectedly, breaking between Jubal and Terrill.

It didn't take long to finish the transaction. They were back in the truck almost immediately, but Jubal hesitated under the wheel.

"I've done what I came to do," he told her. "But I—I don't really—"

How did he say "I'm not ready to take you back just yet—I like it too much that you're here with me, even if you don't understand anything about my life"?

"We don't have to go back now, do we?" she asked in alarm. "We just got here."

His face broke into a sudden smile. "No. We don't

have to. I don't want to, either. So, where'll we go?
It's your call."

She considered him a minute, remembering their
conversation. "Does Edmonds have a mall?"

"I guess so. I don't know."

"Don't you come here a lot?"

"Some. But I don't go to malls."

"Not *ever*?" she asked in amazement.

He flushed. "No. I don't like 'em. They're artificial,
or something. Why would I want to go, anyway?"

Because down inside, you care that you don't fit
in, Terrill thought to herself, watching the still face
across from her. No matter how much you pretend
that you don't.

Twenty-three, he'd said. Maybe he'd always been
on the outside looking in. It was a lonely feeling.
She'd been that way herself ever since Luke died.

But at least she'd dressed as if everything were all
right.

She glanced at his slender body again, at the old
clothes he wore, and wondered suddenly if Jubal even
knew how to dress, if he would know what to choose
to wear even if he had had money. She'd never
thought about it before, that there were actually
people who didn't know.

"Jubal," Terrill said suddenly, "how old is your
mother?"

He glanced at her, wary and puzzled. "Fifty-two."

"And has she ever been to a mall? Ever shopped
for you there?"

"No."

Terrill took a deep breath. "I know what I want to
do. Jubal Kane, I'm going to take you shopping."

"Shoppin'! No, you're not, either," he said forcefully.

"It'll be fun," she coaxed. "And you said it was my
call."

"Aw, Terrill," he said ruefully, "I don't want to."

"Jubal Kane, are you scared of a *mall?*" she asked teasingly.

"No, but—"

"You said you weren't ready to go back to Bethel."

"I ain't ready for a shoppin' trip, either," he said reluctantly, but he turned the truck in the general direction of the Edmonds mall. When he slid into a parking place not far from a Cracker Barrel restaurant sign, he wasn't happy about it.

It took a minute for Terrill to realize part of what was wrong with him, to catch on to the reason he was gripping the wheel so tightly.

"We're just window-shopping," she clarified. "Come on. I've never shopped for a . . . a man before."

"How'd I ever get into this?" he muttered, but he got out of the truck and went with her. And when she stretched out her hand after a moment's hesitation, and he realized with a sudden leap of breath that she was trying to hold his, that she was reaching for him the way he'd wanted to reach for her at the parts store, it was all worth it.

12

"He looks like a damned fool."

That was Jubal's final, unswerving opinion of the mall mannequin they stood in front of. And as Terrill surveyed the plastic model, she wondered with a choked laugh if maybe Jubal weren't right. The dummy had on a bright green pair of baggy pants with a drawstring waist, an orange-and-green over-size shirt that said "Hot Stuff" across it, and a white sweater draped elegantly around his shoulders, its sleeves tied around his neck. A woven cloth band wrapped his wrist, a pair of cat-eye sunglasses dangled from a pocket, and his wig was punky and wild.

"It's not you," she said solemnly.

"I hope to God it's not," Jubal said in indignant relief. "I wouldn't be caught dead in this stuff."

But Terrill was already moving away, tugging him after her. She liked the feel of his hand, hard and warm, long-fingered and strong. Pulling him along was as good a reason as any to hold to it.

"There," she said suddenly. "That's you, Jubal."

He was almost afraid to see what she was pointing at; he'd never seen so much weird junk in his life. Everything was bright lights and brighter colors. The air was heavy with perfume.

But he liked what she had chosen: it was a cotton shirt, tiny greens and browns and a little hint of a peachy color in a small-woven plaid, and over it was a sweater, a pale green in color.

"Well," he said at last, "okay. At least I wouldn't look like Ma's scarecrow in that."

"What's wrong with it?" she demanded, and she reached out a hand to touch the sweater. *Touch me like that,* he wanted to say.

"I don't know." He pointed to the emblem on it. "What's the guy with the horse got a stick for?"

"He's a polo player."

"Well, I don't play that, whatever it is."

"No. But this is right for you. You'd look—it would look good. You would look like you *should* play polo," she argued.

"Oh." But he was secretly pleased that she'd chosen these clothes for him; maybe he liked them. And he liked it because she thought they were right for him.

"Do all these people work in a bank?" he asked at last, gazing around him while she shuffled through another line of clothes—and clung to his hand.

"No," she said with a laugh, glancing around. "Why?"

"Because they're all dressed up like they do. They look like—like your aunt Tandy," he added, nodding down the aisle at a perfume counter where two elegantly clad, well-groomed, tightly girdled salesladies were clustered around a third, who was young and stylish in a red dress with huge padded shoulders.

Terrill smothered a laugh. "Those three work here, Jubal. That's all. They probably don't make as much money as you do working for Henry."

"They don't? But they're so dressed up."

"Most of the time it's just to keep up appearances. Maybe they have husbands with good jobs, so they spend all they make on clothes. Because they want to."

A husband like she'd have someday? The thought made him nearly sick in its unexpected, tearing intensity. Terrill belonged here, with these women. Even if she were only wearing jeans and the pale yellow sweatshirt. She shouldn't be with him, and if she'd been wearing clothes like those women had on, it would be clear to everybody—her included—how mismatched the two of them were today. He hated that thought, too. Unconsciously his hand tightened around hers. "I like the way you look right now better," he said fiercely.

Terrill smiled up at him, startled—and pleased. "I like the way you look, too," she said carefully. This time it came out better, more smoothly than before. They stood face to face in the middle of the department store, caught in their own quiet bubble of emotion, and Terrill felt the tearing of something at her throat.

"Coats," she said inanely.

"What?"

"Coats. They're over there. Let's go look at them"

More than anything else, she hated the brown plaid coat he wore. It was worn, and ugly, and old—and too big. Sometimes when he walked in the office in it, he reminded her of a lost little boy; on those days she had nearly hurt for him, even back when she'd refused even to look directly at him.

Today, because it had not been so cold, he'd left the coat in the truck. She suspected he hated it as much as she did.

She knew which one had his name written on it as soon as she saw it. It was a shining lustrous mahogany leather, styled like a flight jacket, with a rich, thick pile collar.

"This one. This one, Jubal," she told him, tugging it off its wooden hanger. "Put it on. Okay?"

"I don't know. I feel sort of dumb. . . ." His voice trailed off doubtfully.

"Try it on, just once."

"Well . . ."

Reluctantly he took it from her, twisting it in his strong fingers. It felt good beneath his palms, supple and rich.

It looked good under his hands, she thought, watching him handle it.

At last, making a wry face at her, he raised it and hunched a shoulder up to slide an arm in. "What's this?" he asked suspiciously as he did, indicating a plastic piece hanging from the cuff.

"It's to keep people from shoplifting," she told him. "The salespeople take it off when you buy the coat. If you take it out of the store with it still attached—or pry it off—an alarm goes off. I think. I've never tried it."

He fingered it in amazement. "You're kiddin'," he said.

And as Terrill looked at him, head bent, standing there, all dark hair and long fingers and surprised innocence, the truth hit her in the face: she had lost her fear of him, because this man was no criminal. She felt a surge of tender laughter swelling inside her instead. Outlaw Jubal Kane—who had to have the simplest of burglar alarm systems explained to him. Bad boy—who resembled a child caught half in the coat, trapped into fascination by an inexplicable toy.

How had he ever managed to get sent to Lineville?

"Put on the coat," she said quietly. "I want to see what it looks like."

He shrugged into the jacket . . . and the image was gone. Completely.

No child here. No boy. No innocent.

He was all man. All masculine, hard-jawed, sophisticated man, clean-shouldered and long-waisted. The color of the coat highlighted his skin, turned it even more richly tanned, the collar made him look expensive and remote, and the contrast made his eyes glow.

He was watching her face a little warily. "What's wrong? You don't like it? I told you I'd look like a damned idiot in these clothes." He tried to pull a shoulder out of it, but she caught at his hand.

"No, don't. I like it. I like it, Jubal."

He hesitated, looking at her face, hearing the odd tone in her voice. Then he yielded to her tugging hand and let himself be led to a full-length mirror. He glanced in, feeling like a conceited ape—and stared. At last he spoke.

"Is that—is that me?"

This time she couldn't keep the tenderness and the laughter out of her voice. "That's you," she said. "The real Jubal Kane."

"You like it?" he asked her at last, his eyes meeting hers in the mirror.

"A lot."

There was no question as to whether or not they would buy it—they wouldn't. It was an exorbitant price, at least to Jubal's way of thinking. But his hands lingered on it a little as he returned it, and he couldn't erase the startling new image he'd had of himself when he'd looked up into the mirror.

Neither could Terrill, just as she couldn't forget how her stomach had lurched when he took it off and tugged his shirt down from his neck with it for a second. The skin of his shoulder had been brown and smooth—and suddenly she remembered something she'd nearly forgotten: the bite and the scratches he'd had at the mill her first day home.

Something had gone wrong, he didn't know what. She had withdrawn from him, her face still and quiet. And as they walked out of the store, she didn't hold his hand. Instead she shoved both of hers down in her jeans pockets.

"You hungry?" he asked as they sat in the truck in an awkward silence.

"What? Oh, yeah."

"Want to eat there?" he asked, motioning at last toward the bright red-and-white sign of a Dairy Queen that stood at the edge of the mall's parking area.

"Sure."

What in the hell had happened to her? he wondered as they walked up to the counter to order. Then he saw her reaching for her pocket, and his temper flared a little higher. Did she think he couldn't afford to pay for one lousy meal?

"No." He said just the one word, but he said it furiously.

She glanced up at him, at his angry face. "I was just—"

"I know what you were 'just,'" he retorted. "Forget it. Don't even try."

So she didn't, because the bewildered boy of the mall had gone, and Jubal was back with a vengeance. She tried to put her memories away, because she had no right to ask him about them, or any reason to be even curious.

They were just out on a single lark today.

When they pulled out of the parking lot, he didn't ask her where to go this time: he just headed home, back to Cade County.

Damn it, he thought to himself as the miles rolled past. He was supposed to have five hours. And he still had two left—he didn't want to be cheated. But she was so still, sitting there on the other side of the truck, her hair that heavy curtain between them, like always. What if he spoke and said the wrong thing?

Or what if he never said anything at all?

"All right," he muttered. Then louder. "Terrill. What's wrong?"

"Nothing," she answered.

He repeated the word in sarcastic disbelief, then there was another long silence.

"It just dawned on me that I don't really know you very well," she said carefully, at last.

He didn't know what he had expected, but it wasn't that. This meek, cautious answer was all wrong, and it was not Terrill Carroll. But she was at least talking again. And she wanted to know about him. Surely that was a good sign.

"What do you want to know?"

"I'm not sure what I've got a right to ask. As a friend."

A friend. What was she talking about now?

"Ask what you want. What's the big deal?" he replied, impatient and short.

"You know my family. Where I live. My house. A lot about me."

"So? Is that bad?"

"No. But it's not fair. I want . . ." For a minute she didn't know. "I think I would understand you more if I knew the same things about you. I wonder why you do the things you do. I don't believe it's for the reasons Aunt Tandy says."

"Now I'm the one who wants to know—what does she say?" he demanded.

"Let's don't argue, Jubal."

"Then tell me what she says," he returned in rising anger.

"Tandy says that no good—" Terrill stumbled to a halt. "But I know it's not as bad as she says." What was she saying? she asked herself frantically. She was getting in deeper and deeper, and his face was already stiff with temper.

She took a deep breath. There was one sure way to find truth: to seek it out for yourself. She wanted to know what made Jubal the way he was. And if what she found with the request she was about to make was too bad, she could just back away, she told herself. "I want to see Sullivan's Ridge, Jubal. Your home."

Even as angry as he was, he had not been expecting it, the blow to his abdomen that her words delivered.

"I want to see your house."

Girls had been asking things of him since he was fifteen, meaningless things—kisses, dances, a cigarette, screwing around.

He'd thought she'd wanted to know more, like, What kind of man are you really? Do you think we could somehow see each other again? Talk again?

But no.

Terrill Carroll wanted to see where he lived. Where he came from. Such an important detail, the one he'd been judged by most of his life.

Slowly Jubal reached with his right hand for the pack of cigarettes that lay on his dash, pulling a white tube of tobacco from the wine-red package. Then he crumpled the paper container, dropped it to the seat, and put the cigarette between his lips. The amber-colored lighter lay on the dash, too, and he shifted forward to pick it up, to flick it into a tiny flame that he held to the cigarette. Its leaping warmth put a temporary answering flush on his marble-hard chin and lips before he tossed the lighter on the seat, took a drag on the cigarette, and held it away from his mouth, on the wheel.

Then he spoke, calm and easy.

"What makes you think," he said, "that just because I didn't have to work and wanted somebody to run around with this afternoon, and the boss's daughter wanted to run, too—where do you get off tellin' *me* to take you home with me and let you inspect my house? You think your opinion about it matters?"

The blood that rushed to Terrill's face was so thick, it strummed in her eyes, so red it colored her vision. Shock, then embarrassment, shot through her—but all of the other emotions were obliterated by the blazing, white-hot, satisfying explosion of anger that surged all over her body.

"Stop this *truck*." She got the words out somehow, each one climbing higher and higher. "*Now.*"

He shouldn't have said it. He was already bitterly sorry, and he was too late. Jubal could tell all that by the spitting fury in her eyes, the hot red on her cheeks, the way she quivered like a tightly strung string.

"I'm sor—"

"Stop the truck, or I'm going to jump." She meant it. Her fingers were on the latch—the door was opening already.

"Okay," he got out hastily, focusing half on her, half on the road as he jerked the truck over to the side of the two-lane asphalt road. "I'm pullin' over— Don't, Terrill—wait—"

But the truck hadn't even slowed to a decent crawl before she was tumbling out into the dry grass at its edge. He hit the brakes and nearly stood himself on his head when he realized that she'd fallen, tripping in her mad scramble out of the moving truck. But she was up, stumbling, pushing herself off the ground, and as he yanked his own door latch up and threw himself out, she was already on a dead run away from him, her body and long legs lithe and liquid in movement, her tumbling spill of hair a warm banner behind her.

He swore at himself once before he went after her, his boots throwing up little sharp gravels as they tore up the edge of the road. He was fast with his long legs and slim racer's build, but she had a head start and an uncanny knack for avoiding pitfalls. No tripping, stumbling female here.

The wind whipped Terrill's face, cooling the rage and drying anything that even faintly resembled tears. It felt good to run, to leave that obnoxious jackass behind her, and she meant to get away, even when she heard him coming after her.

She flung one look back—he was gaining, leaping in one soaring, graceful movement down the gravelly bank that she'd taken the time to run down, about to fall on her face. He had his arms flung out for balance, and when she turned to run again, she saw in her mind's eye that picture of him, dark and sleek as a jungle cat against the sky.

This time the sob in her throat was dry and painful, because her throat was, too. He was going to catch her. There was nowhere to run, except down this deserted highway.

She pulled up short, forcing panic down, and twisted to face him. Her heart was knocking harshly, her breath tearing through her raggedly, cold sweat drying on her forehead. She was too hot, and she was too scared as he lunged after her.

Terrill had stopped running; she was waiting for him, Jubal realized. Her action was so unpredictable that he slowed automatically, so that by the time he was nearly to her, he was able to slide to a stop, too. His breath was as loud as hers in the still, cold air, and his chest heaved.

For a minute they glared at each other. Then she spoke, her words uneven and choppy.

"I ran—you followed. So now who's the fool?" A gasp for air. "I don't ever want to be with you anymore. But I need a ride home. You owe me that much."

"I'm sorry." He got out the words, quick and fast, before either one of them could do something else reckless.

Her face was scornful.

"Terrill, I only said those things because—"

"You said them because you're ashamed of where you're from," she interrupted rudely, running her open fingers through the top of her hair, shoving the honey-colored strands out of her hot, flushed face. "I want to go home, Jubal Kane." Then she shoved past him, striding back toward the truck in the distance.

He jerked as if she had hit him across the face, and his brown skin flooded with color. "Ashamed!" he repeated.

She just kept walking, and when she got to the vehicle she climbed in, slammed the door, and waited. Eternity must have passed before she heard his steps on the gravel at the door.

Jubal climbed in, too, without a word. He never looked at her, but out of the corner of her eye, she could see long, angry streaks of color on the lean dark cheek turned to her, as though she'd hit him physically and left finger marks. For a minute they sat there silently, two angry, hurt people.

Then he started the truck, and they pulled out on the highway.

13

It took fifteen minutes for Terrill to focus again and realize they had missed the turn into Bethel. Jubal kept going, straight out the highway. But she wasn't sure until the road met the Red Fork River and twisted along beside it. They weren't going west, toward town; they were going north, toward Sullivan's Ridge.

Terrill sat up sharply. "No!" It was the first sound either of them had made, and it broke the silence viciously, like a hammer smashing through glass.

He said nothing. But his foot rode the gas pedal a little more heavily, and they swung around a long curve like a narrow snake sliding through the grass.

"I said no!"

"So jump again." He spoke carelessly, never looking at her. "But this time you'll get killed, and anyway, if I see you reach for the door, I'm gonna get a little faster."

"I don't believe you."

But his foot moved, and the speedometer inched up, faster by another five miles an hour.

Terrill let out all her breath. "I won't jump," she said in defeat. "Did you hear me? Look." She raised her hand from the door latch.

For answer, he lifted his foot off the gas a little, and a little more, and breath crept back into her body as the truck slowed.

"I don't want to see the place now," she told him, trying to be calm. "You've got a problem, Jubal. Nobody normal gets upset when people ask where they live."

He already knew his reaction had been way out of line; he didn't need this sharp-tongued hellcat to tell him so. But she had gone too far; so had he.

"Nobody ever said I was 'normal,'" he answered. "And you wanted to see it, so now you can."

"I've changed my mind."

"Too late."

She drew in an angry, frightened breath, then braced herself, feet against the floor, palms on her knees.

"All right. Show me. Then I'm going home. And I hope I never see you again."

The Red Fork River lapped along the edge of Highway 37 on one side. On the other were tall, rocky cliffs. In the summer they were covered with moss and greenery; now they looked cold and gray.

Jubal and Terrill finally turned to the right, on an asphalt road so narrow that it had no yellow center line at all. The silver ribbon that it cut through the overhanging trees and heavy underbrush was clear before them. The road rose straight up, high into the air, before it twisted and turned between the rises and the hollows on each side of it, still going up.

Up to Sullivan's Ridge.

At four o'clock on a Friday afternoon, with the clouds beginning to filter over the pale sun, it was quiet and lonely. No sudden red-hot bursts of gunfire, no thugs lying in wait on the shallow side of the road, no crazed drunks or mad rapists. Terrill hadn't even known she expected such atrocities, but the relief that washed over her as the quiet woods and deep hollows rolled by was undeniable.

Everybody in Cade County talked about the Ridge. Even as a little girl she remembered Grandpa and Luke recounting lurid tales of bootleggers and knife fights and scandalous misconduct around the ballot boxes here on election days.

As far as Terrill could tell, nothing lived here except squirrels and other woods animals. With the trees in their leafless condition, Terrill could see under their limbs all the long way down into the bottom of hollows in several places. Way, way below her, off the side of the hill, there was the brown glimmer of a creek that rushed along.

Then the land flattened just a little, and things began gradually to appear. First there was a trailer that perched precariously on the side of a rise in a tiny flat spot. A dilapidated tricycle lay overturned in the yard, and a rusted-out automobile sat at the end of the trailer. A black-and-white, short-haired dog ran out after the wheels of Jubal's truck, barking fiercely.

Just beyond the trailer was a weathered barn, one corner propped up with stones; that corner sat nearly in the road under heavy, overhanging trees. Two or three cold-looking Herefords stared at them as they passed, their heads and front legs considerably higher than their rumps, because of the steep slant of the land they stood on.

"Now I've seen it," Terrill said. "Let's go."

Jubal—this Jubal—frightened her. This one was like the man who'd leaned on the City Cafe wall last Saturday, except now he was grim and deathly still, and his face was adult and frozen.

"No," he answered calmly. "You ain't seen it yet."

"I don't want to go to your house," she burst out, panicked.

"I know what you wanted. We're not there yet. Wait."

The houses began to get a little thicker as the road flattened, and they reached the level, stretching top of the Ridge. A small, neat house with a clothesline full of jeans and diapers set off to the right, on another distant rise. Smoke was coming from its chimney.

Terrill looked at Jubal.

"The Bells' house," he answered her unspoken question.

Next came a black tarpaper shanty, with a pack of hounds on the porch.

"Jake Summers," Jubal offered, without a flicker of emotion. "Fox hunter . . . and, once in a while, a drunk."

Terrill said nothing.

A faded red-tiled house with a stack of wood and a worn-out upholstered rocking chair on the porch. "The McDonalds."

More little houses, more old cars, a church, small and peeling under trees so majestic they made the little sanctuary look insignificant and puny.

Then came the center of the Ridge: an old store, tiled in brown, with a high false front, graying wooden steps up to the equally grayed planking of a long porch, two gas pumps in front. A window on the side, at the end of the porch, had white letters painted on it that read "Post Office—Sullivan's Ridge, Tennessee". Across the black screen doors ran the orange-and-yellow line, "Colonial Is Good Bread!"

Inside the long windows at each side of the screen and the door, Terrill could see lights. And a shadowy figure or two, the ones who must have been the owners of the three vehicles parked in front of the porch.

"Ida Fuller's store," Jubal said.

An old school, and more lights, and a few children still scattered on the steps.

And more tiny houses, dotted here and there.

Poverty. Everywhere, there was poverty.

She wanted suddenly to cry. In the cold, gray day, it was a sad place. If the views across the hollows had not been spectacular, if the trees had not been so numerous and so big, it would have been pitiful.

And then he was pulling off the ridge road, onto a graveled one, one so hung over by trees, it was nearly dark.

She sucked in her breath sharply and looked at him. "You wanted to see where I was from," he said, at last returning her glance. "Don't chicken out now." His face was as hard as his tone.

She snapped her teeth together. It wasn't as if she'd done something terrible. What was wrong with asking him about his home? Except that he'd been right; she'd asked for all the wrong reasons.

The road turned, they jounced over a hole, and then the closed, narrow, shadowy lane opened, and Jubal, without warning, stopped the truck. "Here," he said flatly. "I live here."

It wasn't a terrible place.

It didn't look like a hellhole that had spawned a family such as his was reported to be.

Like everything else on the Ridge, it was just poor.

The house was small, with gray shingles as siding. It had a tin roof and a chimney at one end with smoke drifting from it, and a porch ran along the front of it. It was old and had been repaired often; Terrill knew its age because of its style, the way it had two doors that opened onto the porch, one at each end. The doors had no storms; the windows had plastic stretched firmly across them to keep out the cold; an old, brown, cane-bottomed chair stood idly on the porch; and a swing had been lifted to hang against the ceiling, as protection against the damage a winter wind might do.

The house sat in an open, flat spot at the very dead end of the road a hundred yards or more ahead of them, in the middle of the smooth high point. On two sides the land fell away gently from the yard, dropping into deep hollows. But on the right the woods continued stretching, acre after acre, until finally, in the distance, another, taller, ridge began to rise. The top of that steep ridge was so high, it was shrouded now in the cold gray clouds.

Jubal didn't want to move; he wanted never to see the look on Terrill's face. He wondered why she was so still, but rather than read her scorn, he gazed straight ahead, seeing things he'd never really noticed, things that made him flinch a little.

The clothesline over to the side had Ma's mop hung on it by a clothespin; it swayed a little in the breeze. He was lucky she hadn't decided to hang his underwear out on the line today. The flat, low top of the covered well out to the side had empty flower pots and old mayonnaise jars sitting on top of it, a clutter of glass partially hidden by the long, spidery vines of a dead forsythia bush. He hated the junky glasses, had even tried to haul them off, but Ma had protested. She saved everything like that to can in.

At least Ma's chickens had had the good sense to stay out of the front yard today; normally one or two of them could be counted on to greet company on the way across the yard to the porch.

"This is where I grew up," he said abruptly. "Where I live. Not exactly the Carroll farm. So what else do you want to know? Ask around. You'll find out more. I got three brothers, see? David ran away from home sixteen years ago. I was seven. I guess he's dead, even if Ma don't want to talk about it. And then there's Frankie. He got picked up when he was eighteen on suspicion of possession, but they never could prove a case against him; now he's somewhere overseas, working on a pipeline. At least he was the last we heard. Nobody else wanted him, so the government got him. Jarvis had to get married when he was nineteen, and he's got a wife and two kids up at Scottsville. Me . . ." He paused at last, head bent over the wheel, then turned to look up at her. "Me, you already know. Your aunt Tandy told you. So you see, it's just what people call it, a redneck, no-account place. It's where *I'm* from."

"I want to go home," she said quietly, her voice shaking in spite of her best efforts. She was afraid, more than she'd ever been in her life, more than she'd been at the mill. Here, she was on his ground.

But worse than terror, the Ridge—and Jubal's voice—brought despair. She wanted to cry at the sight of this house, and his story repulsed her, even if she was aware that he'd meant for it to. She had made a serious mistake, she'd done this for all the wrong reasons, and now she wanted off this place, and out of this truck, and away from Jubal and his tragedy of a life.

"Yeah," he replied. "I thought you would." He made a quick, rough movement, but only to twist to see over his shoulder and to back the truck down the narrow road. He found an opening among the trees, backed in, then flipped around so that they were heading back out to the Ridge road. It was a fast, twisting glide downhill this time, down the long line of the ridgetop to Highway 37 and the river on the other side of it.

She would have been perfectly happy to let the silence continue, but once on the highway he began to speak, harsh, choked words that spilled out of him as if he had no control. But he kept his eyes away, turned on the road.

"Ashamed. Maybe I was—a little. The same way I was the day we came to move the bed and I didn't know what that bag of leaves was. You made me feel that way then, too. You and your aunt Tandy. You didn't want to know where I lived because I was important to you. You wanted to poke around just to see if it was as bad as everybody said. You're just like the rest of this county."

"That's not true," she whispered, trying to stop his words.

"No?" He shot a glance at her, mocking and angry. "So why, then? You thinkin' about lettin' me be your—what was that you said?—your friend? You figure you might want to know Ma, or come to the house for supper one night?"

Terrill swallowed deeply. "What are you so mad about? My wanting to see the Ridge is no big deal."

"No, nothin' about me is. I'm just like that Ridge; it's a part of me. And I could tell exactly how it made you feel. I knew before we ever went how it'd be. The minute you saw where I was from, it was enough for you. You never even gave *me* a chance, did you? I keep havin' trouble rememberin' who you are, because I lied this morning. That kiss—it was important. I couldn't forget it." He broke off, breathing harshly, his fingers clutching the steering wheel tightly. "But I *will*. I will *now*. It was just a kiss."

Terrill couldn't stand the spill of words anymore; honesty and anguish made for a painful combination. But most of all, she felt compassion for him—a strange mix of pity and tenderness, because in spite of what he said or did, he cared. She felt a surprised gratification that it mattered to him what she thought. How long had it been since she had felt that anybody wanted her approval?

And he couldn't forget one kiss.

"Wh—" She tried again. "Why did you ask me to go to Edmonds today?"

His words rang between them, the harsh, ugly ones he'd spoken earlier.

"I told you," he muttered at last, ungraciously, inviting her to hear the echoing memory.

"You yelled a lot of things at me. Some of them were true. Some. Was it really true that you just wanted somebody, anybody to—"

"No." He cut her off abruptly as they turned into the edge of Bethel.

"Then why?"

"I don't know. But I woulda come on home today after I picked up that part—if there hadn't been you."

"And now, the day's over." What did she want him to say, anyway? He was already saying all the right things, all the things she'd wanted to hear back on that ridge.

He looked over at her at last, his face dark, his eyes an opaque green. "Yeah. All over," he said, and he meant it.

Her mind protested, *But we didn't* do *anything*. Too late to realize now that maybe—just maybe—she wished they had.

Jubal was different, but not because he was bad. He was a little too uncontrolled, maybe, a little too intense.

She did not want him to turn into the silent stranger of the past week. She wanted back the man at the mall—was it only this morning?

But Jubal had other plans.

He let her out a quarter of a mile from the house in silence. Terrill stood in the open door of the truck indecisively, willing him to look at her. Regret and fear boiled up in her.

"Jubal, I was pretty mad when I said some of that stuff—"

"Don't," he interrupted flatly. "It's okay. We're even. I reckon I said too much, too. Anyway, you were right. I'll see you, Terrill." He made an impatient movement, as if to get her out of the door fast.

But she hesitated. "Could we—"

"I'm goin' home," he interrupted. "So I can get things together to come back to make another run to Kentucky tonight for Carroll. I gotta go to work."

She tried again to speak.

"Terrill," he cut in impatiently, "you were right all along when you said you didn't want to remember. We can't ever be 'friends.' It's just took me a while to see it, that's all."

14

She didn't go in the house when she got back to it, her feet dragging. Instead she sat down on one of the rockers on the front porch, huddled down in her coat, feeling confused and regretful. Numb.

Terrill had the strangest feeling that she'd just lost something sweet and precious when she'd erected barriers between herself and Jubal today.

But she didn't sit and brood alone too long, because a big white Buick pulled in the drive and stopped at the gate in front of the house. Two women got out of it.

One had a shiny cap of black hair.

"Hello," Tess Johnson called from the walk as she and the other woman made their way up the sidewalk. "I'm Tess. I thought you might remember me from grade school. Your aunt called our house and asked us to check on you."

Terrill stood slowly. She'd spent most of her life

in the company of other women; it was the only gender to which Rose Hall catered, after all. She liked their company. So why was there something in her that wanted to back away from Tess? She didn't even know her anymore. Maybe it was the other girl's perfection, the way Tess was so overwhelmingly sure of herself, that left Terrill wary.

Whatever it was, it made her stiffly polite and not much more.

"I know who you are. And I remember you, too," she answered as the three of them faced one another on the porch in the long shadows of the autumn afternoon.

"I've seen you at church several times," Tess continued, "but I'm always so busy I never seem to have time to talk much. I barely recognized you the first day. You look so different from the way you looked before you were sent away."

The other girl flushed and coughed a little at Tess's bluntness. "I'm Joanie Crabtree, and don't even try to remember me. You won't. I'm from Chattanooga. We moved here four years ago, when my mother, Wanda, married Tom Townsend, Tess's uncle."

"Your own father is dead?"

"No. My parents are divorced. My actual dad's a big loser, but Tom's been great to me," Joanie said cheerfully. "He treats me like I'm his real daughter. Sort of the way Henry Carroll does you, I guess."

Terrill smiled and said nothing.

"Dad says you're working at the mill," Tess said casually. "We stopped there first, but Rosalie said you were out today. Nobody much was there, in fact."

Joanie slid a wry glance at Tess, one that Terrill caught without understanding.

"I'm only there three days a week. It gets me out of the house."

"Really? Well, some Fridays I cut my lab and drive home early. Like today," Tess said, leaning back against the post near her. In her black jeans and heavy red sweatshirt, she made a slim, vivid splash of color against its white column. "Maybe the next time I do, I'll come by. We'll go to lunch, or something. You could show me around the mill. I've never seen one in too much detail. It might be fun. We could get reacquainted."

Maybe she should fall on her knees in gratitude for Tess's casual offer of friendship, but Terrill just didn't feel like it today. This whole conversation felt strange, and there it was again, that look of amused exasperation on Joanie's face at Tess's words.

So Terrill spoke to Joanie instead. "Will you get to come, too?"

"Probably not. She's the idle rich, but me, I work at the hospital. I'm a brand-new nurse. So what I do depends on my schedule for the week."

Tess straightened. "Well, we've done our duty and checked up on you. Joanie's got to get home, and I've got a date."

"Do you need anything?" Joanie asked hesitantly. "I could stay a while longer. Miss Carroll said—"

"No. I'm fine, just me here by myself," Terrill answered calmly. She watched them as they headed down the steps.

At her car, Tess turned back one last time, considering. "It's Friday night, and you're going to be at home alone? You ought to be having fun."

"Maybe you could go out with some of us some weekend," Joanie suggested. "I know two or three men who'd—"

"No, not a blind date," Terrill said with a laugh and a shake of her head.

"There's somebody you'd like to invite on your

own? That'd be okay, too," Joanie persisted. "I'll bet your mother would like you to get out some, even if she is sick."

Terrill watched the car pull off, and their words danced in her head. But their invitation didn't even tempt her. She didn't want a loud party, or a passive movie theater, or a classic little supper for two in a stilted restaurant.

None of that was rich enough, or wild enough, to satisfy the longing in her veins.

All of it was too smooth, too civilized, its edges too polished.

Making the call to St. Thomas wasn't calculated, but even while she spoke to Tandy on the phone, she knew she was buying herself an insurance policy. If she called Tandy first and sounded normal, Tandy wouldn't call her again that night and discover that Terrill was nowhere in the house to answer the phone.

And she never consciously premeditated what happened, either. She just sat in the room for a while, looking out at the dark, hearing things.

The anger and the despair in Jubal's voice today.

He thought he had been measured by her and had come up far short. That she'd condemned him.

Well, hadn't she?

I can't forget that kiss.

Those words whispered around her head, too. She brushed them away.

It was best not to get involved with anybody like Jubal. It would lead nowhere. She couldn't tell anybody; it would have to be secret; it would be like living with a lie. She could hear Tandy's crisp voice now, laying it out as it really was.

He wore the wrong clothes. He'd been in a prison. He murdered the king's English. He swore like a sailor. He smoked as if he'd never heard of the surgeon general. Maybe he hadn't.

No girl like Terrill should ever look at him.

But . . . his hands were gentle.

His face was beautiful.

His mouth was . . . She buried her own face in her two hands, whimpering to herself like a hurt animal. How many times today had she slid secret, heart-stopping looks over at his wide, mobile mouth and hoped—just a little—that he would break his promise and make one minor pass that involved kissing?

This was only a physical attraction.

But . . . he listened to her.

He believed what she said.

He wanted to impress her, to protect her.

He liked the way she looked.

And—none of all those warm truths were really what decided Terrill; what she kept coming back to was much simpler. He set her free. In the dark night, where nothing mattered, he'd given her freedom to talk, to pour out all her problems, even to tell the shameful story of how Henry hit her. He'd given her freedom today that was physical—where she'd wanted to go, he'd been willing to take her. He was freedom from restraint, from tradition, from expectation, from her mother's illness and her stepfather's hate, from Aunt Tandy's insistence on routine.

He was all that she had craved at Rose Hall. Freedom to run down the highway, to touch the stars, to burn under the hot sun, to break out. Freedom to be the real Terrill.

And if he made her heart beat and throb in her throat, if her hands longed to touch him—that couldn't be helped.

She saw the light across the hollow when it flipped

on, the one on this side of the sawmill. Probably the one at the shop. She knew who was there; hadn't he told her he would be?

It took twenty or thirty minutes to get a big truck ready to run; air pressure had to build up, trailers had to be hooked to tractors—all sorts of little details. She might make it to him before he pulled out—if she ran all the way, if she didn't get caught, if he wasn't in any all-fired hurry to get on the road.

She was going to try it anyway, because she didn't want him to forget that kiss, after all.

He had already climbed into the truck, but the door on the driver's side was still open as Terrill stumbled into the lumberyard and stopped at last, right in front of his lights, trembling from nerves and the exhausting run. She didn't see him when he slid out of the cab—she didn't even know where he was until he stepped slowly in front of it, trapped in its headlights with her, but his long frame was a black silhouette while her face was illuminated. The darkness lapped all around them.

"What are you doin' here?" he asked her harshly, and his words were nearly swallowed by the rumbling dinosaur behind him.

Be brave, Terrill. She took a step closer to him.

"I saw the lights from my bedroom window. I knew it was you. I need to tell you something."

He was already shaking his head. "No. No, you don't. Just like you got no business here. Go home, Terrill."

Another step closer to him; now she could see the gleam that was his cheekbones, and she could make out the top button on his opened jacket.

"I just want to be sure I've got all the facts right,"

she said steadily, tucking her hands in the pockets of her own coat, clenching them until the nails cut into her palms. "You're straight out of some kind of prison. You live on a dirt-poor ridge. You've had a worthless father, and three brothers who're not the cream of the crop. And you never heard of a Gucci label," she said at last, voice cracking just a little in nervous laughter.

He jerked as if she'd hit him with a whip, sucked in a harsh breath at her audacity, and choked out, "You—shut up!"

"I won't. Because it's what you expect me to say. You made sure today I'd know the truth about you. And I do. I know it all, Jubal."

"Tell me somethin' new," he retorted at last, unevenly. "Maybe you feel better now that you've said it. Now get out of my way. I got a job to do." He turned back to the truck jerkily, moving out of the lights.

Terrill caught up to him in the shadows at the truck door, catching his booted foot as he climbed the ladder at the side and got ready to vault in.

"Jubal."

"Damn it," he said furiously, twisting to look down at her upturned face, "I don't want to hear you anymore. I don't want to see you again. I—"

"Do you want to kiss me again?" Terrill made herself stare up at him without flinching, her face as defiant as her words. But somehow, everything sounded and looked shaky, from her voice to his startled face.

Frozen there on the side of the truck, he stared down into her blue eyes a long, long moment.

"What?" he said at last, incredulously, painfully.

"The reason I quit talking today in the mall was because—when you had on the coat, I started thinking how—how beautiful you are—" Oh, great, she thought in hysteria. What every male wants to hear. "And I wondered how many girls you've had. You'd been with somebody when I saw you at the mill that first day." Her voice suddenly got stronger, aggravated and waspish. "And it made—makes me afraid—and— it made me *mad*. There," she finished in a heated rush. She felt ridiculous, standing here clinging to his boot, and quickly she released it and stepped back.

Above her, Jubal felt the blood begin to move in his body again—sluggish and dull, but still moving. Carefully he turned a little and dropped to the ground. Then he regained his balance and stood searching her face in the shadows.

She was offering him heaven—or hell.

If this was just another invitation for a single roll in the backseat of somebody's car, and that was all, he was going to be miserable. He could get that at the Pine. Hell, he could get *that* anywhere.

"Terrill—" *Just come out and say it,* he told himself, and he did, the words harsh, blunt, clear: "Did you come here tonight to get laid?"

She gasped, then pulled back her foot in outrage and kicked him, as hard as she could, in the shin.

And even as he flinched and swore, he understood: it was heaven.

"I should have known, Jubal Kane, that you'd turn anything I said into something—Oh!" The words were smothered on her lips.

It was not like any kiss he'd ever given—or received—in his entire life. He just reached out, grabbed her by the arms, and pulled her into him. She was warm life against his heart, sweet, stinging honey on his lips, dancing fire in his veins. And all of that was before she quit struggling, and slowly wrapped her arms around his waist under his coat, and kissed him back.

They stood there a long, long time, lips locked together. At last, when he set her mouth free, she gasped for breath and spoke. "No," she said, clear and distinctly, looking at his chin.

"No," he repeated, uncomprehending.

"I did *not* come here to do what you said."

"Oh, that," he returned ruefully with a half laugh. "Okay."

That brought her eyes up to his, startled and oh, so close. "Okay?" she questioned suspiciously. "But you said—"

"I say a lot, and mosta the time, it just shows how big a fool I am," he answered slowly, his eyes on her lips again. "Terrill . . ."

Maybe he was asking permission, or maybe he was giving her warning. Neither did any good. She saw his face bending, his lips getting nearer, and she lifted her mouth and touched his before he reached her.

He pulled her even more tightly up against him, his arms shackling her body to his.

She'd never experienced anything like these kisses—sweet, powerful, inebriating. Her heart might burst under its overload, and in desperation she pulled her mouth free from his clinging lips and dropped her face into his shoulder.

He was breathing heavily, each breath lifting her a little, and she felt one of his hands as it touched her hair, caressing it as it fell down her back.

"My God," he said at last. "I wanted to kiss you so bad all week—no, ever since I first saw you."

"We wasted today," she said with a shaky laugh. Daringly, she raised her hand and brushed his lips open a little with one finger.

"You made me promise," he said in protest, catching her hand and holding it against his mouth.

"You acted like it was an easy promise to keep," she retorted.

"Easy to keep! Hell, Terrill, if you knew how much I wanted to touch you this morning and couldn't, you'd think 'easy.'"

"Jubal," she said in a near whisper, her emotions clear for him to see now, "I wanted to be with you even this afternoon, after our fight, after you dumped me on the road and told me to go home. A whole day with you, and I wanted more."

He looked down on her upturned face, raised both his hands to run them through her hair and caress her cheeks with his thumbs. "You went with me today, Terrill," he said tenderly. "You trusted me then. Go with me now. Trust me now."

She jerked under his palms. "Go—now?" she faltered.

"To Kentucky. In the truck," he said, jerking his head toward the big machine at his back. "I'll have you home before dawn—again."

Still she hesitated. "All the way to—"

He interrupted her quickly, persuasively. "Nobody's at your house, Terrill. They won't ever know."

After a minute she shook her head. "No," she answered reluctantly.

"I want you to come. Damn it, you can't just run down here and kiss me a few times and walk away. Not when we could be together," he protested.

"Jubal, you did hear what I said, didn't you?" Terrill asked painfully. "I don't want to go all the way tonight. And I'm not—" she tried to brush away her embarrassment with a quick laugh—"I'm not talking about Kentucky."

He hesitated a minute, then slid his hands down

her neck to her shoulders. She felt his chin touch the top of her head, and his voice was a little muffled and a little embarrassed, Terrill realized in astonishment. "I said that because—I thought maybe the only reason you'd come after me was for . . . for a fast tumble." To anybody else, he could have been explicit—graphic— slangy in his word choice. But to this girl, he stumbled and fumbled for words to soften the blow. "I thought that it'd be something for you to forget the next time we met."

This time she pushed away as if she were too close to a hot stove, and she got out all of his name in one indignant explosion. "Jubal Kane! You've got some funny ideas—wrong ideas—about girls!"

"No, I don't," he said stubbornly. "I know."

She frowned at the conviction in his voice, and he felt a sudden sear of worry that he'd said too much. He didn't want compassion or pity or contempt if she realized how much he'd been stung by the casual assumption—the one Tess had made—that he was just a body to be enjoyed.

He felt like a fool even thinking that way.

It never bothered Bobo or Dusty or anybody else for a girl to make advances, and they preferred that she forget come morning. If he were honest, he'd admit that he'd never minded it that way most of the time himself.

Until Tess had aggravated things.

Until he had kissed Terrill.

He didn't want this particular girl to be easy—that was the whole issue here.

"I want us to last longer than one night," he got out at last, looking out at the darkness because he couldn't look anywhere else.

She swallowed something like a huge clump of tears in her throat and stepped back into his arms to press herself against him, to wrap herself around him, as he hugged her tightly to him. So much heavy emotion might kill, so finally she said in a voice that laughed and only cracked a little, "Are you promising to be good? *You?*"

After a minute, while he adjusted to her altered tone, he said huskily, "I'll be so good that you'll have to beg me to kiss you, if that's the way you want it."

"Not that good," she protested, lifting her face to his.

"Well, maybe you ain't gonna have to beg," he answered teasingly, his hands moving up her back to her shoulders, his lips hovering near hers. "I reckon you could just talk me into anythin'. I got to be careful around you—you can sure talk rings around anybody I ever met, anyway."

"So how come," she whispered just before she kissed him another time, "that I'm the one getting talked into your truck?"

15

"I thought you had to be old to drive one of these trucks," Terrill told Jubal teasingly, watching him run through the endless gears as the Peterbilt picked up speed.

He flashed a grin over at her. "Y'do," he answered calmly. "But it's late, I'm on a back road, and there ain't nobody gonna stop one of Carroll Mill's trucks long as it's mindin' its own business. The mill's too well known. It gives work to a lotta people. Nobody's too anxious to get Carroll upset."

"Oh." Terrill digested all this in a few minutes of silence. Then she had another question. "So where are we going, anyway?"

He told her that, and what they were hauling.

"Engines. At night?"

He answered, "People ship and haul at night all the time. I get paid for it—that's all that's my business."

He said it abruptly, uncomfortable with the sudden remembrance that Terrill at least had a right to ask questions. He didn't like thinking about the fact that she was a Carroll, that he was virtually working for her.

The flashing thought jarred him unpleasantly. He could think of things he'd like to do for Terrill, and with Terrill, but working for her was decidedly out of the question.

"You don't like doing this much, do you?" she asked suddenly, and when he looked over, she was watching him. "So why do you do it? Tell Henry no."

"I have to keep the job," he said shortly.

"The one Henry gave you," she said slowly, remembering Tandy's conversation with Henry. "Got you right out of prison."

Jubal said nothing.

Terrill glanced over at him in the darkness. "Are you going to get mad again if I ask something I want to know?" she asked bluntly.

Jubal returned her look for a moment. "You want to know why I went to Lineville," he said in resignation.

"No. I already know that. But I don't know the reason. Why'd you do all those things?" she asked in hesitation. She couldn't bring herself to say "steal."

Jubal considered her question. He hadn't planned on ever telling anybody. Not that anybody cared; they'd just said, "Did you do it?" and he'd answered, "Yes." That had been the end of it.

But Terrill was asking. He might tell her at least part of the story.

"I can't tell you the other man's name," he said abruptly.

"What other man?"

"The one I was with that night. He'd worked for Carroll for two or three years before the robbery. But he did some kind of extra work for him that summer, and Carroll promised him a big bonus. When he didn't get it, this guy got mad. A bunch of us were hangin' out down at the river that night. He was pretty drunk, and he got this idea that he was just gonna break into Carroll's safe and take the money."

In the little pause that followed, Terrill spoke. "And you? How did you get involved?"

"He'd been a good friend of my brother's before Jarvis moved away. I guess I thought I owed him something. So when he wanted me to go with him, I did."

"But why you?"

"'Cause I can do things with my hands. He figured I could get the safe open. I was twenty. Too dumb to even think about what was gonna happen if we messed up. I guess you could say I wasn't thinkin' real clear."

The self-derision in Jubal's voice made it harsh. Staring out now in the darkness of another night, he could remember the sudden shock of seeing the circling blue lights of Standford's car as it pulled up like a soundless ghost to the office of the mill.

Up until that night, Jubal hadn't even known there was such a thing as a silent alarm that signaled a break-in, not at the business where it occurred, but at a distant sheriff's office.

He remembered the fear that had scattered through him at the sight of those lights—and the way the siren had suddenly cut across the mill yard. The way Standford's voice had sounded on the big horn.

"Come on out," the sheriff had shouted. "We know you're there."

Terrill said quietly, "And you got caught."

"He—the other guy—was gone. I didn't even know when or how. I just laid there, flat on the floor, sweat dripping off me, wondering where in the hell he was. Finally, somebody forced open the door.

That was when all the alarms—the ones the whole world could hear—went off. So loud I couldn't even think. Then somebody—Foster, I found out later— fired a gun in the dark, in the middle of all the noise, not three feet from me."

Terrill swallowed, the sound loud in her own ears. Jubal's voice was still. Emotionless. But there was tension in his body, in the way he sat so stiffly opposite her.

"I never meant to hurt him. He knew that. But I rolled—came up with that letter opener—and when he fired again, I went for him. He panicked, just me and him there in the dark. That's why he kept firing. I got him—by the throat from behind. I coulda killed him then, but I didn't. Just two slashes across his arm. I had to make him drop that gun. Then somebody hit me in the back of the head. The next thing I remember, Standford was throwing water in my face. There was a big light blindin' me, and my head was poundin'." Jubal's voice trailed off, then he spoke again, suddenly. "And I was scared. God, I was scared."

"And your friend?" Terrill asked at last, her voice subdued. She wanted to wince away from the mental picture he'd created for her, but she'd asked for it.

"He got away."

"You didn't tell."

"Why should I? It wouldn't have saved me."

"It's not right. I don't see why—"

"Look," Jubal interrupted, angry, "if you don't like the story, if you don't believe me, what'd you ask me for?"

"I believe you," she said steadily. "Why shouldn't I? You've just admitted to breaking and entering and stealing and then cutting up somebody."

Jubal looked over at her sharply. "I never denied it. You knew it when you came with me tonight."

"You should have tried to explain to the court," she said argumentatively.

He made an exasperated sound in his throat. "Girl, you've been gone from this county too long if you think it'da made a difference. What I did was wrong, but they wouldn't have needed a real reason to send me to Lineville, anyway. I'm Jubal Kane. There wasn't any way out of it, and I guess I deserved it. Ma said I did."

The big truck rumbled on through the night for a while, the two sitting in its cab silent, each casting sliding, unobtrusive glances over at the other, each stiff from emotion.

"Why don't you just say it?" he burst out at last. "You wish you'd never come."

"That's not what I'm thinking," she retorted. "I was thinking that I'm sorry for—"

"Don't be sorry for me. Don't tell me that."

She retorted, a little angry herself, "I'll feel what I want to. I'll feel sorry and glad. Glad I came tonight. I'm glad you told me. I'm glad I'm with you. so *there.* Get your temper up over that, why don't you?"

Her defiant words echoed in the truck, and after a long pause he began to laugh. "Just don't try to jump outta *this* truck," he said at last, still laughing. Then, a little more quietly, "I never told anybody what happened except Ma, and now you. Nobody else ever asked me, either."

Terrill was beginning to smile a little. "So I'll have the distinction of being different," she said flippantly.

"Not different," he corrected. "Special. You're special."

The quiet pleasure in his voice spread through her body, warming her there in the shadows.

After a few minutes' humming silence, Jubal asked, "You tired?"

Terrill sat up a little straighter from where she'd slumped against the back of the seat. "Not much. It's just that it's so dark, and riding sometimes makes me sleepy."

"So go to sleep," he suggested, motioning with his head at the sleeper unit behind them. Terrill had tried fervently to ignore it—the berth that had been fitted snugly behind the truck seats.

"I'm fine," she protested.

He laughed to himself in the darkness of the truck. "I've got to be at the yard by a deadline. You already made me late comin' to the mill tonight— not that I'm complainin'. I'm just tryin' to tell you that I ain't gonna have time to pull the truck over and jump you, at least not on the way up. You can go to sleep if you want."

"Not on the way up!" Terrill echoed, then asked, "And what about coming back?"

"Well," he said doubtfully, "I could work it into the schedule, if you want me to."

He heard the quick breath, then the hint of laughter in her voice. "Thanks," she said humorously before she slid off her shoes and climbed up into the little sleeper bunk, curling up behind him. He had dropped his old coat in it before they'd left the lumberyard, and now she lay on top of it, her face pillowed against its collar. It was almost as delicious as wrapping herself against him had been earlier. She watched his hand on the wheel before her, wondering why she wasn't afraid with him, here at night in this huge machine, leaving the state behind.

Jubal glanced back at her, at the neat little ball she'd rolled herself up into, and a wave of something warm and sweet washed through him. This felt right: he and Terrill, alone together, her safe and sleepy, and him looking out for her. He was—satisfied. That was the only word he could think of.

Reaching his right hand back a little, behind the seat, he fumbled for her and touched her face. He felt her quick start, then she reached up her hand and took his, holding it tightly.

"Don't you need both of these on the wheel?" she asked.

"Not for a few minutes," he said. "I just wanted to see if you were okay." What he'd wanted was to touch her, just to make sure she was really there and this was not a fantastic dream.

"I'm fine," she answered, and she squeezed his hand.

He had to turn loose reluctantly to manage the truck, and when he was able to glance back again in a few minutes, she was asleep, her hair spilled out around her and one hand curled into a ball under her chin.

When Terrill awoke, it was due to two noises: one was the sound of the engine as it cut off, the other was the sound of somebody yelling. She sat up groggily, pushing her hair back, trying to orient herself.

In the darkness, all she could see was Jubal's dark figure.

"Jubal—"

"Shh," he cautioned her in a whisper.

"Where are we?"

"At the yard in Kentucky, where I make the drop. They won't even know you're here if you're quiet."

"Hey, driver," the loud voice called from outside again.

Jubal grabbed the coat from the bunk and pulled it on, then he opened the door and climbed out. Terrill could hear the voice clearly now.

"It's you again," the strange gruff voice said in displeasure. "I told you the last time I wanted—"

"Yeah, I know. But you got me instead. You want this unhooked here or somewhere else?"

Then the voices moved away into the night. Terrill couldn't hear anything but their murmured conversation. As she looked out the window before her, she decided quickly that she didn't like this isolated field. That was all it was as far as she could see, and without Jubal in the truck with her, everything was strange and black. She really didn't know where she was. She'd slept for—two hours? Her watch had a luminous dial that told her clearly she'd been in this bunk for a long time.

When at last Jubal got back in the truck, she was nervous. And he had nothing to say; he just started the motor and waited for the air pressure to build.

"Are you through?" she asked at last over his shoulder.

Glancing back, he smiled at her, completely unaware of her worries. "Yeah, just about. It's unhooked— we've just got to leave it with this guy. And I gotta pull up and hook to the trailer I left here last week and take it home. It's empty." He took a long brown envelope from his coat pocket and tossed it on the truck dash.

Then he switched on the headlights, and they pulled forward in a circle.

"This is a strange place to bring a truckload of engines," Terrill said as he brought the truck to another halt before the empty trailer. "But there's probably a logical reason for it."

Jubal twisted to look at her, his face inquiring.

"I just haven't thought of what it is yet," she said ruefully, answering the look.

And suddenly she didn't care. He was so close, his face teasing and open. He twisted just a little bit more and leaned just a little farther back, and he kissed her.

And it was several minutes—and several kisses—later before he dropped from the truck to hook up the return trailer.

She didn't go back to the other side of the truck on the way home, and she didn't sleep. Instead she sat right behind his right arm, feet dangling out of the sleeper, and they talked.

She told him about Rose Hall.

". . . and the thing that bothered me the most was the routine. Breakfast at seven, lunch at noon, dinner at six. There was never a second that wasn't regulated. If you were five minutes late to meals, you had to miss them." She paused a minute. "Did they do that at Lineville?"

He didn't want to talk about Lineville at all. But at least she wasn't afraid to admit that the place existed. She talked about it as if it were just another kind of school. Maybe she thought it was. "There was a cafeteria," he answered reluctantly. "We stood in line, ate fast, dumped the trays. Nobody ever minded missin' a meal too much. The worst part was havin' to eat 'em three times a day."

"We had classes for everything. All the regular school subjects, and then everything else, just to fill the time," she told him. "I could learn anything, but I couldn't go anywhere. When I finally graduated and went to Belmont, it felt—strange. To be able to walk anywhere. Do anything. Like I hadn't had legs and lungs in a long time, and now I had to learn how to use them again. Maybe I still haven't."

He understood. Oh, he understood. He couldn't tell her what he'd learned at Lineville, but he said slowly, "There was a walk for us. The circle, that's what they called it. It was just a big dirt ring around

a yard. You never went anywhere there, just around
and around 'til you thought you'd go crazy. The
worst part was I woulda—if I hadn't walked that
circle a thousand times. I hated it, but standin' still
was worse. Then they had you. Then you were really
in prison."

Terrill studied his profile. He made her feel little
and her woes seem petty. Rose Hall was a luxurious
gilded cage compared to where he'd been, and she
felt sorry for him when she thought of it.

He caught the expression on her face as he flicked
a quick glance at her and misinterpreted it mostly
because he'd been expecting a reaction ever since
the conversation took off. "You don't like to hear
that I was at Lineville," he said stiffly. "You can't
stand to be with me and think about it. So why
d'you ask me about it?"

"No, that's not it," she said quickly, her hand
going to his arm. "I don't like to think of you there,
that's true, but it's because I don't want to remember
that you were locked up. I've not known you all that
long, but I don't think you belong in that kind of
place."

There it was again—that echo of Maggie's words.

But he didn't have time to think of what she'd
said, because suddenly she bent toward him and he
felt her lips on the side of his throat, just under his
ear. Tentative, shy, light—but it was still a caress. A
voluntary, making-the-first-move touch from Terrill.

He heard her uneven, uncertain breath at his ear,
and he reached up his hand to pull her head against
his throat and hold it there.

"Lineville woulda been a whole lot easier," he
told her at last, his voice as uneven as her breathing,
"if I'd known we were gonna be together tonight like
this, Terrill."

"Rilla," she said slowly.

"What?"

She hadn't asked anybody to call her by the name Luke had given her in years; there hadn't been anybody she'd felt so right with, and she'd tried to shut off that part of her that the nickname seemed to symbolize, the girl who had trusted and loved and believed. It was scary, and risky, to offer Jubal that name, to bring that girl back, but it felt good, too. As if she were whole once more; as if she had accepted herself again. She'd rather be Rilla, to him . . . and to herself.

"Rilla," she repeated, at last, touching his throat another time, daring to slide her arms around his neck from her seat behind him. "It's sort of a nickname. People who matter to me, I'd rather they call me Rilla."

He tried to reach her mouth for a quick touch, but he couldn't and still keep his eyes on the road. All he managed to kiss was the corner of her lips. "When I get back to the mill," he said intensely, "I'm gonna do this right—Rilla."

The name sounded good when he spoke it. "Promise?" she whispered. "Boy, I'm glad I don't have to drive. There's so much else to do over here at the driver's seat." She ran a finger lightly across his eyebrow, down the side of his face, across his cheekbone, and over his jawline—almost exactly the same path she took next with her light, feathery kisses. She stopped with her kiss at the corner of his mouth, teasing where he'd kissed her.

"How many . . . how many guys you ever done this to?" he demanded huskily.

"One," she answered promptly, touching his ear with her lips.

"One!" he exclaimed, and pulled back a little.

"You," she replied tantalizingly. "You're the one."

"I meant—"

"I know what you meant," she said, laughing a little. "The next thing you'll be asking is how many I've kissed."

There was a long, arch pause.

"Well?" he demanded at last.

"You're not the first," she answered teasingly.

"I didn't think so," he muttered. "So how many? A hundred? Two hundred?"

"Well, there was Tony. And Ricky."

"You don't have to give me names," he said, his voice rough. "Or details."

"No?" she asked in disappointment. "Okay. Then I won't tell you that I was ten when Tony kissed me. He was thirteen and we were at a birthday party. He grabbed me in the den, all because his cousin Ricky McCrae liked me and didn't have the nerve—"

"Ricky McCrae!" Jubal echoed. "You mean the fat guy that works at the funeral home?" He could feel relief spreading all over him.

"Does he really?" Rilla asked, diverted, then laughed again. The sound was low and husky against his ear, where her face was. "Well, it figures. He kissed me, too, just to show Tony, and it was a slimy experience. I ought to have known then he was going to be an undertaker."

"And if you're talkin' about Tony Eldridge—"

"That was his name," Rilla interrupted. "I remember now. Is he a mortician, too?"

"No, he's just a creep. Maybe I'll find a reason to hit him one of these days," Jubal said consideringly. "Unless he kissed better." His voice said Tony better not have.

"Better than who? Ricky? No. But then, I don't think I truly appreciated kissing back then. Now that

I'm twenty, I'm seeing things a little different. Or maybe—" Her voice changed abruptly, and her movement away from him was sudden, as if contact with him scalded her unexpectedly.

For an instant he thought she was still teasing—until he looked at her. She was watching him, and her face was wiped clean of the laughter of a moment earlier.

"What?" he demanded.

"Or maybe you just know a lot more about kissing than undertakers and their cousins," she said slowly, as though remembering an unpleasant truth.

"Ter—Rilla, I—" He didn't know what to say. They'd moved out of teasing into dangerous territory—his past.

"How many girls have *you* kissed, Jubal?"

"I don't know," he said honestly.

"Too many to remember?"

He didn't answer, and she edged away a little farther from him. He caught her arm across his chest as it slid from his neck. "Rilla, please, don't," he said, and he was deadly serious. "I never cared before who I kissed, or who kissed me. Now is different. I don't know how. It's been different since the day I first saw you."

"When you had a bite on your throat and scratches on your back and—"

"Rilla!"

"—Ned Standford said they had to wait until dawn for you to come home just so they could arrest you. Well, you won't get back until dawn again today, will you? But I'm not going to do what *she* did, whoever *she* was," Rilla concluded hotly, pulling out of his grasp completely.

"I didn't ask you," he said with rising passion. "I don't want you to be like her. I ain't gonna pretend there wasn't a girl that night; it'd be a lie, and a stupid one. But I didn't even know about you. Not then. Now, I do."

She said nothing, sitting still and silent, staring rigidly out the window to the side. She had turned away from him completely.

"What d'you want me to say?" he burst out at last in frustration, gripping the wheel, wishing he could reach for her, wishing the road were wider so that somewhere he could pull over.

"Nothing," she said at last. "Because when I remember the way you were then, I don't know why I'm here."

"Maybe you should be with some of the men you know in Nashville." He brought the subject up at last.

She jerked in surprise. "What men?"

"You're twenty. You've been at college. How many men have you got hangin' around?"

"I've spent these last years focused on one thing—getting out of school. Doing what I had to do and then being free," she returned.

"But there were men," he said inexorably. "Don't tell me no. There had to be."

She sat stubbornly silent, refusing to tell him anything.

It took another twenty minutes to get back to Bethel and out to the lumberyard—twenty minutes that they passed in silence. Rilla spent them regretting what she'd said. What did she want him to say, anyway? And Jubal sat on his side of the truck, furious with himself for showing his jealousy and for being stupid enough to get mixed up with Tess in the first place. But mostly he was furious with Rilla—how could she just turn everything off?

Why didn't she feel the same strange, strong attraction for him that he did for her?

She had to. He would make her.

He pulled into the lumberyard with dread settling in his stomach. It was almost over—his magical day and night with Terrill. Rilla.

By the time he'd turned off the engine, she was sliding out of the sleeper toward her door. He caught her arm firmly.

"No," he said in low protest. "You can't just get out and walk off, not until you hear what I got to say."

She went still under his grip, afraid to look at him for fear those green eyes would pull her into him again. "So, say it," she whispered at last in the stillness.

"I don't like it that you saw me the way you did here at the mill. And it ain't just the—marks. It's the handcuffs, too, and everything else. But I can tell you this much—you stay away from the college guys, and I'll stay away from other women."

She gave a protesting, disbelieving jerk of her head and shoulders.

"I swear it," he said stubbornly. "Look at me, Rilla. Look."

Reluctantly, slowly, she faced him. He brushed her hair back from her face, then gazed right down into her heart. At least, that's what it felt like.

"So what am I supposed to see? I only had a few dates with a few men," she said at last, and a trace of defiance ran through her voice. "I don't know how to judge them, or what they want, or anything else about them."

"You're a fast learner," he said with a touch of humor. "Rilla, I just want to be with you. Nobody else. There won't be anybody else. Are you listenin'?"

It was much, much too difficult to fight the pull toward him. She swallowed once, then she leaned against his chest, nodding. "There's nobody back in Nashville, Jubal. Nobody at all that matters."

He let out his breath in a long sigh of relief and closed his arms around her. "If there's a way you can forget how I was that first day," he told her bent head at last, "will you try to?"

She looked up at him. "I forget every time I'm with you like this," she said tremulously. Then she put her hands on his shirtfront and said hesitantly, "But we can't be like this, Jubal, except in secret. I know you, but others don't. Not the way you really are. Aunt Tandy and Henry would kill me, or lock me in, or send me away if they knew about us. They'll find out if we're not careful. After Mama is— after she's gone, I won't care what they do," she whispered chokily.

"I can survive for a while like this," he answered. "As long as we're together sometimes. As long as I know you're with me."

Somehow, they had to hold on a while until nobody could stop her if she still wanted to see him. *If.* And he was going to do everything in his power to make sure she did.

He nudged her chin to look into her eyes. They looked black in the dim shadows, and the line of her nose was trim and neat. He traced it down to her mouth, then pulled her to him and kissed her.

He wanted to do more, to open her mouth and push her back against the sleeper and wrap his arms and legs around her, as if he could imprison her heart that way and make it impossible for her to doubt him again.

But instead he just kissed her. Over and over, trying to impress himself upon her.

At last she pushed away. "I've got to go home," she said regretfully.

He let her go, only to walk around the cab of the truck and catch her as she jumped from the steps of the truck to the ground. Holding her up against him, her feet off the ground, he asked her quietly, "And will you remember me tomorrow? Will you think about me?"

"Yes," she told him steadily. "And on Sunday, too."

"I reckon," he said humorously, "that I'm gonna get real excited about comin' to the office on Monday afternoon."

16

It took a long time for Rilla to get to sleep. Maybe it was the nervousness of sliding silently into the kitchen of the dark, empty house, but she doubted it. She just didn't want to go to sleep; she wanted to think of the way Jubal's mouth felt on hers, sweet and hot and heady; of the possessive weight of his hands on her back and in her hair; of the warmth of his body and the narrowness of his waist when she wrapped her arms around him. All those sensations were new and strange and intoxicating.

She closed her eyes and found the distinct lines of his face before her. She heard his words, the teasing ones, the passionate ones, the pleading ones. His words that pressed against her heart, making it ache with a sweet pain.

She could taste him on her lips, and his scent was in her hair.

Maybe she would never sleep again. She had a better way to pass the night—thinking of Jubal.

Tandy had to knock repeatedly on her niece's door Saturday morning before Rilla finally awoke.

"Rilla! Are you all right?"

"Umm, I'm awake," she mumbled aloud at last, blinking at the painfully bright day spilling in her window.

"Thank goodness," Tandy's voice said in relieved exasperation. "We just got home and couldn't find you. I've never known you to sleep this late. Katherine's doing fine—she insisted on coming home, in spite of the surgery."

What was she talking about? Rilla wondered sleepily, trying to marshal her thoughts.

"Come on downstairs and see for yourself."

Sudden remembrance washed over Rilla. The surgery: Katherine was home and alive.

"I'm coming, Aunt Tandy," Rilla said quickly, shoving off the covers. "I guess I overslept. What time is it?"

"Disgracefully late to be asleep still," Tandy answered tartly. "Ten."

Rilla groaned a little, hunting for her shoes. It had been four before she got home. Suddenly a wave of guilt hit her.

As she stumbled into the bathroom, she caught a glimpse of herself in the mirror. She looked perfectly normal, except her pink lips and flushed skin still tingled from Jubal's touch. Quickly she dashed cold water on her face and avoided her own eyes as she did.

Downstairs it was just she and Tandy, who waited patiently, casting only one disapproving look at the clock.

"Where's . . .?" Rilla didn't even want to say his name if it could be avoided.

"Henry left to be at the mill early. Someone was

coming in to see him, maybe. I don't really know. Here—have some cereal or something. You must be starved."

A silence fell while Rilla ate gingerly.

"You don't have much of an appetite," Tandy observed at length. "A good breakfast is the best way to begin a day, Rilla, even if it comes at ten instead of seven."

"I just don't want to eat much right now."

Tandy looked at the cereal Rilla was pushing around halfheartedly in her bowl. "I hope this is not sulkiness on your part because you didn't get to go to the hospital."

For a second, Rilla felt angry. She wanted to tell Tandy sharply that she was not a child. But Tandy's careful face told Rilla that her aunt was worried, and Rilla's own conscience repeated its twinges again. After all, what she'd done last night would be a bigger sin in Tandy's eyes than sulkiness.

"No," Rilla returned abruptly. "I just didn't get to sleep as early as . . . as I usually do, so I overslept. I'm just not hungry. How is Mama this morning?"

"Asleep. They gave her a shot before they sent her home to help her travel."

Now that Rilla looked at Tandy, she could see lines of strain around her eyes. "Maybe I could sit with her tonight," she offered slowly.

Tandy blinked. "Maybe you could," she said consideringly.

"He won't like it."

"Katherine will," Tandy answered calmly. "I'll talk to him, and so will she. He'll do what she wants. It's only fair you should have one night of your own with her. Besides, he stays with her on Sundays so we can go to church. I'll put the cot in there for you, since your bed is upstairs. I can hear from my room, so if she needs anything, and if you don't know what to do, you can call me."

Rilla didn't know why she'd never realized before that Tandy might welcome help, or that Katherine might want her daughter occasionally. But this new knowledge, this awareness of love and the duties it carried, seemed to spring out of the emotions of last night, as though the attraction and the feelings she'd discovered for Jubal had spilled over into her life here, where he was forbidden.

One softness bred another. That thought kept her occupied even when Henry came in as she and Tandy did the dishes.

Rilla ignored him, as she had been doing since the night he'd hit her. He might have been invisible for all the notice she ever gave him, and he returned the favor.

But Rilla got her Saturday night alone with Katherine, and Henry retreated in a somber silence, spending the night shut up in his study.

Before Katherine fell asleep, Rilla finally got up the courage to ask her the question that had bothered her all day. "Mama," she asked slowly, "if you love somebody—really love them—does it make you blind to their faults? Do you see them as good even if the whole world thinks they're not?"

Katherine listened in surprise, then thought about it for a minute. "I don't think so," she said finally. "Maybe you don't like seeing the bad things, but they're there, and you can't avoid them. It never takes long for a man to reveal his true colors. A test comes . . . sooner or later. Then *you* get tested, Rilla. Do you love him enough to overlook the faults, or are they too great? But"—she looked at her daughter on the cot—"a man can be one thing to you, and be completely different toward someone else, even somebody else you love."

They were talking about Henry, Rilla realized suddenly, not about Jubal.

When Katherine spoke again, her voice was calm and determined. "You have to weigh his love for you and yours for him . . . against what he's doing to the other person. You can't be a coward and run from what you find . . . like I've been for years."

"Mama—" Rilla sat up off the cot to lay a hand on the bed beside her in protest.

"But I've set it right, Rilla. Tandy . . . she knows. She says she'll help."

"I've already said that things are straightened out between us, Mama."

"Yes . . . they are. And I'm satisfied. More than you know." Silence reigned in the room for a few minutes before Katherine spoke again worriedly. "The surgery helped, Rilla. The pain is less. But what if I have one of my choking spells tonight? I don't want you . . . to be scared. Not now, or . . . or when the last time comes."

"Don't talk like this. I'll be fine," Rilla answered soothingly, but she *was* afraid, her heart breaking. "So go to sleep, Mama, and don't worry. I'll be here."

Katherine caught at her hands, held them both in hers against her body as Rilla bent over her.

"Just remember . . . when the time comes . . . it won't be me, Rilla. I won't hurt and fight to live. It'll just be my body. Me, I'm going away. Back . . . to the happiest morning, when I ran off with Luke and married him in a little back room of a courthouse in Georgia. Somewhere . . . I could hear a radio playing . . . 'Crazy.' That was the song. 'Crazy for loving you . . .'" Katherine smiled up at Rilla in the darkness of the room. "That's where I'll be. Standing with him in the place where I heard the music. Happy."

After Katherine fell asleep, Rilla turned facedown in the hard little cot, shaking it with her silent, racking tears.

Dying was too hard.

So she made herself think instead of the cool shadows and Jubal's rich kisses. In the memory, she found escape.

By Monday morning Rilla was aching to see Jubal, hoping she could keep her hands off him when he slid into the desk beside hers. But the day was too long for her to wait. Restless, burning up with a electric energy, Rilla could barely concentrate on Rosalie and her numerous tasks.

At two, when the door to the office opened, she was standing near it, waiting, watching, wondering. In the cold light of day, she was uncertain about facing him. What if Friday night—an eternity ago—had been just a temporary fit of madness on his part? And what if she looked at Jubal now and discovered he really was just a roughneck hoodlum?

But his eyes sought her face the instant he stepped through the door, wearing the old coat. Stiff and taut, he stood a second watching her.

Rilla's cheeks flushed, her heart pounded—and his still face broke into a dazzling smile, one she answered.

Then they walked like sedate strangers to the desks, one after the other, past Rosalie as she frowned over her computer screen. And somehow as he put down his papers on the desk, with their backs to the rest of the room, their hands tangled and squeezed, and Rilla found it hard to breathe under his teasing, laughing glance. She was conscious of nothing as they worked except him beside her, and she didn't dare look at him more than once or twice—she'd give the secret away if she did.

She wanted Rosalie to hurry up and leave. Today Henry was in the office with his door shut—she might be able to touch Jubal, to speak to him, if only Rosalie would go off on her bank errand.

But instead she kept working over the computer, and at last, when Jubal could stall no more, he stood to leave.

Longing to speak to him, Rilla looked up and saw the words he'd scrawled across the paper he was sliding slowly across his desk.

The parking lot. He picked up the paper, folded it, and slipped it in his pocket.

There was an urgency in his face when she looked up at him, just before he closed his folder, laid it aside for Henry, and walked out the door.

She watched him from the window in the door; he was heading for the parking lot beyond the shop. Casually, slowly, that was where his steps were leading.

Rilla glanced at the absorbed Rosalie, then at the clock. "I'm almost through with this paperwork," she offered at last. "Do you need me to do something else?"

Rosalie looked up blankly, then her eyes focused on the digital wall clock. "Oh, Lord, is it three already?" she said with a gasp. "I'm going to be late to the bank. Here, Terrill, could you close out this file?"

It took Rosalie ten minutes to get gone. It took thirty seconds for Rilla to get out the door, carrying a handful of papers with her as she went. At least with them she looked as if she were on official business, not out chasing Jubal.

She made a calm-enough walk past the office and

the oak tree, but once around the side of the building and out of sight, she ran breathlessly down the sidewalk, her jacket flying and her cheeks reddened by the chill. By the high wire fence that marked this far end of the parking lot, the end where thick brown ropes of dead honeysuckle vines wove like a dark, complicated lattice through the silver wire triangles, sat Jubal's old truck.

Alone and in the leafless shadows of a sprawled, overhanging sycamore tree.

Where was he?

Her heart thumping in overtime, she waited indecisively. Uncertainly.

Then a movement caught her eye, something over between the truck and the fence, in that isolated corner.

Jubal was standing there, waiting.

Willing her forward.

She ran, twisting between the cars, until she was nearly even with him. Then she stopped, heart pounding, cheeks flushing. He was slender and dark against the blue sky, but his eyes were bright and welcoming, and his hands were reaching for her demandingly.

She was never sure of how they got inside the truck; all she knew was the feel of his lips on hers and his legs and arms wrapping her against him. For a few minutes the only sounds were of their heavy, sharp breaths as they separated, and the sibilant touches of their lips when they met.

Then he pulled away from her mouth reluctantly. "You better come runnin'," he said half-seriously. "When Rosalie Anderson didn't leave, I wanted to die. I waited for two days just to see you this afternoon, and I couldn't even speak to you."

She hugged him fiercely, arms around his waist,

head against his chest. "I know. All I could think of was getting out here before you left. I was afraid I'd dreamed Friday night, or that I really didn't know why you wanted me to come out here."

"Oh, you know," he whispered. "God, it feels so good to hold you." He squeezed her up against him until she could barely breathe, and for a minute it was just the two of them clinging to each other, trying to hold on, trying to satisfy themselves for the hours when they wouldn't see one another.

"You won't be there tomorrow," he said, but it was a question. "But Wednesday—you'll be there Wednesday."

"Yes, if they don't catch me looking at you and make me stay home," she whispered, pulling back to look up at him. "What if I can't keep my hands off you, and I grab you when you walk in?"

He began to laugh. "Try it. We'll find out what happens." And when he kissed her this time, it was slow and clinging. "This corner, and that office, would be lonesomer than hell without you, Rilla," he said at last when they pulled apart. "We gotta think of somethin'. There's gotta be a way for us to be together."

Just then the afternoon whistle sounded, the one that told the workers they had fifteen minutes until quitting time. "Damn it," Jubal muttered in frustration. "How're we—"

But her words cut off his. "I've got to go. They'll catch us. Don't waste time. Kiss me," she demanded, pulling his head down toward her and laughing a little breathlessly. When she tore herself away a minute later and grabbed for the door, she paused to say wistfully, "I'll miss you, Jubal, all day tomorrow."

On Wednesday he wasted no time getting to the parking lot, but he'd barely had time to slide into the truck before she'd followed him. He caught her up without a word and kissed her, and she sighed in satisfaction against his mouth. Her hands, always yearning to touch him, went under his coat, then one slid upward to tangle in the silky dark hair at the nape of his neck.

When he loosed her and she opened her eyes, she had a shaky answer ready. "My gosh. I'm coming out to this parking lot more often."

"No, you're not," he said warningly. "You stay put, right inside that office with your nose to the grindstone, unless I'm out here, too. Behave, Rilla."

She asked impudently, "I'd like to know how you expect me to misbehave when you're not around. There's nobody to be bad with."

"That's good," he retorted. "Just the way I want it."

By Friday he got tired of ignoring her. In the middle of the quiet office while everybody worked, while Rosalie was engrossed in something Henry was explaining to her back in his own office, and nobody was noticing the two of them there alone in the corner, Jubal stretched out his long legs and let his foot touch hers. She jumped, shot a panicked glance around the deserted room and then over at him, and left her foot right where it was. It was a silly thing to do, but he didn't care; he liked the sight of her white leather tennis shoe resting on the top of his boot, just as he liked the light weight riding his foot.

That single innocent touch made him impatient and daring. When Rosalie had gone and Rilla made her escape, when she slid into his arms in the truck that day, he ran his tongue across her lips, forcing her mouth open, kissing her fiercely in a new way. Rilla jerked, startled, but he held her tightly up against him until she stilled.

For once she had no quick answer, no clever retort. She was just very flushed when he let go of her, and she didn't want to look at him when he turned loose.

He pulled her back to him and cuddled her there, wondering if he should have done it. Maybe it was too soon. But that daily touch of the lips and one hug or two was all he had to look forward to. Fifteen minutes every other day.

He had to have more. He'd been thinking about a way to accomplish the feat, and he had only one desperate idea.

"Rilla," he whispered against the top of her head, "meet me tonight. At the mill again."

In his arms, Rilla went still, but her heart gave a heavy thump. These rushed, cautious quarter hours were not enough for her, either, but night meetings were dangerous. Still, she wasn't surprised by his demand; she'd already figured out it was the only way she was likely to be with him for any length of time.

"I want to see you," he said urgently, intently, above her head, and she could feel his fingers spreading on her back, holding her fast to his chest. "I'll wait at the mill. Ten—eleven? Tell me when."

She wanted to, but nerves and her wincing conscience made her hesitate, then push back from him to look up into his eyes. They were impatient and pleading.

"God, Rilla, don't you think I wanta come to the door of your house and do it right?" he burst out at last in the heavy silence. "But I *can't*. They won't let me."

His words tore at her heart, and as always, she hid emotions behind words of her own, teasing and bold. "Are you going to put that silver tongue of yours to such . . . such creative use as you just did a minute or two ago if we meet tonight?" To save her life, she couldn't have stopped the flood of color that washed up into her cheeks.

He pulled in his breath. He was right; it had been too soon, and she'd hated it. "No," he answered shortly. "Since you don't like it."

She laughed a little. "Oh, I think I could—like it . . . after a little practice."

What had she just said? Jubal wasn't sure he'd heard. He stared a minute at this teasing devil, oh, so close, and pure excitement rose in him, trying to push laughter up out of his lungs. "Come here," he said threateningly.

"Who, me?"

"Yeah, you." And when they were nose to nose, he whispered, "Tell me what time to be there tonight. I'm willin' to practice—'til you get it right."

"Eleven," she managed shakily. "Turn on the light at your shop so I'll know you're here. I'm the only one"—he was so near that she could barely think— "who can see the mill from my win—"

His lips closed over hers, and the word was silenced between them.

The night was clear and brisk when Rilla stepped out into it, and her first impression was of a dark, stretching sky sprinkled with bright stars, like so many fireflies pinning up a deep, billowing canopy. She was a little bit scared; after all, it was nearly eleven o'clock, and she was out here for a deliberate, illicit meeting.

But the cold air blew away many things—the memory of Katherine's face tonight, pale as a porcelain effigy, and the emotions and fears that kept the house on heated edge. The wind swept things to her as well, such as the heady anticipation of being with Jubal. He was waiting—she knew it for a certainty the second the light had come on, the minute the wind blew around her, inviting her and tugging her toward the mill.

The truck was in the deep shadows of the alcove between the office and the mechanic shop. She had no hesitation about what she was supposed to do now, and neither did he. He just pulled her into that warm little world they were creating.

But tonight was different. Tonight there was a reason and an intent for being here; tonight they had time—time to savor and to slow down and to explore at leisure.

Somehow he knew of her fear. Holding her next to the warm length of his body, he kissed every inch of her face, the sides of her throat, down to the neck line of her sweater. All slow, gentle, all tender. Then he kissed her fingers and pulled her hands to his face.

It was easy after that. All she had to do was pull his face down to hers. His skin tasted clean, and his lips were willing to cling to hers—and do nothing else.

Yesterday it would have been enough.

But today she had learned something more, so that this time she was the one who opened *his* mouth.

She heard his quick intake of breath and felt the catch in his throat before she slid both arms around his neck and gave herself up completely to this erotic kiss. His tongue answered hers, demanding and swift, and his hands moved restlessly up and down her back.

"Is this practice?" he murmured at last when they pulled apart reluctantly. "I don't reckon I'm gonna make it to the real thing if this is just a trial run. I thought you didn't know how to do that?"

"I didn't. I don't. But I thought about it a lot after this afternoon. I think I'm inspired," she said solemnly.

"I said it before—you're a fast learner," he assured her.

"So I don't need to practice anymore?"

"I *didn't* say that," he answered. "A little extra practice never hurt anybody, did it?"

When as last they broke apart this time, both of them were panting. She said with a tremor in her voice, "I don't think we'd better do any more of this for a while."

He would have kissed her again, but, regretfully, he pulled away. His ragged breathing told him that maybe she was right.

"All right," he answered. "But don't go back home. You just got here. Are you cold?"

"Only a little."

He twisted sideways. "Turn around," he suggested.

"What for?" Somehow his words had been provocative and not too safe.

"Because that way I can hold you and we'll both stay warm. We'll talk—or just sit here."

She hesitated, then slowly did as he asked. So they wound up with him leaning against his door, and her back pressed against his chest. He had one leg up on the seat beside hers, so that she sat in the protective *V* his body made, his arms wrapping her warmly around her stomach, his chin pressing against the side of her temple.

With the steering wheel on one side and the back of the truck seat on the other, she felt safe, nearly hidden, here in the shelter of his arms.

"This is nice," she said at last, her head on his chest. "Why can't we sit like this in the office? I bet

I'd be the best, most cooperative secretary that Henry ever had."

"Not me," he said ruefully. "I wouldn't hear one word the man said. It's rough enough havin' you beside me. I keep tellin' myself not to move, not to look at you because they might notice. Him and Rosalie, they keep their eagle eyes on you."

"I'm getting used to it. He's the same way at home."

"How'd you get out tonight?" Jubal asked curiously. "Will they notice that you're gone?"

"No. Tandy's too busy with Katherine—and Henry, he won't let me come in Mama's room at night when he's there. Not since the night he hit me," Rilla said quietly, without emotion. But she pushed a little deeper into Jubal's arms. "I'm supposed to stay upstairs. In my room."

"You don't get to be with her at all?" he asked in surprised sympathy, pulling her tighter and tighter.

"On Saturday nights. Tandy persuaded him. Or maybe Mama did. Once she wouldn't have said a word to Henry, but now—" Her voice stopped abruptly.

He felt her regret, heard her swallow harshly before she spoke again. "I wish she hadn't waited until she was dying."

Even her last word was clear, but it was an effort.

His chin on her head, his hands and arms warm around her waist, stroking her stomach almost unconsciously, Jubal asked quietly, "How much longer?"

"For Mama? The doctor says spring—maybe." Somehow it didn't hurt so much to say the words because she accepted them as she did everything about her, without a struggle, with calmness.

"That's rough," he answered somberly. "I'd hate for it to be Ma."

"Is your mother like mine?" Rilla asked curiously.

He gave a sudden, deep chuckle that reverberated against her back. "Hell, no. Mine's not about to let up on me. She's got these big ideas for me. Sometimes it's funny what she thinks I can do." Then his voice quieted again. "And sometimes it kills me that I can't be what she expects."

His words might have been Rilla's. She'd thought them herself all too many times. Now, without a sound, she twisted sideways to wrap herself more tightly against him, hugging him to her. "Your mother must have a lot of faith in you," she said slowly.

Jubal shrugged, the movement rubbing against her back. "Yeah, I guess. But it's more than that. She's no fool about me. She's just like a bulldog that won't give up. 'You're gonna get there, Jubal,' she says, 'but you got to keep workin' at it.' It was how she got me through high school when I wanted to quit."

"But you made it. You graduated," Rilla said, and her voice had a question in it.

"I made it. Got a real live diploma," he conceded. "I was nearly nineteen, and then I went straight to prison." His voice was ironic, a little hopeless.

She laid her fingers over his lips, quieting him. "And you made it through there, too. It's over, Jubal. Now you're free to do what you want. Whatever you like."

He was quiet a minute before he smiled down at her. "You might be right. I'm likin' what I'm doin' right now pretty well," he answered teasingly, letting one hand slide up and down her side suggestively.

"Do you, Jubal?" she persisted. "Do you like what you're doing? Are you going to keep working for Henry when your probation is up?"

He hesitated. "I thought maybe after Christmas I'd go to Nashville. It's busy there, and things are shiny new. Too many people, and I don't like cities, but maybe there'd be a job for me."

"You're leaving," she repeated quietly. She'd been half-afraid that this would be his answer; most of the county was hoping it would be. But not Rilla. These last few days she'd tried not to think of Jubal's future, or of anything else beyond right now. Couldn't bear to, because that meant she had to consider Katherine's death. "Did you ever think, Jubal, that life's too hard?" she asked slowly. "That it's not fair?"

He watched her face a minute before he laughed a little in confusion. "You're askin' *me* that kind of question?"

"I just think that somebody who's been through the things that you have would be bitter and hard. But it feels like I'm the one that's bitter, not you."

"You're the one havin' the worst time of it right now, Rilla," he said gently, letting his hand slide up to her nape, under the fall of hair. "I'd be meaner than hell if I had to live with Carroll. But it'll pass. Things will get better."

"How do you know?" she whispered in despair. "What's so good about your life that you believe that?"

"I don't think it's about havin' a good life all the time," Jubal answered, stumbling a little. "Maybe it's just knowin' you're not alone. Sometimes when I'm up on Copper's Bluff or"—he shivered a little—"when I was at Lineville, in all the places I should have been alone, I wasn't."

"What does that mean?" Rilla persisted.

Jubal hesitated before he finally answered ruefully, "Damned if I know. I'm just tellin' you how I feel.

But Rilla, you're not gonna be left alone, no matter what happens. I'll be here if you need me."

"You said you were leaving to go to Nashville," she pointed out reasonably.

"Maybe I don't want to much right now," he offered at last, pressing the side of her face into his throat and against his chest to bend his head over hers. "But I can't go on workin' for Carroll. Never mind why."

She sat too still in his arms, and he dropped a kiss on the top of her hair. "I'll come back. Every weekend if you ask me to. I keep thinkin' that maybe it'd be easier out there where they don't know me." He paused, striving to be casual. "You'll be back in Nashville, too, someday, won't you?"

"I still have a year to go at Belmont," she answered slowly. "I thought that I was coming home for good, Jubal. Every morning in the middle of Rose Hall, I'd look out at the old stone fence that ran around the grounds, and across the top of it I'd see tall buildings and the way things were so crammed together. One skyscraper right against another, and I'd want to be home so much I could taste it. A part of me shriveled up from thirst, waiting to get back. But . . ."

Rilla sat up suddenly, pulling out of the warmth of Jubal's arms. "But when I got here, it was all Henry's ground. Even Daddy's mill. Mama gave it to him. Sometimes I want to fight that, and scream and struggle. But mostly I'm tired of fighting. I don't know what I'm going to do. All these years spent trying to come home, and now I don't even have a place here. I can't stay with Henry once Mama is gone. And I can't bear to go back to living half a life, caught in Rose Hall with Mrs. Denton and all those other girls, either, even if it is the only home I've got where they all want me."

One of Jubal's arms went to the back of the seat on his right; the other, he laid across the top of the steering wheel. "Maybe . . . maybe you belong with somebody else besides any of them," he suggested daringly.

She twisted to look at him, but there were no words.

"Unless you wouldn't want to," he began slowly, "we could see each other when you go back to Nashville. Out there, in the open."

"I don't know yet what this is between us," she whispered painfully. "I'm just trying to hold on to my heart until I figure it out."

"Me, you mean?" His voice was hoarse. "And when you do get me all figured out and find out that I'm only Jubal Kane, what then?"

"If I didn't want to be here, if I didn't like what I've found when I'm with you, Jubal, I'd already have stopped meeting you. Just like you would have me." She leaned closer to toy with the buttons on his shirt a minute, the heat of his leg as it lay along the length of the seat warm against her hips. "You're the one going away before we even get a chance to meet like normal people."

"I wish," he said suddenly, "that I could take you out. Like I guess the others you've been with have done. We could just walk into the movies, or go to a cafe, and nobody would care."

She put her hand over his mouth. "I'd say no to the others if they asked me right now. Maybe we'll do all of that someday, Jubal, if you still want to when this thing with Mama is over. I'm not saying no to *you*, am I?"

Above her hand, his eyes watched her a long, waiting moment, then they began to smile reluctantly. "Well," he said in dubiousness as he caught her hand and pulled it down, "I thought I heard you say no about one thing." He didn't let her answer, just rushed on. "I never meant to tell you any of this, but I wonder what's gonna happen when Christmas is over and I won't be around the mill anymore. I just want to make sure this is not gonna end because I'm a hundred miles away during the week."

She leaned against him again, still as a mouse, considering. "Then do something else, some other job, that keeps you here, Jubal. Don't go away without me."

"*What?* Tell me what. I've been through it and through it," he returned bitterly.

"There's a way. You'll find it—and a job—and I'll help you. I'll show you what to wear, tell you how to say whatever it is you want to say, if you need me to. If that's what's wrong."

If there was a hidden sting in her words, Rilla didn't realize it, and she didn't give his anger time to grow. She rose on the seat in front of him, her hands sliding up his neck to his face, her lips caressing his cheeks.

"You're smart enough to do anything you want, Jubal," she whispered passionately, her face nearly against his. "I've seen it in you, all these weeks I've been sitting beside you at the desk. You do your job, and you're not half trying. You're Henry's best mechanic. You're your mother's best son. Can't you try hard to stay here and—and be *my* best?"

The stark, heavy silence echoed with what she had said. She was half-afraid of her own words; they promised too much, demanded too much.

He said hoarsely. "Your best—what? *What?*

"Whatever you want to be," she faltered.

"I want," he said slowly, "to come up to your front door and ask for you, and I want your people to let you see me. I don't want them to care if I—if Jubal Kane—is the one taking you out. I want people right here in this county to change their minds about me. I don't want to have to run away from everything I am and everywhere I belong." Doubt and despair crept into his voice. "I don't think I can make that happen. There's too much wrong. And I don't know how to begin to change *me* so that I can change *them*."

"You can do anything, Jubal," she whispered. "*We* can. I know."

"Maybe I never really tried before," he said almost to himself. Without realizing it, he had her wrapped up against him again. "Never gave a damn before. Until you."

17

Now they rarely met in the parking lot; it was too open. But Jubal and Rilla had Friday nights—and then they added Tuesday nights as well—from eleven until one. Always secret, always a mingling of passion and compassion for each other in their private world.

They kissed, they caressed, they talked, they dreamed.

Rilla told of her mother. Of Luke. Of Tandy. Sometimes, unwillingly, of Henry. Jubal never condemned, never seemed shocked, never seemed bored.

Jubal talked of his mother, his plans, sometimes of Lineville. He had never in his life had anybody like Rilla to talk to before. Somebody who wasn't surprised because he had feelings and thoughts, somebody who let him reach for the ideas and emotions he'd kept hidden for so long. Before her, girls had been just for a good time and a quick release. If he did without one for months, it was a physical pain. Now there was more—being without Rilla from night until night was a mental anguish, too. He kept saving things in his head to tell her, trying to remember them.

Not that he didn't feel the relationship's physical edge keenly. There was too much contact. He knew it, so did she, but they couldn't stop—wouldn't stop—the torturous pleasure of touching and tantalizing.

She learned to kiss hotly, to tease with her mouth and her tongue, to torment him in all sorts of delicious little ways, but he had nobody to blame but himself, because he taught her most of them. Some of her new knowledge she gained through her own daring experimentation. That was how she came to unbutton the top three or four buttons on his shirt and rub her hands over his collarbone and along the T-shirt he sometimes wore. On the nights he wore none, she touched his smooth bare chest and buried her face in his throat and bit at his ears.

He let her, encouraging her to touch him by sitting under her hands and never losing control, never going too far. Once in a while he brushed the top of her breasts with his lips or his open palm. He touched her knees familiarly. But he forced himself to stop his own kisses and caresses when she wanted him to.

She was the best thing he'd ever had in his life, the closest he'd ever come to heaven.

Not that they didn't argue. She was sharp as often as she was gentle.

Once they argued over his cigarettes. He had started to put one between his lips, and she had reached up and pulled it from him, her eyes teasing and tentative in the dim light.

"Don't smoke," she told him.

"Why not?" he asked warily.

"Because I . . ." She hesitated, then started again. "I like the way *you* taste instead."

He heard what she was really trying to say, that she didn't like the taste of the cigarettes when he kissed her, and it embarrassed him.

"I didn't know it bothered you," he said stiffly, looking straight ahead out the window.

"It's a weakness in me," she said with a laugh. "I like the other things you do with your mouth better," she added provocatively. "And besides, I want you to live to be a hundred, so we can keep meeting in this truck."

He didn't want to be pacified or teased, and he remained stubborn and silent, unmoving.

She took a deep, aggravated breath. "Oh, all right. Here." She tossed the cigarette back at him. "Smoke. Die young. See if I care."

"I *like* to smoke," he said argumentatively.

"I don't," she retorted.

"And you don't want to kiss me when I've been smokin', either," he replied flatly. "Is that it?"

She looked at him in exasperation a minute, then her face broke into a slow, reluctant smile. "I want to kiss you anytime," she answered resignedly. "So you win."

He looked down at the cigarettes. He didn't think he'd like it if Rilla smoked, if she tasted like nicotine and tobacco. What was she doing to him? he asked himself wryly.

"I'll make a deal with you," he told her abruptly. "I won't smoke while I'm with you. Or before I'm gonna see you. How's that?"

"Are you implying," she began in mock indignation, "that I'm going to kiss you every time we're together?"

"I was kinda hopin' it. That was gonna be your part of the deal."

"Well," she said in a slow, thoughtful voice, "it might work. If I were doing a good deed—kissing you to keep you from smoking, you know—I might be willing. How often do you think you'll have the urge to light up?"

"Right now," he began, leaning closer to her, "right now I'm about to die for one." He paused suggestively, and he brushed her lips with his thumb.

"I hate to see you suffer," she said, laughing under her breath.

"I can't help it," he told her. "I'm addicted."

"Oh, great," she whispered back. "That's the best news I've heard today."

Jubal didn't know where they were going; he just knew where he wanted to be—with her.

She made him feel sure and confident, clean and hopeful.

Ma noticed the difference in him. He could tell she knew something was going on. Maybe it was the sudden penchant for neatness he'd developed, or the way he began to look for another job. Not in Cade County, but quietly, in the neighboring counties, where people didn't know him very well.

He put together a lot of facts about himself. A sort of résumé, that was what Rilla called it the night she helped him start it. Just for himself, just so he could see what he could do.

He spread it out on the kitchen table one night after work, and when he looked up from it in frowning concentration, he caught Ma watching him from where she was washing dishes.

"I'm gonna get a new job, Ma," he said, suddenly confident.

Pleasure sparkled in her hazel eyes. "Believin' in

yourself is half the fight, Jubal." Then she walked over to the table, dish towel wrapped around her wet hands, and looked over his head at the list for a long, long moment.

"Ida tells me that there's a man named Hank Barlow who just moved in over at Glover. He's got money and he's looking for a crew. I don't know what kind. Ida says he might get the bid on that contract for the new school at Edmonds if he can put a crew together fast enough. He might even cut Lloyd Allardt out of a chance of building it, and an Allardt has built everythin' that's been built around here for the last twenty years."

"Barlow. But that's the Yankee," Jubal said slowly.

"So I hear. People don't like him. Enos James had a cow to get loose on that big farm of Barlow's, the one he bought when he rolled in here from Royal Oak, Michigan," Maggie said calmly. "Enos never has kept his fences up. His cows have grazed off of his neighbors for years. But instead of just callin' Enos to come and get the cow like everybody else does, Barlow got all up in the air and butchered her. Then he sent Enos half of the meat, and Barlow thought he was doin' the right thing. He can't figure out why everybody's mad at him."

Jubal's mouth quivered in exasperated amusement. "He's a damn fool."

Maggie made a silent facial expression of agreement. "But the fact is, Barlow's got money, and he can't get men. Not any good ones, like you'd be. They're scared of the Allardts, and they don't like him."

"He doesn't know me," Jubal said slowly, looking down at the paper. Barlow. Maybe there was hope. He'd done worse in his life than work for a Yankee.

"Reckon you've quit thinkin' about goin' to Nashville." Ma said it matter-of-factly.

"I don't know. It depends. But maybe I'll stay for a little while longer."

"Good," she said on a deep note of satisfaction.

Maybe Rilla and Ma had more in common than they could ever dream, he thought wryly.

Bobo noticed the change in him, the very next time he tried to get him to go to the Lonesome Pine and Jubal refused. It wasn't that he didn't sometimes miss the place; once in a while, he wished for its loud, noisy friendliness and its raw electricity. It wasn't that he didn't need a girl—in fact, sometimes after a date with Rilla, after all that kissing, he'd wonder if he'd make it without one.

But the Lonesome Pine wasn't part of the bright dream that had Rilla at its center; it only made his dissatisfaction and his hunger worse, and it never satisfied, just as the girls there never did.

Bobo looked at him in disgust after Jubal refused his invitation for the third time, then threw up his hands and turned to walk away. But he stopped abruptly and wheeled as a thought hit him. "It's a girl, ain't it?" he asked. "You got one somewhere you're seein'."

Jubal couldn't stop the hot flush that slid slowly, betrayingly, up into his face, and Bobo, seeing it, said in triumphant relief, "I knew it. A woman." Then he laughed. "Hell, I shoulda figured that if you wasn't goin' to the Pine, it was because you had somethin' private goin'. Hope you're gettin' lucky, boy," he said suggestively, grinning.

Jubal didn't answer; it was better that way. And his face didn't even reveal the fact that Bobo's comment made him angry. He *was* lucky, but not in the way Bobo meant.

Not even Henry Carroll bothered him lately. Katherine was sinking fast—somebody said she had to have oxygen part of the time now, just to breathe—and when Carroll wasn't with her, he was in his office, brooding, pondering, sitting in a silent, moody, black trance.

Jubal tried not to think of the man, or of the woman dying in the house across the hollow; he just kept hoping that things would work out, even if he didn't know how.

Rilla alone understood Jubal's exuberance: she shared it. What nights she didn't spend the hours between eleven and one with him, she was thinking of him, dreaming of the way his body felt, the way his mouth and skin tasted, the way she could never get enough.

Sometimes she'd look over at him out of the corner of her eye in the office, and a hot rush of sweet pain would shoot through her. Those long, agile fingers with their pronounced knuckles: she had caressed them, kissed them in the darkness the night before. His hair, that stubborn, heavy, soft wave just behind his ear: she had pushed her hand through it. She'd touched him, held him; she knew things about him.

Let the rest of them pull away, or be afraid, or whisper and speculate. Rilla knew the truth. Nights with Jubal Kane. She had them.

The man of the still face and dark reputation was pure delight, and she meant to hold on to him.

The knowledge brought changes in her.

Tandy noticed. Not that she complained, because the new Rilla was quieter, more abstracted, less likely to denigrate Henry or argue with her aunt. Tandy, ironically, became more sympathetic, more lenient, certain that her niece was grieving over Katherine.

Henry, too wrapped up in his own woe, didn't see anything different. He was silent and apart now, and though Rilla sometimes looked and found his carefully blank stare on her face, they rarely spoke.

Rosalie probably noticed a change: Rilla's ability to concentrate dropped, in part because she couldn't seem to focus on anything but Jubal in her good moments and Katherine in her bad ones and in part because the late hours she was keeping often now, coming in stealthily at one, so wild and keyed up that she didn't sleep until nearly dawn, were making it difficult for her to work.

Katherine knew. Rilla told her, at least in part. She couldn't let Mama die without sharing this part of her life. So one Saturday night when it was just Katherine and her in another painful vigil, Rilla told her half-asleep mother about Jubal. Oh, not much. Not his name, or the bad things. Just how much he cared, how good he was, how beautiful. Maybe Katherine understood her daughter's emotions. She caught her last words, and asked croakily, "Luke was beautiful. Inside. Is your . . . friend?"

"Yes. In his heart and everywhere else," she answered, laughing.

"Be . . . sure," Katherine faltered. "Don't get hurt. Don't make a mistake."

"I won't, Mama. I promise," she told Katherine solemnly. "I think he loves me."

18

"*There was an* old movie—years and years ago—called *The Man Who Played God.* Have you ever heard of that movie, Kane?"

Henry Carroll asked the question out of the blue, his hands in his pockets as he gazed out the window of his office, across the hollow toward home.

"No," Jubal answered finally.

"That'd be something, wouldn't it? To set things like you want them. To put your life in order. Get rid of the things and the people that make living wrong. To stop people from dying." Carroll might not even have been talking to Jubal; his words were little more than murmured musings.

It made Jubal uncomfortable; he stayed silent.

"I'd like to try it." Carroll turned abruptly from the window, his odd behavior falling from him. "But what would I know about playing God? I can't even keep one down-at-the-heel mechanic like you in line," he mused.

"All I'm complainin' about is the drivin'. That wasn't part of the job," Jubal said patiently. "I've hauled two on pure luck. If I get caught—"

"You won't get caught. It's a back road, and I know both DOT officers for the area. I *know* them." Carroll said it meaningfully.

"Let Bobo do it. Hell, I'm already on the edge. He ain't on probation, and it's *his* job," Jubal said stubbornly. "I'm involved too much. This ain't right."

Carroll snapped his hand against the desk in an efficient, fierce movement. His black eyes glittered with fury. "Don't you tell *me* what's too much, or what's right. You're here because I made it possible. You knew the score. I'm sick of the bellyaching. Don't be a fool, and stop pushing me. I may not be able to play God too often, but you're right where I want you, and it's where you're going to stay, if you've got a lick of sense."

Jubal's face was white, and he straightened until his shoulders felt stiff. "You make me think of somebody else I know. But I'm through with her, just like I want to be out of this rotten, no-good deal with you. When this probation's up at Christmas—"

Henry laughed, a low, silky sound. "So that's what's in your head. That's the reason for this minor rebellion. I've taught you all the tricks of the game, put you in the middle of it, and now you think you'll walk."

Jubal knew better than to answer this man with the glittering eyes; he'd said too much already. So they faced one another like predator and prey. Jubal was pretty certain he knew which one of those he was in this twosome.

"We'll see," Henry concluded suddenly, and sat down on the chair behind the desk. "We'll see, won't we? But I don't want to hear any more from you,

Kane, except when you come to tell me tomorrow morning that this load's been delivered. Now get out of my office, and take your scruples with you. Where in the hell did you get them, anyway?"

"What are you doin' out here?" Jubal demanded irritably that afternoon when he went to the Peterbilt to drop the paperwork into it.

Bobo Hackett was just hauling himself backward out of the passenger side, and Jubal's curt question surprised him so much that he jumped, missed the step down, and fell clumsily to the ground.

"Jubal!" he exclaimed, hauling himself up. He stared at the man opposite him a minute, then dusted himself off with shaky hands. "Hellfire, boy, you scared the daylights outta me."

"Seein' you's not doin' much for me, either," Jubal said, pulling himself up by the route Bobo had tumbled past. He tossed the packet onto the sleeper, and as he jumped down, Bobo watched him uneasily.

Jubal snorted. "If you're thinkin' that I'm wantin' to punch you a good one for not takin' this load, then you're thinkin' right. Dammit, Bobo, this is your job. I'm doin' enough already."

"Talk to Carroll about it."

Jubal gave his opinion of Carroll in one ugly word. "And if you like drivin' so much that you're out here hangin' around the truck—"

"I was just out here lookin' for a knife I lost last week when I hauled a load of logs from the timber reserve up at Dural, that's all. I ain't wantin' to drive tonight. Guess I'll go to the Pine."

"Yeah? Well, you have a good time," Jubal returned shortly. He wouldn't get much of one; there'd be no seeing Rilla this particular Friday night.

*   *   *

Carroll showed up at eight at the mill yard that night, just as Jubal finished checking the straps that held the load in place. Standing under the purply security light, Carroll waited until Jubal had finished before he spoke.

"Make sure these engines get delivered and dropped before eleven-thirty tonight. Stick to the same routine you used the last two times."

"I tell you what, Mr. Carroll," Jubal said quietly, gazing down on him from the driver's seat, "why don't you haul the damn load yourself?"

Carroll smiled. "Be careful, Kane. Be careful."

Anger pushed him along that night, and he made the trip in good time.

When he got headed back, he was too tired to sustain the anger. He'd worked all week, been with Rilla one night, and worked two long overtimes to get these engines ready. And to make matters worse, Carroll expected him to show up for the half day that the mill stayed open tomorrow, Saturday.

Maybe it was a good thing that he didn't see Rilla on Saturday nights. If he'd thought he could, he'd be fool enough to meet her there again and lose another night's sleep.

He didn't need to do that; he was dog-tired. In fact, he was having trouble staying awake now, nearly hallucinating because he was so exhausted. He could have sworn there were blue lights flashing in the heavy trees up ahead, just beyond the curve.

They had to be an illusion. This was the middle of nowhere, the middle of the night . . . and when he'd glimpsed those lights, they'd looked like the ones used by police for a roadblock.

No, it wasn't the police.

When the big Peterbilt swung around the curve, Jubal found out what it was and lost his sleepiness.

It was the DOT. Great watchdog of American highways. The Department of Transportation.

"I *know* them," Carroll had said just today.

Damn you, Henry Carroll. What are you trying to do to me? I thought you had this all fixed.

No CDL. None of the right permits. And he was underage for this kind of driving to boot. Big, big trouble.

The man who flagged him down shined a giant flashlight up into his face when Jubal opened the door. Jubal winced, blinked; all he could make out was the officer's chin. Pointed and young.

Don't give anything until they ask for it, that was the rule to play by here.

"Yeah?"

"Identify the truck and yourself, driver."

"The truck's from Carroll Mills in Bethel, Tennessee. The name and number are on the side. I work for the mill."

"Out awful late, aren't you, for a sawmill truck?"

"I just haul where they tell me, when they tell me."

"Where's the trailer?" The officer swung the lights beyond the back of the truck. Nothing but a set of wheels there.

"I left it at a pickup yard with the load on it."

"Um-huh."

Dammit, who did the man think he was? A doctor examining a patient? And where were the important questions, like, Where in the hell is your CDL? Jubal felt sweat on his neck and back, cold and clammy here in the chilly night.

The man examined the back of the tractor, circling it with his light. Jubal waited, keeping quiet and still, until the door on the passenger side opened unexpectedly and the officer hauled himself up inside the cab.

"What are you doin'?" Jubal demanded roughly, startled. In the cab lights, the officer was pale and red-haired. He looked all of eighteen, and he was very, very pleased with himself.

"The DOT has the right to search any and all trucks, inside and outside." The flashlight swung to the sleeper berth. "Turn off your engine, driver."

The officer's free hand slid over the sleeper berth, then went to its edge, his fingers slipping down between the heavy mattress that filled it and the metal rail that held it in place. Searching.

Jubal didn't turn off anything; instead he froze as a hundred clamoring alarms went off in his head.

Carroll. This was Carroll's doing. *Be careful, Kane,* and that smug-as-a-damn-cat smile.

And Bobo. My good old buddy Bobo.

A setup. *A setup.*

The officer knew exactly what he was looking for, and when he pulled it from its hiding place at the edge of the mattress, Jubal found out, too.

He stared at the plastic bag and the white, powder-like substance it held.

Suspended disbelief—this couldn't be happening.

A tiny blood vessel roaring in his ear.

And off in the dark, shadowy woods beyond, past the malicious, triumphant eyes of the DOT officer opposite him, Jubal heard the wind shrill even over the sound of the big engine. Over the sound of his heart.

"A little something to ease life's pain, driver?"

No. No. *No.* I'm not getting involved in somebody

else's schemes and taking the rap for it. Never again, he thought wildly.

Jubal didn't remember even planning what he did. Panic and fury drove him to it.

He just leaned across the cab and with one hand snatched the bag. With the other, he gave the officer the hardest shove he'd ever given anybody.

The officer screamed, made a futile grab at anything, dropped the flashlight, and toppled backward out of the open door into the shadowy night.

The truck lunged forward, black smoke shot from the stacks, and Jubal, who'd never turned off the motor, never dropped below fourth gear, went through six more in less than thirty seconds.

He scraped the side of the DOT car with his wheels as he shot past it. Shouldn't leave it parked in the middle of road, he thought viciously. When the truck screamed around one of the hairpin curves and an overhanging oak branch got in its way, he tore off the mirror on the right side and dented the still opened door. Like a careening drunk, the Peterbilt slid sideways and skidded in loose gravel before it slipped onto the crumbling narrow shoulder of the road.

Running an inch or two from the deep black hollow at the road's edge, an inch or two that separated living from dying.

Fighting to control the big machine. Fighting to hold on to the wheel and his life.

Patchy fog swirled like a gleeful demon in his headlights, blinding him, and he wrenched the wheel to the left.

No brakes. Don't hit any brakes. Not here, or me and this truck are going straight to flaming glory by way of a Kentucky hollow.

When the mad fog cleared, he was in the middle

of the road, riding the faded white line. Still alive, out where the road was smoother, wider.

No DOT, no officer, no blue lights in his rearview.

He slowed a little, but the truck and his heart were both still making eighty when he finally hit the dividing point in the road, one highway east, one south to the state line.

Beyond a store that advertised Kentucky lottery tickets for sale in the silent little circle of buildings that made up the town of Gamaliel at midnight, he stopped.

That was when his hands began to shake. He wanted to climb down out of this truck if he could make his legs walk; he wanted to throw up.

But first, frantically, he searched the interior of the truck. Nothing else but this one bag, and he opened it to let the contents pour out the window. Then he threw the bag to the wind.

By the time he got outside in the cold air, hugging the shadows along the side of the truck, he wasn't sick anymore. Breathless, furious, afraid—he was all of that, instead.

Carroll had tried to frame him tonight.

And Bobo.

He'd been the one who first came to Lineville, to tell Jubal what Carroll wanted to do. "All you have to do is work for him, and he'll get you out." That was the one conversation Jubal had never told Maggie about.

Bobo had a dozen epithets for Carroll when his back was turned, none of them complimentary, but he always went when Carroll crooked his finger.

He'd gone to this Peterbilt this afternoon, and he'd planted what looked like cocaine in his friend's truck. Jubal had never touched drugs in his life. Even Frankie, hard-core as he was, hadn't messed around with anything except homegrown marijuana, and even that on a small scale.

When Jubal hoisted himself up into the Peterbilt for the rest of the trip home, he had two thoughts.

He wondered what was going to come out of his scuffle with the DOT—he'd be damned if he'd admit that the man even stopped him when he got asked.

And he told himself to get a grip on his foaming temper: he didn't want to kill his low-down, back-stabbing good ol' buddy Bobo when he found him. He just wanted to beat the hell out of him.

At one thirty in the morning, the Pine was beginning to wind down so Autry could go home at two.

The only people left in this place were the band, gathered around a table in a far corner, a handful of people at the pool table, Bobo Hackett—and an acquaintance.

Dusty Bainbridge.

He'd actually brought Dusty to the Pine. Jubal couldn't stomach him with his body-builder, weight-lifting body and big mouth, the one Dusty had been honing on him for weeks now. The man was a bruiser and a bully, and he liked to fight.

Maybe Bobo meant for Dusty to do his fighting tonight, maybe he'd brought him for protection just in case Jubal got free from the DOT and showed up, but that was just too damn bad. Grimly, Jubal shoved his way past the chairs to get to the two of them. Bobo saw him coming; he'd been watching the door. Now he jumped to his feet, already beginning to talk.

"You keep away from me, Jubal. Whatever your problem is, it's got nothin' to do with me. You—"

Jubal grabbed the front of Bobo's black sweatshirt and stepped right into him. Bobo gaped up at him.

"How you doin', good buddy? Bet you're real surprised to see me here. Maybe you thought I'd spend the night somewhere up in Kentucky. All cozy, locked up tight."

Bobo swallowed, then tried to laugh. "I don't know what'n the hell you're talkin' about."

"I'm talkin' about"—and Jubal's voice got louder and louder—"a little problem I had tonight. About a 'knife' you went huntin' for in my truck."

At that moment, Dusty intervened. "If you're lookin' for a fight, Kane, don't just stop with Hackett. I'm here, too."

Jubal's gaze switched to the other man. "You stay the hell outta this. When I'm through with *him*"—he gave Bobo's shirt a hard jerk—"then we'll talk, or fight, or whatever else it is you've been pushin' me to do ever since the first day I came to work at the mill."

Jubal's hand jerked Bobo's shirt a second time, knocking Bobo onto the chair beside him. The people left in the bar had realized what was happening; the band members edged a little closer, watching, listening, waiting right along with the few frowsy-looking customers still standing around.

"We're gonna talk about how I took the rap for you once, Bobo," Jubal said menacingly, his face not six inches from the shorter man's. "About how you set up this job for me with Carroll. An' about how I wound up in front of a DOT officer tonight with a little cargo I didn't know I was haulin'. An' most of all"—Jubal's words got quieter, softer, but more dangerous—"about how I ain't goin' back to jail, not for Carroll, not for you, not even for St. Peter."

"You're crazy. Get off." Bobo gave a hard shove that sent Jubal backward, forcing him to turn loose of the shirt. "I ain't tellin' you nothin'."

But Jubal came back instantly to stand his ground.

"I reckon we'll see," he said somberly, and hit him.

Autry came out hurriedly from the bar, a glass and a towel in his hands, soap up around his arms. "Y'all ain't bustin' the place up, now!" he yelled.

Band members scrambled to safety as Bobo stumbled backward into them, blood splattering from his nose, and he swore in surprise and pain as he fell into the wall.

Dusty made a dive for Jubal, roaring like a bull ape, knocking him flat on his back, but before he could do more damage, Autry and his bouncer had him, hauling him off.

"You can damn well wait your turn!" Autry hollered. "Get off. And take the two of them outta here," he shouted toward the band members. "Take it outside, or I'm callin' the law!"

Jubal pulled himself to his feet, knocking away the drummer who meant to haul him away. "I'm willin'," he panted, his face red. "I'm *ready*. Get outside, Bobo. Unless you're gonna hide behind Bainbridge again."

Bobo was still feeling his nose, looking at the blood in stupefaction. Then his gaze shifted to Jubal and his face went dark with fury. "Hell, yes, I'll fight you. You lead the way."

It took eight and a half minutes to beat Bobo's face to a bloody pulp, and Jubal didn't fare a whole lot better. Bobo was older and heavier, but Jubal had grown up with Frankie Kane, who'd fought with the best of them, or with his little brothers if all else failed.

And Jubal was aflame with fury.

"Now you tell me *why*," he said panting, looking down at the bloody face under him.

"Hell, no." Bobo flared weakly, trying to rise. But Jubal's hands shoved him back down.

"Have it your way, then. But if you don't talk, I'm goin' straight to Ned Standford. I'll tell him ever' damn thing I know."

Bobo stared through his swollen eyelids. "I never thought I'd live to see the day that a ridge runner would run to the law, and you a Kane, at that," he gasped.

"Don't give me any talk about what I ought to do," Jubal said derisively. "I told you—I'm never goin' to jail again. And if I wind up framed for somethin', I'm takin' you down with me. Carroll, too. I mean it, Bobo. I swear to God I do."

"You'd turn us in?"

"In a minute, you bastard. Stick it to you just like you tried to do me tonight," Jubal answered, his voice implacable.

Bobo breathed heavily a few minutes before he finally spoke again. "Let me up, then. I'll talk." He had to prop himself up on the hood of a nearby truck, but Bobo managed to stand in the dark, quiet parking lot.

Autry had cut off the lights and shut the doors; his big bouncer guarded it now, fifty feet away, making sure nobody else got outside to horn in on this fight.

"He ain't gonna let you go, Jubal."

Jubal frowned. "What?"

"Me'n you, we know too much. We know those big engines are stolen straight out of some factory, smuggled out part by part." Bobo stopped to spit blood on the ground, groaning as he straightened. "Hell, I even seen the man from that plant that gets 'em out once. Wouldn't recognize him again, don't know his name, but he don't know that. Scares me to death. He's some big executive with the company he's stealin' from. An' you, Jubal, you put them engines back together. You do all the paperwork, the real papers an' the dummy papers. We've both hauled 'em to a buyer. Carroll's got your signature on ever'thing, and mine on whatever's left over."

He grunted painfully as he tried to straighten.

Jubal felt the tightening of muscles in his throat; his voice was hoarse. "I know all that. It was the deal. If he'd get me out of Lineville, I'd do it, until the end of probation. And he can't show those papers to the police without them knowin' he's been involved. He's not got me that way. That way's a standoff."

Bobo tried to snort. "That's what tonight was about. He has two DOT officers in his back pocket. They leave the road wide open for him. But the man tonight—he was a phony. Part of the setup. You was supposed to think he was real, that he'd caught you with coke and was gonna write you up. But it was nothin' but sugar. Carroll was goin' to act like he got you out of trouble with the DOT, but he was gonna keep the report. Hold it. Have it over your head. Make you think he'd use it against you if you left the job."

Numbness settled over Jubal; it didn't even feel as if he were there. He was only watching the scene. Bobo peered at his dark, terrifying face.

"I didn't have no choice, Jubal. He don't need me. What I'm doin', any fool can do. But you, you're the whole works. You got them hands, and you know how to make things run. So Carroll says to set you up, or else he takes me down. An' Lily, she's pregnant, Jubal."

There was a long, long pause. Jubal could hear himself breathing, could feel his heart slowing down to a heavy, painful thud . . . thud . . . thud.

"Carroll's in it, too, up to his neck."

"You can't prove nothin' if you go to Standford. Even if you could, I might go to jail; you sure as hell would. But Carroll ain't comin' down. Any paperwork, or anythin' that'd prove him guilty, he's got it hid somewhere, I think, in that office. I can't find it, but I know it's there. Don't ask me how I know."

Bobo looked away from Jubal's face, lighted by blazing eyes. "I ain't got nothin' against you, Jubal," he protested defensively. "You did me a favor—went to Lineville 'thout a word about me. I did you one. You wanted out. I got you out. What'd you expect? That Carroll would just let you go, like he said? You ain't that dumb. An' he's payin' you, ain't he?"

"You son of a bitch." Jubal's voice was heavy. There was nothing left to say—or do. So he turned and strode away toward the dark dawn.

The bouncer moved from the door behind him in relief, and the instant that he did, Dusty spilled out of it.

Jubal was already at his truck when Dusty started after him.

"Kane!" he bellowed. "You promised me a piece of your hide. I been waitin' for too long just to see how tough a pretty boy like you can be. You ain't runnin' now."

"Wait, Dusty," Bobo called feebly.

Jubal knew he had two sore hands, a jaw that ached, and ribs that made him feel as if he'd been squeezed by a bear. But his heart was pumping with fury; his whole body felt outraged.

He turned back to Bainbridge. "I'm through runnin'. Come and take me down—if you think you're big enough."

19

"*Kane's not here* today," Rosalie said in surprise.

"He's not?" Rilla's heart fell a little. The best thing about Monday—or any day—was seeing him at work.

"Neither is Bobo Hackett, or Dusty Bainbridge. Of course, Bainbridge has missed a few Mondays before. Too much of *this*"—Rosalie raised her eyebrows and made a mime of drinking with her hands—"on the weekends."

Rilla stared. "You don't mean you think Jubal—"

"I used to. But he's been steady as a rock since he came to work here." Rosalie grimaced. "I never thought I'd hear myself say that about a Kane. But maybe eight months is his limit. Maybe he had a spree this weekend. Can't ever tell about those ridge runners."

She clucked a little as she swung back around on

her swivel chair. Beyond her, Terrill sat wordlessly, torn between her anger at Rosalie's words and the reassurances she was giving herself: Jubal wouldn't behave that way. He wasn't that kind of person.

That afternoon, Bobo came in to work at last.

When Carroll called him in, Rilla, Rosalie, and a buyer who'd come to the office to pay his bill all stopped and stared.

Hackett's face was black and blue; one hand was wrapped and bandaged.

"That must have been some fight he was in," the buyer commented dryly as Bobo went into Carroll's office. "I wonder what the other man looks like?"

The other man.

Without a word, Rilla went to the filing cabinet. The door to Henry's office was near and not shut completely.

". . . in the hell went on?" Henry was saying angrily.

"There was a fight at the Pine, that's all," Bobo said evasively.

"A fight."

"That's right. Me and Dusty and . . . and Jubal."

A long, pregnant pause.

"Now there's what I wanted to know. At last," Henry said smoothly.

"It was no big deal. Dusty made some smart-ass cracks about Jubal being such a pretty face, and Jubal finally got mad."

Henry's voice was slow in coming and sarcastic. "And he didn't say a word about getting stopped in the Peterbilt Friday night?"

"No, and I was waitin' for him to. I was gonna play dumb. I thought it fell through, but maybe that was why Jubal wanted to fight. He came in red hot. I got away light compared to Dusty. He won't be in to work for a week or two."

"I don't give a plug nickel about Dusty," Henry said dangerously. "But Kane—"

"I didn't know that kid had it in him to fight like that," Bobo interrupted hurriedly. "And I don't know who won. Jubal fell first—he was all beat up. But he drove hisself home. Dusty had to be carried."

"I really don't care." Henry apparently threw papers on the desk; Rilla heard their swishing sound and the *plop* as they hit the surface. "You know what I want to talk about. The deal went wrong Friday night."

A pause.

"It did?"

"I suppose you didn't know that?"

"Why would I? Who'd tell me, except you? I couldn't say, 'Did you get stopped?' to *him*, could I?"

Rilla moved away from the door unobtrusively as Carroll's footsteps neared it. His hand appeared momentarily at the crack between the door and the jamb, before he slammed it completely shut on Hackett's cautious voice.

All Rilla understood was that Jubal had gone back to that bar where he'd once met a girl who'd put her mouth on his throat. She couldn't stand the thought, so she went to the water fountain in the far corner, trying to wash away the lump in her throat.

He'd gone to pick a fight, just the way Bobo Hackett would have.

And Dusty Bainbridge.

Rilla couldn't reconcile the Jubal she knew at midnight with the man Bobo had just described.

That man—Bobo's Jubal—was the one she'd first met here in this office.

Hell-bent. Bad.

She felt somehow betrayed by what Bobo said had happened. Uncertain. Afraid.

Why, Jubal? Why?

Or have you been lying to me about what you are?

Sleet was falling in a thin, cold sheet when Jubal reached for the light switch, the one that would turn on the electric bulb in his shop at the back of the mill. It was the light Rilla could see the most easily from her window.

His hand wavered and fell.

They'd never met on a Monday night. She might not know that he meant the light as a signal, or that it was he.

But by now she had to know what was wrong, why he hadn't been there today. And if she'd heard he'd been in a fight at the Pine, he was pretty sure there was going to be some explaining he had to do.

On the other hand, maybe he should just leave her alone. He was nothing but trouble. Even knowing that what he was doing was wrong, he'd tried to justify it, to tell himself he had to get out of Lineville, that it was Carroll's scheme and he was just a tiny, reluctant part of it.

But when Bobo had his deeds put into stark, black-and-white terms Friday night—putting together stolen engines—it had left him squirming with guilt.

Ma didn't know what her son, the one she hoped and prayed for, was doing. Not what kind of dirty little deal had really taken him from Lineville. She'd be heartbroken.

And Rilla. When this had first started, he'd never thought she'd become so important to him. She'd kissed him, touched him—and he was neck deep in a cesspool of dishonesty. He'd put hands on her, knowing he wasn't fit to.

He was right down there with Henry Carroll, whom she hated. Linchpin in her stepfather's upwardly mobile little business. It damn well served him right to have Carroll turn on him now. Like Ma would say, you reap what you sow.

But Rilla didn't know. Nobody was going to tell. Maybe, Jubal thought, he wasn't doing anything any worse than a hundred other men did every day in boardrooms and under the table.

He wasn't going to hurt her or bring her down with him. He just needed to see her. And she needed to see him, now, so she could view the damage Dusty had inflicted on his painfully tender face. Otherwise she'd react at work Wednesday in front of people.

That was a good rationale for signaling her tonight.

Airy little gusts of fine sleet still blew in when he finally switched on the light. They peppered his legs, and he tried not to shiver so his ribs wouldn't hurt when he did. But the cold little pellets felt good against him; they chilled some of his anxiety.

Even a man like him needed a woman like Rilla, he thought.

He needed her to lay cool fingers and warm lips on him.

Even if she didn't, if she spit at him like an angry cat, it was better than remembering Tess, or Carroll, or Bobo. She'd make him believe that he had some good in him, no matter what anybody else said.

Forgiveness or anger—which would she bring?
Come on, Rilla, whatever it's to be.
Hurry, while I'm still standing.

*   *   *

He was under the awning, his face and shoulders deliberately in the shadows, leaning heavily against the door frame. She saw his old boots, his jeans, the red plaid of the flannel shirt as it hung around his hips.

Sleet crackled against the side of the silent building as they stood for an instant facing each other. It stung her cheeks and hung, a sparkling captive, in the fur of the hood that lined her face; it pattered on his boots and against his dark hands as they lay in the folds of his arms, crossed against him.

Then he moved silently to reach behind him and turn off the light, leaving them to stand in darkness.

Each waiting.

"You came," he managed at last.

"You turned on the light so I would," she returned quietly, wrapping her arms around her waist to keep warm.

He took a slow step toward her. "I guess you heard why I wasn't at work today."

"I heard. You were in a brawl at the Pine with Bobo and Dusty." Her voice was cool and reserved. "You beat up on both of them."

Anger. It was going to be anger. His shoulders slumped a little; he was too tired for the emotion, after all.

"I didn't go lookin' for trouble, Terrill."

"Didn't you?"

"Somethin' went wrong with the delivery Friday night. Part of it was Bobo's fault. I got mad. An' I went to find him."

"How lucky for you that he was at one of your favorite dives," she said with cold irony.

"I only went because he was there," Jubal returned after he'd considered her words. "Bainbridge was with him."

"You went because you wanted to fight," Rilla said flatly.

A long pause, while sleet danced around them.

"I *had* to fight," he answered finally. "You can only push a man so far, Rilla, and I've been shoved around for a long time."

She moved a tiny bit, almost uncertain. He wanted to plead, but he didn't. He had pride left, at least.

"So you shoved back. And what did they . . . did they do to you?" Her voice shook a little.

"They didn't kill me, at least." His voice was wry.

Now she was the one who stepped toward him, and her hands came up unexpectedly to touch his face.

His wet skin quivered under her fingers as she traced his features, finding the swollen side of his face first. He heard the breath in her throat, saw the gleam of her eyes, as her hands slid over his cut lip, his sore jaw, his abrased cheek, his eye—

"Umh." He made the sound involuntarily, trying not to pull away. "That hurts."

Her fingers weren't angry at all; they were soft and gentle. But then she grasped his chin, turning his head a little while her gaze tried to assess him.

"Your face is a mess," she whispered after two attempts to speak.

"You oughta see the rest of me," he said, trying to ease the tension. His hands clenched at his sides. He wanted to reach for her, but then his temple began to throb viciously, and he backed a little away from her to rest against the shop door.

He'd thought the sleet would keep him more alert than this.

"No. I don't think I want to." She stepped away, too.

"Why don't you just come out and say whatever it is that's botherin' you, Rilla?" he asked quietly.

She looked away, out at the empty mill yard. "Tonight you're like the man you were the first time I ever saw you. I don't know you. You scare me."

"Don't know me? I'm exactly the same one I was the last time I was with you," he returned, and a flare of temper edged his voice. There was fear, too: he needed her to believe he was of some account. Had she quit now?

"I don't like you fighting at a bar," she said tightly.

"I had to. Don't you understand? If I'd taken what they were doin', I'd be—" He couldn't think of words, so he tried again. "A man can't let this world, or even a woman, castrate him. Not if she expects him to be worth havin'. You're strong, girl. Sometimes you remind me of your aunt. And that's okay, if you'll see that I've got to be, too. I have to try to hold my own."

"And this is the way you do it?" Her voice cracked; her composure shattered. She wanted to cry for his face, for the way his skin had been feverish to her touch, for the brutality he'd waded into. She wanted to hate him for going to a place she was afraid of. And it poured out in her words. "Where's the man I meet at night, Jubal?"

He didn't answer.

"The men I know—the ones I'm used to—don't fight with their fists. They act like gentlemen."

He stood like a statue, looking down at her. "Men like Henry Carroll, you mean?" he said bitingly. "There's a 'gentleman,' now. But you know what? I don't think Dusty, or Bobo, woulda understood what I had to say any other way. I don't reckon I coulda done it any different, either."

"So you don't care what I think. You don't care that I can't stand to see you hurt like this." Her voice caught, then cracked with temper. "What did you come here tonight for, anyway, Jubal?"

He started toward the truck, moving stiffly.

"What?" she called after him.

"I reckon you better go home. And while you're at it, find one of those 'gentlemen' to push around. Me, I'm gonna quit hangin' around like some stray hound, waitin' for a pat from you."

"You can probably get that"—Rilla called after him on a hard sob as he opened the truck door—"from one of the girls at the Pine."

Maggie's face was rigid as she dabbed Jubal's bare back and side with a stinging antiseptic. Flinching a little, he tried not to grimace; his bruised face was too sore to allow much movement without an equal amount of pain.

"I hope," Maggie said in little short bursts of effort as she pulled a bandage over a long cut from Dusty's ring, "that she was worth this, boy."

"It wasn't over a girl," he said somberly.

Maggie screwed the cap back on the antiseptic before she walked around in front of him to stare at his bruised face. "You're lucky that this eye's not swelled shut completely this mornin'."

"I'll be lucky to walk," he groaned, trying to get up with the least amount of effort.

Maggie watched her battered son a long, silent moment. "You're beat half to death, but you managed to drag yourself outta the house late last night. You're gonna have to end the thing with this woman, Jubal. She's bringin' you nothin' but grief."

The hard jerk of surprise that hit him made him grunt in pain. "What woman?" he asked at last.

"The one that's been takin' you out of the house all hours of the night. You think I don't know? Whoever she is, she's had you goin' for nearly two months. I

hope she's decent, but at the hours you're keepin',
I'm afraid it ain't likely."

His face, the side not mottled purple and black,
flushed red as he spoke abruptly. "She's a good person,
Ma. That's the trouble. She's not the kind of girl that
belongs with me."

Maggie spoke sharply. "I reckon you better tell
me what that means. You're just as good as—"

"Ma." His flat voice cut off her comment. "She's different from me. She's got too much. And maybe I've
done too much."

"Did she tell you that?"

"No. But her family's not the kind that's gonna
want her mixed up with one of us from Sullivan's
Ridge." He took a deep, steadying breath. "I gotta
lay down. I'm feelin' pretty bad. Guess I won't get to
go to work today, either."

Maggie followed him into his little bedroom and
watched as he eased himself down on the quilt.
Along his chest and side, the dark bruising from
Dusty's fists showed up viciously against the creamy
fabric of the domestic that the quilt had been pieced
with. "Jubal, this ain't . . . you ain't foolin' around
with Lionel Johnson's daughter, are you?"

He hurt too much to react, but he stared up at his
mother in exasperation. "No. There ain't nothin'
good about Tess. What grapevine did you get that
off of, Ma?"

Relief made Maggie's face lighter. "Ida said she'd
heard it." She hesitated. "Jubal, listen to me. I don't
see how this woman can be any good for you, but
maybe I ain't gettin' the whole picture. You just
remember—any girl that ain't willin' to take you for
what you are, who can't see the truth of you—she
ain't worth havin'.'."

Jubal might have laughed, but that hurt, too, so

he settled for a huffing sound. "That sounds good, but it don't work that way."

"You fought over her, and she don't even—"

"I told you, no. She didn't like it that I'd been fightin'. So mad that she might be through with me." He said it moodily, turning his face to the wall. "I need to rest a little while, Ma."

Tuesday nights were ones he usually spent with Rilla. He didn't go.

But he faced Carroll on Wednesday.

"You tried to frame me," he said steadily when he walked in the office.

Carroll looked up from his papers. Sitting there on his big chair, his big gold watch glinting on his arm, his gold eyeglasses hooked over his nose, he looked expensive and professional. Too big a man to dirty his hands with a piece of work like that setup.

Too big a man to be involved in receiving stolen property, too.

But he didn't even try to deny the charge. "And the trying is what matters, isn't it, Kane?" he drawled, leaning back on the chair. "I hear things didn't go according to plan. And I gathered that you took out some of your frustrations on Hackett and Bainbridge."

"When what I needed to do," Jubal said quietly, "was to take them out on the person really responsible." His gaze never wavered from Carroll's face as the other man tossed his pen to the desk.

"But you won't. Because I'm not denying a thing. Yes. I meant to set you up. And even if things didn't go as planned, they made my point clear. You can see now how easy it would be for me to cost you everything, Kane. This little event with the DOT failed. The next time I decide to do something like this, it'll work. You won't even see it coming. So don't do anything that requires me to take such an action again."

The room was so quiet that Jubal could hear Rosalie's voice from the one beyond. Nothing distinct—just a jumbled sound.

"How long am I goin' to be your slave, Mr. Carroll?" he asked bitterly. "When is it enough?"

"I'll let you know," Carroll said calmly. "I assume you're here to work, despite the fact that you look like hell. All you've got to remember is just to do your job. Then everything will be fine."

"Here, Miss Carroll," the young, rawboned man said cheerfully as he handed her three invoices. Charlie Danson did requisitions; he was the kind who smiled a lot and made others smile back.

"What are these for?"

"Most of them are requisitioning parts for that truck that Jubal Kane tried to ride to hell Friday night," Charlie answered, grinning at her.

"What?"

"Kane hit a patch of fog coming off Black Mountain. Door's messed up, mirror's gone. I'm surprised he's still alive to tell the story. There are deep hollows on both sides of those curves. Two people have been killed there in the last three years."

Rilla stood slowly. "Jubal was in a wreck?"

"If it had been anybody else, it'd have been a wreck," Charlie corrected. "Jubal pulled it out of the spin. My daddy says he must have some of his grandfather's blood in him."

Rosalie chuckled unexpectedly. "I hadn't thought of Elijah Kane in years. He was a bootlegger. A whiskey runner," she told Rilla.

"That old man made Thunder Road look tame. He

could drive anything. If Jubal didn't keep to himself so much, I'd rag him a little about him. But I don't know how he'd take it," Charlie concluded, "so I do what he does. I stay quiet."

Rilla watched him go before she looked down at the papers in her hand. "He could have been killed," she told Rosalie.

"Probably. He was driving the truck Bobo drives. Some of the men think Hackett had done something careless—or left something undone, which is also careless—that caused the whole thing. And *that* caused the fight afterward."

"He still didn't have to fight," Rilla said, but her hands shook a little as she laid the papers down.

"He really made a mess of that handsome face," Rosalie said wryly. "Only a mother could love him the way he looks today. . . . Good gracious, there he is now. Is it two already?"

Jubal never even looked at Rilla as he sank onto the chair, careful and slow. Like Rosalie, she wanted to wince away from his bruised face, but compassion and regret flooded through her.

She didn't understand him, and she hated the thoughts of the Pine, but she wanted to tell him that she didn't want a gentleman, after all. Just him, whatever he was. Just time to sit in the circle of his arms. But last night he hadn't come to the mill.

She glanced at him surreptitiously. Rosalie was wrong; more than his mother still found him pleasing to watch.

"Oh, Terrill, I meant to tell you." Rosalie's face was alight with humor as she gathered things for her bank trip. "Charlie Danson's from an awfully good family. He's working his way through the community college over at Edmonds, too, at night. Almost ready to graduate."

Rilla pulled her gaze from Jubal's bent head. "He seems nice," she said in mild surprise.

"He is. He asked me to point all of that out to you, since you don't seem to be noticing it on your own. I said I would, to keep him from coming in the office six or seven times a day." Rosalie laughed. "He's wearing out his shoes."

Rilla flushed to the roots of her hair, not because of the woman's words, but because of the way Jubal had tensed and gone completely still. She never looked at him; she just knew. "I thought he was supposed to come that often."

"Honey, I haven't seen Charlie's face in this office more than twice a week since he came to work here. *Until* you showed up. Give old Charlie a break, okay?"

The door had barely shut behind her before Jubal was rising, pushing away papers. His face was dark and quiet.

"You didn't tell me you were in an accident." She kept her voice low so that Henry in the office beyond couldn't hear.

"I wasn't. It was just a—a thing that happened. An' I didn't hear you askin' too many questions."

"Jubal—"

He looked back at her as he opened the door. "Charlie Danson's a pretty good guy, Rilla. We're the same age, the two of us. But you know what? Sometimes I feel a hundred years older."

The November moon made the night bright as a summer dawn; with its help, Rilla could make out his shape as she neared the truck parked in the alcove. His head and shoulders were against the window in the far door, his legs stretched out on the seat. She took a deep breath of relief. He'd come.

She opened the door and slipped in quietly as he pulled himself upright. There was silence for a minute while both looked out the front windshield.

"I didn't know if you'd come, an' I don't know what I'm doin' here," he began without preamble.

"I know why I came." Better to get this over with right up front. "To tell you that I was scared and jealous Monday night."

"Jealous! Of what?"

"You went back to the Pine, where the girl is."

"What girl?" he asked slowly.

"The one you'd been with the night of the mill robbery."

Her steady voice brought a flush to his neck; he felt the heat at his collar. "She ain't been there in a while," he said brusquely. "And even if she was, I don't want to be with her. Ever. But I told you that."

"Good. I wanted to hear it again," Rilla said huskily.

The moon poured down on them in the long silence. Then he wrapped his long fingers tightly around the steering column in front of him, leaning his forehead against the top of the wheel. "There's a lot of things you don't know about me, Rilla. Things I've done, and I ain't too proud of 'em. You wouldn't like them, just the way you didn't like the fight."

She looked down at the lapels of her coat, trying to swallow the lump in her throat. "You said you had to fight, Jubal."

"I did. But there's people who probably would have handled it different. Who *could* have, who wouldn't ever have got in a situation like I was in. People like Charlie."

"So you came here tonight to hand me over to him?" Her voice was stronger; it pulled his head up.

"Is that why?" she persisted. "You want me to walk up to him on the mill yard tomorrow and put my hand on his, or invite him to the house, or go out with him alone and let him kiss me—"

"No!" He pushed away from the wheel, and it swung a little with his force. *"No."*

She waited, still as a statue, until he finally looked over at her before she spoke.

"You didn't come to be noble, Jubal." There was a rich thread of tremulous laughter in her words. "I know what you're here for. For this."

Closer and closer to him on the seat she came, so close she could hear the rapid beating of his heart in the solitude of the bright night.

"You came to hear me say that I don't want Charlie Danson. And all those 'gentlemen' I threw at you the other night . . ." Her whisper trailed into nothing. His eyes were so green, they looked lit from somewhere behind.

"Not them, either, Jubal," she finished.

"So who?" he invited thickly, watching her lips, close, so close.

She rose like the wind, sudden and impetuous, to press her mouth to his. "You," she breathed into him. "You."

His resistance, already weak, collapsed as she pressed herself against him; his hands reached and closed fiercely around her neck, tangling in her hair to hold her to him, refusing to let her escape.

They broke apart at last, dragging for breath.

"Don't tell me anymore about other men I belong with, Jubal," she whispered passionately.

"Then don't talk to me about 'em, either, Rilla," he returned with equal passion.

"And don't tell me who to love. Whatever you are, it's what I want."

He fumbled for her mouth again, but her lips traced down the bruised side of his face, finding each tiny cut, each hurt. Down his throat, to the V of his shirt.

His skin tasted like salt, and soap, and some tangy after-shave. And when he winced away from her fingers on his side, Rilla went a little insane. She gathered the T-shirt and the thermal shirt under it into her hands and pulled up on them until they slid free of his jeans.

She heard his sharp intake of breath, felt his hands clench her shoulders in shock.

Gentle, smooth, careful. She was all of that when she slipped the two shirts up his lean brown torso.

"You said you didn't want to see the rest of me, the other night," he panted above her.

"Because I was scared of what they'd done to you. And of you. Oh, Jubal." Her voice held pity and regret because even here in the moonlight, he was a mass of abrasions and contusions. His smooth skin was dark and vicious in coloring. "Does it hurt?" Her fingers caressed him.

"Rilla—"

Without volition his hands found her head, urging her down. In a silent yielding, she obeyed, her lips cool against his hot skin. His heart knocked against her.

But when she bent to kiss his stomach, right above his belt, he reacted, violent in his movement, clamping her head against him.

Holding her for a long, long moment.

She moved against him at last, rising up his chest, and his hands slid down her, not to pull away, but to brush freely across the swell of her breasts, cupping them.

She tore from him with a strangled cry, her hands going to her heart.

They watched each other for a pounding moment while he tried to speak and she fought the shocking waves of pleasure.

"I'm sorry," he pushed out at last. And his hands reluctantly tugged down the shirts she'd pushed up. "I won't do it again. I didn't mean to—" He cut off his own sentence. "Hell, that's a lie. I meant to, Rilla. I wanted to. You were touching me, so I touched you." Breathing too hard, too fast.

"I did it because you were hurt." Her voice might have been a defensive child's. She didn't feel like a child.

He pulled himself together.

"Hurt, and sore, and bruised up, but, Lord, Rilla, I ain't *dead.*"

The words were so indignant that after a moment's hesitation, she laughed. Not a great laugh, but it was one nevertheless.

"It's not funny. You nearly killed me," he protested.

She caressed his face for one long moment while they watched one another. "I've got to go," she said at last, unsteadily, "before we—"

"I won't do any more," he interrupted pleadingly. "I promise."

"I want to stay so much it hurts," she managed quietly. "And that's why I have to go. But there *is* a promise I wish you would make me, Jubal."

"I can't promise never to fight, if that's it."

"No, not that. Promise me you won't go to the Pine again. Something bad happens every time you do."

Jubal made a sound half sigh, half laughter. "You and Ma," he said in mock exasperation. "You're movin' in on me, you know it, girl? First my cigarettes, now the Pine. But it's okay. I'll stay away."

"Just like that?"

"Rilla, look at me." He reached out to tilt her chin up to him. "There's a lot of things messed up in my life right now. You're what's right with it. I won't go. I don't like it much, anymore. There's nothing there for me. Everything I want is right here, even if I don't deserve it."

She nodded wordlessly, then smiled half-tremulously. "I'd seal this deal with a kiss, but even sick as you are, there's nothing wrong with your hands," she said teasingly.

He promptly slid them behind his back. "Look—none."

She considered the situation. "No cheating?" she asked dubiously.

"No cheating. Honest Jubal Kane, that's me." His mouth twisted in wryness.

He got his kiss, but for all their teasing, there was a self-derision in him that she didn't understand. And to save their lives, they couldn't make it light and fun. It held passion, and frustration, and hunger.

Hunger unsatisfied.

$\overline{20}$

Dusty came back to work on Monday.

He and Jubal met in the yard in front of half the mill that bright morning, and most of the place held their breath.

"You don't look so tough today, Kane." Dusty said it pugnaciously enough, but he made no menacing moves, no swaggering gestures.

Jubal laughed. "No. I guess not. I sort of look like you. You gonna start pushin' me again, Dusty? Because if you mean to, start hittin'. I'll hit back. I mean for it to end, one way or the other."

The loosely formed bracelet of men around them pulled in a little tighter. Dusty looked first at Jubal's set face and then at the waiting ones. He looked down at his own hands, still split at the knuckles, as red as his face.

"You fell first, Kane. I won that fight."

"If you say so."

"I ain't fightin' again to prove a point I've already

made," Dusty rumbled, but he was blustery and defensive.

Silently Jubal stood his ground, and it was finally Dusty who stepped away. When he did, the circle spread apart; men went back to their places, mumbling to themselves.

And Jubal stood in the middle of the sunny, cold mill yard. He didn't know how, but he'd just won.

It felt nearly as good as when he walked away from Tess.

The other men knew it, too. Something changed overnight. Nobody called him "ridge runner" anymore. Two or three nodded or spoke when he passed.

He wondered how something as terrible as that night could produce good, but it had. When he worked alone in the shop, hating what he was doing, forcing himself to face the reality that he couldn't get out of it, he wondered ironically if any good would ever come of *this*.

Henry Carroll would get rich off of it. Now there was real compensation for Jubal.

But he had another worry—a sweet worry—that took his mind off Carroll: Jubal was willfully letting the situation with Rilla get so out of hand that he was having trouble controlling it.

He knew the two of them were pushing their limits. Rilla knew it, too. But she didn't really understand how close to the edge he actually was.

If she'd understood, she would never have come to work today. It was a Thursday; she wasn't supposed to be at the mill.

But just moments after he'd settled into his customary seat near Rosalie, the door had opened, and he'd looked up and felt his heart jerk a little.

Rilla stood there, flushing as she mumbled something to the secretary about forgetting to finish her paperwork the day before. ". . . and I had some free time now," she concluded.

"Gracious, you didn't have to come today just for that," Rosalie answered in surprise. "But it's perfectly all right with me."

And as she slid into the chair near his, Rilla finally shot a glance at Jubal. It was half-shy, half-provocative, and he knew damn good and well what she was doing here: she'd come to see him.

Looking might be enough to satisfy her. She seemed content enough, now that she was close, to do her work and nothing more. But her unexpected appearance set off those darker, more aggressive emotions that he'd let loose after their argument and hadn't been able to fight since.

At this very instant she was making his nerves spark, as she stretched her legs out lazily before her desk. It was the way she always sat, but today, he was as jumpy as a Mexican bean.

Then she stepped on the heel of her right shoe with the toe of her left one and her foot slid a little way out of her sneaker. The sock she was wearing wasn't particularly erotic; it was blue, with a big pink hand that appeared to wrap her heel and ankle, and splashed across the side of the sock had been a big white "Gotcha!"

He wished, without even realizing where his thoughts were going, that it was his hand, that he could pull up the bottom of her jeans and run his fingers up the long, smooth calf. He had one luscious memory of being tangled in her flailing legs in the darkness at the mill, the night he'd first caught her there.

And while he was sitting on his chair, frozen in place by his thoughts, she crooked her arm and bent her elbow up over her head to pull her hair off her face. She looked up as she did, and catching him staring, she made a wry face and gestured with her pen down at her papers.

The contact released him from his still state, and he felt a sudden flame streak through him. Hastily he glanced down at his own work.

VIN numbers.

The words danced in front of him. What in the hell was a VIN, and what did it have to do with him, anyway?

When the hour of torture was over, when he couldn't stand it anymore, he pushed aside the folder and said quietly, "Rilla."

She shot one glance over her shoulder to where Henry's door was shut; another one at Rosalie's desk, empty now that she'd gone to the bank. Then she looked at him.

"The parking lot," he demanded urgently, his voice a tight thread of sound.

They hadn't met at that spot in a long time, and as she returned his gaze, she flushed, then nodded.

She was a little slow in getting there, and he was impatient as he reached for her, taking time only to think fleetingly that he was glad she liked kisses with open mouths and teeth and tongues, because that was exactly what she got, pinned there against him so tightly that he felt every rib—and every curve as well.

Rilla kissed him back; her mouth softened under his and moved against his invasion. But when he had to break the kiss just because it had extended beyond all decency, even for an illicit parking lot caress, she put a hand against his chest, right over his thundering heart, and pushed back. Leaning against the prison circle of his arms, she murmured questioningly, "Jubal?"

He looked at her, then lifted one hand to slide his widespread fingers through her hair, just as she had in the office, and he deliberately tangled the strands around his hand and caught the back of her head.

"You know what you were doin' with your feet a few minutes ago?"

"My feet! I wasn't—"

"Don't do it anymore," he interrupted darkly. "You're drivin' me crazy. And I think I just screwed up that damn paperwork," he added gloomily as she began to laugh. He put his hand over her mouth and said quietly, "Meet me tonight, Rilla."

The laughter fled, and she pushed his hand away before she stepped back farther from him. "It's Thursday, not Friday," she said reasonably, but her voice shook.

"What difference does that make?" he demanded in frustration. "You came to work today. We both know why—because we never see each other enough. Two hours, two nights a week—that's all we get. Damn it, Rilla, don't we deserve more time than that once in a while?"

She touched his face. "Yes," she agreed, and tried to smile. "Just—be nice when I come tonight, Jubal."

He was too far gone, too worked up and wrung out, to be here. But he told himself that he would be satisfied just to meet her, then he'd send her home immediately. He'd find some excuse.

Good intentions, that's what they were. Lies, his conscience accused, because the intent was never really there. All along he'd known what he would really do; he was mush where Rilla Carroll was concerned. The minute she slid into the truck, bringing a rush of cold air and her own sweet scent, he was telling himself that only a fool would send this warm and willing girl with her bright eyes and her tender mouth back to an old-maid aunt and a rotten-to-the-core stepfather and a dying mother.

He'd keep her just a little while.

She kissed him differently. It was nearly shy, a quick, warm brush on his lips, and she was edgy in her motions.

"What's the matter with you?" he demanded at last in frustration as she avoided his hands for the third time.

"It's too much," she said at last reluctantly. "The way you're acting."

"The way I'm actin'!" he echoed before he got angry. "You wanted me to be this way," he accused. "Now you're chickenin' out."

She had no denial, but she twisted her hands nervously. "Let's do something we've never done before, Jubal. Let's drive."

"Drive?" he repeated, not comprehending.

"Surely nobody would catch us if we just went for a drive," she said nervously. "Just for a few minutes. Instead of . . . sitting here. We could talk, maybe." Her cheeks were stained red, and she wouldn't look at him.

Rilla had solved their problem. She was doing the right thing, just as he should have done. Why, then, was he not relieved?

"Drive and talk," he repeated. "Okay. We'll drive."

They circled down by the dark river, avoiding town, and headed out on the lonely stretch of highway that ran north. The only light in the truck was the yellow-brown glow of the radio; for miles the only sound was the low voice of the deejay. Finally Jubal reached over and flipped everything into silence.

"I thought you wanted to talk," he said at last.

"I did. I do. But it's such a . . . a pretty night—" She didn't even try to finish the sentence. The night was cold, the moon often hidden by heavy, banking clouds, and the wind sullen as it pushed at the truck, trying to whistle it off the road into the dark, overgrown hollows. Nothing pretty about any of it.

"*I* want to talk," he told her flatly, glancing over. "About the way you're sittin' over there huggin' the door. Why?"

She could see his tall, lean body as it folded behind the wheel. But his face was half-hidden, his right shoulder hunched up to let his wrist ride the top of the steering wheel and his fingers wrap under and around it.

"I don't know," she said, and at last slid across the seat until she was brushing his coat. He glanced over his shoulder at her, but he didn't drop one arm around her as he usually did.

"Better be careful," he drawled sarcastically. "You might get too close. And I might just reach over and get you." The last word was too husky, too suggestive.

"I think," Rilla said in a still, careful voice, "that you'd better take me home after all."

Anger spread out over him, making his face hard. Without a word he made a quick turn into a dirt road that led into a hay field, lying open and black in the night. Then he backed onto the highway, letting the wheel slide under his hand carelessly. They hit the asphalt road in a spray of gravel, and the sound of the tiny rocks peppering the sides of the truck told of his anger better than words.

Rilla kept sliding glances up at his still, dark face, and little nerves tingled in her fingers and legs. He said nothing. Not a single word.

"Listen, Jubal, the only reason I want you to take me home is that I'm not in a very good mood. And I'm tired. Can't I be tired just one time?"

"You want me to take you home because you're afraid," he shot back, but he never looked from the road. "Afraid because of the way I kissed you at work today."

"That wasn't a kiss," she denied, cutting across the memory, angry herself. "It was more like—"

"Like what?"

"Never mind. I just don't want to do it anymore."

He drew a deep, steadying breath, then shifted his hands on the wheel so that he could drop the right one and fumble for his cigarettes in his shirt pocket, somewhere under his coat. He'd no sooner brought out the pack than she protested involuntarily, "No. Don't smoke."

His hands stilled on the pack. "If you think I'm gonna try to kiss you good night, forget it. And I'll smoke if I want to."

She gave an angry flounce away from him. "Okay. Go ahead, then. What's a kiss from you anyway?"

"That's what I thought," he muttered, and he threw the cigarettes violently against the door at her feet. "So I'll get you back to your damn house as fast as I can. But don't give me any of those big-eyed stares tomorrow. I don't need any girl playin' games with me, and I'm tired of layin' awake at night thinkin' about touchin' her and kissin' her and makin' love to her—"

Good God, what was he saying? He cut off the hot words as quickly as a sharp ax slicing off a tree limb.

But she had heard; her breath whistled a little because she sucked it in so sharply. "Stop it, Jubal. You're—you really are scaring me," she said shakily. But for all her words, it wasn't fright that was zinging through the air. Sexual tension sizzled instead, quick and intense.

Swearing violently, he slid the truck into the dark shadows of the trees just beside a dilapidated, lop-sided shack that once had been an old grocery store. A rusted tin sign that was nailed on the side flashed in his headlights, momentarily proclaiming Levi Garrett as a chewing tobacco. When he cut off the engine and the lights, they were all alone in the black shadows, just them and the wind and their beating hearts there beside the deserted little road.

"Don't, Jubal," Rilla said tremulously, her voice shaking.

"Don't—don't—don't. That's all you say anymore," he flung back at her. "Half of the time you want me, half of the time you run."

Her voice was pleading and desperate; she had to make him understand. "If I quit running, I'm going to do something stupid. I'm going to say, 'Jubal, *don't*. Don't stop. Touch me. Please, touch me,' and—"

Her words broke, and she moved, violent and quick, as if a dam had burst inside her, leaping at him. Her arms went around his neck, her mouth finding his.

As he fell back against the door, he had one last thought that made good sense: he knew enough to clutch at her ribs under the jacket and pull her back with him.

Rilla had never kissed like this in her life. What-ever had ignited in her that afternoon out in the chilly parking lot exploded now like a flame fueled by gasoline. Every move he made, even the shape of his mouth, pulled her to him. She wanted him, not his anger, so she treated him to her version of his own kiss today, and he nearly burned up under her hands and her lips.

When it was over, they were both struggling for breath, she was half on his lap, one leg poking in his stomach sharply, and his hands were up under her pink plaid shirt against the warmth of her shoulders.

Looking down on his face, with heavy passion darkening his eyes to black and making his mouth look nearly sulky, she whispered, "I didn't mean it, Jubal."

"The kiss?" He stumbled over the word, bewildered. His tongue didn't seem to remember how to talk.

"No. I mean, yes—I did mean the kiss. I didn't mean all those other things, about not liking it when you kissed me today. I liked it too much, don't you see? Just the way I liked the other things."

He lay still a long, long time, then he turned her loose. "Don't tell me this, Rilla," he said swallowing. "Not here. Not now." He tried to sit up, pulling at the steering wheel, easing her backward, off of him.

"But you knew it. You started it. You're the one who kissed me this afternoon."

"That's because"—he braced both his hands on the steering wheel before him and pushed against it, preparing for his confession—"that's because I was starin' at your legs in the office and thinkin' how I'd like to see them just once." He stopped, ran his hand over his damp face, then he laughed a little. Too husky, too breathy, but it might pass as laughter. "It's those socks you had on; this is all their fault. No, that's a lie. I think about what you'd look like without those jeans all the time. At work. At home. God, I can't even see you walk across the mill yard without dyin'." He couldn't quite keep the resentfulness out of his voice.

She had gone still, as though his words had stunned her. But her cheeks were flushed even in the dim moonlight. She never took her eyes off his face, and when she spoke it was almost without volition, intense and focused.

"Why don't you ask me, Jubal, what I think about?"

He'd been running his hand around the top of the ridged steering wheel unconsciously; her words stopped the motion on the instant, the breath caught in his throat as he stared at her.

"I don't stay awake at night. I sleep. And it's just as bad. Do you know what I dreamed about last night? Why I had to see you today even though I was scared to? I dreamed"—she reached out and touched his shirt lightly—"that we were in a field, in the hot sun, and I reached out like this, and unbuttoned your shirt, and slid it off your shoulders . . ."

Her hands slipped up to his shoulders, and his heart pounded wildly under the touch, the blood beating in his ears as her breath warmed his cheek.

"And your skin was brown, and as hot as the sunshine."

He grabbed for the handle of the truck door, swung it open with such violence that he nearly tore it off its metal hinges, and plunged into the cold wind.

"Jubal." She didn't call after him, or beg, or tantalize. It was just his name, clear as crystal.

He stopped where he stood, a few fast-traveled yards from the truck. But he didn't turn around. He wasn't that big a fool. "What are you tryin' to do to me?" he said, groaning, and he shoved his hands into his back pockets forcefully. "Maybe this is fun to you. I reckon it is to most girls. But I don't like it, Rilla."

"Jubal."

Reluctantly he swung around. Rilla was standing outside the truck, too, but still inside the shelter of its door, and the dim yellow light behind turned her into a silhouette, but one with substance and glinting hints of color. Then she raised her hands, and her elbows went out at angles on each side of her waist. Paralyzed, he saw the movement, then heard the snap and slide of her jeans.

"My God. Rilla—"

"You said I didn't have to be afraid. That I could trust you, Jubal."

"You can't trust any man this much, or push him this far," he gasped out. "Why are you doin' this?"

For a minute she just stood there, and he could hear her ragged breathing even across the distance. Then she dropped her face into her hands and began to cry.

"I don't know," she choked out. "I really don't understand. Sometimes I hate you, Jubal Kane, because you make me do things. I don't want to be like this. You've been with other girls; they've . . . seen you. Me, I know what I want. I want to be married to the man I first make love with. I want to wait. It's just that the dreams are of you. Why don't you leave me alone? Why don't you let me sleep?"

She sounded confused and angry. The night slid by in a waiting stillness. Then Jubal broke it, and his voice held a decision.

"Rilla. Look at me," he said, and the words shook in the wind.

He didn't even stop to consider. He just reached for the front lapels of his jacket and slowly, deliberately, pulled it off, twisting out of it. It dropped on the ground behind while she stared. Then one hand caught at the unbuttoned old plaid shirt, and he slid out first one arm, then the other one, and the shirt joined the jacket on the ground, falling into a silent puddle at his feet. The whole world waited for a drifting eternity.

"I'm . . . I'm scared," she whispered finally, and her teeth chattered a little.

"Don't be." Jubal said it so quietly that it nearly floated away on the cold breeze. "You want to see me, then look. Even if it's all you want to do, just look. I want you to."

He never took his eyes off her as he crossed his arms in front of him and his fingers found the bottom of his black T-shirt. In one quick, fluid movement he had pulled it up and *swooshed* it over his head and off his arms. Stripped to the waist, the wind chilling his hot skin, he stood holding the balled shirt in one hand—and he waited.

Even in the shifting shadows, Rilla could see the clean line of his neck, could see where his waist narrowed into his jeans and how the tops of his shoulders gleamed like the polished cherry of the table in the dining room. Few bruises were left to mar his skin now. An arrow of flame shot clear down to her toes.

Too late to turn back now. *This is wrong,* her mind whispered weakly. But she had started this, caught up in the wild heat of the day's events, and now she was going to have to finish it in the decided chill of the night. His eyes were like emerald pinpoints in the darkness, and she swallowed panic.

"You don't have to," he said, but his voice was ragged.

She barely heard him as she pushed the open jeans down past her hips. The soft, oversize shirt hung to the tops of her thighs. Then she bent her knee out sideways and, stooping a little, found the heel of her shoe. It came off as if it had been greased, and she dropped it with a thud. Hooking her fingers in the bottom of the jeans leg, she tugged it off, pulled her leg free as she balanced one hand on the truck door, and stood erect, only to repeat the process.

There. It was done, and a fifty-dollar pair of jeans lay in a heap by her feet. Her legs were shaking with cold and nerves and reaction, but she stood still.

Jubal stared, transfixed; he didn't need anything to live except the sight of Terrill, half-dressed. She was exactly as he had known she would be, slender and graceful and provocative.

He started toward her slowly, savoring the new details of her that each step brought him, and the thudding of his heart was everywhere. In his throat, in his wrists, in his fingertips. Everywhere.

"Rilla," he whispered at last, as he stood inches from her. She was struggling with fear. "D'yu know you're the prettiest thing I ever saw in my life, baby?"

He pulled her against him. Her face and nose pushing into his bare chest and her hands clutching at the skin of his back were erotic, forbidden pleasures that he reveled in. She was shaking as if she had a hard chill, and her fear and the way her hands clung to him momentarily diminished the pure hot flame of his lust. That, and his sudden amused realization that she still had on a pair of white socks. At least these didn't seem to have hands on them. He laid his cheek against her hair, caught between soft tenderness and sharp desire.

"I'm freezing," she mumbled, and her mouth moved against his skin like the brush of a moth's wings. He had to swallow a lump of emotion that choked him before he could tell her in a voice tight as a coiled spring, "Go on. Get in the truck."

He was already turning her around to help her in, when she hesitated, twisting back into his body. "My clothes."

"I'll get them," he said, and his voice made her

stomach lurch. Too smooth. Too purposeful. And his face had the same intent, heavy look it had worn earlier in the parking lot. It was the same way he'd looked in her dream and when she'd kissed his stomach.

"Jubal—"

"Go on."

Rilla reluctantly sat down on the cold vinyl of the seat. The ridges of the upholstery rubbed the backs of her thighs as she scooted to the far door, and her feet hit the gearshift in the floor before they brushed the rough texture of the floor mat.

She watched Jubal's shadowy figure as he rose from collecting her clothes off the ground and wadded them against his own clothes, and as he bent to scoop them up in his other arm, the same slant of light that had made his shoulders gleam earlier played across his long back. He was not heavily muscular, but lean and sleek and dark as a panther. She could still feel the hard silk of his skin under her fingertips.

He straightened and turned, and the flaring attraction she was feeling turned to panic. Too late, she knew exactly what tonight was: it was a game. A dangerous sexual game that she had initiated because he was an intoxicating drug in her bloodstream every waking hour since the Monday he'd run his hands over her breasts, and because she had never felt so powerful as when she forced reaction from him.

Time now to pay.

He swung into the truck, slamming the door behind him, and when the reverberation died, there was just the two of them.

She reached for the clothes on the seat beside him, and in a smooth movement, he pushed them into the floor. Right out of her grasp.

Rilla looked at the tangled heap, then back at his face. And a huge knot settled in her throat.

"In a minute," he whispered. "That's all." His eyes scorched her, and his face was predatory. One hand on the seat, his weight resting on his knuckles, he lifted himself a little and edged forward. Closer to her. Again. Again. Until her back was against the door behind her, the handle hurting her spine.

"Jubal." A gaspy whisper on his skin, that was what her words amounted to.

"C'mere." His hands were at her waist, fingers biting through the heavy cotton shirt, and he was lifting her. Her legs bumped his in the rough denim, and the left one bent at the knee, sideways, as it pressed the length of his thigh. Her right one he pulled across him, and as he did, his rough palm caught in the warm hollow at the bend of her leg. Leaning a little, lifting a little, he kissed her knee, and his hand lingered and stroked and soothed the slender calf, reluctant to move on, until he closed it around her ankle, and he stripped off the sock. His rough fingers tickled her sole as they handled her foot.

This time when he moved, he reached behind him to wrap her leg about his naked waist. Then he lifted himself into the V of her body, inside the other leg as well. He was still, then, passive and waiting, and the contrast with his prior aggression was so strong that she understood what he was telling her. Her captive—if she chose to lock him there.

"This is where I want to be, Rilla," he whispered, and his face was so close, she felt the movement of his lips. "Ever since the day I first saw you, I wanted your legs around me. I wanted *you*."

She loved him.

Never admitted before, never spoken, but those words were already more than so many broken syllables: they were a simple truth. If he had been rough or violent or if he had tried to force her, she wouldn't have known. But then he wouldn't have been Jubal, who had a secret gentle heart and tender hands.

It was easy to slide her arms around his warm neck, to put her lips on his and open them invitingly, to yield to his passionate kiss. His heart—no, it was hers—was beating in heavy, painful strokes. It was trying to tell him a secret, if he would only listen.

And when the kiss broke, they took time only to shift their head positions, and another kiss began, warm and wet. Her hand slid up the base of his skull, pushing the thick, dark hair up lovingly into tufts that she clutched in her fingers. His own hands fumbled for and found her skin, and it chilled in delicious goose bumps as he brushed his open palm up under the shirt. Up and around her side, stroking, circling on her back.

He pulled his lips away at last, mumbling, "God, oh, God," and he kissed the side of her face again and again, working his way past her ear and her jaw to her throat. His hand—the one not riding her like a warm brand—lifted her hair away, and he kissed the soft skin he'd just bared behind her ear. Then his whole body jerked, rising into hers, and he went still.

For one minute, Jubal turned to stone in her arms. No movement. No breath. No words. The relentless silence pressed on—on—on. Then she felt his chest move against her as he gasped heavily, felt his hands as they gripped her arms tightly.

"If you—if you make—one more move, I'll—I don't want to stop, Rilla—I—and I ain't got the right—"

The voice of her conscience—that creature that Katherine and Tandy and Mrs. Denton had all nurtured—was there with her now, whispering no.

But something stronger had her in its grip; she couldn't bear to let him go. So instead she rose to his lips, stopping his words, opening his mouth, insisting that he answer her passion.

He shuddered beneath her hands, then pulled away to look down in her face one long, searching moment. "So be it, then," he muttered almost to himself. "But you better mean it, Rilla. For God's sake, mean it. No matter what."

Her trembling hands went to the front of her shirt and began to unbutton it. "I don't think I can make it one more night without this. Please, Jubal, please—"

Something inside him crashed and shattered, and his body relaxed as his arms gathered her to him, hastily, clumsily. She was a precious weight in his arms, a warm soul against his. Alive with fire and passion. And when he laid her back on the seat, her hands clung to him, her kisses stung his skin like potent bees.

Honey and lightning.

Sweetness in his heart, flashes of white fire in his head.

I hold her.

Mine.

He pulled her other sock from her foot. Finished unbuttoning the shirt, spread it wide lingeringly.

Every inch of Rilla's skin felt electric; silky nerve endings tingled even in her toes. Her skin was flushed as she looked up into his intent features.

"I'm gonna do this right, Rilla. Because I love you, more than I've ever loved anybody in my life."

And the little voice that had whispered so persistently was washed away into oblivion by a huge sea wave of thick emotion.

His hands slipped beneath the shirt to loosen the scrap of satin and lace that separated him from her breasts. She waited for the touch of his mouth, heart thundering. Instead he kissed her from shoulder to shoulder, then slowly downward.

She heard his heart.

She heard her own breath. She felt his lips . . . at last. She gasped, shivering from the delight of his touch. Allowing it for a few moments before she pushed him from her. His eyes were hot and dazed, and it took a minute for him to realize what her hands were doing, that she was urging him away from her enough that she could spread answering kisses against the skin of his chest.

She struggled to rise above him a little, sliding her hands through his thick, dark hair as he looked up at her a moment, a passionate supplicant.

Nearly face to face, he spoke.

"I've been with other girls, Rilla," he said honestly, catching at her when she gasped and jumped back. "I'm tellin' you so you'll know that I mean what I say. This is different. None of 'em was like this. Tonight is because I love you. I want to forget everything else but that. But there's things about me you don't know. Maybe you need to hear them first."

"I know what I want to know," she managed.

"And you're willin' to take a chance on me? I want it to last forever. If that's too much, if you ain't sure, then you say so. Tell me that you've got other things you want to do, that you don't want to be tied to me. I ain't gonna lie and say I won't touch you tonight anyway. I know better. I think I've got to have you, no matter what. But don't let this be a lie. Tell me the truth about what we're doing tonight."

Jubal wanted to hide somewhere instead of looking straight into her eyes, but that would be a lie, too, so he made himself face her, his soul stripped bare before her.

The whole world really was beautiful tonight, Rilla thought. The moon half-hidden behind the clouds, its glow reflecting off a dial in the truck, the lingering scent of tobacco and leather. He was beautiful, too, this man kneeling before her, hazy through her tears. His stubborn, clean jaw; the determined green eyes; the heavy dark hair that curled around his neck.

She touched his lips with her fingers, and he didn't move. Still as a statue, waiting.

"The truth is, I love you, Jubal. I don't want anybody else. Not . . . not ever," she whispered shakily.

Her shirt came off effortlessly. He crushed her to him, tumbling her backward onto the truck seat; his shoulder struck the wheel, but he barely noticed as he pulled away to look down at her, to slide his hand down her throat, brushing his palms across her breasts freely now. His hands were satin and steel as they caressed her.

Dimly, in the heat of the growing passion, he felt her fingers sweep down to edge under the waist of his blue jeans.

He broke the kiss and rose above her long enough to shuck away the jeans and his shoes, this time hitting his hip on the wheel of the truck; to look down on her aroused, warm face and the tumble of her hair; to push his bare feet against the door in the cramped space.

When their breaths were harsh and loud across the silence of the truck, when she was quivering beneath the weight of his body, he tangled his hands in her hair, twisting her face up to his, trying to remember why he had to be slow.

She was new to this; the shock of it was in her face, as well as the pleasure.

This was what he couldn't let himself forget: she'd never done this before.

"It might hurt." Such an effort for him to breathe. "I don't want to hurt you."

Urgent, pleading, he dropped a hundred heated, frantic kisses across her throat.

Hard to remember how to talk, she thought. She'd been all sensation for so long. "You can't help it, Jubal. I want—"

He sealed off the words with his mouth and moved decisively against her, catching her rough breaths in his throat, riding the jerky motions of her body, soothing and settling with the open palms of his hands.

Touching Rilla. Making love to Terrill. At last, at last.

Then she gave a cry, jerking under him.

Jubal stopped all motion. He was hurting her.

"I don't know what to do," he gasped in helpless dismay. "I never was with a virgin before."

She was pulling in long breaths, twisting her cheek to pillow it against the back of his hand, the one beside her face.

"Listen," he said in frustration. "Just forget it, baby. We'll wait a while. An hour. We don't even have to do this at all." He smoothed the hair back from her face, holding himself up on his elbow. "It's okay."

But her eyes blazed blue right up into his, and her hands pulled at him. "Please, Jubal, please."

For one moment he tried to resist her, pushing himself up, his arms shaking.

But she came up after him, her lips searching, seeking, finding his face, and his capitulation was easy, so easy, his body eager to follow her back down.

She was wild when he touched her again, struggling against his careful handling, awkward and beautiful in her innocence and inexperience.

"Easy, easy," he was murmuring, a soothing, mindless chant he measured out as he coaxed a heated magic with his hands.

"Jubal. *Jubal.*" She rose up frantically to meet him, clutching at him, and with her movement the heat rippled like hot liquid through both of them.

Then it exploded, and fire roared through the night.

"Rilla!" He cried her name across the flame, fitting her to him, carrying her up with him as they swirled in the blaze, both fed and consumed by it.

Then they collapsed together.

When Rilla began to cool again, when she could think and see, the internal flames had died down until they were just gentle licks of light from the glowing amber radio dial. She was shivering, but sweat was damp on her body.

He was there, brushing the hair off her cheeks, whispering nonsense caresses as she clutched at his shoulders, crowded together with him here on the truck seat so that she felt his very breath.

"I love you, Jubal Kane," she said raggedly.

He laughed, exhausted and exhilarated. "I love you, too. You—you won't be sorry tomorrow?" That same insistent question.

She slid her hand down his heaving chest, pushing him back until she could rise. They twisted uncomfortably in the narrow seat, so that he slid under her and she looked down on him, her hair spilling over both of them.

"As long as you remember that I don't share, either." Her eyes sparkled. "I may not be your first, but—" She paused meaningfully, bending forward to bite the sweaty flesh of his shoulder before she soothed it lovingly with her tongue and her lips.

"Keep remindin' me like this," he advised, laughing a little in relief as his hands wrapped possessively around her bare waist.

Her fingers brushed his throat. "I'll murder you," she said, her voice fierce, "if you let one of those 'other girls' near you after this. *Nobody* touches you. Nobody puts a mark on you like the one you had." Her hands lingered, a threat at his throat.

"Nobody," he agreed, his voice meek, and reached for her.

"Except me," she flashed mischievously, resisting him.

Jubal was no fool. He knew what to say. "Except you," he answered obediently, and this time she let his tugging hands pull her down to him and into his kiss.

21

Daylight brought recriminations.

Jubal woke up with her dazzling, echoing words in his ear and a stark fact in his heart: a man didn't take a woman like Rilla on a hard seat in a cold truck without honesty, without protection, and without marriage.

At the thought, he sat straight up in bed.

There it was. The reaction that was going to mark him forever as the uncool, unhip, unsophisticated redneck son of Maggie Kane: he thought in terms of marriage. Even with the whores at the Pine, or the girls who'd come on to him out on the Ridge, or Tess—it had been in the back of his head that he was doing things with them that belonged in marriage, that they were wronging somebody down the line who'd want a permanent relationship.

"A man keeps his mouth an' hands to himself," Maggie used to tell him and Jarvis and Frankie.

Between the memories of Jarvis's shotgun wedding

and Maggie's words, he'd been careful with girls. But until Rilla, he'd reassured himself with his very caution and pushed away any uneasy twinges of conscience. Maggie was from a different time and a different age, anyway.

But now, markers had finally come due. Maybe there really wasn't any getting away from your raisings.

He loved Rilla. Wanted her.

But she had another year of college. What was he doing with a college girl? He worked in a sawmill.

The thought staggered him when he really considered it.

And he was doing something illegal. He hadn't told her the truth about that. Couldn't.

Rilla hadn't realized what she was doing last night; she'd been caught up in the sexual tension that constantly strained between them.

This morning she'd come to her senses and despise him when she realized what he'd taken. Him, marry Terrill Carroll? It was laughable.

And he'd let what was their one and only love-making happen in a *truck*. Treated her as if she were Tess Johnson.

Jubal was pretty certain he'd ruined everything.

He'd be lucky if she didn't hate him.

Men are after only one thing, and they've got a thousand ways to get it.

That was how Mrs. Denton always admonished her girls.

Jubal had not even had to try last night, Rilla thought miserably; she'd practically thrown herself at him.

Now had she become just another girl to him? Somebody to avoid?

But when she twisted her face into the bedclothes, she saw his face, she heard his voice.

And she felt his hands touching her.

No, she didn't really think he'd been like that with anybody else.

It had been too real.

He was standing in the parking lot when she walked through. Watching her. Willing her to look at him.

When she didn't, he swung through the cars impatiently, trying to get to her. Only two or three men were in the lot; he didn't care, anyway. He had to know.

When he fell in step with her, she shot a sideways glance at him. Her cheeks were flushed.

"Hello."

"Mornin'," he said. *Get it over with,* he told himself. "Are you all right?"

Her cheeks flooded even more scarlet. "I'm fine." The she asked daringly, "Are *you?*" He caught her cheeky grin as she headed off through the mill yard.

She was flushed and shy in the office, but she nodded when he slid the note across her desk that asked her to come to the parking lot. "I had a phone call." She explained her lateness there in a rush of confusion. "Joanie Crabtree. That's the first time she's ever called."

"Guess there's a lot of first times for you lately," he said quietly, and bent to her lips. One sure way to find out about Rilla—the truth was always in her kiss.

He came up smiling. "See you tonight," he said huskily.

*   *   *

How do you face a man you've been intimate with, Rilla wondered that night, especially going back to the same situation?

But it didn't take long to find out.

He was standing outside the truck; was he as reluctant to get back in it as she?

"You're late." His voice was abrupt.

"I didn't want to come." She could be short, too.

"Didn't want to come! Why not?"

"Because of what happened last night." She'd said it all now. "I'm not ready to do that again, Jubal."

"I didn't ask you to, did I? But I thought you liked it." His voice was stiff with injured male pride.

"I did. But it's too big a thing for me to do again, for a while." *Until I know where we're going,* she thought. *And the way you're acting, I can't tell.*

"I don't want it to happen again like that, either," he said finally. "You deserve more than this truck, Rilla. Sometimes I hate it. It shouldn'ta been like that. But I lost my mind for a while." His voice was tense and regretful.

Relief chased through Rilla, relief and tender laughter. He'd worked himself up into nearly the same frenzy she had.

"You're right. You did it all," she said solemnly. "I protested."

"There's something I've got to tell you, and I don't want to," Jubal said miserably, without even registering her words. "But you need to know."

Rilla pushed her hair back and felt a little apprehension. "What?"

"You could be . . . Oh, hell, I did something really stupid last night. I didn't—you could be pregnant, Rilla."

She took a deep breath. "I thought about it this morning; it was just one time."

Her calmness threw him completely. He stared, nothing but green eyes and amazement.

"And if I am, it wouldn't be the first time two people parked and created a baby, would it?" She tried hard to be breezy.

"No, but I never did before," he retorted unsteadily. "You don't care?"

"It depends."

"Depends! On what?"

"On what you do. You're the big unknown here. What will you do if there's a baby, Jubal?"

He raked his hair back with both hands until it resembled a bushy pompadour. "I'd—I'd be its father."

"We already know that. But last night you talked about forever," she whispered.

He swallowed. "Rilla, I've been thinkin' that maybe last night was something you're goin' to regret. You made promises, too. But I'm not holdin' you to 'em. The first time's like that for girls, and—"

"Are you telling me that you don't want me anymore?" she asked in rising temper.

"I'm tellin' you to look before you leap," he said stubbornly. "I'm Jubal Kane from Sullivan's Ridge. Do you know what that means around here? I've been in prison, I work at the mill. You're not like me."

"You think all these nights together have been a mistake?" she asked, her voice soft with danger. "Then why didn't you leave me alone, Jubal? Back when I still believed what everybody said about you? Why did you spend weeks with me, proving everybody wrong?" She laid both hands on his chest, giving him a rough, furious shove.

"And when this thing with your mother is over?" he persisted uncomfortably. "Will you need me—want me—when you go back to normal living? Because I'm

sick and tired of these nights. I want to walk down
Main Street in broad daylight with you. How's it goin'
to feel then to be with me?"

"Are you accusing me of using you?" Her eyes were
sparkling with temper.

"No."

"Yes, you are. I never knew what you thought of
me before, but I do now. You think I let you be with
me in ways, in ways nobody else ever has, and it was
just some kind of comfort because my mother's
dying. Do you know what that makes me? What it
makes last night?"

"Here—wait—I didn't say any of that," he protested
in confusion. "It's not what I meant." He caught her
wrists.

"Then I guess," she said, trying to wrench away
unsuccessfully, "that you'd better speak what you
mean, Mr. Kane."

"You be still a minute," he told her sharply, sliding
his hands up to her forearms to hold her firmly. "Be
still and listen, dammit."

Tossing back her hair, she glared up at him. Her
eyes were too bright as he gazed down at her, and
his own face softened. "I'm tryin' to do the right
thing, Rilla. For you."

"No," she whispered, bracing herself against his
hands. "You're doing this for *you,* Jubal. Because
you're scared to death of what it'd be to go out there,
in broad daylight on Main, and let them see you like
you really are."

He didn't make any answer.

"Do you love me?" she whispered.

His throat worked.

"Answer me. Do you love me, like you said last
night?"

"*Yes.*"

"You said you'd be a father to a baby if there was one. But *me,* Jubal, what will you be to me?"

His hands tightened painfully around her arms; his face twisted. Then he turned loose and stepped back.

"I've been ever'thing a man can be to the woman he loves. Except—"

"Except a husband."

Her words swirled around them before she continued, more quietly, "Did you really think I would let a man go as far as you did last night without meaning to marry him?"

"You got carried away. I let things—"

"*Tell* me. Did I make love with you last night and not mean it?" Her voice was insistent, rough, demanding.

He had trouble with the word, so he shook his head. Then he found his tongue. "No."

"So say it. Ask it. One little question."

"You can't marry me," he said instead, torn between hope and agony. "No matter how much I want it. And I want you bad enough that I let last night happen even knowin' it wasn't fair to you."

A pulsing moment full of pleading silence and throbbing emotion slid by.

"You're right." Rilla swallowed the lump in her throat. "I can't marry you. You're letting yourself be measured by this town. By your own insecurities. You don't believe in yourself, so what difference does any of this make? You could have had me, Jubal, if you'd only reached. And I'm pretty special. I believe when you don't. You made me believe. Who knows what else you could have done?"

She whirled to run, already halfway across the mill yard before he came out of his stupor.

"No—Rilla—" He caught up with her in a mad dash,

snatching at the back of her coat. "You don't know all of it."

"I don't want to hear it anymore, Jubal. Stop beating yourself to death. *Grow up*," she said brutally.

He jerked as hard as if Dusty's fist had hammered him again. In the moonlight his brown face was white.

Reach, reach, Rainey said.

Better things.

You could have had me.

Without a word he gave her coat a hard yank. She stumbled back into him with a muffled cry of alarm, but he caught her hand and jerked her around to him.

"You know what, Terrill Carroll?" he demanded, angry huffs of breath coming between the words, "you got the *damnedest,* most smart-aleck mouth I ever heard on a woman." With his free hand he cupped her jaw in his palm, his fingers pressing frantically up to the edges of her mouth. "And you know what else? You can just put it to some other good use besides blessin' me out. I want it sweet and *quiet.*"

Even in her state of shock, Rilla might have split something back at him, but she never got the chance. His mouth stopped her words, so insistent that she nearly collapsed against him.

Into the small of her back he pressed her own hands, forcing her up high against him, cutting off breath, making her heart clamor.

"All right." He spoke quickly, before he ever turned loose of her. "You said it. You said I could have you if I reached. Wouldn't listen to reason. So, will you marry me, Rilla?"

She had to try twice. *"Yes."*

He let his breath out in a rush, struggling before he spoke again. "And if I try—and I will—and I turn out to be just me, nothing more, will you still be with me?"

"I'll take you just the way you are now, a man with a good heart, like my father," she answered tremulously, between tears and laughter. "Anything else is just extra." She laid her lips against his throat, kissing the pulse that throbbed under his skin, her face wet against him.

He couldn't talk for a moment, clasping her tightly. "I'm gonna give you a lot of extras, Rilla," he swore at last, his words passionate and husky above her. "There's just one thing I've got to clear up. One thing I'm ashamed of. But it's not anything to do with us. You're never goin' to be sorry, Rilla. I promise."

"Do you know what time it is?" Rainey queried as he pulled up his left overall strap and latched it shut. His big black hands rubbed over his old face, wiping away the night's sleep.

"I reckon it's nearly six," Jubal tried to say calmly. "Still a little dark. But I had to come early because I got to be to work early today. And I want to do this now." No point in telling Rainey he hadn't been to bed at all, that he'd felt so good since about midnight that he could have been high on something.

But then he was. On love, on Terrill, and on belief. *She believed.*

"You wanta do what now?" Rainey asked suspiciously, eyeing Jubal as the two of them stood on the little porch of Rainey's house. It smelled a little like wet dog; the source of the odor wagged his hound-dog tail between them, thumping it against Jubal's leg in his enthusiasm.

"Remember what you told me once? About how to show yourself you're gonna do something better? Be somebody more?" Jubal looked dead at Rainey. "I want you to do it for me, Rainey. Baptize me."

Rainey's mouth fell open; his hand dropped nervelessly to his overall front. "Boy, are you drunk?"

Drunk on self-confidence and a woman's love.

"No, I ain't drunk. I just want to be baptized. Right now. I brought extra clothes."

Rainey stared, fumbling futilely with his overall straps. "I b'lieve you sure enough mean it, Jubal."

"I do. You gonna do it for me?" Jubal questioned anxiously.

Rainey pulled his head back and puffed out two or three breaths, grinning at him in slow delight. "I knowed you since you and them brothers was born. I put up with enough devilment from you and Jarvis and Jonah till I got a right to this baptizin'. Let me get my hat."

As he opened the screen door he paused, looking through it toward the horizon, where a November sun was coming up, as bright and cold as last night's moon.

"It's a good day to start new," he remarked to that sun.

The Red Fork River lapped inquiringly against Jubal's bare feet, tugging at the old blue jeans as he waded out in it, right into the tendrils of smoky fog that curled around him. The water took a bite out of him, wondering what kind of man came in November and plunged in.

"Cold as ice, Rainey," he said apologetically to the old preacher who sat on the rock laboriously unlacing his boots. "Reckon we'll both be blue when this is over."

"Whiter'n snow, boy, whiter'n snow." Rainey

stuck a toe in. "Well, you're gonna remember this, Jubal. No forgettin'," he said ruefully. "Whuu-ee."

"I ain't gonna forget," Jubal vowed, and the turn he made in the waist-deep water sent a swirl nearly to the bank on the far side.

"I got to ask," Rainey said as he waded slowly out to him, "if you made everything all right, Jubal. With your own heart."

Jubal waited until the old man looked up; Rainey had forgotten and left on his hat, and he had to peer up from under the brim. "I've done a lot of things I ain't proud of, Rainey. Sometimes I felt like I was just runnin' in place. And always afraid. Scared I was gonna do it wrong, so I did. But from this day on, I mean to try something else. Like you said."

"There's wellsprings of faith some men find." Rainey came to a halt in front of Jubal. "I've been waitin' a long time for you to find one. Where, Jubal?"

Jubal dipped his hands in the river and rubbed them, wet and cold, over his face. "She loves me, Rainey. And I love her."

"All right." Rainey nodded sagely. "More men than you have found their God—and theirselves— through a woman. Is it the lastin' kind?"

Jubal laughed a little, his face still as he looked at the rising sun. "I ain't gonna outlive this love. Not if I live to be a thousand."

Rainey considered, shivering a little, before he spoke, suddenly brisk. "Then let's get on with it 'fore we freeze, boy. My bones wish you'da got salvation in July, not November."

Jubal reached out and lifted the old brown felt hat from Rainey's white curls. Rainey looked at it blankly, then took it and gave it a wild toss, meaning to catch it on the big rock at the river's edge. But the river caught it gleefully and carried it away instead.

"That's all right," Rainey said philosophically. "I'll give it the hat on account it's gonna give me back a brand-new man. You, Jubal."

22

Fitting the puzzle together.

He twisted and pushed and tightened. Head bolt into block. One part of the engine into another. Putting together the big dark heart of a truck.

His head reassured him that it was all right, that he had to do this if he wanted to stay free.

Keep pushing.

Keep tightening.

But his heart was a different matter: it kept remembering the light in a girl's eyes last night and the light of the rising sun shining bright as hope in his face this morning when Rainey pulled him up out of the water. The last engine he'd ever put together for Carroll's schemes, that was what this was. He had to see that it never left this mill. He had to stop its shipment, and the shipment of two others that were slated to be finished and hauled in nine days.

Keep puzzling. How?

He knew the obvious thing to do.

The up-and-down, black-and-white solution was to go to Ned Standford and tell the truth.

But Henry Carroll was respected and powerful. Did Jubal have the proof to make Cade County listen? It wasn't as if they'd take the word of a Kane against a Carroll.

Worse, if Jubal went to the cops, he'd be breaking that unwritten code that ridgerunners lived by, the one that said they settled their own problems. Nobody ran to the law, because the law didn't understand them, anyway.

Jubal wasn't sure he could stomach getting involved with men such as Foster and Malone, and Sullivan's Ridge was liable to turn on him even faster than Bethel if he did.

But wasn't Standford different?

And was this really fear that was holding Jubal back? He was dog-sick when he considered the real possibility that in taking Carroll down, he himself was likely to wind up back in prison.

But this couldn't go on, not if he'd meant all the things he'd said and done with Rilla.

He didn't have many options.

So when work ended at noon that Saturday, Jubal found a phone in a quiet corner of Bethel, and with hands that shook, he called Standford's office.

"Sheriff's not here," a voice informed him. "He's gone to see his daughter in Indiana over the holidays and won't be back for two weeks. He left me in charge. This is Malone."

Malone.

Quietly, Jubal hung up.

What was he thinking, running to slime like Malone?

You can do it, he told himself. You got yourself into this mess. Surely now you've got the guts and the brains to get yourself out.

Get out smart, too—get out alive and free.

Don't stay under Carroll's thumb like Bobo.

Bobo.

At two o'clock on Saturday afternoon, Jubal raised a reluctant hand to bang on the door of Lily Clayburn's trailer. From inside came the sound of a television blasting; from the pen at the end of the trailer, a dog snapped and snarled at him.

Bobo was here. Too late for work, too early for the Pine. It was risky to talk to him. He couldn't be trusted. But, once again, Jubal had few choices.

Lily's eyeglasses made her brown eyes huge and round as a startled owl's; they took Jubal by surprise, too. She usually wore contacts.

"Jubal!" She clutched the doorknob, nervous as a cat.

"I want to see Bobo."

"I don't want any trouble. If you come to start another fight—"

"Who is it, Lily?" Before she could answer, Bobo himself strode into the living room, his hair standing up like a porcupine's quills, his white T-shirt hanging loose over baggy pants. His face darkened. "What d'you want, Jubal?"

"To talk."

"You coulda talked at the mill yard any time these last few weeks. But now you're a big man. Even Dusty keeps his mouth shut. So why come here?"

"Bobo." Lily's voice held a warning.

"I didn't hear you talkin' to me, either. But I didn't come about that. I came because the way I figure it, you owe me."

"I owe *you?*" Bobo gave a huff of ridicule.

"That's right. You want to talk outside?" Jubal didn't know exactly how much Bobo told Lily about his doings, but his attempt to shield her failed.

"I got no reason to. She knows anythin' you want to say." But Bobo was wary.

"I've got some private things to talk about. Most of 'em about Carroll." Jubal shot another pointed look at Lily as he shut the door behind him.

Bobo didn't move.

"I'm not about to leave," Lily said firmly, gripping the couch arm. "Don't even think I will, Bobo."

Jubal shrugged. "Then you'll have to hear. Once I stayed quiet for you, Bobo. And a few weeks ago, when they dragged me back in because the mill had been robbed another time, you spoke up for me before they even asked. They let me go because I had alibis. You were one of them. Bobo Hackett told how I'd rode to the Pine with him and had been there until after midnight."

The other man frowned, trying to search his way to what was coming. "I came through for you, didn't I?" he demanded pugnaciously.

"Except it was a lie. Me and you and the Delaneys, all in a back room shootin' pool until eleven. Then you said you had to make a trip to the john. But you know what? You were gone over an hour. Maybe Bobby and Rick were too drunk to notice. Not me."

The hands of the other man shook, and into the silence in the room came a sudden burst of excitement from the television set, where a football game roared. The Oilers and the Saints.

"I got to talkin' to—"

"No." Jubal leaned heavily on the door behind him. "You didn't talk. You left. Because when I went outside at midnight to get my coat outta your truck, it was in a different place. The hood was still hot. But you were already inside again, tellin' ever'body about the woman who'd stopped you and come on to you. Bobo, there wasn't any woman who'd kept you talkin' anywhere."

"What'n the hell would you know?" Bobo demanded defensively, but he was panicked. It was in his eyes. "All you could see was that Johnson girl. You went outside to go with her. You think we didn't know who—"

"I don't care what you knew." Jubal watched him steadily. "The fact is, you weren't my alibi that night. *I was yours.* And the Delaneys, they never even caught on that you were gone, so they made even better alibis."

In the silence, Lily had begun to cry.

"You were the one who broke into the mill a second time. Not me." It wasn't a question; Jubal knew it. It was written in Bobo's face. "Because under my coat on the seat of your truck was a flashlight. A big black one with a gold stripe down its side. It had been on Carroll's desk that afternoon when I took the paperwork to him."

Another wild shout from the Oiler fans. Bobo reached over and jammed the buttons, sending the ball game into oblivion.

"Hell, Lily, I didn't take anythin'. I swear it." Bobo moved roughly over to the couch. "An' I wadn't with a woman, neither. Not that night. Not in over a year." His hand wavered and dropped from her direction when she scooted farther away, down the couch.

"That's two times I've been quiet for you, Bobo. How many more do you expect me to cover for you? I reckon you're just plain no good. You'd tell a lie even when the truth would do."

"It was a setup." Bobo said it to Jubal, but he was pleading with Lily. "I did it for Carroll."

"He keeps you real busy," Jubal said sarcastically.

"But I don't care about any of that. Like I told you, you owe me. An' I only want to know one thing: you said he kept papers. Where?"

"Listen to me," Bobo pleaded with him and Lily both. "It's the truth. The son of a bitch robbed his own mill. Had *me* do it. That afternoon he brought me in, showed me the safe, showed me how to open it. That night, when I got there, he'd already took care of the alarm on the door, made it look like a burglar had detoured the electric circuit. All I had to do was open the door, go to his office, and open the safe. There's a blue light on a panel inside his desk. When it comes on, it means the silent alarm's gone off. Soon as I set it off, all I was supposed to do was run. So I did. I didn't take one damn thing. I just broke in and triggered the alarm for his inner office while Carroll set at home with his sister. She's the perfect alibi. Nobody would ever doubt Tandy Carroll's word. There wasn't no money, no papers, in there when I opened it."

"That's a lie," Jubal said flatly, tiredly. "I took him paperwork just as work closed. And there was money on his desk in a wrapper there. Ever'body else was already gone. He always put it in the safe. Ten minutes later, I watched him drive away. Empty hands. I was at work late that night, too. Nearly until eight, finishing up with the loader. He didn't come back, and Tandy Carroll told Standford he was with her until the alarm went off."

"No, no," Bobo returned eagerly. "He's got another place, a secret place, he keeps things. In the office. You wanted to know about the papers. That's where they are."

"What secret place?" Jubal wanted to shake Bobo until his teeth rattled, until the truth fell out of him. *If* it was in him.

"I don't know. I think it's hid in the wall some-where. The one between the offices. One of those wires from the alarm—it runs along the floor to it. They ain't no reason to wire an inside wall unless there's somethin' behind it. And that's what he did. Put all that money in another safe. I broke into an empty one, just to make 'em think the place had been robbed. Then I ran across the field, the same way the Carroll girl comes ever' mornin', to my truck. It was parked right in the Carroll drive. Just at the gate."

Jubal considered the words, then the source. "I don't believe any story this crazy," he said at last. "You took that money. Not Carroll. He had no reason."

Lily stood, her face red from crying, her body still so slender that she gave little hint of her pregnancy. She pulled down her equally red sweater decisively. "I told you, Bobo, I'm not puttin' up with this. My baby don't need a daddy this bad. I don't say one word about you goin' off with the Delaneys ever' Friday night, but right here's where I draw the line. You get your things and you get out."

"He took at least fifty thousand dollars from the regular safe," Bobo said forcefully. "I saw that much in a marked wrapper when he showed me how to open it. The insurance replaced it."

"But why?"

"How'n the hell do I know? Maybe it was just because his sister interfered. She bought logs on her own, stuck her nose in his business, and he didn't like it. So maybe he didn't pay for 'em. The insurance did. He can't stand to have his plans messed up, and he's got his own ideas for the money the mill makes."

"But that's—that's crazy."

"So is he. You know why I think he really did it? Just to prove he could. Maybe he even used the insurance money to pay for the engine parts that you put together. They're dirt cheap anyway, bein' stolen, but he don't turn loose of nothin' if he can find a way to hold it. This way, the parts would be free and clear. All profit. He's nuts, Jubal. Said once to me that he had to make a cool million, and when he did, he was gonna show it to Luke." Bobo took a deep breath. "Hell, I chilled right down to my toes. Luke Carroll's as dead as they get."

Jubal felt the chill himself, and the dog outside must have, too. He howled into the still afternoon, the sound dying hard.

"If he's so crazy," Jubal asked, choked, "why don't you get away?"

Bobo sat down weakly on the couch. "You know why. The same reason you won't ever. He knows too much. He's got proof. An' he figures that even if we talked a little before he got to us, nobody's goin' to pay attention. We're just us."

For a minute the old despair filled Jubal. But he made himself remember the sun in the morning sky and the girl at midnight.

"I'm tired of bein' just us." He turned back to the door and opened it. "And I'm tired of Henry Carroll."

Lily stepped out silently onto the porch with him.

"You better let him stay, Lily," Jubal said flatly. "He's got nobody else."

"Do you want me to iron your blue dress for you for church tomorrow?" Tandy stuck her head in Katherine's room to address Rilla as she sat on the rocker beside her mother's bed. "Since you're going out for dinner, I thought you'd want to wear something special. I've already got the iron hot."

"It'll be fine, Aunt. Thanks."

"Where are you . . . going tomorrow, Rilla?" Katherine asked quietly, her blue eyes brutally beautiful in her thin face.

"Joanie Crabtree called. Wanted me to come to lunch."

"You need to be out some. Joanie's a . . . sweet girl." Katherine's hand reached up to her pillow, to catch the cotton case and worry the corner between her fingers. "Sometimes you and Tandy . . . sometimes it seems like you've become her daughter already. Not mine."

"I'll always be yours, Mama."

"It's all right. It's the way I want it . . . to be. Tandy's never had anybody to . . . to make over. I want to smile to see her acting like . . . like some mother hen with you. It was my plan, you know." Katherine tried to laugh. "You'd come home, Tandy would . . . take to you—she always had a weakness for you—and I would—"

Rilla stumbled out of her chair hurriedly, finding the bedside in the dim, dusky room and sinking onto it. "Mama."

Katherine looked at her, and the blue eyes held frustrated anger behind the sheen of tears. "I wasted years, Rilla. Now I can't complain . . . because I'll never know a single part of your life."

She pressed the palms of her hands against her eyes. "I don't want to die. It's not fair. *I don't want to die.*"

There was absolutely nothing Rilla could do to soothe her mother, to stop her own heart from breaking.

No antidote for this grief.

Holding Katherine's wrists, Rilla pulled them to her lap. "Don't cry," she soothed, speaking to herself as well as to her mother. "Don't cry, Mama, and I'll tell you something that only the two of us will know. I haven't told Tandy. Remember the man I told you about? Well, I was right. He does love me. And I love him. I'm going to marry him, Mama."

Clutching at the loose shirt Rilla wore, Katherine whispered, "I want you to be happy."

"I will be."

"Would I like him?" Katherine questioned wistfully.

Looking down on the doll-like figure against the pillows, Rilla made a decision.

Henry couldn't dispose of her anymore. She wouldn't let him. And Tandy had to know about Jubal sooner or later.

It was time for this love to step out of the shadows.

"I'll bring him to you," Rilla promised her mother. "He'll come once I talk to him, I know."

". . . so what I'm working my way up to saying is"— Joanie took a long draw of air—"that Dr. Jones asked me if I wanted to be the nurse with your mother the last few days. And with you."

Her voice trailed off as Rilla's face registered her meaning. The two of them sat across the tiny table for two at the Wayside Inn, halfway between Edmonds and Bethel.

"Is it that soon?" Rilla could talk about it now without a break.

Wordlessly Joanie nodded. "I'm new to this. I've seen people die before, but I wasn't the nurse in charge. If you want me to be the one, knowing that, I'm willing. There needs to be somebody." Her brown eyes were frank and anxious.

"Why did you decide to be a nurse?" Rilla asked, trying to pull her mind from Joanie's revelation—*It's that soon*—and think.

Joanie laughed. "It's my way of being the rebel of the family."

"Oh, one of those," Rilla teased a little.

"I've heard you're one, too," Joanie said quietly. "All I've ever found it meant was that you hurt more and feel more, because you're trying to follow your heart."

"*My* heart's mixed up," Rilla answered. "Sometimes it's as happy as it has ever been. Sometimes I think I'll ache for the rest of my life for Mama. And sometimes, I'm just guilty because I'm going to keep on living and she has to die. Just help her, Joanie."

"When the time comes, Terrill," Joanie promised, "I'll be there."

Bobo was right. There *was* something different about that wall, Jubal reflected as he eyed it Monday.

A closet was housed behind it, that wall that divided the general office, where Rosalie and Terrill worked, and Carroll's private one, but the closet was only about four feet long. The wall itself continued another four feet beyond that, just as wide as if the closet were still caught between its smooth surface and the paneled one that was the next one over. Was it just an empty space? Or more?

And there was a tiny wire running to the wall; Jubal traced it with his eyes while Carroll flipped through his paperwork. That wire ran right along the base of the wall, close to one of the grooves in the paneling, and disappeared into a corner, the very corner where the burglar alarm system was housed in a box on the back outside corner of the mill office.

He didn't know enough about alarms to tamper intimately with individual wires, thought Jubal. So the whole system had to go. Somehow, this week, because Thursday was Thanksgiving. The entire mill would be empty for four days.

Time enough for him to make the hit and retreat to safety.

"You want *what?*"

Rilla caught at Jubal as he flung himself backward against the high fence in their corner of the parking lot. "She's not going to live much longer," she pleaded, "and I want her to know you."

Jubal laid his head back, staring up at the sky in shock. "I can't just walk in and— What would I say? An' you know what they'd do? Girl, they'd find a reason to lock *me* up and they'd chain *you* to their side until one of us dropped dead from old age." His voice was rough with panic.

"Jubal." Rilla caught his face with both her hands, forcing him to look down on her. "We'll have to, if not this week, then soon. Let's stop meeting in the dark. You said you wanted to. Come and sit on the living room couch." Her voice laughed. "Henry can only have a stroke once, and Aunt Tandy won't send me back to Rose Hall now."

"Oh, God," Jubal moaned feebly. He'd told himself after that trip to the bottom of the river that he'd stop swearing so much, so this had to be prayer. "I want to, Rilla, but—"

Rilla pounced. "But you'll do it."

"I guess I'll have to. I need time—some time to think. When are you wantin' to talk to her?"

"Maybe this weekend."

"This weekend?" he stumbled. "Thursday, that's Thanksgiving."

"Well?"

"You'd be with your family then. And I'd rather come the first time when Carroll's not there."

"Oh."

"And Friday, I may have to—" He stopped, wondering why he just couldn't go ahead and tell her.

"What?"

"Rilla, I've got to do something, that's for me, so that I can be free, so I can feel—"

"Something to do with your probation?" she interrupted, puzzled, giving him a way out at last.

"Yeah." Relief swept over him.

Dubious, she examined his face. "Jubal, if you're afraid, just remember, I'll be there with you, right beside you."

Flooded with a sudden wry tenderness, he leaned out a little to catch her and coax her closer. "That's one thing I'm countin' on."

"This damn clutch is slippin'," Dusty announced to Jubal as he looked over the big truck. "It's got to be fixed."

"Okay." Jubal motioned down toward the shop. "I just pulled the loader up. It needs work, too. So I guess you'll have to park your truck over there." He motioned to the distant alcove between the mill office and the shop. "I'll try to get to it tomorrow. Hey, Dusty."

Dusty turned an irritable red face toward him.

"Better stay back from the edge. The land slopes. Angle the truck nose toward the office. You wouldn't want to start rollin' and wind up in the bottom of that holler." Jubal nodded toward the deep, dark abyss that lay between the mill—just beyond the office—and the Carroll farm.

Dusty snorted. "I'm a better driver than I am a fighter, Kane. I know how to park it."

His swaggering vault up to the cab took away a little of Jubal's twinge of conscience. Dusty knew a lot, that was certain; he parked the truck at exactly the right angle on the slope, just the right distance from the corner of the building.

And Dusty made sure that it would never roll to the hollow, too. The wall of the office would stop it first, the wall right where the alarm system sat.

But there were things that Dusty didn't know, such as the fact that his clutch had been tampered with and that he'd been lured right into the position of leaving the truck with Jubal.

And he was off in the front of the mill yard when Jubal climbed in from the back side to release the brakes.

But he knew three minutes later when the big tractor slammed with the force of a train into the side of Henry's office.

The impact crushed brick and dented aluminum siding; it made a grinding, crunching uproar and jarred mortar dust in a wild dance.

And it set every burglar alarm in the place into a mad jangle of sound and light and confusion.

"What in the hell did you think you were doing?"

For once Carroll was not cold and icy and contained. His hair stood straight up, his face shone purple red, his whole body quivered with rage.

"I put on the brake. I'd take an oath on it," Dusty explained and groveled and kowtowed for the third time. "But it was actin' funny all day. Clutch not right, air pressure not right. I told you, it's why I brought the damn thing in to Kane. And he's told you—it ain't my fault."

"That's right," Jubal interposed. "I told him to

park it, that I'd look at it. And I did. I hit somethin', jarred somethin'. The brakes didn't hold."

"Goddamn it, do you think I'm blind? I *know* they didn't hold," Carroll shouted in high dudgeon, and the burglar alarm, for some reason known only to itself, went off again, just as erratically as it had been doing for the last twenty minutes. "Get me some aspirins, Rosalie!" he shouted at the woman who hovered nearby. "Look at that wall. Do you know how much money it'll take to replace those bricks and redo that siding?"

Most of the workers—those who weren't blind and dumb—were milling around outside under the oak tree with Carroll and Jubal and Dusty. Malone's patrol car with its flashing blue lights sat pulled up to the office; so did Foster's. The two of them were still trying to control the maddened alarm.

Over on the office porch, Rilla stared wide-eyed at the damage, hoping to escape the sound of Henry's fury as he berated Dusty and Jubal by turns.

An adventurous photographer from the *Cade County Examiner* snapped pictures as Buddy Waller's big wrecker struggled to pull the big truck from its sloping, nosedived position against the wall, his own engine moaning with the strain.

"Somebody's going to pay for this, I swear to God!" Henry roared.

"I told you, it's my fault," Jubal said quietly. "So if you're gonna fire somebody, fire me." His face he could manage, but the taunt that threaded through his voice was beyond his control.

Carroll stared, then began to calm. Around them, men waited. "That'd be the easy way out for you, wouldn't it, Kane?" he said finally, inexplicably. "But don't get cocky. Your time's coming."

The silent challenge lay between them. Rilla

could read it in their posture, even at a distance too great to hear their words: Carroll, square and pugnacious, faced off against Jubal, slender and defiant.

Hold your own, she wanted to tell Jubal. *Don't let him back you down. I can't stand to see him rip you up for a mistake.*

Then Henry reached out, pushed Jubal out of the way, and walked over to Malone. Closer to Rilla.

"Damn thing's tore all to pieces," Malone told Henry decisively. "Foster's tryin' to disconnect it, but it's the fanciest piece of work I ever saw, especially for a sawmill out here in Cade County. Sheriff might know what to do, but he's outta town. You'll need to call the people who installed it—"

"I've already done that," Henry snapped. "They think they can't work until Monday. Said just about everybody had gone home early for the holiday tomorrow. That means you'll have to patrol this place once an hour every hour, Malone."

Malone snorted. "The last big robbery in this county was right here three months ago, Mr. Carroll. Still no explanation for that one. Sheriff says he's kinda gettin' tired of this mill havin' problems. I'll run a patrol by the place once in a while during the day, but Foster's the only one on duty at night. He don't like leavin' the office before ten much unless there's a call."

"You two are real lawmen, aren't you?" Carroll said sarcastically.

"Well, look at it this way: we're all you've got."

* * *

"You did it deliberately," Bobo accused. He pulled off the navy cap he wore, running a hand through his thick thatch of reddish-blond hair.

Jubal leaned up against Maggie's porch post carelessly; his coat caught so that it bunched at his waist and opened in a V toward his throat; it made him look bulkier than usual. When he finally spoke, his warm breath made another puff of smoke in the chilly Wednesday night air, one that matched the thin line drifting from the cigarette he'd just lit.

"I wasn't the one who pulled the truck in, Bobo. Dusty did. You really don't think he'd do anything for me, do you?" Jubal told himself: *Laugh, be calm, don't react.* "And anyway, what good would it do me to wreck one of Carroll's trucks? I'm gonna be the one who'll have to fix it."

"You can't fool me, boy. That alarm is gone. Shot. Because you wanted it to be. Because you mean to get into Carroll's safe and get those papers." Bobo laughed, the sound unsteady. "Anybody else, I'd think they were goin' for money. But you got this weird streak of honesty, or something. You're some kind of dreamer, always believin' in good. You can't stand what you're doin' for Carroll. Me, I ain't dreamy one damn bit, but I'm sick of Carroll lookin' over my shoulder. He's had you a few months. I been caught near five years. That's enough."

Bobo's agitation kept him pushing out words, and it made his whole body tense. He slammed his cap back on his head and stuffed his hands into the pockets of his red plaid jacket. "I want to go with you, Jubal."

Jubal froze for a second. "I don't know what you're talkin' about."

"Don't you get too big on me," Bobo returned, his temper rising. "There was a time when you was a kid that you begged to run with me'n Jarvis."

Jubal twisted, giving the cigarette that he hadn't

touched yet a hard, angry fling out onto the wet grass. "Maybe so, but it was a long time ago. Before I knew what a Judas you could be."

Bobo flushed, then grunted heavily. "I reckon I deserve that. But I want out, too. I want to make sure you get all the papers about me."

"You're crazy. Have you even been listenin' to me?" Jubal demanded, walking to the steps.

Bobo waited a stretching moment, until the silence forced Jubal to look back at him.

"Say what you want to say," he told the younger man. "But you need to know one thing. There's that other alarm. The silent one. You remember it, don't you? Well, you didn't take it out. It's hooked up from inside his desk. I saw the way it works when he cut everything off to show me how I was supposed to break into the safe."

Jubal felt his throat close up a minute; he never moved a muscle. "I'll tell you what, Bobo, why don't *you* break into Carroll's office if you're so wild about it? If you've done it so often?"

"'Cause I ain't got hands like yours. Steady as a rock. It ain't gonna be nothin' to you to disarm that office, not if I'm there to show you where everythin' is, to tell you how to do it." Bobo's voice ended on a pleading, waiting note.

Jubal finally laughed. "Just go home, Bobo. You got Lily and a baby waitin' for you, and you're out here believin' fairy tales. You think I'm some kinda secret agent or something?"

Every time Rilla looked at Katherine, she remembered: This was the last Thanksgiving.

It was in all their faces, in their eyes when they met. Henry was so miserable that Rilla couldn't pretend and laugh anymore, so at six she left them alone and went upstairs.

"Rilla!" Tandy called up those stairs to her, sounding both curious and surprised, "There's a phone call. A man. He says he's a friend. I hope his manners are better than I think they are. He wouldn't give a name."

Rilla ran down the stairs, as surprised as Tandy. "Maybe it's somebody from the university," she offered. "Hello?"

"Rilla?"

Jubal. It was Jubal. She sucked in her breath sharply, twisting to see who was nearby. Nobody. "You're calling me," she said blankly.

He laughed. "Feels weird, I know. It felt real strange to dial the number. I even had to look it up."

He'd kissed her, and drawn off her clothes, and made love to her, and he'd never called her. It struck her as funny. Humor in the middle of this nerve-racking day.

"You said we had to stop hidin'. I guess this is my first step," he told her at last.

"I like it," she answered, ridiculously pleased. "You have a nice voice."

"Yeah? Well, you've got a lot of nice things, too," he said, teasing and rough. "I sort of need to see you tonight. We can't meet at the mill—those patrols—but I can come to the end of your road at the gate. It's takin' a chance, but—" His voice stopped, waited, then resumed. "There's too many people in this world, y'know that?"

"Where are you?"

"At Ida's store. So, will you meet me?"

"Is this a proposition?"

"I already made one of those. You said yes." No teasing now. His voice was quiet.

"It's yes now, too, Jubal. At eleven."

Just a friend, she told Tandy. He'd said he was coming to visit sometime.

Without a word, he unzipped the light jacket she wore, slid his arms around her waist under it, and drew her up to him.

"I want . . . I *need* to hold you a minute, Rilla. That's all."

He buried his face in her hair, letting his heart beat steadily against her. For a confused minute she thought he was at peace. But above her he spoke, and his voice was urgent and pleading.

"I know I probably should let you go. Just like I knew better than to make love to you. But I ain't a saint. I don't want to be. I just want us to be together."

She pulled back a little, to look up at him in puzzlement. His jaw was clenched; his eyes burned bright.

"I want that, too, Jubal."

"There's something more. I want you to believe in me, Rilla, okay? No matter what happens or what people say. Everything I've been with you, all that's the truth. D'you hear me?"

She nodded at last.

"There's something I've got to do tomorrow night. It's not exactly right and it's not exactly wrong. But it's the only way. When it's over, then we'll be all right."

"But—"

"No. No questions tonight. Tonight I need something different. You just remember that I want to be that 'good man,' Rilla, the one you said I was."

She lifted her hands to caress his shoulders. She could feel the tension in him. The waiting. The anxiety.

"I'll be here when tomorrow night's gone, Jubal. Come and see. No matter what," she whispered.

*   *   *

She stopped cold in the entrance to the dark kitchen. A shadowy figure was seated at the table, facing the door, and the air felt tight, suspenseful.

"Where you've been?"

Henry Carroll.

His voice was dangerous silk, his whole body still and coiled. The old terror that he'd generated in her as a child writhed in her stomach again; she thought she'd conquered it.

"Out walking," she answered nervously, pushing the door shut. Her fingers were clammy on the knob. "What are you doing up, Henry? Communing with your inner being?" That was better—rude and flippant.

"Walking at midnight? And it's how cold? Thirty-four degrees?" Henry stood slowly, a black bulk in a shifting, underworldlike room of shadows. "I know it's cold. Because I went outside, too. Worried about the mill, I guess. And who did I see running—not walking—down the road? You, Terrill."

She heard breath—a stricken intake of it from the darkest corner of the room. Not Henry. Not her.

"And there was someone waiting," he whispered. "A man."

"Stop playing these games, Henry." It was Tandy in the corner, her voice frighteningly stern. "Turn on the lights."

In the glow of the bulb above the sink that Henry flipped on, Tandy's face was grim and white. Henry's just looked satisfied.

Blood pounded in Rilla's temples. *Don't be afraid,* she told herself. *It's time to tell, anyway.*

"Sit down, Rilla." Her aunt's voice was firm, her lips compressed.

"No. I'll stand." *The better to fight you with,* she thought fleetingly.

"You met a man at midnight at the gate. We've got nothing against you bringing your men friends here. You know that. So why sneak and meet him?"

"I could say that I do it because I want to, Aunt Tandy," Rilla answered steadily while her heart beat madly in her chest, "and it would be nothing to you. I'm an adult. I can live as I please."

"Not in my house," Henry said softly.

"Is it your *house* now, too?"

"No—no bickering," Tandy intervened. "You're right. You don't have to tell his name. But that only makes it look worse. And he's not much of a man, or he'd—"

"I never said I wouldn't tell you," Rilla interrupted, but she was dreading every second of this ordeal. "I mean to bring him here, to see Mama soon. So you need to know. His name is Jubal."

The silence grew as wide as the sea, as wide as Tandy's eyes, as wide as Henry's shoulders as he heaved them up.

"What?" Tandy whispered, her hands nervously smoothing over each other.

And Henry began to laugh.

"You heard me."

"You've been meeting *Kane* at midnight? Maggie Kane's wild son? Dear God. *God.* Rilla, you don't know what you're doing. Do you know what he is? Do you know what Kane will—"

"His name is Jubal."

Tandy stopped dead in her tirade. Against her yellow bathrobe, her hands looked stiff. "And you know all about him, I suppose," she said quietly. "How long, Rilla, has this been going on?"

"Too long for you to stop it now, Aunt."

"She's a little tramp." Henry said it triumphantly. "Just like I always knew she would be."

"That's enough." Tandy flared at her brother. "All these years, and you've always been half the problem. Now you get out. *Out.* I'm the one who'll handle this."

Henry's mouth drew back in a thin line. "You're such a fool, Tandy. There's nothing for you to handle. I'll pull him in line Monday morning. Now I know why he's got so damn sure of himself with me. As for her, send her back to Rose Hall—"

"You can't make me go, Henry. Never again," Rilla said passionately.

"Or better yet, since she likes them so much, give her to the Kanes."

The kitchen door shut behind him on the words.

"Why him, Rilla? No, don't answer. I already know. His looks, I suppose," Tandy said implacably. "Henry has so much to answer for. He told me he'd keep Kane away from you at the mill. So I let you walk right into his hands. Oh, God."

"You don't even know him, Aunt. You don't know how kind he can be, or how he—" She stopped, floundering helplessly.

Tandy sucked in her breath. "And just what do *you* know about him, Rilla?" Her cheeks had two red spots, one high on each side.

"I know that he's a hard worker, that his mother—"

"No." Her aunt shook her head. "You know what I mean. How far has this gone?"

Rilla swallowed, cheeks flaming. "I don't have to answer you. It's nobody's business."

"I'm not asking so I can get vicarious thrills. I'm asking to try to help you. Are you a virgin, Rilla?" Tandy was right on her now.

Tell the truth. Tell the truth, she urged her tongue. "We made love. Don't start, Aunt Tandy. He's the only one. I mean to marry him. Sometimes I already feel married to him."

"*Marry* him!"

Tandy's breath was ragged as she walked to the kitchen table and fumbled for a chair. She sat there for so long, staring at her hands, that Rilla moved away.

"I'm sorry. But I love him."

Tandy twisted to clasp the back of her chair. "Wait. You'll hear what I have to say, and I'll say it. Because I care about you. I never thought I'd see the day I'd be talking to you about the likes of Kane. I don't even understand the attraction. But let me tell you what I do understand: this is not Nashville. Maybe you can behave any way you want there. This is Cade County, full of people who know each other—and you. One of the facts of life here is that your 'Jubal' can't do anything for you except give you a reputation. His whole family except his mother—they're bad blood. You can't marry him. You may not know that, but he does. Dear God, you're a *Carroll*." Tandy's laugh was nearly hysterical.

Rilla had to catch at the nearest wall before she could speak. She'd never seen Tandy so upset or her eyes so angry. "I can't believe you're saying this. Nobody's 'bad blood' just because of his family."

"No? Maybe not," Tandy returned. "But you can only be what you're taught to be, and this—this Jubal was raised out on that ridge with all three of his brothers. His good-for-nothing daddy, too, until he got killed. Now you tell me how he's going to be different from them. They're all he knows. All of it, except what he learned at Lineville."

There was a silence.

"I can't make you understand." Rilla had never felt so utterly without weapons in this struggle with her aunt. "You have to know him. Please, meet him. Talk to him. He *loves* me, just the way I am. He's a little shy, not too sure of himself. I think he's afraid of you."

Tandy put both hands to her temples. "Terrill. We're talking about Jubal Kane. This is the same man who robbed the mill. Who went to prison. Who had a whore from the Pine as an alibi three or four months ago. Don't be a fool. You've made a huge mistake. We can't recall it. But we don't have to dwell on it, either. It's not even all your fault. I hold him responsible. He was born old. Too old for you to know how to handle."

Keep remembering, Rilla told herself. *Remember Jubal the way he is. Don't let her sway you.*

But her aunt was so sure, the facts so right.

"Please, please, meet him, Aunt. I can't give him up. I love him."

Tandy looked at her niece's pleading face. "All right." Her eyes were hard, implacable. "I'll meet him. And when I'm through, you'll understand clearly why this is an absurdity. So will he. And Henry Carroll will fire him Monday. This time, I mean it."

23

The phone rang early the next morning, breaking the heavy silence between Tandy and Terrill that persisted in the kitchen.

"Want to go Christmas shopping?" Joanie demanded as soon as Rilla answered. "Everybody else crowds into Nashville today. Why not us? We could make a whole day of it."

Rilla considered the question, then considered spending the day with Tandy's disapproval.

"I'll be ready by—when? Ten?"

"Great. Tell your aunt that we might not be back until late. *Really* late. We'll go to a movie tonight if we don't drop dead on our feet at the mall. Okay?"

The whirlwind on the other end of the line stilled as Joanie clicked down her phone. Rilla put down her receiver more slowly, contemplating her aunt.

"That was Joanie. I'm going shopping with her today in Nashville."

"Then I'll say now what I've been trying to find a

way to say all morning." Tandy opened the almond-colored dishwasher to remove the plates from the night before. "I thought for an hour or two last night that nothing could be worse than the fact that you've . . . been intimate with Jubal Kane. But then I remembered that you mean to *marry* him. Rilla, you're compounding this mistake. And I blame myself for it."

"You! But it's got nothing to do with you," Rilla protested.

Tandy sat the plates on the breakfast bar with a rattling snap. "Yes, it does. I've also stressed sexual purity. Maybe I've made you feel that because you've given him your innocence, you have to marry him. But you can forget and get past the—"

"I've already told you," Rilla interrupted stubbornly. "Get used to the idea, Aunt Tandy. Jubal is here to stay. Once you know him, you'll understand."

"No. I won't. Not ever." Tandy reached for the plates again to hide her agitation.

"Where's Bobo?" Jubal demanded of Bobby Delaney as he stood leaning against the flashing jukebox in the corner of the Pine.

"Like always. At the pool table," Bobby said lazily. "I'm gettin' tired of it. I think tonight I'll see if there's any other action in the place. C'mon, Jubal"—he tugged Jubal's sleeve in the general direction of a table full of females in the corner—"let's me'n you—"

"I just need to see Bobo," Jubal interrupted, shrugging away. "I'll leave the action to you."

Over the heads of the crowd, he saw the man he was looking for. Bobo was talking, gesturing with the pool cue, but he stopped in midsentence, his face comical in its surprise, as he saw who approached.

"You said you wanted to help." Jubal spoke so low

that no one else in the crowded, noisy room could hear. "So it's now."

Bobo stared, swallowed, sweated a little. Then he carefully laid down the cue.

"I'll meet you out front. My truck." Jubal was twisting through the crowd again even as Bobo caught the tail end of the words.

They were three miles down the dark highway before Bobo managed to speak. "Why?"

"Why what?"

"Why'd you come after me?"

"You said you had a reason for gettin' in that mill. Malone goes home at six. Foster didn't run a patrol until ten last night. It's after seven now. So I don't have long to find this safe you claim is there. I need help, and you're the best I've got." Jubal speeded up a little as the road straightened. "But if you screw up, you're goin' down, Bobo. With me or without me. I don't care."

Bobo sat silently in the shadows. Then he nervously rubbed the sleeve of his coat over his damp face. "Life's funny, y'know? A few years ago you were a know-nothing kid that did just what I told you to do. You froze up in a robbery that you never shoulda been in. Now, you're tellin' *me* what to do. But, hell, I ain't proud. If it gets me outta this mess, I'm willin'."

They parked behind the old water tank and walked a half mile in the dark to get to the mill.

The front door was easy: Bobo had his key.

The door to Carroll's office was more difficult. It had a complicated lock, and Jubal was not an expert at picking locks. So he did it a different way: he took off the whole doorknob, lock and all. It took a while under the wavering light Bobo held for him, and his hands were so sweaty that he had to stop to rub them down the front of his shirt several times. Then, once the door was opened, he put it back together. Tomorrow there wouldn't be a trace that the door had swung wide for him tonight.

"Bet this ain't what Mama meant for me to be doin' someday," Bobo said humorously as they slid into the dark office.

"No," Jubal agreed. "Got a feelin' we didn't take that lock out the pretty way, but it's done. Where's the alarm?"

Bobo motioned with the light to the desk. "I'll tell you where. I ain't too steady, and it don't take much tamperin' to set it off."

Under the dark edge of the desk, far right corner, was a panel with two lights, one white, one indistinguishable in the darkness. "That's good, real good," Bobo said heavily. "Only time you got to worry is when that second one glows in the dark, as blue as—as—that Carroll girl's eyes. Then you're in trouble. It's gone off at the police station then."

Caught under the edge of the desk, Jubal twisted his neck to look back at Bobo, hunched behind him, his face ghastly in the upward glow of light from the flashlight in his hands.

"That'd be some kind of blue," Jubal said steadily.

Bobo returned his stare. "That's what I thought. Something's goin' on between the two of you. Because while I was watchin' you, tryin' to figure out what you was up to, I caught her watchin' you, too. You're crazy, Jubal, if you're plannin' on tryin' somethin' with her."

"I'm crazy if I don't." His voice was sure. "But first I gotta get out of tonight alive. I'm gonna do exactly what you said Carroll did: I'm gonna detour the circuit, lead this alarm right back to the box, and leave that wall wide open. The minute that light glows—if it does—it means I've made a mistake, and we've gotta get out of here."

"For God's sake, don't make a mistake," Bobo returned fervently.

This time Jubal stripped off his coat, not only because he was burning up with nerves, but because inside it he had the tools he needed to make this work. Then he bent his will—his attention—his energy, to the task.

Don't think about what you're doing; the fantastic act of sitting in the floor of a lonely mill office really committing a crime—again.

The law was black and white. Maybe it could never understand that he was caught tonight somewhere in between. Walking in the gray.

All Jubal himself understood was that he was doing this tonight for a different reason, for an honest motive. And because there was no other way, not if he wanted a real life. Not if he wanted to be free.

Sweat dripped off the end of his nose as he worked. Almost through. Almost . . . Almost.

The patience of a saint—somebody once said that, but his patience was wearing thin, his nerves at the breaking point.

"There."

His one word was gasped, and he heard Bobo's answering puff of breath.

"No lights. None. Now what?"

"Now's the real test. Now I cut the original wires." *Let me have done this right,* he prayed. Did God answer the prayers of a man breaking and entering?

Clip.

A long silence.

"Well, do it," Bobo growled in frustration from his watchful stance at the desk.

"It's done." Jubal sat back on his haunches and breathed, laughter and relief threading through his entire body. "Done, and no alarms went off. Now, where's this secret place you're so sure of?"

"I don't know exactly how to get in it. But I've caught him there, in that corner, more'n once. And I could've swore one morning—don't laugh—that the whole wall moved." Bobo reached out a hand, then pulled back. "You sure this is clean?"

"As a whistle," Jubal returned. "Are *you* sure?"

Bobo's hands slid up the wall, down it, across it, while Jubal waited, his heart beating too strongly.

"Damn it!" Bobo muttered in frustration. "I *know* something's here. I *know*. But—"

"Here. Let me see." Jubal pushed him aside impatiently. Time was ticking . . . ticking . . . ticking. Already three minutes after nine.

Slow down, slow down.

He told it to his own fingertips as they began at the top of the paneled wall and traced down, painstakingly slow. Tedious.

Beside him, Bobo ran his whole rough palm over another portion of the wall.

Another slow search with his fingertips. Caressing the wood of the wall. *Show me.*

Rather be tracing the tender curve of one girl's lips, he thought, nearly wild with nerves. Rather run my hand over her smooth skin. Under the bend of her knee. Hadn't let himself think of that too much. Too dangerous.

"Goddammit, where is it?" Bobo burst out in frustration.

Clock said 9:15.

"Maybe it opens with a—"

Jubal never finished his sentence. It was under his fingers, smooth and flat, just like the center of a knothole, one of many in the middle of the pine paneling. But it pressed inward; he felt the tiny movement, clock jumped another minute, he pushed, and the wall in front of him slid back.

In all of his life, back on an uncomplicated, redneck, out-of-step ridgetop, Jubal had never seen, never heard of, never imagined that somebody in Cade County, an apparently normal person, would have a walk-in safe hidden discreetly in a wall with sliding doors triggered by a mechanical lever.

"I think"—he choked—"that when I get out of here, I want to go up to Copper's Bluff and stay there. Just give me some air, and you can have these dirty little secrets."

"I knew it. First I thought I was crazy to think it. But it kept hittin' me. There had to be a hiding place in here. And, by God, there is," Bobo crowed.

Clock.

The clock said 9:18.

"Hurry. We've got to find somethin'."

Jubal pulled the light from Bobo's limp hand, swung it around the black space in front of him. The beam caught momentarily on some rich color on a shelf; Jubal swung it back.

"My heart ain't gonna take much more," Bobo moaned.

Money. Neatly stacked greenbacks with nice, tidy, proper bank wrappers around each loaf. Divided into what appeared to be piles of five thousand dollars. Made up of crisp, innocuous hundred-dollar bills.

"There's gotta be a hundred thousand dollars there," Bobo whispered. "Carroll's a fool leaving that much money in this safe."

"Maybe it's for some kind of deal that's about to go down," Jubal offered, "or maybe—"

"Or maybe he can't turn loose of it. Maybe he's a basket case that likes to hold on to it and brood over it," Bobo returned viciously, reaching out to touch one of the packets.

"We don't want the money." Jubal said it forcefully. "We want the papers. Where?"

And that was the one thing the safe didn't contain. No papers. Not on any of the side shelves. The two walls had no shelves; they were smooth, coated in steel.

9:30.

I've done all of this for nothing, Jubal thought sickly as Bobo searched one side and he searched the other.

More money, three or four thousand, in another corner.

Where were the papers?

The flashlight in his hand drooped as his own hopes did, pointing toward the floor of the safe.

Wooden.

In the middle of the steel walls and high-tech alarms, a wooden floor with a ring in the side of it.

"Move," he told the man crammed into the tiny space beside him. "Step outside for a minute."

He bent, his fingers reaching. This was too easy. Was it? Then he fumbled, found the big ring, and pulled up.

"Nothing. No lights," Bobo informed him from the desk. "No alarms."

The flashlight revealed it all: a wide crawl space, maybe four feet by six feet, under the floor. Lined in brick. Jubal dropped into it feet first and wound up with the wooden floor at waist height on him. Maybe three feet deep.

"There they are."

His voice was quiet but triumphant, because right there, on top, was a black ledger. Relief swamped him even as he thought that it was typical of Henry's peculiar mind-set that this ledger was hidden more securely than most of the money.

"That's what I'm bettin' on," he told Bobo fiercely. "It's where he records all those serial numbers before I change 'em. God knows what else he puts in there. Now let's get it all out of here."

By 9:47 every ounce of paperwork had been crammed into two canvas bags.

They left another cool ten thousand in the bricked hole.

"That's more money than we'd make in—"

"*No.*" Jubal said it flatly. "I'm no thief, no matter what I'm doin' tonight. Let him have his money. Maybe he can buy peace with it when Katherine Carroll's gone."

"Yeah." Bobo drew back quickly. "Let's get the hell outta here. I've been wipin' the place down, clean of prints, as we went. It won't take long to finish it."

9:50.

As Jubal swung himself up out of the hole in the ground to sit on the floor, his feet dangling into the gaping space, Bobo shivered.

"That'd make a hell of a grave, wouldn't it?" he said quietly, and they closed the wooden door over it.

He rolled down the truck window and let the cold air rush in.

Now that it was over, now that he'd pumped himself full of nervy adrenaline, he was weak and shaky.

Bobo laughed every few minutes, like a man half-drunk. They were nearly back at the Pine to pick up Bobo's truck when he spoke.

"I hope we got enough, Jubal. He's got more on me than on you, and it's gonna take a lot to convince him we mean business."

"We've got it. That ledger. He records it all there. I did the paperwork, remember? And I once saw the account. Carroll was always on to me to make sure nothin' that went in it fell in anybody else's hands. Ever' folder of paperwork sealed."

Bobo fell silent, not speaking again until the Pine came into view. It was at its hottest at ten-thirty; cars were everywhere.

Jubal was quiet, too, because the truth had just hit home: he was free from Carroll, free from the deal, free to face the sun and stretch out his hand to Rilla.

"I'll see Carroll at work first thing Monday," Jubal told Bobo. "Maybe even before he catches on to what we did to his alarm."

The only place to park was at the edge of the woods, and the two of them climbed out into the night simultaneously.

"I ain't lookin' forward to what he—" Bobo's words were cut off by a woman's cry.

"No—I said *no*—"

"Listen, honey, you been askin' for it all night long. You'll damn well take it now, and like it."

It was Bobby Delaney's voice, hoarse with anger and raw with frustrated passion.

Another scream from the unknown woman, this time cut off sharply.

Bobo moved uneasily, and when he did, Jubal caught sight of the car parked ten feet away in the dark shadows of the trees. The back door was open. Something—the woman's foot, maybe—kicked it, making it jar and vibrate.

A smothered curse from Bobby, a sobbing moan from the woman, then another cry.

"Ah, hell, what's he doin' to her?" Bobo said reluctantly.

A big white Buick.

The second Jubal recognized it, a wave of disgust and resignation swept over him. The next second he was moving forward.

"Bobby!" His voice cracked across the cold parking lot, ringing clear even over the sound of music and muffled noise coming from the Pine. "Let her go."

He didn't want to be a part of this. Every time he thought of Tess and what he'd let her do to him, he felt dirty. He didn't want to remember her. In Rilla's arms he'd found something entirely different.

But he knew Tess Johnson: she was high-handed, imperious, immoral, and completely used to getting her way with men.

And he knew Bobby Delaney: he took women at face value. If she came on, he gave back. Rough. Direct. And he'd never heard of letting a woman change her mind, not once the party started.

Jubal despised both of them as he looked down at their struggling, tangled bodies.

"Bobby!"

Delaney went stiff. He spoke without even lifting his head. "You get the hell outta here, Jubal. You ain't been interested in this one in weeks. Too late to want her now. Tonight, she came on to *me.* Now this is between me'n her."

Beneath him, Tess was crying. "Jubal—pl-please—don't—don't leave me—" Her words were slurred crazily.

"Don't be a fool," Jubal said fiercely. "I ain't doin' this because I want her. But I'm tellin' you, Tess ain't nothin' but trouble. I know. And what's gonna happen when you get through here? You'll have to let her go. If she tells her old man, or the law, you're lookin' straight at a rape charge. And the way you're treatin' her, you're gonna deserve it."

In the heavy, empty pause, Tess sobbed quietly, desperately.

"She's not worth it, Bobby," Jubal urged.

"Then you tell her to stay the hell away from me," Delaney exploded in embarrassment, frustration, and temper. He pushed himself out of the car, hair wild and face bloody from scratches she'd inflicted, and began to zip his pants. "She came to my table, ran her hand up my leg under it, said I—"

"She does it to everybody," Jubal cut in. "Just go home. You can't go back in. She's scratched you all up."

Delaney put a hand to his face, and his fingers came away sticky and red. "Damn wildcat," he snarled, and stalked off toward his truck.

Jubal waited while Tess struggled up, while she tried to adjust her clothes, while she cried . . . and cried.

"Come on," he said shortly, reaching a hand in the car. She clung to it, let him pull her out, where she stumbled and fell against him. "You're drunk," he said in realization.

Both of her arms wrapped around his waist as he tried to move. What was her perfume? What did she call it? Obsession. It had clung to his skin after every night he'd been with her. Nearly forgotten, it rushed back now around him. "Stand up," he commanded, trying to peel her off him.

"Ju-Jubal. *My* Jubal. I thought he was your friend. . . ."

"No friend of mine."

"But he . . . wasn't like you," she said, finally looking up to see him.

Tess Johnson—the one he knew—was gone. In her place was a terrified, dazed girl with her hair rumpled, her makeup smeared, mascara streaking her cheeks, and a mouth that shook when she tried to talk.

"He hu-hu—He hurt me." She had to concentrate on the verb to speak it.

"That's what you wanted, idn't it? It's what you come here for. To get with some man—any man in a car. To use them, or like tonight, get used." Jubal pushed her away, caught her shoulders, shook her a little. "You gotta quit, Tess."

"Oh—God—sick—I'm sick." She moaned, falling back against the car.

Now Jubal could see her clearly: the tiny bruise at the edge of her mouth, the torn shoulder of her red silk shirt. "Go home," he told her with finality. "And stay away from this place from now on. You don't belong here."

"Jubal." For the first time he remembered Bobo standing in silence in the shadows. "She can't drive. Not like that. But she better get outta here. So had you. Bobby's still over there, nursin' his pride, and he's liable to decide to come back."

He couldn't leave her. Where were all her friends now? he wondered. All that crowd she usually came here with?

"Get in the car," he snapped. "If I get caught with you, in this condition . . ." He shuddered at the thought. "You're not worth the trouble you cause, Tess," he said brutally as he bundled her onto the passenger side of the Buick. "Bobo, I need you to drive my truck. Follow me."

"Where?"

Jubal hesitated. "I don't know," he said helplessly. "Tess, listen. *Listen.* I gotta take you home. To your daddy's—"

"No." She said the one word thickly, but she was definite. "Party . . . there . . . tonight. Joanie's . . . to Joanie's. They're gone. Ju-Jubal, I think . . . I'm . . . throwing up. I'm—"

"What did Tandy say when you called?" Joanie demanded from the couch. Her feet were propped on a fluffy pillow in the middle of the den floor of the Townsend house, her toes wiggling luxuriously. "Gosh, my feet are tired. Too much shopping."

"That Katherine is fine—that she understood it was late, and that it was a good idea for me to spend the night. Where are your parents?" Rilla asked curiously.

"Gone to a party at the Johnsons'. Anyway, they live on that side of the house"—Joanie pointed languidly in the direction of a dark hall—"and I live here. The only thing we share is the kitchen in the middle. It's great—I get to be at home and have privacy, too."

The room was almost dark, just the two of them in the tiny light from a small reading lamp on an antique drop-leaf desk in the corner.

"Thanks for the sleep shirt," Rilla offered dubiously, looking down at the silky garment, its low-cut lapels decorated lavishly with pink hearts.

"It was a Valentine's Day present from James Henigar," Joanie said, rolling over to her stomach with a laugh. "He wrapped my engagement ring in it. If you don't like that shirt, I've got a blue one somewhere. It has Garfield on it. He's drooling."

"Did James give you that one, too?" Rilla asked with a laugh, sinking onto the sea green carpet that Joanie was wallowing on like a contented cat.

"You better believe it. What do your boyfriends give you?" Joanie's head came up curiously.

"I've never had too many."

Joanie made a disbelieving sound. "You're joking, aren't you?"

Rilla looked down at the pink hearts. "I didn't say there wasn't one special one. But my family can't stand him."

Joanie sat up slowly, pushing herself off the floor. "Do I know him?"

"I doubt it." It felt strange to talk about him, here in this house, out in the open.

"What does Tandy—"

But Joanie never finished her sentence. Outside, in the dark on the brick patio, someone knocked over one of the wrought-iron chairs that stood near the hedge.

Both Joanie and Rilla went still.

"What's that?" Joanie demanded in a hushed whisper.

"Just your parents, maybe?" Rilla offered reassuringly, but she was coming slowly to her feet, moving to the French doors that led outside.

Joanie shook her head. "Too early, and they use the other doors."

Straining against the night, Rilla could hear voices. Low, hushed. A protest, a laugh. Whoever it was, he wasn't trying to be completely silent.

Joanie startled her by coming up behind her on stealthy feet, and the two of them listened.

". . . make you want me again . . . the night . . . just spend the night . . . nobody will know. . . ."

There was a man's murmured protest. Something in his voice triggered sensations in Rilla. Who?

". . . won't brush me off . . . touch me and you'll see. . . ."

"This is far enough. You can make it from here."

And then she knew: it was Jubal.

Joanie gave a sudden heave of relief. "Oh, for crying out loud, it's Tess. She's done something stupid and now she's afraid to go home again."

With an exasperated gesture, she flipped on the patio lights, flooding the backyard with brilliance. Catching two shocked people in the big beams not twelve feet from Joanie as she flung open the door.

Tess Johnson, half-dressed and disheveled, clinging to a slender, dark-haired, tall man whose left arm wrapped her to his side. Supported her. Held her.

I once thought this could never be, Rilla thought. The one clear sentence in her jumbled head. Then another one: *Maybe it wasn't a whore I was with. Maybe it was a little china doll.*

His eyes were green as grass even at this distance. And when he caught sight of her in the open door, behind Joanie, he staggered as if he'd been hit right in the solar plexus.

"R-Rilla!" he gasped.

But her heart was breaking. *Tess and Jubal.* Lies, all lies. Just as Tandy had said.

Without a word, Rilla turned past the other girl and ran to Joanie's bedroom. Where were her clothes?

She had to go home.

Jubal practically dropped Tess onto the lawn at the patio's edge.

"Rilla!" He went after her—he had to explain— and got stopped short by a stunned Joanie Townsend.

"What—"

"I've got to see her."

"Who?"

"Rilla. Terrill. She thinks I'm with Tess." Jubal wanted to shove Joanie out of the way, but he forced himself to stand still. "Let me in."

"I don't even know you, nothing except what Tess has told me," Joanie retorted unevenly. "And look at the condition you brought her home in. I ought to call Ned this second. I can't let you in."

"I didn't touch her," Jubal denied passionately. "She just nearly got herself raped by a man at the Pine, and I brought her home. A friend's out on the road in my truck, waiting for me. Now, I want to see Rilla."

Tess had made it to the door by now, raking one hand back through her hair with shaky fingers. "And here I thought you dumped me for some noble—r-reason," she said, her words still a little slurred and sloppy. "Because . . . I wouldn't make an . . . honest man out of you. And it was . . . only 'cause you found . . . her."

She slid down to sit in the open door, leaning her head against the jamb carefully. "D'you know he . . . said no, Joanie? To *me*?" she asked plaintively.

"Believe me, Tess, if you live long enough, there'll be somebody else who'll say it," he said furiously. There was a time when he couldn't have stood up to her like this; Jubal didn't know why, but he knew that being with Rilla had given him the ability to hold his own with Tess now. Rilla had talked to him, responded to him, loved him. It had changed him.

He had to see her.

"Please," he managed at last to Joanie. "I've gotta talk to her. I won't hurt her."

But before Joanie could move, Rilla came back down the stairs, completely dressed.

"I want to go home," she said distinctly.

"Rilla—"

"Don't say anything to me. I know what I saw, Jubal."

"I just brought her home from the Pine—"

"You said you wouldn't go there anymore. Joanie, come on. If you don't take me home, I'll call Tandy."

"No, don't call. I'll take you," Joanie said fervently.

"I was at the Pine," he began again, doggedly.

Rilla flung back her heavy cloud of hair. "The first day when I came home, when you had your back scratched and your neck marked, was she the one?"

"None of that matters. It was a long time ago. Tonight when I—"

"Was she the one?"

Jubal answered at last, reluctantly, "Yeah. She was the one." He felt the slow crawl of hot color up his cheeks.

Rilla's face went white, not red, and at the door Tess laughed. "Don't tell me he's been taking you up to Mason's Point, too. Tell me something, Jubal, honey, how many backseats have you been in?"

Maybe Rilla heard or maybe she didn't. She just plowed on. "You kept telling me there was something wrong. Something you had to do tonight. Something between us. I don't understand it, but I know one thing—we're through."

Rilla stepped out of the door, brushing past him, and he caught her arm roughly.

"You're gonna listen," he said forcefully, "if I have to hold you down and make you. I didn't do anythin'. I love you. *I love you.*"

His passionate words rang across the night. Joanie and Tess, frozen in their places, might have been forgotten by the two caught in the well of anger and emotion.

"I see how much you love me. You don't know the rules, then, if you think this is love," Rilla said scornfully. "Aunt Tandy was right. You're bad blood, Jubal Kane. *Bad blood.*"

Caught so close to him, she could hear the beating

of his heart. See his face go still. Sense the terrible halt to his emotions.

She had known instinctively how to hurt him the worst. He'd let her get that close, at least.

"Bad blood?" he echoed at last, tonelessly, and he dropped her arm. Hope, and something else, died out of him. Then he moved away, his face cold and his voice dull. "She's got no right to say anything about me, or my people. And you don't, either."

Rilla didn't have to break loose. He pushed around her, striding blindly across the backyard of the Townsend house, the old coat he always wore flapping around his waist.

Rilla choked down an insane need to cry, to run after him, to plead. He had completely betrayed her.

"I want to go home, Joanie. Now."

24

Nothing could reach Jubal anymore. Nobody, either.

Maggie tried once she realized that something was desperately wrong with him. He didn't talk, he barely ate, he stayed outside as much as possible that Saturday and Sunday.

At last she asked her quiet son a direct question, sitting at the supper table on Sunday night while he looked at his food and did precious little else.

"She's done something, ain't she?"

He didn't pretend that he didn't know who she was talking about. "I don't want to talk about her. Not ever."

"Who is she, Jubal?"

"Makes no difference. Not now."

"At least tell me what she's done so I can help you," Maggie said at last.

His jaw tightened and he shook his head. "She didn't do it. I did. I believed in her."

"Jubal, I don't like beggin' for a woman I don't even know, but if she loves you—"

"No," he answered, and he didn't even sound like himself. "She doesn't."

Rilla didn't cry.

At first there was too much anger and outrage.

Jubal had really been with Tess. She had been the one to put her lips against his throat. She had been the one he'd incited to such frenzy that she'd clawed his back.

It had been bad enough in the abstract; now that it was made concrete, now that she knew it really was Tess, it seemed a thousand times worse.

And she'd let him do the same thing to her, Terrill. She had believed him. How could she have been so gullible? So blind?

Maybe at the end Jubal had intended to end his affair with Tess. "There's one thing I'm ashamed of," he'd said. And it would have been difficult to come out in the open and marry *her* if Tess were still around, Rilla supposed with an ironic ache in her heart.

She, Terrill Carroll, had actually been a big enough fool to think of marrying Jubal.

He didn't love her. He couldn't. He deserved whatever she could say or do to hurt him.

"About this affair with Kane," Tandy began determinedly on Sunday afternoon.

"No." Rilla said it flatly. "There is no affair with Kane. I've been thinking, and you're right."

Tandy's mouth fell open. "Just like that?"

"I learned some things about him at Joanie's. Things

I don't want to talk about. And I don't want to hear about him ever again. It—it hurts too much." Her voice didn't waver until the end, when it nearly cracked completely.

Tandy's hand pressed her shoulder in vast relief. "Thank the Lord that you've come to your senses. And I won't even wonder why, I'm that glad. We won't speak another word about him."

Jubal was already waiting when Henry Carroll arrived at work Monday morning, thirty minutes before anybody else.

"A little holiday goes a long way, eh, Kane?" Carroll asked ironically as he unlocked the front door.

Jubal shifted the folder of papers from his right to his left hand. "Long enough," he returned somberly. "I just have somethin' I need to show you once we get inside."

"Some problem with your work?" Carroll quizzed, and they moved through the empty outer office to Carroll's own door.

"You might call it that," Jubal agreed, watching as Carroll fumbled with the lock he'd taken apart two nights earlier.

When Carroll swung his big briefcase onto the desk, he looked over at his mechanic. "Well, what is it? I hope it's nothing . . . personal."

Jubal caught the inflection but didn't understand it and was in too big a hurry to care. He wanted this over so he could get out of here before he had to see Terrill.

"It's to show you this." From the folder he took two pages full of scribbled numbers and slanted writing.

Carroll took off his long black overcoat, tossed it

over his chair, and reached for them. "If this is a mix-up or something you've been—" His words faltered as he realized what he was holding, and his face drained of color.

"Where'd you get this?" he asked in a voice quiet and menacing.

"Out of a big black ledger, one that used to be hid in a crawl space under your fancy wall safe." Jubal never moved, never took his eyes off Carroll. "And that's just a samplin'. I've got it all, *Mr.* Carroll. All of it."

First there was anger.

Then disbelief replaced it in the black eyes that threatened him. Without a word Carroll strode around the desk, heading straight for the wall.

"The clip I made in the circuit is on the left, two feet from the corner." Jubal was trying to keep his voice emotionless, to deny the licks of triumph and relief shooting up from his stomach. He had Carroll where he wanted him. No need to push farther.

When the man straightened and turned, the disbelief had faded into outrage and, under it all, fear.

"What do you want?" he gasped furiously, foam flecking his lips. In his hands the paper crumpled.

It was hard to look at him—like looking into the flaming heart of a volcano. A soul ablaze. Jubal stared, and for the first time he understood Bobo's fear. *Maybe he's a basket case. . . .*

"I want out of this crooked deal. Out of the mill. You tell the probation and parole board I've been a good little boy. Get me my release. And I want Bobo Hackett laid off, with an unemployment check until he gets a new job. That's all."

Carroll circled Jubal like a wolf about to pounce. "You're such a hero, Kane."

"No hero," Jubal returned somberly. "If I was, I'd

turn you in and let the heat fall, even if some of it fell on me. Because we both did it, one of us for money, one of us for freedom. We're both guilty by law. But the world will go on even if I go back to prison—I'm the one who won't. And Ma won't. And"—he took a long, deep breath—"I don't see that I'm a bad enough person to deserve that."

Jubal registered his own words with an odd sense of relief. Did he believe that of himself?

Carroll dropped the crumpled papers in the trash can at the edge of the desk. "Maybe you even think you deserve a reward," he said sarcastically. "Maybe you want Terrill."

A tremor of surprise slid over Jubal.

"That's it, isn't it, Kane? Oh, I've seen the two of you. Caught you with her one night."

Breath tangled in Jubal's throat. "Makes no difference now," he answered croakily. "I guess we're through, anyway. She doesn't know about any of this. Got nothin' to do with it. Except, she's another reason for you to quit and me to stay quiet. It'll hurt her if this comes out."

"And you don't want Terrill hurt."

Jubal said nothing.

His very stillness, his control, sent the other man's spinning.

Carroll suddenly reached out and swept the big briefcase from the desk in a flaming rage. It slammed into the chair, tumbled down its side, crashed on the floor. And when the loud commotion faded, he hissed in Jubal's face, "Son of a bitch! Think you're somebody? Think you'll stop me? Do you think any of you will?"

"I can't live your life," Jubal said steadily. "I'm havin' a hard enough time with my own. You'll do what you'll do, but I'm out of it. You have to let me go."

He was nearly to the door when the man answered. "I won't be taken down by—a—a—"

"A Kane from Sullivan's Ridge?" Jubal returned. "That's the problem with you, Mr. Carroll. With a lot of people. You can't see past what you think I am. And I'm a whole lot more."

"You're fired, Kane!" Carroll shouted after him.

"Good," Jubal answered simply.

Rosalie kept sending scurrying little looks over at Terrill as the morning progressed. Rilla was aware of them, but so nervous over the fact that she'd have to face Jubal today for the first time that she didn't inquire about Rosalie's odd behavior.

Henry had been gone since before Rilla came in.

At two-thirty, unable to stand the tension, she finally asked, "Where's Jubal? He's late."

Rosalie pursed her lips and laid down a pen carefully. "I wondered if you knew. Mr. Carroll said he had to fire him early this morning. I knew there'd have to be a good reason for him to get rid of his boy wonder."

Rilla stared. "Fired him? Why?"

Rosalie flushed a little. "Don't *you* know?" she asked pointedly.

"No, I don't."

"He said it was because he'd caught the two of you together and he wasn't going to put up with it," she answered bluntly.

"You can't just fire him," Rilla protested hotly to her uncle that night.

He was very quiet, very restrained. "I have."

"But his mother—she still depends on him. And his probation. What will—"

"That's been cleared up."

"You fired him just to hurt me, Henry. Just because you thought I cared."

"Tandy tells me that it's over between the two of you. Kane told me the same thing this morning. so why would I do it to hurt you? I fired him because I wanted to."

"Because he was with *me*. Because he stepped out of line with *me*."

"Believe whatever you want. And you're damn well right—he was way out of line."

"I know you were probably trying to do the right thing," Tandy said in quiet reproof, "but I don't think it was necessary to tell the whole world about Rilla. I've had phone calls off and on all day about it. It has created unnecessary gossip, and I hold you directly responsible, Henry."

When the next morning dawned, Jubal was waiting at the river.

Like an iridescent bird that was struggling to spread its wide wings, some shimmering emotion kept stirring down inside him.

"I'm a whole lot more," he'd told Carroll.

The sun edged slowly upward, and it was just as he'd known it would be: crystalline, brilliant in its pink-and-gold glory.

Terrill had been the only good thing he'd ever had in his life. For her, he'd tried.

Now he'd lost her.

Worse than that, he'd discovered that she didn't believe in him any more than anybody else did. He'd done everything for nothing.

The rays of the sun angled across the water now, hitting it in shattered prisms of light.

But in trying for her, he'd created another man. The man he was now.

He'd tried for Terrill, but he'd done it for himself, too, because he had to. Because he'd reached a crossroads. Couldn't go back, didn't want to go down.

The water began to dance under the beaming, sparkling rays.

I know what I am. Not a hero, but not a villain, either. I walked away from Tess, stood up to Dusty, just won against Henry Carroll.

I can do more than this world ever dreamed.

And when he hit the last thought, he understood: he believed in Jubal Kane . . . and that was enough.

His heart might break because Terrill hadn't, because he loved her, but he would still survive. He couldn't go back to what he'd been before her, whether she wanted him or not. Whether he wanted *her* or not.

Rainey was standing silently at the big rock right behind him when Jubal turned from the flaring sun and the vibrating water. His eyes were nearly blind with light, but he felt Rainey's huge, rough hands as they caught his face, cupping his jaw and cheeks in their giant grasp.

"You've got it, boy. Don't know what or why," Rainey said huskily, "but it's in your face. Now you hold on to it. *Hold on.*"

The inner man might crave the sublime, but the outer man was a different story. He needed things ridiculously mundane.

So Jubal took money from what he'd saved and went to Edmonds. Hated doing it, but he kept remembering the things that Rilla had taught him, one way or the other.

I'll show you how to dress, how to talk.

That was important. He'd figured out that much.

Straight to the bright lights of the big mall, to a department where he'd walked with another, barely able to concentrate on anything at the time but the hand she'd slipped into his.

But he remembered enough to know where to go, what to ask for.

Under a garland of flashing Christmas lights, he found shirts like the one she'd picked out. Not the same colors exactly, but he figured they would do.

"I want this," he said awkwardly to the manicured-and-styled saleslady he'd been half-terrified of that day two months ago.

"And is this the size you need?" she simpered, looking over her glasses. "Arm length correct? Collar style correct?"

"I don't know," he answered, trapped and helpless. Rilla. She should have been here. But she wasn't.

"Don't know?"

He gulped and made the terrible admission. "I never really bought my clothes before. My mama, she usually—"

"Well, bless your heart," the lady cooed. She came out from the counter and patted his arm. "You men look like you could conquer the world, and most of you are totally lost when it comes to shopping. Honey, I've got a son who's exactly the same. Now let me show you . . ."

He sweated through most of the ordeal and just plain hated being told to go inside a tiny cubicle and take off his clothes, but he did it.

And once he finally made the woman understand that he had just so much money to spend, once she began to see that she had a mere babe in the woods on her hands, she got protective. Downright zealous.

He bought a shirt and a pair of pants and a pair of

boots. No idea if he was getting the right kind, the kind Rilla would have chosen. But he and the saleslady plowed on anyway.

And then he asked for one more thing: "I want a coat," he said simply. Rolled up in his shirt pocket was exactly the amount of money one certain jacket was going to cost.

Then he discovered the jacket was gone.

His industrious helper finally hunted up one close to it in style. And in the end, he spent all the money he'd brought with him.

Still, he figured it was worth it, if his plan worked.

Jubal wore the clothes for the first time on Thursday when he went to ask for a job with Hank Barlow.

Maggie's eyes sparkled under tears when she saw him.

"Why are you cryin'?" he asked uneasily. "Don't you like 'em?"

She nodded, swallowing, catching the nearest chair back with her twisted fingers. "It's just that . . . you're changin'. I can feel it, down inside."

"What are you talkin' about?" Jubal said, half-afraid himself of what he was doing.

"It's nothin' bad. It's got to happen if you're ever gonna do anything with your life. But it's hard to let you go, Jubal."

"I'm just goin' to see about a job, Ma."

"You know what I'm talkin' about."

Barlow couldn't see him until after lunch, a friendly receptionist told him, and her gaze slid over his face, the jacket, his legs, with an avid approval that had Jubal nearly blushing before she was through.

To escape, he wandered outside the office onto the paved side lot. In the back was a big orange building with the sound of voices drifting from it, and he made his way toward it, wondering what work here was like.

So familiar. He'd been in a hundred places like this. Stretching concrete floors, walls hung with tools, two or three men arguing over a broken-apart loader in the back.

Arguing about what was wrong.

Jubal listened a few minutes, finally walking up behind them. What they knew about big engines was next to nothing. Jubal caught on to that fact quickly. And in the middle of the noise, he spoke up.

"The only thing wrong with that engine is that it needs a new head gasket," he said calmly.

The two men who were arguing stopped and stared, silently demanding to know who he was.

"I'm here for a job. But I can show you"—then he remembered the new clothes—"or *tell* you how to do it."

"The day I let some yahoo from off the street walk in here and start bossing me around," one began.

The dirtiest one of them all was up to his arms in grease, bent over the machine itself. He looked up at Jubal in disgust. "You know so much, tell me how. I'm the only one working, it seems."

So Jubal did.

And when he came back that afternoon after lunch and walked into Barlow's office, the same man who'd been bent over the loader, who'd taken Jubal's instructions most of the morning, looked up at him from behind the desk.

Cleaned up now, but still the one.

He was brusque and to the point. "I'm Hank Barlow. I didn't catch your name this morning."

"Kane. Jubal Kane."

Not even a reaction. No recognition at all. "You want a job. That loader was worth one. I've got two openings. One for a laborer to help the carpenters. Other's for a shop foreman over the heavy equipment and four men. You've already met two of them. You look awful young to hold that kind of job, but you knew what you were doing this morning. So speak up. Which one of those jobs are you here about?"

You can't do it, a panicked voice inside him said. *Too inexperienced. Too much a Kane.*

And a stronger one: *Reach.*

"The foreman's," he said, and the word was only a little strangled.

He told Maggie that night and watched her face light up as she shared his minor success. But he wanted to tell Rilla, wanted her arms to reward him, to reach for him and hold him.

That night when he couldn't sleep, it wasn't even excitement that kept him awake. It was longing.

He wanted to make love to her again, in a real bed, with time to stop and savor and caress. He wanted to sleep with her, to wake up with her.

But he couldn't. *Bad blood.*

So he pushed and shoved the memories back into some dark closet.

By Friday the news had hit the Ridge. Ida got it from Jake Summers, who'd heard it from another fox hunter out of Bethel.

By Friday night Maggie Kane knew it, too.

"Jubal." She stopped him that night on his way out to the porch. "I saw Ida this afternoon. She came up to visit a little while. She told me that there's a lot of talk down in Bethel about you gettin' fired from the mill."

"I didn't get fired. I wanted out. I told you that.

But I reckon Henry Carroll's tellin' it a different way. It's all right with me, but he's lyin'."

"And is he lyin' when he says he caught you with his stepdaughter?"

The words stopped Jubal, held him in place as he stared back at his quiet mother. "He never 'caught' us, not in the way you mean. But he found out."

"So it's true. She's the one."

"She's the one." He repeated the words blankly, trying to ignore the tearing pain.

"The one who hurt you." Maggie turned away, her voice suddenly stronger. "I'm glad. Do you hear me, boy? Those Carrolls are as high and mighty as God Himself. And this girl's aunt, she's not the kind who'd ever take to you, Jubal. They're all stiff-necked and proud. Let it be anybody but one of them that you finally wind up with."

He didn't mean to defend Rilla, but he couldn't stop the words. "You're wrong, Ma. Maybe she didn't care enough in the end, but Ril—Terrill, that's her name, she cried and hurt and felt just as much as you ever did."

"And that's why she dropped you."

"She thought I was—I was going out on her with another woman. And instead of giving me a chance, instead of believin' a little, she—" He broke off.

"She acted like a Carroll," Maggie finished, and Jubal, unwilling to hear any more, turned away and went outside.

On Saturday Tandy decided that she and Terrill would go Christmas shopping along with the rest of the world. She'd rarely let her niece out of her sight this week, and Rilla didn't care enough to fight anymore.

Besides, there was good news: Katherine was

better. Actually better. She'd been completely without pain, able to breathe more easily, for four days now. It was reason for a celebration, so Henry spent that Saturday afternoon with his wife alone, and Tandy and Rilla headed off into the bright, cold sunshine.

"What do you want for Christmas this year?" Tandy asked, trying to rouse Rilla from the quietness that was becoming habitual.

Jubal the way he used to be, she wanted to say. "It doesn't matter," she said instead.

Bethel was busy. It had no mall, only stores clustered around the square and down Broad Street, but it was still the largest town in any direction for a fifty-mile radius. People were everywhere, and the drugstore had big speakers hung outside that played Christmas carols at full blast.

A week without Jubal. A week of rage and pain, wondering where he was.

"Look at the Christmas tree," Tandy said appreciatively, pointing to one in the front of the bank as they parked.

They wandered in several of the stores. Rilla had already bought her presents the week before with Joanie, but she found a delicate crystal ball with tiny figures in it, one that glowed from a soft inner light, and she wondered if Katherine would like it.

She saw exactly what she would have given Jubal just as she left one of the stores, on her way to meet Tandy down the street: it was a muffler, soft and green, as richly green as his eyes.

She was an idiot. She was moping over somebody who was nothing but trouble. From the very beginning he'd been bad news, and Tess had only helped her to remember what she already knew: Jubal Kane was wild, rednecked, unfaithful. Like his brothers, he was on a road going nowhere, except possibly to hell.

She made her way outside, and the first thing she saw was Jubal himself, not on the path to destruction, but on one of Bethel's sidewalks. The sight stunned her so much, she couldn't move. He had his back to her, his hands shoved down in the pockets of a new leather coat, and he was talking to somebody.

A woman, an older woman. She wore a blue dress, with a long black coat over it. Her shoes were flat and black and serviceable, and she had a bag hanging over one arm in a firm sort of way. She nodded at something he said, then Rilla saw her pat him on the shoulder once.

His mother. This was his mother, this old-fashioned figure.

The woman turned and caught Rilla as she stared, and before Rilla could move away, Jubal, too, had glanced around inquiringly. He looked older today than twenty-three, she thought fleetingly, just as panic and his green gaze settled on her. Strong, dark emotion chased over his face, and the way it twisted his features before he controlled it made her unable to move.

She just stood there, staring at him, wanting to scream at him. You hurt me, she wanted to say. You hurt me. She pulled in a long, shivery breath and turned blindly away.

Then he called her name. It came unwillingly, as though it had been torn out of him.

"Rilla!"

Just keep moving away from him, she told her panicky feet.

But his long-fingered hand was on her shoulder, grasping it, stopping her movement, pulling her around to face him. Her heart jumped in fear and painful longing as she jerked away from him and twisted to blaze, "Stop grabbing at me."

He looked down at her, swallowing so harshly that she heard him, and he stuffed his hands into the pockets of the coat.

"I thought I never wanted to see you again," he said, "but now I reckon I've got something to say."

"Well, I've got nothing to say to you at all," she shot back. Then, before he could hurt her, she said it herself, "How's Tess?"

This time he didn't show surprise, and he didn't flush. He just said forcefully, "I ain't been with Tess in the way you're talking about since the night before you came home from Rose Hall. But that's not what I wanted to tell you."

"She said you've been in the backseat of a car with her," Rilla burst out. The words had rung in her head a thousand times; she hated them. She couldn't forget them.

"I never was with her after you." Simple, direct.

"But you said you couldn't be with me that Friday night. That you'd done something you were ashamed of."

Harder for him to deal with that. "I had. But it had nothin' to do with Tess Johnson. It was something I had to make right with another man. I'd tell you all of it, but there's other people involved who'll get hurt."

Sudden tears burned in the back of Rilla's eyes, and she turned away hastily. "I don't want to hear it."

He caught her again, above the elbow, and this time he held on as he turned her to him again. "It can't matter now, anyway. I reckon we're through, like you said. You think it happened because I was sleepin' around and doin' you wrong, but it didn't," he said intently. "I didn't. And you think you're the one that's been hurt, but you're not."

She gave a hard jerk, trying to escape, but he held on.

"You wouldn't let me explain that night. Never gave me a chance. But I mean to now. I took Bobo to the Pine to pick up his truck. We didn't even go in. Tess was there. She's there a lot. It's where I met her. She was drunk and she'd come on to the wrong man. He had her in the car. He meant to rape her. So I got her out and brought her home. I never touched her."

Rilla looked past him at the nearest store window, where three paper angels stared back. So did several curious, wide-eyed shoppers, watching the two of them out there on the street.

"Do you believe me?" he asked at last, quietly.

No answer. She tried, but the tears she'd denied all week were burning in her throat now as well as in her eyes.

"That's all right. Don't matter now, anyway. Because we might get past Tess somehow, but we can't get past what you said to me." He loosened his grip.

She took a step away but stared up into his dark face, mesmerized.

"You told me all those times that we were together—the night you let me make love to you—that you believed in me. You made me believe in myself."

The Salvation Army bell ringing from the street corner sounded as loud as an angel chorus in her ears.

"And it was nothing but a lie." His face was made stern by bitterness. "That's when I saw you were a lie, too. When it came down to the wire, I was just 'bad blood.' You know how many times I've heard that? But I won't let you take me down, Rilla. I've come too far. It's my turn now: I've just stopped believin' in *you*."

"Terrill!" Tandy was hurrying down the sidewalk to her, trying to save her from Jubal.

Across the way, the druggist was leaned up in his door, listening.

And Jubal's mother watched quietly.

All of them were witnesses, Rilla thought in some corner of her mind: they were there to see her heart shattering into a million pieces as Jubal turned loose completely, stepped back, and walked away.

That Saturday night, when it was just the two of them, Katherine said huskily, "Why does it . . . feel like there's . . . something wrong with you?"

The words startled her daughter, who'd been smoothing the covers over the bed, and she looked up into Katherine's eyes. They were too close for Rilla to pretend or dissemble, so when Katherine touched her face with her thin, narrow fingers, everything in her crumbled.

She blinked and her face twisted as she fought back tears.

"There *is* something bothering you," Katherine said in certainty. "What? . . . What, Rilla?"

"He did something that hurt me, and I hurt him back, Mama." The confession was only an anguished whisper.

"Who?" Katherine asked in surprise. "The man you've been telling me about?"

"Yes. I hurt him too much, and he . . ." She dropped her face into the pillow beside Katherine's. "I loved him."

She felt her mother's hand on her head, light as a ghost's touch. "Why can't I keep the people I love? What do I do that's wrong?" Rilla asked, her voice broken and muffled in the pillow. "He's gone. And you're—" She couldn't finish. She was crying so hard, the bed shook with her tears.

Katherine laid her head on her daughter's. "It's not . . . your fault . . . Rilla. Love works miracles. If . . . he loves you . . . he'll be back."

"And you, Mama?" Rilla asked painfully, her face hot and tired and aching against the wet pillow. "When will you come back?"

Katherine's stroking faltered and stopped. "If I had the power . . . to come back . . . and it could make . . . you see that I . . . love you, I would. Someday you'll see that I do. You'll see how I've tried—to show you."

"I don't want you to die," Rilla whispered, her throat heavy and clogged with tears. Raising her head, she looked at her mother and said the words she'd tried to so many times before. "I love you, Mama."

Katherine's expression lightened a little as she lay back on the pillow. "I thought . . . you'd never say it. But I knew. Don't be afraid to love, Rilla, even if it hurts. It's an old line, but it's true. Love is . . . all that . . . all that matters when it comes time to die."

"And it works miracles." She repeated Katherine's words with a touch of bitterness.

"Even if it doesn't . . . it's all there is," Katherine whispered in finality.

25

On the next Saturday, the day warmed up unexpectedly, and the thermometer outside the kitchen hit fifty-eight degrees. Sunshine glowed on the pink-and-white coverlet on Rilla's bed, and the kitchen was nearly hot by the time Tandy finished cooking breakfast and making two pecan pies.

Katherine was still feeling better, so much so that she sat up half-reclining, on pillows in the bed, and listened in quiet amusement when Tandy took a storytelling spell and told the funniest, most scandalous tales about half the residents of Cade County.

Henry stayed in his study, turning papers, worrying over some glitch at the mill.

On Sunday, Katherine's good days ended.

She woke up weak, and by the afternoon she could barely draw in breaths.

At midnight she had a choking spell and spit up blood.

Monday morning she choked again, and Dr. Jones

was at the house by six-thirty. By seven Katherine was breathing more steadily.

Rilla hung by her mother's bedside until Henry demanded that she go to work.

"No. I want to stay. I *will* stay."

"You'll do as you're told. Katherine's already better. Now, do you go on to work or do I drag you out?"

"I hate you," she choked out.

"Hate away," Henry answered implacably. "You're doing Katherine no good here, crying and dragging at her. Do you think she wants you to see her like this?"

Rilla looked down at Katherine, who had her eyes closed. Everything about her face was shuttered and shut down now, except for the white line of her lips as she breathed in harshly through her mouth.

"She knows you love her, Rilla," Tandy said as she let her out the front door. "She never doubted it. But if something is wrong—she doesn't want you to be here. She told me so."

"But I want to be. What about what I want? Promise me—promise me, Aunt Tandy, you'll call me at work if she gets worse," Rilla began desperately. "You said once that you would."

Tandy hesitated. "Oh, all right. But she's had these spells before. It's just that it's been a while. By the time you get home this afternoon, she'll be waiting for you to tell you to tell her the news. So don't sit around today listening for some phone call of doom."

Rosalie took the message from Tandy at 9:43, and she relayed Tandy's two words to Rilla just as she hung up the phone. They were simply, "Come home."

Rilla looked at Rosalie, and a hard black weight settled in her chest. But there was no surprise. She'd known this morning. In the middle of the fear on her way across the field, she wanted Jubal with such a ferocity that it sent a lance of pain through her.

At the door of the farmhouse she hesitated, then reached for the cold brass doorknob. But it twisted, and as the door opened without her help, she looked into the face of Joanie Crabtree. "I told you I'd come, Rilla, when it was time," she said simply.

I didn't hear any music, Mama, Rilla thought quietly. *Not one strain of "Crazy." I hope you heard it.*

The Baptist preacher cleared his throat again against the chill of the day and held down more firmly the thin pages of the Bible that the wind kept whipping up, here at the foot of the open grave in this little cemetery.

". . . and as the weaver folds his loom when the weaving is completed, we here today fold the fabric of the life of Katherine Carroll. We are left with the joy of knowing she is free from her terrible pain . . ."

And free from Henry.

Henry. The way he turned on me when Mama was finally gone, the tears for her still in his eyes, and lashed out at me. "Are you happy now, Terrill?" he said. "Katherine begged me to keep you from seeing, made me promise. But you. You made me break that last promise to her. You had to be here. You and the damned ghost of Luke Carroll."

The sun broke through the clouds just as the service finished, and the wind felt almost warm as the crowd turned to leave.

That was when she saw Jubal, a long way away, over by the old iron gate.

For a moment Rilla's heart doubted. It didn't look like him. This man could have belonged anywhere in his neat shirt, his tan-colored slacks, the leather jacket he'd worn that Saturday on the street.

She watched him as Brother Sams bent over Tandy to speak to her as they sat on the folding chairs under the funeral canopy, as the gravediggers began to drop loud clods of dirt into the grave.

Look at the man by the far gate, Rilla thought. Block out the sounds.

The way he moved, the lean build, the dark hair. New clothes or not, it was Jubal.

Without a word she got up and walked to him, not caring who watched. He straightened at her approach.

"Hello, Jubal."

"Rilla. Are you . . . are you all right?"

You asked me that once before, she thought quietly, but she only nodded. "I'm glad you came. I didn't know you . . . the clothes."

"I never saw you in a dress before, either. You look real pretty." He looked out over the crowd, shoving his hands in his pockets against the cold. "You're gonna be okay, Rilla," he offered at last. "Aren't you?"

She nodded wordlessly. What else could she do?

This close to him—to the sound of his voice, the green of his eyes, moody and dark today, to the warmth of him, it felt as if she were home. He *was* her home, and it had been a long time since she'd been there.

But he just touched her face with his hand, and finally, he turned away.

T. G. Watson adjusted the little gold glasses on his nose and spread several papers out on the kitchen table in front of him.

"I appreciate your taking the time to let me go

through this today, Tandy, Henry. You, too, Terrill."
His slow, even voice was nearly genial, and there
was a trace of sympathy on his face and in his brown
eyes. He was the senior partner in Cade County's
only law firm, but with his rumpled tie and his
graying hair in its odd Dutch-boy cut, he looked like
an absentminded eccentric. "It's barely January . . .
holidays just over. I might have waited longer to
read y'all this will, but I'm going to be in Memphis
for the next two or three weeks."

Rilla stared stonily at the calendar on the wall,
the one with the Sunbeam bread girl smiling down
at her. She knew what day it was: January the third.
Katherine had been dead three weeks today. The
longest, darkest three weeks of her life.

Henry was dark and silent, too. He had little to
say to anyone anymore. Now he twisted his coffee
cup in its saucer, staring down into the black liquid
Tandy had poured for him. The lawyer's cup was
empty; Tandy Carroll made good coffee.

Only Tandy had any life about her, and she was
overdone and brittle. Too talkative. Too bright. She
acted almost nervous, Rilla thought in slow surprise.

Watson was still explaining when Henry interrupted. "Just read the will," he muttered. "Get it over
with. I can't stand much more."

Rilla watched her stepfather as the lawyer's voice
began its droning, "I, Katherine Carroll . . ." Henry
looked ill, his face gaunt and shadowed, his movements slow. He had loved Katherine. Rilla could admit
that now. Loved her too much. He had passed through
the entire funeral as though it had no reality for him,
and he had refused even to look at his dead wife.
Katherine had been right about him; he needed her.

Rilla wondered with an unexpected stab of pity how
Henry could bear to go on living in misery like his.

Katherine had left all of the money to Henry, the lawyer announced. She'd left him any personal items in the house that he wanted. She'd left him half the farm.

To Rilla, she left the house and the surrounding fields.

"And now for the business," Watson announced briskly, and Terrill shut off the sound of the lawyer's words, watching her stepfather's face.

It was his reaction that told her first that something was wrong. Henry looked up at Watson, his face betraying shock and agitation, and he half rose from his seat.

"What? What did you just read?" Carroll said harshly, choking on the words.

Tandy had gotten very still, her hands clasped together, but her face was calm and resigned.

Watson flicked one look at Rilla's aunt, then said soothingly, "I'll read it again, Henry. It's in her exact words. It says, 'Upon my death, the sole ownership of Carroll Mills shall revert to my daughter, Terrill Leigh Carroll, with the provision that she seek the advice and help of her aunt, Tandy Carroll, who shall act as financial officer of the mills, and her uncle, Henry Carroll, who shall be offered the position of manager until Terrill reaches the age of twenty-five.'"

The words registered in Rilla's mind slowly, then the meaning hit home: Katherine had taken the mill from Henry. The slow realization began to bleed into Rilla's soul. She knew why Katherine had done it: "You'll see how I love you," she had said. She had returned Luke's inheritance.

Katherine had betrayed him and taken the mill away to put it firmly in the hands of his brother's child. That was how Henry would see it. Tandy knew his reaction. So did Rilla.

For a long moment Henry hung there, half suspended between standing and rising, and if a knife had been stabbed through his heart, he could not have appeared more stunned or hurt.

No one spoke.

Finally Watson said mildly, "The next paragraph makes provision for each of you—Tandy, Terrill, Henry—to receive one-third of the mill's income for the rest of your life. After Terrill reaches twenty-five, however, she may choose to replace either of you in your positions. Should you die, the mill reverts completely to her or to any heirs she might have."

"I c-can't believe Katherine . . . *my* Katherine, would—" Henry broke off the stumbling words, to pass his hand over his stiff face. His eyes were staring and frightened.

Another long silence, then Watson said pityingly, "I know it's difficult to understand. But she was my client. She wanted this. She tried to be fair. And I've been instructed to give you a sealed letter which she dictated to Tandy for you to read. I believe she sets out to explain—"

Henry's head jerked toward his sister, still standing stiffly at the sink. "You knew," he whispered harshly, his face blood red and accusing. "You knew all along."

Tandy flinched a little. "Henry, you've got so much. You can't just cut Rilla off."

Henry Carroll's lower jaw was chattering with every loud breath he took. He looked once at the wide-eyed, terrified face of his stepdaughter. Everything was unfocused—except the hate.

Then he turned, knocking over the chair with a loud crash, and he slammed out the door into the cold January day, into the stray, drifting snowflakes that had floated down off and on all morning.

*   *   *

That night when Rilla awoke in the dark, she thought immediately of Katherine, and for the first time in weeks there was a tingly, tentative happiness. In her gesture with the mill, Katherine had proved what she had said. She had believed that Rilla wasn't entirely to blame for the problems with Henry.

Most of all, she had welcomed Rilla back again. She had given her the mill outright; the gesture said, You belong, Rilla. Come home.

Then she shivered, and pulled the quilts up higher around her. Henry was terrifying. He hadn't returned yet, even though Tandy had taken his supper to the mill in desperation tonight. She said he'd been locked inside his office, but he wouldn't talk to her. She'd finally left the meal sitting on Rosalie's desk.

Rilla knew what Tandy wanted and what Katherine had wanted: they wanted her to try to talk to him. Even wanting to do the right thing, even grasping vaguely that Henry's pain was far deeper than hers and was somehow tied up with a feeling of betrayal, Rilla couldn't bring herself to say anything yet.

She resented and disliked him, but even more, she was afraid. There was evil in him, a dark rage, and it was directed right at her.

Only Jubal had ever made her feel safe, protected from Henry's menace. In his arms Henry had seemed so far away that he couldn't reach her. She had almost forgotten her stepfather's malevolence.

In the arms of Jubal, wrapped tight against his body, Rilla had been free from Henry.

She was beginning to think that maybe Jubal had told her the truth.

From this distance of days and across all the grief, Rilla remembered too many things. And she began to reason: when had Jubal ever had time to carry on an affair with another girl? Between work, and the trips to Kentucky, and their midnight meetings, he'd been half-exhausted some nights.

And it had felt as if he loved her.

God, I think I was wrong, she thought in a frantic half plea, half prayer. But I can't get to him. I said too much, and I never understood how it would hurt him.

Even if I tried to get him back, I don't think he would ever come.

Restlessly Rilla pushed back the covers and did as she did too many nights: she padded across the cold wooden floor in the chill of the room and stood staring out the window at the mill across the hollow, where she'd met him so many times.

Carroll Mills. It belonged to her, really and truly. Her place in the world.

But Jubal wasn't there. Everything was dark and silent on the distant hilltop.

26

The January day was freezing, the streets of Nashville slushy with a mix of ice and rain that had been falling for several hours. It had wet her hair and her coat as she had walked through it on her way across the Belmont campus. By the time she got back to the car late that afternoon, her fingers and her toes were cold.

Rilla was trying. Really trying. Back in school, commuting three days a week, helping at the mill the two others. Nobody but her and Tandy now. Henry spent his days in the bedroom or sitting out on the hill. "We're going to have to get him help if he doesn't come out of this," Tandy said worriedly.

The men at the mill hadn't caught on yet that anything was wrong because there was little work anyway in January when the weather was this bad.

Rilla made one decisive move the first day she came back to the office: she had Jubal's desk moved so that her heart wouldn't freeze up every time she walked in and looked at it.

She'd heard that he'd taken a job over at Glover. A foreman over there, somebody said in surprise, for a crazy Yankee who didn't know any better than to give such a job to a Kane.

There was a college senior studying to be something in the music industry who asked Rilla to lunch one day after class. She went, and she wondered where Jubal was.

The man across the table from her that noon was exactly the kind she'd always planned to marry. But he wasn't Jubal.

Sometimes at night she put her hands over her ears to shut out her own words: "You're bad blood."

And then his: "I don't believe in you anymore."

"It's been eight weeks, Jubal, since you left her on that street. Now why can't you leave her in your heart?"

"I'm tryin', Ma. I just worry about her, that's all. What's she doin' since her mother's dead? Is Carroll treatin' her all right? I heard she got the mill. He ain't the kind of man to take that. I know things about him that make my skin crawl. I keep thinkin' maybe I should try to tell her some of those things, but I don't know what good it'd do."

"I don't mean to hurt you, Jubal, but it's best if you let the Carrolls take care of their own. Find another girl."

"No."

There was silence in the warm kitchen with only the sound of the soup bubbling between them. Jubal stared out the kitchen window at the bare, frozen backyard, and he said in a calmer voice, "I don't want to talk about it, Ma. I ain't ready to forget yet."

She stirred the soup once. "And when will you be?"

"When I know she's not cryin' at night. When I know she's safe."

"Then it sounds to me like you're waitin' for her to find another man."

He only flinched a little, but he bent his head to lean it against the window.

"I wish," Maggie said suddenly, "that you'd never laid eyes on the Carroll girl."

Rilla fell asleep at last, but she awoke again in the dark, and her face was wet. The remnants of the dream that had made her cry still clung above her. Katherine had been there, in the room, begging Rilla to come with her somewhere.

The clock in the hall struck, on and on, while Rilla counted. Twelve. Then she twisted in the covers restlessly, remembering. Friday night, when she used to meet Jubal.

She couldn't be still and think of him, so at last she threw back the covers and paced to the windows, looking out to search for the moon. But it was gone, hidden under the heavy gray clouds that had smeared the sky like cold soot all day. The weatherman had forecast snow.

Longingly she looked toward the mill, and—

Rilla sucked in her breath sharply, and as her heart began a heavy, painful thudding, her fingers clutched at the curtains nervelessly.

A light.

There was a light at the mill.

Jubal.

Oh, God—Jubal. After all this time, could it be?

Nobody else ever came to the mill at midnight and turned on the little light at the storage building. Nobody. Henry had been in the house most of the day. Hadn't been to the mill once this week.

And the light wasn't going out. To her, it appeared to be burning brighter and brighter.

It might be Jubal. He might really be back.

The thought terrified her, making her shake and shiver. But nothing—not fear, not the winter cold, not the long weeks of painful silence—could keep Rilla from going to the mill.

She might have a final chance to know the truth, a last fleeting opportunity to say what she needed to say.

As she stumbled into the edge of the dark yard and stopped, panting for breath, she caught a sharp, acrid odor. Somewhere in the night, something was burning, and there was an ominous, heavy feeling in the air that made her steps to the alcove cautious and timid.

But Jubal's truck wasn't parked there.

Rilla swallowed the lump of disappointment that rose in her throat, nervously tucking the long strands of her hair behind her ears.

If the truck wasn't here, where was it? Who had turned on the light at the small storage room? Fear danced in her blood.

She crossed quickly to the little building, circling to the back side where the door and the light were. It was on, illuminating the open door, and beyond the door, the tiny light inside the building burned dimly, too.

Her heart beating in quick jerks, Rilla peered in cautiously. Nothing out of place except an empty canister, one of the ones the mill sometimes used to haul fuel, which lay turned over in the floor.

Then Rilla pulled back into the shadows on the

far side of the building, thinking frantically. Whose keys could open the storage room?

And the answer came quickly: Henry's. She remembered clearly a square, triangular key with a strip of red tape on it that had read "3." The storage room was building three.

Unless someone had stolen the keys. Or picked the lock. Or—

A muffled, distant popping sound floated across the cold night air, reaching her in the darkness. She strained to hear it again. The office. Was it from the office?

Pulses were beating all over her body in fluttery, frightened movement, and her feet felt like two blocks of ice. The she caught it again, the smell.

Rilla made the trip to the office in blackness, edging around the dim circle of purple light from the security pole, sliding down the front of the office in the shadows between the shrubs and the wall. She should go home, but the night pulsed with tension.

She slid her hand along the panels of the door from her position, flattened against the wall, and the door swung inward a little, already open.

Rilla stifled a high, quick scream.

Smoke.

A heavy black cloud hung at the ceiling, hovering like an ominous canopy over the rest of the room, reaching in a long dark finger toward the door she'd just opened.

Heat shimmered from the direction of Henry's office, billowing out against Rilla's petrified body, warring with the cold, snowy air at her back.

Fire. His office was on fire behind that closed door!

The crackling and snapping were much louder now, and something crashed and crumpled resoundingly somewhere beyond, like a stick of kindling collapsing on a great bonfire.

Rilla tried to take in a gust of air to scream. Instead she got a mouth full of smoke and something that tasted of grit, and she began to cough and gag, stumbling backward into the night as another gust of heat slapped her down.

And as she sprawled there in the darkness on the cold ground, sucking in fresh air, she saw the flames shooting up from the roof of the mill itself.

The whole place was on fire. Every building.

And once the blaze spread to the stacks of dried lumber, Carroll Mills would be a roaring inferno.

The telephone on Rosalie's desk—Rilla had to get inside long enough to call the fire station in Bethel. There wasn't time for anything else.

Now she was prepared for the high cloud of smoke and heat, and she crawled along on the floor, facedown. Only twenty feet to the telephone.

Almost there, in the shadow of the desk and the wall, she raised up to fumble for it.

A dim figure stumbled through the open door, catching Rilla completely off guard. She fell between the desk and the wall, straining to see the flitting shadow, terrified. It twisted once to look back out the door, gazing toward the mill, where flames were already licking through to the night . . . and Rilla recognized him.

If every bad feeling, every horrible dream, every ounce of hate, she'd ever felt for Henry Carroll had been poured back into her all at once, Rilla could not have been more violently sick than she was in the instant she recognized her stepfather, standing between flickering light and dusky shadow. Her stomach jerked, and she clapped a hand over her mouth to keep herself from retching. In a hideous blaze of illumination, she understood.

He had set fire to the mill.

Shaking violently, biting her own hand to keep back the sound of the choking whimper that erupted in her chest and pushed into her throat, she tried to think past Henry's lunatic hate and the sensation of unreality.

She watched Henry as he suddenly moved to look at the canister he held in his hands, then all around him consideringly. After a second or two he came to some kind of decision, moving out of the door toward her.

She shrank further back into the shadows, heart thudding in the back of her head as though her brain would explode. She had to get out of this doomed mill. As soon as he moved far enough away from the door. Out. *Out.*

He was pulling long strips of rags from his pocket, dropping them in piles around the door. And while he worked, he talked. Explaining, wheedling, reasoning with somebody Rilla couldn't see.

"It's for the best, Kathy," he said over and over. "You'll see. It needs to be finished, what's between you and me and Luke. Trust me, Kathy."

The canister made an ominous *thud* as he sat it down on the thin carpet.

"Terrill doesn't know how to run the place. She never really wanted it. She just didn't want me to have it. You can see that now, can't you, Kathy? And Luke has got to understand once and for all that he can't come between us. The mill was his weapon, don't you see, Kathy? But no more."

He began to cough as he waded farther into the room, into the cloud of smoke. She saw the big black letters on the side of the fuel container clearly; they spelled DIESEL.

"He got to Kane through Terrill, Luke did. Too afraid I was going to succeed. Afraid I was going to be successful."

He crooned the words as he sloshed the diesel around the entrance, dripping it down the drapes at the side window, letting it soak into the carpet, pouring it carefully over the scattered piles of rags.

Get away from the door, she screamed at him silently as she huddled under the desk. *Move away!*

"Not long now, Kathy. Not long."

The first pile of rags must have had gasoline on them as well as diesel. They ignited so violently that the flames *whoosh*ed up in a mighty yellow gust of intense heat that scorched his face painfully and left him coughing and gagging.

Stumbling back as the pile blazed into red glory, Henry gasped for air, then struck the second match.

This time he jerked away immediately, but this blaze was slower to start. It took a few seconds before a line of fire shot up the drapes.

More smoke was pouring into the air, rising in black gusts to the ceiling, and the room was already an orange maze of delicate hot trails that crisscrossed the floor, following the various paths of diesel, casting dancing, hideous shadows on the ceiling and walls.

When he turned his back on her to look toward the door, Rilla's iron control broke. She had to get out. Only twenty feet—she would run free into the night, then. Away from this crazy world of fire.

She pushed off the floor, hard and fast.

Run. *Run.*

Just as she made the final lunge for the door, his hands caught her.

"No! *No!* Let go of me!"

She struggled and fought and kicked against the

grotesque black monster that grasped her, her hands wet with sweaty terror, his strength magnified by sheer insanity. Writhing against his arms, she twisted to slap and scratch at his face, to pound at his legs with her feet.

Fighting for life.

He would kill her.

"I don't . . . want . . . to—die!" she screamed in bursts of sound. Not to him, but to the night beyond.

Henry's eyes blazed with fury, his hair stood up like a wild mane. "You won't ruin this, too," he panted, and turned loose of her with one hand. "I'll put you where you'll never ruin anything again."

For one minute Rilla thought she would be free.

Then he hit her in the side of the temple with something hard and heavy. Everything blurred . . . so still now . . . so quiet.

Sliding downward toward the orangy, crisscrossed floor. A loud alarm went off somewhere. In her head?

Cheek against the carpet. His shoes. She saw his shoes.

One last coherent thought: I never meant to die in a fire.

27

The pounding on the door was so loud, it sounded like Judgment Day, that was what Maggie was mumbling as she went past Jubal's room in the night to answer it.

He fumbled for his pants, wondering what was wrong, but before he could get them fastened, there was a loud commotion in the living room and the sound of voices.

"Get Jubal up. *Jubal—*" Bobo Hackett practically fell into the dark room, fumbling for a light switch.

"What? What is it?"

The light came on with a snap, revealing Bobo wild-eyed and frightened. "It's the mill—and Carroll—and the girl."

Fingers of fear played up his spine as if it were a piano. *I knew—I knew something was wrong,* he heard his own brain say.

"What? *What?*"

"Whole mill's on fire. They think Carroll set it. And they think the girl is in it."

He couldn't move for a minute. Even his heart quit. *Step,* he told his foot, *step into shoes.*

No time.

"Where do they—" He couldn't finish the question, and his body released so that he could move again, scrambling for clothes.

"She went to the mill, Jubal." Bobo said it with certainty. "They found her footprints. They're still searching the grounds, the house. And they found Carroll."

He was moving so fast he went past Maggie like a shot; her face was scared and white.

Out the door, down the steps, into the open door of Bobo's truck.

"Where?"

"In his office. Dead from smoke. Suicide. He'd barred the doors from the inside. Tandy Carroll's out there, on the edge of a nervous breakdown. Whole town's out there. God."

It was snowing. Heavy, wet flakes of it were pelting down against the windshield. In the lights of Bobo's truck, it was a blizzard striking at them. The wipers clacked rhythmically, pushing them away.

"Hurry."

"I'm goin' as fast as I can."

"Where do they think she is?"

"They don't know. If she was in the mill itself, or your shop, or the other three outbuildings, she's— It's too late. They're gone. But—"

"For God's sake, Bobo, tell me," he said hoarsely. He was hurting everywhere.

"They put out a lot of the fire at the office. Long enough to drag him out. One inside wall had collapsed. She could be . . . be under it."

"*No.*"

*   *   *

Hell must look like this, he thought.

Wild red streaks of pure fire jumping and dancing against the midnight sky. White snow falling before it, into it.

Past it—he ran past it.

People screaming and crying as they huddled at a distance. The curious, the fascinated.

Fire engine.

Police car.

Ambulance with a black, grotesque shape under a sheet just beyond the open doors.

What was left of Henry Carroll.

Don't think about it. Keep going.

The office of the mill looked as if it had been electrified; its perimeters glowed orange. But it stood. It still stood.

The sound of a woman having hysterics. Tandy Carroll, locked in Ned Standford's arms as he tried to hold her back.

"Where's Terrill?" Jubal demanded, his voice harsh and rough.

"Get back, Jubal! How'd you get through?"

One of the firemen, his face grimed with sweat, reached for him, and he sidestepped.

"Where is she?"

"How'n in the hell do I know?" Ned shouted in frustration over Tandy's head. "Get me one of those paramedics, Foster. Dammit! They chopped through a back way and found *him* in the corner of the office beside a damn-fool wall of steel. It didn't burn like the rest of 'em did. Otherwise he'd have been—" He broke off, remembering Tandy. "Where's that medic?"

The man who rushed up from the ambulance tried to pull the struggling Tandy away from Standford, away from the fire that blistered Jubal's skin and crackled like something wild and manic behind him.

Soot and ash blew past into the white blaze of snow all around them, a black-and-white warring of the elements. A loud alarm went off somewhere as a distant pile of flaming lumber fell through on top of itself, a deadly pyre.

Beside a damn-fool wall of steel.

He knew where she was.

Oh, Rilla, Rilla. *That'd make a hell of a grave, wouldn't it?*

He ran—ran. Past more firemen. "Stop him!" the fire chief roared somewhere as he shot past. Straight to the back of the office. A corner where he'd once jammed a burglar alarm.

The firemen had chopped through the outside wall right through the aluminum siding, through the wooden studs. And once inside, they'd discovered they couldn't hack through the wall that ran perpendicular to it, because it was coated in steel. So they'd abandoned it.

He fell through the crude, smoky opening just as one of the firemen lunged for him, choking on the fumes and the odor of the chemicals they'd sprayed here, in this office.

Right here, in this corner, Carroll had died.

Right here, he'd hidden Terrill.

I know him. I know him, Jubal thought. Please—please—let this work. Let this panel still slide.

It was hot to the touch, burning his fingertips.

Don't die, Rilla. Don't be afraid. I'm coming.

He couldn't see at all. Smoke gagged and blinded him; his eyes teared until he had to twist his face toward the shattered wall beside him where snow and fresh air poured in from the night beyond.

Flames danced across the horizon beyond the snow, out in the lumberyard. He saw them as he stood plastered to the wall, facing the cold night, while his hands fumbled up and down blindly, feeling, feeling.

I've got to find it.

The face of one of Bethel's firemen—James Bennett—appeared in the opening, his head dusted with snow.

"Kane—" He couldn't see him clearly in the dark swirling smoke. "Kane! You've got to get out! This building's still on fire at the other end! Where are you? It could collapse—"

His fingers found it. He pushed it, pushing at the wall, praying that the spring action that the button released would work. *Push harder.*

Slowly, ponderously—and only halfway. But it was enough. The wall slid open.

Fresh air here—no smoke yet.

He fumbled for the ring, stooping to yank up the wooden trap door with all his strength, letting it slam against the steel wall opposite him, trying to see down into the black pit.

Please, let her be here. It's the only way she'll still be alive. Please.

He had to lie on the floor to reach his hand down into the hole, and nearly jumped out of his skin when he touched warm flesh.

Rilla.

His chest was heaving against the sooty black floor when he reached both arms down into the hole, wrapped his hands around her clothes, and pulled.

She was a dead weight.

Not dead. Not dead.

He pulled her up enough to see the white of her shirt. He had her by the shirt. She was on her side.

His arms were about to give way under the strain, his shoulders aching and cramped as they tried to fit into the miserly distance that the wall had opened.

But he couldn't let go of her.

Then the fireman was above him, legs straddling his hips, reaching down to grab at her, too.

A belt loop. Bennett caught a belt loop, that was all, but it was enough. The added impetus let Jubal yank her up.

The shadowy outline of her face, her hair spilling to the side, her head lolling over.

Legs still caught under the wooden door.

One more brutal pull, and he had her. That hellhole, a night of flame, and all of Henry Carroll's evil couldn't hold her from him.

Won again, he thought wildly, and clasped her up against his chest.

Bennett stumbled up, off him, choking and coughing as the smoke began to pour into the space between the walls.

"Gotta . . . get out," he gasped to Jubal, motioning toward the hole where they'd crawled in. He clambered through, grunting as Jubal staggered and stood, a sweet burden against his heart.

She had to be alive. She was warm.

At the hole in the wall, Bennett stretched out his arms to take her.

"No," he croaked, his voice like sandpaper. "No."

And he maneuvered himself through, still clutching her to him.

Bennett roared in mad relief to anybody who'd listen, "We found her!"

Jubal followed with his limp, rag-doll burden as Bennett swept them through the other staring firemen, the policemen, right into the wide, cleared circle that had once been the mill yard.

Full of white, pristine snow.

Ringed by the fires of the outer buildings on one side.

By waiting, staring people on the other side of the barriers.

There, in the fiery light, he dared to look at her.

Her face was bruised, but she was alive. Unconscious, but breathing.

Face, hands, arms, legs.

All that was Rilla.

Here, against him, heart beating.

That was when he gave out. His own legs folded under him; he felt himself go to his knees. But he didn't turn loose.

Tandy Carroll was sobbing at the edge of the circle. "Oh, God—oh, God."

And the whole beautiful river might have rushed through his blood.

Hold on.

I held on, Rainey. I didn't let go. I got her out.

Now it wasn't Tandy crying anymore. It was him. *He* was the one weeping as though his heart would break. Tears dropping on the quiet face of the one in his arms.

He slipped farther, sitting on the ground now, clutching her to him fiercely.

"Jubal." Somebody was speaking his name. "Son, give her to the medics. They can help her."

Ned's voice. Gentle, soothing. He could trust Ned. Could hand her to him before he collapsed completely.

Baby, he thought, looking down at her, you made it. Gonna get to live a long, long time. Long enough for me to tell you that I don't blame you for not believing. Long enough to tell you that you were the best thing that ever happened to me, even if we didn't make it.

He let them pull her from him and from his racking sobs, giving her to the world again, to all these staring people.

Somebody dropped beside him in the falling snow, and her arms were bands of steel around him for a moment as she pressed him to her, like a mother hugging a child.

It was Tandy Carroll.

28

He slept at last, just as a white, snowy dawn crept over his windowsill.

His sleep was not the dark, cool oblivion that he'd been seeking, the one he hoped would give him respite from the red-hot flames that still danced in his memory; instead he dreamed of running through a fire time after time, but never running fast enough to get wherever he was going.

But it was still a relief from the emotional drain and the physical exhaustion that had dragged at him ever since he'd returned home at four A.M. this morning to find Maggie, pale and terrified, waiting in the yellow glow of the tiny living room lamp.

Ida had been sitting with her, her presence proof that all of Cade County, from Sullivan's Ridge down to Bethel, was a part of this terrible, restless night and the tragedy at Carroll Mill.

Ida had already heard what had transpired there ninety minutes earlier. She and Maggie had watched

Jubal in a silent agony until Ida finally spoke. "That was a mighty big thing you did tonight, boy."

He hadn't even answered; instead he'd walked to his bedroom and fallen facedown across the bed, dirty, smoky, singed clothes and all.

And with his awakening this morning, he looked out on the frozen world with only one thought in his head: She was alive, somewhere in Cade County General.

He knew what he was going to do, too; he had as much right as anybody to see that girl. He had to, just to reassure himself that Rilla really had come through in one piece. That she really was able to breathe and walk and run out where the air was pure and sweet.

He put gas in the truck at Ida's, not paying much attention to those gaping at him in the store, but when he paid his bill, Ida spoke.

"You goin' to see her?"

"Yeah."

"Well, you wait just a minute." Ida hurried to the back room and came out with a cake tin in her hands. "I've had this fruitcake baked since Christmas. It's homemade and rich as sin. You take this to her, and to her aunt. I heard Tandy Carroll hadn't moved out of that hospital since she got there. No fit food at a hospital. If I had something else ready, I'd send it."

Jubal looked down at the red-and-white tin. He felt ridiculous holding it, would probably feel even sillier when he gave it to Tandy, but he couldn't tell Ida that, so he just mumbled his thanks and left.

At the nurses' station, he stopped to ask a young woman on duty where the room was. She turned flustered and pink.

"Oh, it's you, Mr. Kane. Well, Miss Carroll's not

letting anybody in to see her, but I'm sure she'll let *you*. She's just down the hall in the waiting room."

There were two people with Tandy, all of them sitting on tiny red plastic chairs. One was Joanie, distant and clinical in her nurse's white uniform, the other Ned Standford. Jubal stopped in confusion, but when Tandy saw him, she stood, as worn and gray as he felt.

"She's there," she said simply, pointing to a door across the hall.

It was hard to push open the door, but his first glimpse erased most of his fears. Rilla asleep, that's all he saw as he looked down on her. Her cheeks had color, her fingers on the bedclothes twitched.

A huge dark bruise colored her right temple. Carroll had done it, Jubal knew instinctively. Twice I let Carroll hit her, he thought, and now I'm glad he's dead.

His fingers brushed the bruise, remembering her touch on him after that fight at the Pine, and impulsively he leaned over to press a kiss against the mark.

She moved a little, and his heart jumped. *Wake up, Rilla.*

"Actually, the fact that Henry knocked her unconscious may turn out for the best," Tandy said unsteadily from behind him, and he flushed in surprise, moving from the bed.

"If we're lucky, she'll never remember much of what happened. Never even know what he . . . he tried to do to her," Tandy finished.

"But he didn't."

"No, and I owe a debt of thanks to you."

Her gratitude was spoken quietly, but he didn't want it. He hadn't gone in that burning mill for her or Rilla, but for himself, so he could keep on living.

"Mr. Kane, I can't ever tell you how much—"

"Don't."

The word was rough and rude. He didn't know how to make it any other way.

Tandy paused, watching him. Then she walked to the window and looked out on the icy white world outside. "Could I ask you something? How did you know where to find her? I've been around that mill all my life and I never once saw that hole in the ground."

"Because Carroll made it. He was as dark and secret and insane as it." He'd make no apologies for what he was saying about this woman's brother. "I knew him."

"I thought I knew him, too." Tandy brushed a hand across her face. "I never thought even once that Henry had it in him to kill. Or if I did, I denied it to myself."

She turned to look at him across the sleeping girl. "And last night," Tandy whispered with effort, "I discovered that Jubal Kane knew how to cry."

His throat moved convulsively as she watched him, her face like breakable porcelain.

"You love her."

Jubal looked down at his hands blindly.

"She'll wake up, Mr. Kane. Any hour now. I keep holding on to that thought while I go through all the horrible necessities of arranging a funeral, and dealing with the insurance people, and talking to Sheriff Standford."

A long, pregnant pause.

"He tells me that there's money in that godforsaken hole. Hundreds of thousands of dollars. Do you know where it came from?"

Jubal was tired of half-truths and staying quiet; last night had been too gigantic a tear in the fabric of his life for him to keep lies shrouded in it now. He didn't even consider the outcome; he just said, with little or no emotion, "Call him in."

Tandy knew instantly what he was about to do. "I hope I have the strength to hear this," she said with effort before she crossed to the door.

And when Ned Standford entered, his face keen and expectant, Jubal faced the sheriff and Tandy Carroll across the white, still bed and told it all.

Confession at last.

Tandy didn't move when he was finished, but her fingers gripped the sheets until the knuckles shone.

"Is there . . . is there any way we can give the money back?" she asked finally, glancing from Jubal to the motionless sheriff.

"I don't know who the man was who got the engines to Carroll. He was an executive with the corporation that made them. I think he fixed things so that the corporation never even knew the parts had been built, let alone stolen. But there was a ledger from the office. All about Carroll's end of the deal. Serial numbers and phone numbers, and haul dates, and everything else. I'll give it to you. I took it when I left the job."

"You took it?" Standford's voice was sharp.

"I told him if he didn't let me go, I'd find a way to let it fall into the hands of the police." He reached to brush the back of Rilla's fingers as they lay on the bed. "She said she loved me. For her sake—and for mine—I couldn't stand to keep on doing it. But it's caught up with me anyway."

Tandy watched his movement, and her eyes searched his face before she at last broke the quiet circle of emotion. "So it comes down to two choices. The sheriff can try to return the money, and probably send you back to prison. That's one choice, maybe the morally truthful one."

Jubal swallowed harshly. "I always heard, Miss Carroll, that you didn't know how to live anything but truth. So I guess you'll have to now. And you, Sheriff, you'll have to do the same."

The three of them watched each other, each searching and waiting. Then Tandy moved to clasp her hands together.

"You know something, Mr. Kane? I'm forty-seven years old. Unless—no, *until* Rilla wakes up, I'm all that's left of the Carroll family. It's taken all of this to make me understand how wrong it is to accept anything as absolute. I've spent my life hiding behind safe little rules and black-and-white commandments. But today I have to find the courage to think for myself."

She walked with jerky movements around the bed, until she was standing so close to him that she laid her hand on his.

"There's what is truth, and then there's something greater. There's what is *right*. I can see now that they're not always the same." She took a long, steadying breath, then looked at the other man. "I hope you understand what I'm saying, Sheriff."

"What I understand," Standford began slowly, "is that it serves no purpose for you to be goin' back to Lineville, Jubal. Or for Maggie and Tandy to be put through a scandal like the one another trial would cause if this business ever came out. I'll make a call to the Cummins corporation and suggest that they've got a bad apple somewhere high up, and all that money . . . well, Tandy can donate it to one of her charities if she wants to. But you, Jubal—" the sheriff paused, then said offhandedly, "if I never saw that ledger—and I don't reckon it'd do me any good to see it—I'd have no case against you."

A gust of wind and snow rattled the window, and the rough sound cut across the quiet room as Jubal registered what Standford was trying to tell him.

"A fire burns everything in its path," Tandy said at last. "Dreams and buildings and people. Let a fire have that ledger, too, Jubal, because you earned your absolution—if that's what you want."

Dead silence between them.

Only Rilla made a sound as she moved a little on the pillow.

He couldn't speak at all, so he nodded wordlessly, then looked away. There on a chair beside the door was the red-and-white tin, right where he'd deposited it.

"There." The word was choked as he motioned toward the chair. "Ida Fuller sent that to you."

"I don't think I've had a gift from Sullivan's Ridge before. Tell her it's appreciated," Tandy said.

His hand reached out and brushed away the hair that clung to Rilla's throat and spilled down on her shoulders in the white gown. She moved a little, letting her cheek rest on his hand, just as she had the night they'd made love, a whole eternity ago.

"She's been tossing around like that since noon. The doctor says it means that she's coming out of it," Tandy whispered.

Like lustrous shadows, the lashes lay against her high cheekbones. He memorized her face, the line of her throat. "You're free, girl," he said huskily. "Just like you were always wantin' to be."

He couldn't think of anything else to say; he'd reached the inevitable end, where all was said and done. He had to leave her and go back to his own life.

He was at the door when Tandy called his name in surprise. "She'll want to see you. Aren't you coming back?"

"You—you tell her. Say that I was here," he said. "That's all."

"But I thought you loved her!"

He ran a hand over his face in frustrated pain. "What'd you expect me to do, Miss Carroll? Stand around waitin' for her to wake up and fall in my arms because I pulled her out of a fire? I'm the same man she quit believin' in two months ago. She'll know why I left. But"—he hesitated—"but she knows, too, that if she needs me, I'll be on the Ridge."

At two o'clock on Sunday afternoon, while most of a scandalized Cade County flocked to Henry's funeral, Rilla lay on a narrow hospital bed watching the snow drift past her window. Frost made odd, lacy patterns in the high corners.

Her head still throbbed, but she hadn't rung the nurse yet to ask for any medication. She wanted to be alert, awake, to try to think.

Part of her shuddered in sick horror away from what Henry had intended. Her stomach still roiled at the last clear memory she had—that of him standing in the doorway, holding a canister of fuel.

But most confusing of all to Rilla was what she felt spreading through under the terror, the emotion that was trying to push out all the others: it was relief, and maybe even joy.

Henry was gone.

Maybe Tandy grieved him; maybe she had recollections of a different man, back before his obsession with Katherine and his hatred of the brother who'd taken her away.

But not Rilla. The world somehow felt lighter, cleaner, more normal.

Sanity was out there somewhere.

So was Jubal.

Surely he would come to her. Surely he still loved her.

*   *   *

"So, you see, you have options," T. G. Watson told Rilla the following Friday as she and Tandy sat in his office on the square in Bethel. She had just checked out of the hospital. "The sensible thing to do—the thing most young women in your situation would do—is to sell out. The farm, the timber reserve at Dural, all the heavy equipment still left, right down to any contracts the mill might be able to hold on to with different companies. You'd be very comfortable—downright wealthy, Terrill. And you could live wherever you choose. Nashville, Atlanta, even New York if you wanted to."

The silence in the room was broken at last by the sound of a car horn outside, where people moved slowly down the slushy street.

Tandy said nothing, just sat with both hands crossed in her lap as if to make it clear that she was out of this decision.

Rilla pushed the coat off her shoulders; it was too hot in this stuffy room. "Do you know what happened to me while I was in that hole in the ground, Mr. Watson?"

T.G. glanced uneasily at the remnants of the bruise on her face, then at Tandy before he cleared his throat. "It was the most unfortunate—"

"No, I don't mean that. I mean, in *here*." Rilla put her fingers to her head. "And in *here*." To her heart. "It didn't even happen in the mill, so much as it did later. When I woke up, I knew what I wanted. I don't want just life. I want *my* life. I haven't gotten to live much of it yet."

"This money will enable you to travel the world, Terrill. You could—"

"No." She stood, the soft red shirt a warm foil for

the spill of rich, honey-colored hair around her
shoulders, and went to the window. "You're doing
it, too, Mr. Watson. You're giving me what *you*
think is the life I should live."

A silence before she spoke again.

"Do you know what I want? What I think life is?
I've thought about it a lot since Mama died. I came
out of that fire understanding it. It's the little things.
The way hay sticks to you when it's cut in Grandpa's
fields. The way roosters crow in the morning. It's
this town square, and those hills, and the river. And
do you know what else it is, Mr. Watson?"

He shook his head.

"It's me, being just what I am. I'm not Katherine
Carroll. I'm never going to be, don't even want to be
anymore." Rilla drew in a long, rough breath, half
laughter and half tears, her eyes wide and glittering
with emotion. "If I don't follow the rules and do
what women like me—whatever that means—are
supposed to do, then it's nothing to anybody except
me. I'm going to be what I am, and give back what I
can. I mean to live here. It's where I belong. If I go
away, I'll come back here. And when I die, I'll sleep
here."

Watson broke the long silence at last. "Well," he
said, then shifted on his chair. "I guess," he said
humorously, "that this means you don't plan to sell."

Snow was still falling when Rilla and Tandy went to
the bank the next week.

"I declare, I never saw such heavy snows," Tandy
said as the two of them stepped out from the Ford into
the icy white drifts that lay against the parking curb.

"I think somebody's trying to clean up the world
of the mess people have made," Rilla answered as

she swung across the patch closest to her, bracing herself with a hand on the icy hood of the car.

Tandy patted her arm as they merged at the door of Citizens Bank. "You're fine, Rilla. Don't think about it. Even your face has healed. And you know what you want. That's half the battle."

I know what I want, she thought. I want Jubal, too. My heart hasn't healed. Why doesn't he come?

Inside, one of the cashiers, pretty and blond, caught sight of the two of them. She laid down her money tray, came out from her window, and hurried over.

"Miss Carroll. And Miss Carroll." She beamed. "Mr. Johnson is expecting you. I'm supposed to take you right up to him. How are you doing?" The last she asked solicitously of Rilla, her face sympathetic, her voice as hushed as if they were in a library.

"Fine, thank you." Rilla tried to make it polite, but she was tired of the shock and the awe and the tippy-toe gentleness everybody used around her.

But the pretty blonde wasn't through yet. "I saw your Jubal Kane the other day, over in Glover. I told my husband that if I hadn't loved him first, and if Mr. Kane didn't belong to Miss Carroll, I'd lose my heart to him."

Rilla looked down at the front of her coat, where her hands gripped the lapels tightly. "I'm sure he'd be flattered to hear that," she managed, her voice steady.

Tandy intervened. "We'll see ourselves up, Mrs."— she peered at the woman's name tag—"Simmons."

"Oh, but Mr. Johnson—"

"We'd rather." Tandy said it firmly, reaching past the cashier to open the door marked STAIRS. "And we'll climb instead of riding the elevator. There's no point in encouraging laziness."

The cashier's mouth moved as if she meant to protest again, but Rilla and Tandy had already stepped through, the creased fold in the back of Tandy's straight blue skirt swishing past the door as it shut.

"No, no, and no," Johnson said furiously, his palms planted so firmly on the glass top over his oak desk that they might have been glued down. "A woman and a girl cannot run a sawmill full of men. You've tried this before, Tandy. Didn't you learn your lesson then?"

Tandy's back never even came close to touching the rose brocade of the wingback chair she sat on, and despite the two red spots burning in each cheek, her voice was steady. "Yes. I learned a great many things. Because of that debacle I think I can do a better job this time."

Johnson took a deep, soothing breath. "Now, look. You have other, more viable options than trying to rebuild a mill. Have you considered them?"

"Every one," Rilla answered, her figure slender and as upright as her aunt's in the smoothly fitting, delicately embroidered dress of creamy wool. "And I know that here is where I belong." She gestured firmly at the floor. "The mill needs to be here, just like I do. Do you know how many families depend on it? Most of those men don't know anything but work in a sawmill. Now what will they do? The nearest one is all the way over in Macon County, and they've already got a full crew."

"Don't you think the whole town's thinking about that?" Lionel demanded, pulling his glasses from his nose so roughly that they threatened to pull his ears off. "The thing to do is sell. Sell to men like Allardt and Henigar and me. We'll rebuild the mill, hire managers. You can finish college and teach or sew or whatever—"

"My degree is in management," Rilla interrupted. "And I grew up around that mill. I know how to grade lumber, how to tell oak from pine, walnut from beech, maple from pecan. And Aunt Tandy knows finance. She's always been an accountant and a bookkeeper."

"You don't know men!" Johnson practically roared, coming up out of his chair. "Good God, girl, you hadn't been home but a few weeks before you got hooked up with Jubal Kane! The rest of this county may put a halo on him these days, but I'm not so sure myself."

Rilla's face was as white as the dress, and Tandy broke in.

"Without Mr. Kane, Rilla wouldn't be here. She made an excellent choice, I'd say. And I don't think you're such a fine judge of character yourself, Lionel. You trusted Henry implicitly."

Johnson sat down again heavily on his chair of oxblood leather.

"We intend to pursue this idea," Tandy continued. "Somehow."

"With what? The insurance has refused to pay," Johnson said insistently. "Arson and suicide cancel out policies, Tandy. I'm trying to save you and this girl from your own—" He broke off.

"Our own stupidity?" Tandy snapped, and now the red spots on her cheeks blended perfectly with the fire in her eyes.

"I didn't say that. But rebuilding the mill is important enough that it shouldn't be turned into a frivolous undertaking that's doomed to fail because two women decided to dabble in the timber business. Because you've always had a yen to do this kind of thing, Tandy, and now you're dragging your niece into it, too. I know you, woman."

Rilla made it to the chair in time to catch Tandy as she shot up out of it, her blue suit coat flapping briskly.

"Mr. Johnson," Rilla said to the banker, who'd reared back fearfully at Tandy's movement, "if you knew me at all, then you'd know that I make up my own mind. I know that we may have trouble with a mill. But I hope you're not turning us—and our collateral, all that timberland—down flat just because we're women."

"I'm trying to stop you from losing everything," he said obstinately, sliding a hand into the collar of his white shirt and pulling it away from his throat as if he couldn't breathe. "You need a man to help you, dammit. You bring me one that's live and kicking, one that can do it, and then we'll talk about a loan. And if my saying that is discrimination, then hell, call the ACLU. And yes, Tandy, I swore."

"I think *you'd* better call the doctor," Tandy snapped, snatching up her purse. "You appear to be on the verge of a stroke, Lionel."

"He's right, you know," Tandy said as they sat in the living room. It was a place they rarely used, but tonight, with light snow still falling, they'd lit a fire in the huge fireplace at one end.

Rilla sat on the piano bench on the opposite side of the room, watching the flames. Gentle and contained now. Outside, smoke still drifted from piles of charred sawdust and lumber, even after two weeks. She didn't like to look at the grotesque heaps and odd shapes that lay blanketed by the snow.

But the white purity of it had won after all: it was still falling, still smothering out the fire. Still anxiously patting down and smoothing over the newest grave in the family cemetery.

"Lionel was right today," Tandy continued, "because most of those men will only respect another man. We need a man."

Rilla twisted to look at the ivory keys on the piano behind her. "I need one, too, Aunt Tandy," she said quietly. "I'm going after him. Now, tonight. And I'm not above bribery. I'm going to offer him a third of the mill. The third that would have been Henry's if I'd chosen to sell it to him."

Tandy's hands stilled on her needlework. "He'll think it's out of gratitude, Rilla."

"You understand better, don't you, Aunt? It's out of necessity."

"I'm hardly the one to understand anything about Jubal. I discovered I didn't know him at all."

"I've waited all these days for him," Rilla said painfully. "And I don't understand, either. What kind of man loves me enough to risk his life but not enough to forgive me?"

Tandy had no answer, so she sat silently on the chair for a moment. "Lionel still won't go along with us. Jubal is too young, too much a Kane even now. And Jubal may not agree, either."

"I'll find a way," Rilla said in determination, laying her fingers on the ivory keys. "Even if they say I'm crazy. One of the crazy Carrolls."

Tandy stood, the firelight behind her sending her shadow across the sea green carpet. "Don't, Rilla. We'll be fine."

Rilla's fingers had found the melody now. "Crazy for cryin' . . . crazy for tryin' . . ." whispered the keys.

"In spite of Lionel, I think asking Jubal is a good idea. It's not like we're getting anywhere on our own with this plan," Tandy said, smiling wryly.

Under Rilla's fingers, the music finished.

". . . crazy for lovin' you."

29

Working for Hank Barlow wasn't the easiest job in the world, thought Jubal as he made the long trip home that Friday night through the light snow. The man kept erratic hours, he had a fierce temper, he was brusque and short, he had enough money to think he was God.

Barlow didn't understand southerners much yet, either, and their antipathy didn't help matters. He didn't know what to do with their politeness, sometimes taking it for just plain two-facedness. He was here simply because he'd married a younger woman who thought she was going to be the next Reba McEntire, so he'd brought his little darling to Mecca.

While she pounded doors in Nashville every day, Barlow went about the business of making money sixty miles away in Glover.

Barlow was growing increasingly frustrated with the blocks being put in his way by locals, who'd seen northerners invade, take over, and change whole sections of the state, and by the men who'd controlled business in the area for years and weren't about to give up their territory to a foreigner.

"You know any of these damned Allardts? Or that Johnson in Bethel?" Barlow had demanded of Jubal once he'd found out where Jubal was from.

"Yeah, but we're sorta from different sides of the tracks," Jubal had answered caustically.

"I'm getting tired of butting heads with them over everything in sight," Barlow had said. "One of these days I'll find a way into that little county, and we'll see how tough they really are."

Jubal stayed quiet and went about his business. He got along with Barlow, and the only time he'd had trouble with the men, right at the beginning, Barlow had backed him completely. He didn't even mind Barlow's ways. For one thing, the Yankee was fair; for another, he wasn't Henry Carroll.

There was Carroll again.

Why couldn't he just forget him?

And when was this gaping wound that Rilla had left in him going to heal?

Three months now since the night at Joanie's, when he'd thought he hated her. Two weeks since the fire, when he faced the fact that he loved her, probably forever. *I ain't gonna outlive this love.*

He was caught, dangling helplessly between the two extremes. He wanted to go back to her, but he'd learned one thing from Tess that applied here: a woman who didn't believe in a man, who put him down, could break him. His heart, his spirit, his soul.

On the other hand, Jubal's mind argued, maybe Rilla had had cause to hurt him.

For her, it had been about getting back at him over Tess. And on his own count, he'd been doing something illegal the entire time he was with her.

But he wanted to get beyond all of that. He wanted to forgive her. He wanted her to ask to be forgiven, so they could try to make it right.

But not a word in two weeks.

He'd walked into a fire for her, and she couldn't even come. Had nightmares still.

Of course, he'd made it clear at the hospital that he was through. But he'd tacked on one last sentence: "I'll be on the Ridge."

It wouldn't work between the two of them . . . but he couldn't live without her.

Jubal didn't know what he wanted anymore. Couldn't go to her. Why didn't she come to him?

Didn't want gratitude, but love might do the trick.

Maggie had supper waiting for him. He could smell homemade bread as soon as he waded through the snow far enough to stand in the bars of yellow warmth that the living room lights sent spilling outside.

The moon was trying to show now through the snow clouds; its rays struck the tin roof where snow had melted around the chimney. A quiet, still night . . . one that made him wish he could lie wrapped in warm quilts with—

No.

He halted his poignant, willful thoughts and crossed the porch, stopping to bump snow off his boots at the door.

Maggie opened it for him.

"You're terrible late. I was beginnin' to think you had trouble on the road."

"No, no trouble. Just workin' overtime, like always."

They were sitting at the little table, his meal just barely begun, when he heard the sound of a car coming down the road to Maggie's house. The rutted

lane was packed with snow; the huge trees that
shaded it in the summer kept out the winter sun, too,
so that the snow took a long time to melt along the
road.

"Who in the world could that be?" Maggie went
to the window to peer out. "I don't know the car,
but it's comin' awful slow."

He walked to the window in his sock feet. The car
was dark and shadowy, but something about its
outline was familiar.

Maggie realized who it was first, just as soon as
the slender figure stepped out of it. "It's her," she
said flatly, and in her face there was fear and anger.

Jubal knew who she was talking about before he
took his next breath. He yanked aside the ruffled
cotton curtain at the living room window, searching
for her, needing to see her. Breathing hard now.

She looked different. Wore something white and
creamy—a dress—under the long dark dress coat.
Boots that slid tightly up the curve—that delicious
curve—of her leg. They were cream, too.

Wading through the snow to get to the little
house that he'd once been afraid to show her.

Why?

"Jubal, she's not the kind you need," Maggie was
saying with a hard insistence at his elbow. "She's
too . . . too rich, or somethin'. You get yourself
an easygoing one, one who'll not ask much of
you, one that laughs a lot. Look at her. She ain't
gonna live with you long, boy. You're a common
man."

Rilla was at the steps now. He could see her in
the light from the window. Hair pulled back. Face
hesitant. Scared. Of what?

"Listen to me. A woman that you love enough to
nearly die for in a fire, she's dangerous. I can't lose

another son, Jubal, and that's what I nearly did. Because of her."

Maggie's eyes were wide and pleading, full of tears as she caught at his arm. Slowly he let the curtain drop.

Then she knocked on the door.

The two inside looked at each other.

"Open the door, Ma." He had to struggle to say the words.

Maggie Kane's stern face terrified Rilla.

"I'm—I'm Terrill Carroll, and I came to—"

"I know who you are. And who you came to see." Maggie's resigned words sent a wave of color to Rilla's hairline. "Come in."

Jubal was standing in the middle of the little living room, where the ceiling was lower than she was used to. For a minute her hungry eyes saw nothing but him, sweeping from his sock feet, up his blue-jeaned legs, past the white, long-sleeved placket-front shirt, pausing at its open, V neck where his throat rose from it, to his face.

Fierce green.

Hurriedly she let her gaze fall again. The white shirt had dirt and stains on the sleeves up to the elbow, while the rest of it was startlingly clean.

He'd just got home from work, she thought. He'd taken off the flannel shirt—he still wore one over the other, the arms rolled up. The discolored sleeves showed that.

That odd little bit of familiarity soothed her. Comforted her.

After three months, maybe they weren't total strangers, after all. In a minute she might find the courage to look at his face again.

"Hello, Jubal."

"Hello, Rilla."

Voice still husky. So dear.

"I came to see you for a reason." What a silly thing to say. Everybody came for reasons.

"Let me take your coat."

Close enough to her now that she could touch him. Behind her, pulling the coat away. Fingers at her neck, making her entire spine tingle.

"I was eatin' supper," he offered at last after he laid the coat across a chair. "Just got home. You want some?"

She shook her head wordlessly before she managed to speak. "Go ahead and finish. I'll wait."

He hesitated, then Maggie solved the problem.

"Go on into the kitchen, Miss Terrill. I reckon he ain't gonna eat much if you're out here." Her voice was flat as she motioned Rilla through the door.

Maggie Kane looked like a gentle, good-hearted woman, Rilla thought. She had a soft cloud of silver hair that curled around an open face. Her mouth looked as though it enjoyed laughter, and her eyes were hazel with dancing green flecks in them.

So why was she so full of disapproval and unhappiness? Rilla wondered. Because she had come?

The kitchen was long and narrow, with the stove and refrigerator at one end, the table and chairs at another. A row of windows, etched now in snow, ran along the section of wall by that table.

Jubal sat down awkwardly where his half-empty plate was, trying to swallow food without choking on it. For a while the only sounds were of the wind outside and the fire that crackled in the wood stove in the living room just beyond.

"I hear you're working in Glover. A foreman," she said at last.

"I heard you went back to college," he returned.

"I did. I only missed a week because of the—the fire. It didn't make a ripple at Belmont. To them, it was just a little extra trouble when they had to let me make up work I'd missed."

He took a sip of the coffee that Maggie had set at his elbow.

"Jubal, I don't know how to say thanks for my life," she burst out hurriedly.

"I don't want you to," he said in fierce determination. "I did it because I wanted to know you were alive somewhere in this world. And because—I was the one who knew where that crawl space was."

"I don't care why you did it. The end result is that I'm still alive, and I've found out that I like living." She could look at his face now, trace with her eyes the pure line of his profile, the sensual curve of his lips. His hair was different. Neater, shorter, brushed carelessly back. He'd had the wave behind his ear cut severely away.

No, she didn't like changes. They were proof that the two of them had been apart, that nothing remained the same, after all.

"What did you come for, Rilla?" he asked at last, a dark urgency in his voice.

Maggie bustled around them, taking away the plate, the cup. "I'll do it, Ma," he said impatiently.

"You tend to your company," she said calmly. "I'll tend to my kitchen."

"Well?" he demanded when Maggie had retreated.

"I came to . . . to make you an offer."

"An offer! Of what?"

"Today Tandy and I went to the bank. We asked Lionel to use a two-thousand-acre parcel of timber as collateral and make us a loan. It was worth every penny that we asked for."

Jubal watched her face as she talked. Still so vibrant, so alive with color and energy, that it nearly took a man's breath away. He knew her, even after all this time. Knew her so well that his hands ached to touch her. Knew her well enough that he understood already what she'd wanted from Johnson.

"You're gonna build the mill back."

"Not if Lionel has his way. He wouldn't even listen, Jubal. He said we didn't know how to handle the crews. That we needed a—a man to work with us."

Maggie went still at the sink beyond them.

Jubal went sick. It took a minute for it to happen, for the rich expectancy that had thrummed in him from the minute she'd stood on the porch to fade into bleakness. She didn't want him. She wanted a—what? A foreman, too, like Barlow?

Rilla watched his face and panicked. What was wrong? She stumbled on, letting her hands clutch at the pale yellow tablecloth. "I wondered if you'd consider being that man, Jubal. You could do it. I know you could."

"Don't start believin' in me again, Rilla," he said brutally, leaning away from her. "Your kind of faith nearly killed me the last time."

A dark flush rose up her cheeks. "I'll make you a partner, Jubal. Give you a third of the business. That's what Tandy will have. What I'll have. We'll be equal."

"Except—what'll you do about my 'bad blood,' if it crops up again?" He pushed himself away from the table, and as he stood, she did, too, her eyes as blue as a stormy sea.

"I've never said it, have I? Never told you that I'm sorry," she said steadily. "I know now—too late—that we were on completely different wavelengths that night. To me, it was just about Tess. I thought she'd taken a man who was mine, and he'd let her. I said the first thing I thought of, but not because I didn't believe in you. I said it out of jealousy. Just jealousy. It's one of my sins where—where you're concerned."

A man who was mine.

It rang in his head as he confronted her. *I'm still yours, Rilla. Can't you see that? That you're branded on every part of me? Ask me for something more than this partnership. Where's your courage now, girl? Where's that wild daring that let you meet me at the mill in the dark midnight?*

But he couldn't say that out loud.

"You had a right to say it, maybe," he managed. "I was puttin' together stolen—"

"Tandy's already told me."

He hesitated. "And you're still askin' me to be a partner, knowing that?"

"Did you want to put together those engines?"

"*No.*"

"Are you doing something illegal now?"

"You know I'm not."

"Will you ever again?"

"No, Rilla. Never."

"Then what are we talking about it for?" she demanded quietly.

He swallowed, then his face relaxed. "How would I know?" he asked ruefully. On a night like this, under the terrible pressure of standing here so close that his breath nearly stirred the soft hair at her temples, but not touching her—on this kind of night, he couldn't find any good answers.

He turned away, blind with need. Trying to hide it from her, knowing what he had to say.

"I can't do what you're askin' me to do, Rilla."

He heard her sharp intake of breath.

Rilla felt the pain right down to her toes. She

looked away from the long line of his back, down the kitchen where Maggie stood, turned from them toward another window.

"Don't act surprised. You knew what the answer was gonna be." Brusque now, trying to brush off her hurt.

"Why? Because you can't forgive me?"

"I forgave you a long time ago," he said. "But I won't let you pay me for—"

"It's not payment for my life, Jubal."

He looked down at his hands, wondering when she would step away so he could think clearly. "Whatever it's for, I don't want it. They'll say you gave me everythin' I'll ever have if I let you do that."

Frustration nearly choked Rilla. She wanted him. *Wanted* him, this stubborn man who stood so close that she could feel him breathing.

"What do we care what people say, Jubal? They never knew me. They never knew you, either. Let's do it *our* way."

"Your way, you mean. And you're forgettin' one thing. I'd have to live with me if I let you hand me that mill after all that's been between us. The first time I ever saw you, I had on handcuffs. It made me sick for you to see me like that. But if I let you do this thing, it'll put me right back in a different kind of handcuffs." His voice was thick.

She caught him by the arm at last, the contact scalding. He flinched, she trembled. When there was a dearth of touch, every tiny one was too much. She couldn't pull him around, her hand was suddenly too weak; so instead she pulled herself about to face him, oblivious of everything except her own pain.

"You talk about what's been between us." Her words were choppy and passionate. "About how this started. I came home still a child, at least in some ways. You scared me to death, but I needed you. My buffer against Henry. My help for Mama. But I'm not a child now. That fire burned away any last traces of childhood. The only thing that's left is you, Jubal. You're all that's in my heart. I'm not sorry for any of the things that we've done. I love you."

He caught her by the shoulders. "Why didn't you ask me for somethin' different, then? Why didn't you say, Be my husband?"

She reached up, caught his hands, pleading with him. "Because I know now that you're a man of pride, Jubal. I've learned it the hard way. It'll never work if we can't be together as equals. And I want to hold on to you forever. Be my husband, if you'll be my partner, too."

His hand tightened, his face twisted in anguish. "I *can't*."

"You'd work for it. All of it. Jubal, please, what do you want me to do? Give it up? Give it away? To who?" she cried, her hands sliding down his arms to his chest, where his heart was beating frantically.

"There—there ain't no answer," he said at last, struggling with himself. "We're two different people. I never knew the first time I kissed you it'd come all the way down to me changin' my life for you, but it did. I ain't sorry, either, like you're not, but the funny thing is, it's pushin' us farther apart. Because now I know that real love ain't about two people goin' to bed together"—he slid his own hands to her neck, locking her in a hard hold—"even if, God knows, I'd give a good part of what's left of my life just to lay down with you one more time. Just one more, Rilla."

His hands pulled her so close, she could see the tiny pores in his skin, so close that his eyes scorched her—then clamped down, letting her come no farther.

"But real love's all mixed up with self-respect. You think you're givin' me that when you offer me your mill? I want you, Rilla. But I can't. I *can't.*"

"Did you ever stop to think what I want?" she demanded huskily, letting her fingers clutch and tangle in his shirt. "I want pecan pies in the winter, and tall corn in the hot summer, and the sound of the mill saw cutting across the hollow on a dusty day, and someday, babies. Green-eyed babies. Eyes like yours, Jubal, as deep as emeralds."

He laid his hand across her mouth to cut off the words, nearly frantic with pain. "Stop," he moaned. "You know what you're doin' to me, and it ain't fair."

She watched him silently, but she let her eyes plead for her, and after a moment's hesitation he groaned and pulled her to him. His body, his arms, his smell . . . at last she had him again, and she clutched him tightly to her, to hold on as long as he would let her.

Jubal let out a hard breath. "Okay," he said with finality. "I can't take the mill, but I'll work for you." There should have been joy in his capitulation; instead there was defeat. "I once said I'd never do it, but I didn't know then how love could break a man. So I'll work."

Rilla stood body to body with him, the two of them locked together in the tiny kitchen, and felt the newborn hope begin to die out of her. She was so close that the buttons on his shirt dug into her, and his hard fingers on her back tried to pull her even closer.

Instead they might never have been farther apart.

Rilla held on one last moment, her arms trying to crush him to her. One last time to remember what it felt like to hold him, to listen to the sound of his heart beating life's blood through him.

Then she let her senses open wide and spread beyond him, to the sound of the icy snow scattering across the windows, to the more distant sound of Maggie Kane crying quietly in the far reaches of the kitchen.

She'd forgotten Maggie completely, didn't know why she was crying, but the sound could have been her own.

Then Rilla broke away.

Jubal made a protesting sound and tried to stop her.

"No." Grief was washing over her in waves, sweeping and shattering against her heart. She made herself look into his face, his dark, dangerous, beloved face. "I don't want a hired hand, Jubal."

"I'm not—"

"You can't do it my way." She cut through his words with painful ones of her own. "I don't see how I can do it yours."

He let his hands fall from her, his eyes dark and shadowed. "So what will we do, Rilla?"

"I don't know," she answered. "Maybe I'll just pine away for you." Hard to be flippant now, but she wouldn't break down. "Or maybe I'll just have to get on with living. The mill needs to reopen. Too many jobs at stake. So I'll go on. Somewhere I'll get the money, and somebody else to be the . . . the hired help. Somebody I don't love."

"I want to say yes. Don't you know that?" Jubal demanded passionately. "It'd be the easy way."

"And you won't take it," Rilla finished resignedly. "Or me. Well, I learned something else in that fire, Jubal. Life's too short to grieve forever. Someday, maybe, there'll be another man who'll take me with all the trappings, and I'll still have those babies, even if I won't love him the same."

His face was stricken. "Rilla—"

"Don't," she said raggedly. "I've offered you everything, and you've turned it down. So at least let me get out while I'm still fighting."

He was aching so much he couldn't move, so he just watched as she crossed to the door and left the room. She was leaving.

"Jubal!" It was Maggie at his elbow, so insistent that he heard her even over the pain snaking through him. "What, Ma?" His voice was just a rough thread.

"You can't let her go."

Maggie was the one crying. Not Rilla. Jubal registered the surprise even over the searing in his chest.

She never cried.

"She loves you, Jubal. I can see it now. Never thought I'd ever watch a Carroll cry over one of mine, or beg and fight for him like this one's doin'. She means it. I've been as blind about her as Bethel used to be about you. She's the one. I—I—" She choked on the words, finally pushing him in the direction of the living room, where Rilla had vanished.

Rilla.

There was the pain again, and there was the slamming of the door.

She was at the dark edge of the wooden porch when he yanked open the front door; the boards were cold and wet under his socks, and the light wind cut through his shirt.

"Rilla—" What could he say? "You're killin' me. You stick a knife in me with this partnership, and when I do the right thing, you twist it by tellin' me you'll find another man."

She wanted to give in, but she couldn't. "What do you want me to do? You know that Terrill Carroll and Jubal Kane belong together. It doesn't even sound farfetched anymore, not even to Aunt Tandy."

Her eyes were so bright with longing, with anger, with grief, that they nearly mesmerized him.

"I deserve a better choice than this, Rilla. I walked through that fire for you, and now you can't even be kind? You're offerin' me *charity*."

The anger won in her. She stepped close to him as he shivered against the cold. "I'd take it from you, Jubal, but then, I'm not as proud as you Kanes are. And I'd give you everything I've got, if you're willing to accept. So take it from me, and then take me along with it." She couldn't fight it anymore, so she lifted her mouth to find his in the kiss they'd been waiting for, aching for since three months ago. It was hot and hard and dark, wild with need and anger and pure lust. His tongue thrust into her mouth, his body pressed against hers, their hands were frantic and rough with each other.

Then he pushed her away, his hands trembling on her shoulders. "Give me time," he said, gasping. "Let me think about it."

Her face was suddenly so alight that he had to look away, out into the snow.

"Oh, Jubal," she whispered. "Oh, Jubal."

He struggled with himself a few days, trying to remember why he should say no.

For one thing, he wasn't going to be any help in her fight with Lionel Johnson and the powers in Cade County.

For another, he was scared. This was reaching so high it was ridiculous.

But Terrill Carroll was his, and he'd take the head off any man who tried to get close enough even to *think* of giving her those babies she'd talked about. In fact, Jubal got pretty aggravated at Rilla herself when he remembered that she'd even threatened to consider somebody else. But, he thought wryly, she knew exactly what buttons to push to get to him.

Why shouldn't he, Jubal Kane, be the one to run that mill? He could do it; he was doing fine with Barlow's crew; he knew how.

He was a different man than Cade County thought.

The battle was nearly over inside him when Maggie finally took up arms in Rilla's defense.

"When are you gonna quit tearin' yourself apart, Jubal?" she asked him.

He knew what she meant at once, although they hadn't talked about it since the night Rilla had pulled off down the same snowy lane she'd come to him on.

"I've just never done anything like this before, Ma," he said in quiet anguish. "I wish I was the one givin' Rilla somethin'."

"You are. Your whole life, your hands, your back, your sweat. She told you that." Maggie had gone over to the enemy with a vengeance.

"You know what I mean. People only see dollars and cents. I ain't gonna know—I'm *not* gonna know what to say or do when Johnson and Allardt and all the rest of 'em are involved. I'm not good at anythin' that matters to people like them."

"You're good at lovin' that girl," Maggie said insistently, touching his face with her gnarled hands. "That's what matters to her. And you're gonna do the rest right, too. It's funny, Jubal, how a body can pray and ask, and then not even see when the answer to that prayer is right there."

She laughed a little, remembering. "Be careful what you pray for, you might get it," she whispered. "She was standin' right in front of me, offerin' you every chance I'd ever wanted for you. Love, too.

And I couldn't see it because it was so much more that it scared me. She did, too. But I'm tellin' you that what's happenin' is right. You're where you're supposed to be, Jubal. Don't get cold feet now."

Maggie watched him Friday night as he shrugged into his new coat, surveying the clean-shaven face, the hair, the clothes.

"Guess you're goin' to see Terrill," she observed.

Silently he reached into the pocket of his jacket and pulled out a tiny square box. Maggie took it, opened it carefully, and smiled down at the diamond that shined up at her.

"Not the biggest stone in the whole world," Jubal said with a touch of rue, "and at that, I'll be makin' payments most of next year on it."

"She ain't gonna care about the size of it."

Jubal shook his head quizzically. "You sure did decide you liked her awful fast, Ma."

"I don't know her. I ain't sure how much I like her yet. Maybe we won't get along at all. But it don't matter. I told you, Jubal, she's the one meant for you, and I don't reckon I've got much to say about it. But"—Maggie smiled up at him—"she's gettin' somebody to be proud of."

He made a grunting sound, but her words soothed the anxiety in him. Then he forgot his own careful grooming and ran a hand back through his hair in tension.

"Well, I gotta—"

"Jubal, wait."

"You about to give me the lecture you always gave Jarvis?"

"No. I reckon it's too late for that anyhow, ain't it?" Maggie asked knowingly as she went to the shelf behind the door and pulled down the black purse she always carried.

"You readin' minds now?" he demanded.

"No. I just watched the way you were with her— the way she touched you—and I knew. But I do have somethin' I want to give you." She opened the purse, removed an official-looking document, and offered it to him.

"What is this?"

Maggie looked down at the paper he was turning over and over in his brown hands. "My grandfather, Lehman Copper, loved the Bluff better'n anythin'. He died up there somewhere, and nobody ever found his body. Then the Bluff came down to my daddy, and then to me. You can't farm it. Too hilly. It's not much good for anythin' except dreamin', and growin' trees. Some of 'em have been there for three or four hundred years, Jubal, long before me. The top's so high up that there's not many good ones there, I don't reckon, and it'd be too hard to get to 'em, anyway. So maybe . . . maybe you could leave those, the little ones."

He heard the break in her voice. "You're givin' me the Bluff?" he asked, uncertain, amazed.

"I never thought about the timber on Copper's Bluff bein' worth so much, but Ida said it was. So I asked her last week to get somebody to come and look it over. I didn't know it'd be that much money. Here, here's what he figured."

Maggie laid another paper in his hands, and Jubal gaped at the sum written there.

"But Ma—why?"

"So you won't have to go to the Carrolls empty-handed. So you'll have something to use as your part of the deal. A man's pride is an important thing. Important enough for me to tell you that if you need to—to log at Copper's Bluff"—her face twisted a little—"it's all right. I don't know how I can stand to see some of those trees come down. They're old friends. Part of the dreamin'."

She worried the straps on the purse, struggling to keep on speaking. "But I'll stand it. For my sons. Because I'm countin' on you bringin' Jarvis home and givin' him a job," she finished in agitation.

Then he understood.

She had laid her entire life in his hands. The one heirloom that she possessed, the towering cliff that as a boy he'd thought reached clear to God.

Maggie had held him, taught him, loved him even when he'd gone to Lineville. Now she was turning loose of him with the very best that she had.

He didn't know how else to tell her—they weren't people of pretty words or casual handshakes—so he just pulled her to him and hugged her as fiercely as if she were the child and he the parent.

"Ma, I—" He swallowed down the tears. "I'll use it as a part of the collateral. Like Rilla's using hers. Once they know the timber's there, it'll be enough. Maybe I'll never have to touch it. I'll try, Ma. I swear I'll try."

He'd never in all of his life walked down a fancy brick sidewalk, one brushed clean of snow and slush, and climbed the steps to the front door of a girl's house. Never rung the doorbell and waited with a pounding heart until her aunt opened it and looked out at him inquiringly.

"Miss Carroll."

"Oh, Jubal, it's you." Her stern face broke into a smile. "She's upstairs. Come on in—you can wait right there, in the living room."

So he stood waiting in the middle of the room

with the piano, remembering what it had been like the last time he'd been here.

He heard her mad rush down the stairs.

She saw him just as she got to the bottom step, his face tense and quiet, the coat opened to reveal the lean, slender body, and she halted, trying to control her soaring emotions.

He'd come to say yes. She knew, and she couldn't stop the happiness.

"You've got on blue jeans," he said in relief. "You look like my girl again."

"I always was your girl." She took a step toward him. "You came to take the partnership, didn't you, Jubal? Please, say you did."

"We're gonna have to talk about that, Rilla, but yeah, I want it. And I want somethin' else, too," he drawled, his face as full of danger as it had been all those months ago. "Another kind of job. Come over here."

She eased to him, face upturned. "Which job?" she managed.

"Offer me one that takes up all my nights," he whispered, his hands reaching for her, one at her waist, one tangling in her hair. "One for the rest of my life."

His lips were so close now, his eyes scorching her skin with their intensity.

"Jubal—" She could barely speak, her heart was beating so. "Will you—"

"Umm?" Only a fraction of space between their lips now.

"Will you marry me?" All in one rush, the words came.

"That's the one," he whispered, and right there, in the middle of the Carroll farmhouse, one room away from her aunt, he pushed her up against the piano and let his lips and his hands reclaim what was his.

30

"Lionel's called an open meeting at City Hall, Jubal," Rilla told him at last as they sat watching the flames dance in the fireplace at the Carroll house, raising her head from his shoulder to look up at him.

The arms around her tightened. "I knew there was somethin' wrong," Jubal said. "You've been too quiet tonight. Is the meetin' because of me?"

Rilla hesitated, letting her hand caress his shirt-front.

"Tell me the truth," Jubal demanded.

"Partly. He was having an apoplectic fit when he called Aunt Tandy. He said you weren't what he had in mind when he told us to get a man into the business. He wouldn't even consider the collateral. This meeting is to try to bring the town around to his side. To put pressure on us."

Jubal's face was stern. "I told you."

"It's more than you, Jubal. He wants the mill,"

Rilla said quietly. "The meeting's at five this Friday. We all need to be there."

That took his eyes off the dancing fire. "Rilla, I ain't any good at that kind of thing," he said, panicked.

"Daddy hated it, too, but he did it."

He ran his free hand—the one not behind her back and around her waist—over his face. "Tell me somethin', girl, how come lovin' you is so hard? Why couldn't you just be a plain person? No mill, no nothin'," he said only half in jest.

"Because I was made for you," she said teasingly. "And you're not the average Joe yourself."

Her face was warm and full of laughing, flickering shadows from the fire as he traced her cheek down to her mouth with his hand. "Firelight sure looks good on you," he whispered.

She swallowed. "Sometimes I hate it. Sometimes when I close my eyes at night, all I can see is fire against the sky. The mill roof blazing. It's the last thing I remember before—"

His hands tightened on her. "He came so close, Rilla. I've asked myself how he ever got his hands on you."

"I saw a light at the mill," she said simply. "When I saw it, I hoped you were waiting. So I went."

He pulled her to him, shackling her against him so tightly that she could barely breathe. "And nearly died," he said roughly. "I've had some bad nights, too. But soon we'll take care of all that. Just push away the bad ones when they come and make some good memories instead."

Jubal hadn't shown up.

Rilla swallowed her own nervousness as Lionel Johnson walked across the crowded, overheated, noisy little room at City Hall and leaned over her and Tandy.

"Your boy's not here, Terrill, and it's already a quarter after. I have to start the meeting." His face was triumphant, his air superior.

"You don't have to do any of this, Lionel," Tandy returned, "but you're going to anyway. So get on with it. I despise idle threats."

Lionel flushed angrily and straightened.

Where was Jubal? Rilla wondered as Johnson crossed to the little podium in the front of the room. He held up a hand for silence.

"All right, people," he roared across the chattering crowd. "Let's have some quiet so we can get started. Everybody knows what we're here for. Not long ago, one of our businesses burned. It took a lot of jobs, and most of us want to see it opened again. We want the mill to be prosperous again. We're here to see if we can't find a way—"

The sound of the back door creaking open pulled Rilla's head around again, just as it did everybody else's, and Rilla's heart gave a huge leap of relief.

Jubal had entered. Late, but here.

He had on the clothes he'd worn to Katherine's funeral, and as he came up the aisle under the inspecting eye of everybody in the room, a dark flush climbed up his throat. But he kept his eyes locked firmly on Rilla's, and she ached in sympathy for him.

It must have been torture to run that gauntlet, to come face to face with old enemies. Most of the families in the town had a representative here: the Allardts, the Johnsons, the Henigars.

Red Sinclair, Charlie Danson, even Dusty—all of them were here, men whose livelihood depended on that mill.

Jubal made it to her in the silence, his shoulders straight, his face steady. Rilla felt a stab of pride in him; he looked capable and right.

As he sank onto the chair waiting beside her, Johnson swept on with his speech, ignoring him.

"We all understand that businesses ought to be run by people with experience and a record of success in business. Of course, we want those people to be respectable and civic-minded, too. Tandy Carroll, for example, is certainly that. But when it comes to good business sense, we have her past record to—"

The door opened a second time, louder and faster than when Jubal had entered. This time it was a massive, middle-aged, prosperous-looking man with a shock of graying black hair. He looked about him belligerently, with an air of authority that nearly rivaled Johnson's.

In fact, Johnson bristled all over at the sight of him. "What are you doing here, Barlow?" he demanded, forgetting his speech completely.

The one he addressed paused in the act of sitting down. "It's an open meeting," he said calmly, his words clipped off in the sound peculiar to south Michigan. "And I came for Kane, there. I'm on his side in this."

Lloyd Allardt in the front row said just loudly enough to be heard, "That's a good pair, those two. And we don't need either of them in Bethel."

Before Rilla or anybody else could react, the door opened yet a third time.

"Is nobody punctual around here anymore?" Lionel said grumpily, but his mouth fell open in surprise at just whom the door had admitted.

It was Maggie Kane, and Bobo Hackett, and an old black man twisting a new felt hat in his hands. Beside her, she felt Jubal's shock as he half stood.

"Ma!" he exclaimed. "Rainey! What are you doin' here?"

It was the old man who finally answered. "We

thought you might need a little help, Jubal," he said mildly. "And besides, it's time us from the north end of this county had a say-so in some things. You're still one of us, ain't you? Even if you are gonna marry her." Rainey nodded at the wide-eyed girl behind Jubal.

Rilla's cheeks flushed as darkly as Jubal's; they hadn't announced the marriage formally yet, in spite of the ring she'd been quietly wearing.

But Jubal relaxed a little as he stared at Rainey across the avid crowd, then at his mother's calm face. "Yeah," he said at last, smiling. "I'm still one of you."

Allardt stood abruptly, speaking to Johnson. "Are you going to let a bunch of rabble-rousers disrupt this meeting, or are we going to get on with it? I refuse to sit here listening to this assortment of people any longer. What is Cade County coming to when we can't call a public meeting without outsiders and hooligans and ridge runners barging in and taking over?"

A murmur of voices went up at his words. Johnson, his face flushed in anger, spoke to the crowd. "Let's get back to the business at hand, which is whether—"

Allardt interrupted again. "Just lay it out cold, Lionel, and stop this fancy footwork," he demanded. Then he turned to look back at the crowd and at Jubal, still standing across from him. "We all know what we want," he told them. "We want a mill run right. Two women can't do that. And as for Kane—" He gave a snort of incredulous laughter. "Hell, I remember when my brother shot and killed his old man because he was a thief. And Kane here, he's no better. There's not a man in this county who'll work for him. And do you really want the world to turn

upside down? To have *this* crowd from the Ridge"—
he jerked his head toward Rainey and Maggie and
Bobo—"hanging around the mill?"

Allardt's voice rose with the fervor of a tent
revivalist's, just as Rilla felt shocked fury rising in
her. She surged to her feet beside Jubal; the tension
in him was so strong, she could almost feel it
vibrating.

"Why don't you deal with the present instead of
the past, Mr. Allardt?" she demanded hotly. "And
deal with the issues. Let us show you on paper how
we can finance and manage this mill. As for these
people—" She looked at Maggie, too.

"No, don't." Jubal's voice was choppy, but it was
decisive. "Like Rainey said, they're *my* people. It's
for me to defend them. To defend *us.*"

He was shaking with nerves and tension, his face
sharp and angled, his eyes bright. Rilla could see his
agitation in his hands before he shoved them in his
pockets. Then he looked out across the sea of
absorbed faces. "You can't find one bad thing to say
about Ma or Rainey, even if you tried. As for me,"
he said clearly, "I've made mistakes. I ain't denyin'
that. I don't know all that my daddy did, or my
granddaddy. But I know what I'm tryin' to be. You
might not trust me now; that's all right. But you
watch me. You judge me on what I do in the next
ten or twenty or thirty years. An' whenever you're
ready, you make up your mind. If I have any luck, or
any willpower at all, you're gonna have to say, 'Jubal
Kane's tryin' to be a good man.'"

His words challenged the quiet crowd before he
turned back to Allardt and Johnson. "If I'm the reason
you ain't—*aren't*—gonna help these two," he said,
nodding at Tandy and Rilla, "then I'll stay outta the
mill. I've got a job I can go back to. If nobody'll work

for me, like you say"—another line of red edged to
his cheekbones—"then so be it. But don't turn them
down and take away ever'thin' they want to keep."
He looked at Rilla beside him. "She can do just
about anythin' she puts her mind to. She'll do this if
you give her a chance."

There was a long silence in the room, broken only
by the sound of Rilla's sobbing intake of breath.

Then Rainey spoke, his voice quiet and sure.
"There's those that'll work for you, Jubal, no matter
what Mr. Johnson says. My boy Jonah, he will. And
he'll be glad to get the job."

Johnson recovered from the shock of actually having
Jubal face him down. He ignored Rainey. "Let's don't
be simpleminded about this. Workers are not the only
problem. Technology, worker efficiency, investment
procedures, capital outlay—all of these factors have
to—"

Red Sinclair came violently to his feet. "Ah, *hell*,"
he said furiously, cutting across Johnson's words
and startling the crowd again. "All I know is that *he*
talks like me." He pointed at Jubal. "And I can't make
a damn bit a' sense outta you, Johnson. I'll work for
you, Jubal, if you'll tell *her*"—he nodded at Tandy—
"to keep her Bible away from me."

Then Red turned to nudge the one beside him.
"C'mon, Dusty, get up. You know you'd rather have
Kane than Allardt or Johnson. He'll get down and
fight with you. Or maybe come in a fired mill after
you. They can't even see you."

Somebody laughed, somebody swore, and Dusty
Bainbridge stood up reluctantly.

"All right," he said, not looking at Jubal.

"I don't give a damn how many of you stand with
Kane," Johnson roared suddenly. "The simple fact is
that my bank is not about to loan the money that's

needed to reopen the mill to him, or Tandy, or Terrill. Is that clear?"

"It looks like I got here just in time, then." Hank Barlow's big body resembled a mountain as he shrugged himself up to join those standing. "Kane spent most of the morning talking and persuading and explaining to me about this mill and this meeting. Then I spent this afternoon thinking, calling people to check what he'd told me, trying to come to a decision. He asked me to back the mill financially." Under his bristling eyebrows, Barlow's eyes searched Rilla's surprised face and Tandy's stunned one. "And I've made up my mind, right here and now. I'll loan you the money at two percent lower than anything Johnson might offer, if you'll agree to it."

The listeners erupted in surprised chatter.

"And in return, this Yankee gets a toehold in our county," Allardt told the murmuring crowd furiously. "Then it never stops. My God, people, they've taken over Nashville. Even the damned mayor's one of 'em."

"It sounds like an offer that should be considered," Rilla returned slowly, "no matter where Mr. Barlow is from."

"You're not considering taking a loan from him, are you?" Johnson demanded incredulously.

For the first time in this whole mad mess, Tandy spoke, her voice clear and calm. "I think you were complaining earlier about my head for business, Lionel. Now we can put it to the test, can't we? Mr. Barlow is offering us the money that you won't let us have, and at a lower percentage rate. Even to me," she concluded dryly, "his offer makes sense."

As she stood, too, Johnson gasped, "But, Tandy, you don't even know him. We're from right here in Bethel. You've known us all your life."

"Good businessmen don't let sentiment get in the way of making money, Lionel," she said calmly. "Well, Terrill, should we talk to Jubal's ally?"

Rilla looked at her aunt, then at Barlow and Rainey and Red and Dusty. A fairly motley crew. But Charlie Danson was standing now, too, and Rosalie Anderson. Joanie was with her, smiling at Rilla. The crowd was beginning to move a little, getting the incredible idea that Johnson and Allardt were about to lose for the first time in years, and to a Kane.

Jubal looked as if he'd been knocked to his knees, staggered by the thought that this handful of people were standing *for* him, not against him.

For him.

"Which ally, Aunt Tandy?" Rilla asked shakily.

The meeting between them and Barlow lasted until nearly eleven o'clock that night, while they hammered out details there in the back room of City Hall.

When Tandy was through with him, Barlow went home with three new business partners and a new-found, fervent respect for southern womanhood.

And outside, in the dark hall, Jubal pulled Rilla up against him tightly. "I was scared to death this afternoon," he confessed to the top of her head. "I never expected those people—"

He couldn't finish the sentence.

"You'll live up to every expectation they have of you, Jubal," Rilla said tenderly, looking up at him in the dusk, "and more. Look what you did with Barlow."

He didn't answer; instead he ran his hands over her shoulders restlessly. "You're gonna have to marry me for sure now," he managed huskily. "Rainey told ever'body. Can't jilt me, can you? Make it soon, Rilla." His mouth lowered to hers. "I want to be with you. But most of all"—his eyes burned even in the shadows—"I want to go to bed with you. The idea's eatin' me up. A real bed—and you."

The night janitor found them there in the hall a few minutes later, oblivious of the world, and went on about his business, muttering to his broom, "Them two better get married fast, that's all I can say."

31

He went to the river early on the morning of his wedding, two weeks later, during Rilla's spring break.

Today the water was frozen and chill, not moving. A third snowstorm had hit the night before, thick and wet in the March night, and now it coated everything in sight. But he knew: under that snow, under that ice, flowed the river. Always going to be there for him, full of promise.

Just like Copper's Bluff.

Just like the woman he was marrying today.

How had Jubal Kane, late of Lineville and despair, come to be this man, the one who believed in a thing called hope?

He didn't know, he didn't question.

He just accepted.

*   *   *

The church was full.

Most of the people from Sullivan's Ridge who came had never been inside it before; Maggie, who had been, wasn't used to sitting on the front left pew. They were all as uncomfortable as the groom and his brother Jarvis, the best man, but they were still there.

Jubal wanted to do this the right way, so that this whole town could see what he and Rilla had between them, but it was—next to the meeting at City Hall—the hardest thing he'd ever done.

He longed for the nights in the truck when it had been so simple, just the two of them and love. For one moment as he stood at the altar, nearly strangling over the high collar and tie that matched his black tuxedo, watching the flickering candles and the minister's serious face, the smell of white roses strong in his nostrils, he wondered if this was really Jubal Kane standing here.

But that was before the "Wedding March" began, before Joanie came down the aisle and stepped aside. Before Jubal saw past the rows of faces to the woman who watched him, eyes clinging to his, as she stepped toward him.

They'd done things in such a hurry that there'd been no time for him to stop and really think about what this moment would be like.

She was all he'd ever wanted: the mane of honey hair, blue eyes above high cheekbones, slender body, and long legs. All of that and a tender heart wrapped in gleaming white satin.

For one flashing moment Jubal remembered the girl she'd been at the mill that first day. Scared of him, scornful, dismissive. He saw her in passion, then in flames, now in this church.

Love could do almost anything. Because of it, he stepped out and took her hand, and the rest of the world fell away.

They came back to the farm after the reception to change clothes. It was just the two of them now; Tandy had moved back to her own house in town a week ago.

Rilla let Jubal pull her up the snowy steps to the farmhouse door, and when she looked up into his dark face and green eyes, her heart hung in her throat.

"I think I'm supposed to do this now," he drawled, and swung her off the snowy steps to hoist her up against him. "Or don't people do it anymore?"

"We will," she whispered.

"Except I ain't got it figured out yet how I'm supposed to get this door open and hold you at the same time," he said teasingly. "Whole lotta dress here."

It spilled like the snow over his black tuxedo coat, covering his hands, falling to his legs as she lay against him.

"I could help you," she offered, reaching down to the brass doorknob.

Once inside, he set her on her feet and pushed the door shut behind them. But he held on to her wrist when she turned.

"I have to get changed, Jubal, if we're going to be in Nashville in time for the plane."

"Rilla Carroll—"

"Kane," she flashed, grinning at him as she reached up to loosen the tiny coronet that had held up her veil.

"Rilla *Kane,*" he said forcefully, "I appreciate

your aunt Tandy givin' us a trip to—Where are we goin'?"

"The Cayman Islands."

"Wherever that is, but the fact is that I ain't—I'm not spendin' my weddin' night on any airplane. I'd be just as happy never to set foot on one."

Rilla looked at his determined face, at the way his shoulders were square and pugnacious under the black jacket, and her heart began a steady thump—thump—thump.

"But you have to fly to get there," she said tremulously.

"I called Joanie last week. She said she'd get us another plane, tomorrow night. I reckon she did." He reached up with his one free hand to tug at the bow tie, pulling it loose before he twisted the button on the collar open.

"You just rearranged Aunt Tandy's honeymoon plans?" Rilla got out, and she put *her* free hand up to his collar to help him.

"That's right. I like your aunt well enough, but I know what I want to do on my weddin' night, and where I want to do it without her givin' me any advice. I'm starting with her like I mean to go on."

His face was daring and bold as he pulled Rilla's fingers down to his second button, urging her to unfasten the white shirt down to his waist. Beneath it, his skin was brown and warm.

"I see."

He caught her hand, held it to him. "I got dressed up, wore a tie for you, went through . . . What was that awful thing we did last Thursday?" he demanded.

"A counseling session. The minister does it for all the couples he marries, Jubal."

"I did all of that, then I stood and let you put cake in my mouth in front of all those people. A grown man, Rilla, and I hate cake. Now I think I deserve a little something for my efforts."

She whispered, "I think you do, too. It's been a long time, Jubal." She didn't mean to cry, but the words shook.

"And I don't plan on lettin' you rush off into your bedroom and change into one of those fancy dresses, either. I been thinkin' that I'm only gonna get one chance to take a weddin' gown off a woman"—he laid his hands, brown and lean, against the creamy skin of her breasts, right where the scalloped lace of the dress edged them—"and I'm gonna take it, and enjoy it."

She caught his wrists. "I think you have good, good ideas, Jubal. But then, I've always believed in you."

He searched her face. "So you're not gonna be mad if we're a day late on this honeymoon?"

"*This* is our honeymoon." She pulled away, catching his hands as she did. "In our house, in our bed. We can build a fire in the living room, and I'll show you where all twenty-four of the buttons are on this dress—"

"Twenty-four!" He groaned.

"And then maybe you could build another one of those fires you're so good at. In here." She pressed his hands against her waist, lifted her lips to his.

"I love you, Rilla," he whispered passionately.

Outside, the snow drifted down in white, clean sweeps, turning Cade County, Tennessee, into some ethereal land of dreams.

Epilogue

The bright, sweet smell of spring hung in the air four weeks later when Jubal kissed Rilla on the front steps of his mother's house.

"Want to go to the base of Copper's Bluff with me?" he demanded. "We might find wildflowers bloomin' already in the woods over there."

She kissed him back. "I want to, but I think I need to say some things to your mother. Things like 'Thanks for the son.'"

He laughed up at her from two steps below. "Maybe she was glad to get rid of me. And maybe, when you get through thankin' her, you can come and thank *me*."

"In the woods?" she asked dubiously.

"There's all sorts of things to do in the woods," he retorted teasingly. "Why d'you think Red Ridin' Hood hung out there so much?"

Rilla watched him go, letting her laughter chase after him.

The remnants of the Sunday dinner they'd had with Maggie were still on the table when Rilla went back in and tried to do exactly what she'd told Jubal she meant to do.

"You were the right one, that's all," Maggie answered, her hands smoothing over each other. "I'd been waitin' so long for somethin' to happen that I almost gave up, and then there you were."

Rilla pulled her legs up to her chest and wrapped her arms around her knees as she sat on the wooden stool in Maggie's kitchen. "I don't understand, but—"

"The morning Jubal was born, I looked down in his face and I saw green eyes, Rilla," Maggie said calmly. "I'd asked for a sign that he'd have something better in his life than any of us had ever had. His eyes—they were the sign."

Rilla was still a moment. "I don't know anything about signs from God, Maggie," she said. "I just know that even back when I thought it was crazy to love him, it still felt right."

Maggie's laugh was low, rich, satisfied. "It was never crazy, except in the way that real love should be. And I knew it was supposed to be you from the night you came here, when you told him about green-eyed babies. Green as emeralds, you said. I see them that way, too. But you know what? If you asked Ida, or your aunt, or anybody else but me, to look into Jubal's face"—she took a deep breath—"they'd tell you that his eyes are gray. Stone gray."

Rilla felt Maggie's rough fingers reach to caress her own hand, she heard the blood beating somewhere in her body, but she couldn't move. All she could do was keep staring into Maggie's sympathetic, knowing countenance.

"But," she choked out at last, "they're not. They're green."

"To you," Maggie agreed firmly. "And to me. But to the rest of the world, Jubal Kane's eyes ain't green at all. Did you hear me, Rilla?" She reached out and patted the shocked girl's face. "Not green at all," she repeated quietly.

AVAILABLE NOW

THE COURT OF THREE SISTERS by Marianne Willman

An enthralling historical romance from the award-winning author of *Yesterday's Shadows* and *Silver Shadows*. The Court of Three Sisters was a hauntingly beautiful Italian villa where a prominent archaeologist took his three daughters: Thea, Summer, and Fanny. Into their circle came Col McCallum, who was determined to discover the real story behind the mysterious death of his mentor. Soon Col and Summer, in a race to unearth the fabulous ancient treasure that lay buried on the island, found the meaning of true love.

OUTRAGEOUS by Christina Dodd

The flamboyant Lady Marian Wenthaven, who cared nothing for the opinions of society, proudly claimed two-year-old Lionel as her illegitimate son. When she learned that Sir Griffith ap Powel, who came to visit her father's manor, was actually a spy sent by King Henry VII to watch her, she took Lionel and fled. But there was no escaping from Griffith and the powerful attraction between them.

CRAZY FOR LOVIN' YOU by Lisa G. Brown

The acclaimed author of *Billy Bob Walker Got Married* spins a tale of life and love in a small Tennessee town. After four years of exile, Terrill Carroll returns home when she learns of her mother's serious illness. Clashing with her stepfather, grieving over her mother, and trying to find a place in her family again, she turns to Jubal Kane, a man from the opposite side of the tracks who has a prison record, a bad reputation, and the face of a dark angel.

TAMING MARIAH by Lee Scofield

When Mariah kissed a stranger at the train station, everyone in the small town of Mead, Colorado, called her a hellion, but her grandfather knew she only needed to meet the right man. The black sheep son of a titled English family, Hank had come to the American West seeking adventure . . . until he kissed Mariah.

FLASH AND FIRE by Marie Ferrarella

Amanda Foster, who has learned the hard way how to make it on her own, finally lands the coveted anchor position on the five o'clock news. But when she falls for Pierce Alexander, the station's resident womanizer, is she ready to trust love again?

INDISCRETIONS by Penelope Thomas

The spellbinding story of a murder, a ghost, and a love that conquered all. During a visit to the home of enigmatic Edmund Llewellyn, Hilary Carewe uncovered a decade-old murder through rousing the spirit of Edmund's stepmother, Lily Llewelyn. As Edmund and Hilary were drawn together, the spirit grew stronger and more vindictive. No one was more affected by her presence than Hilary, whom Lily seemed determined to possess.

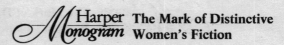

Harper Monogram The Mark of Distinctive Women's Fiction

COMING NEXT MONTH

FOREVERMORE by Maura Seger

As the only surviving member of a family that had lived in the English village of Avebury for generations, Sarah Huxley was fated to protect the magical sanctuary of the tumbled stone circles and earthen mounds. But when a series of bizarre deaths at Avebury began to occur, Sarah met her match in William Devereux Faulkner, a level-headed Londoner, who had come to investigate. "Ms. Seger has a special magic touch with her lovers that makes her an enduring favorite with readers everywhere."—*Romantic Times*

PROMISES by Jeane Renick

From the award-winning author of *Trust Me* and *Always* comes a sizzling novel set in a small Ohio town, featuring a beautiful blind heroine, her greedy fiancé, two sisters in love with the same man, a mysterious undercover police officer, and a holographic will.

KISSING COUSINS by Carol Jerina

Texas rancher meets English beauty in this witty follow-up to *The Bridegroom*. When Prescott Trefarrow learned that it was he who was the true Earl of St. Keverne, and not his twin brother, he went to Cornwall to claim his title, his castle, and a multitude of responsibilities. Reluctantly, he became immersed in life at Ravens Lair Castle—and the lovely Lucinda Trefarrow.

HUNTER'S HEART by Christina Hamlett

A romantic suspense novel featuring a mysterious millionaire and a woman determined to figure him out. Many things about wealthy industrialist Hunter O'Hare intrigue Victoria Cameron. First of all, why did O'Hare have his ancestral castle moved to Virginia from Ireland, stone by stone? Secondly, why does everyone else in the castle act as if they have something to hide? And last, but not least, what does Hunter want from Victoria?

THE LAW AND MISS PENNY by Sharon Ihle

When U.S. Marshal Morgan Slater suffered a head injury and woke up with no memory, Mariah Penny conveniently supplied him with a fabricated story so that he wouldn't run her family's medicine show out of town. As he traveled through Colorado Territory with the Pennys, he and Mariah fell in love. Everything seemed idyllic until the day the lawman's memory returned.

PRIMROSE by Clara Wimberly

A passionate historical tale of forbidden romance between a wealthy city girl and a fiercely independent local man in the wilds of the Tennessee mountains. Rosalyn Hunte's heart was torn between loyalty to her family and the love of a man who wanted to claim her for himself.